I0717128

PRAISE FOR
PEAK
BOOK THREE OF THE JACK HARPER TRILOGY

"Barlow ends the Jack Harper trilogy with more of what hooked fans from the start—inventive plotting, consistently high stakes, and emotional realism… Echoes of real-world events bring deeper darkness, and brighter light, to Barlow's finale."
—Kirkus Reviews

"*Peak* is full of nonstop surprises. Just when you think things have gone as far as they can, Barlow pushes you over the edge again... and again! A great book you won't want to put down."
—Yvonne Navarro, Author of *Highborn* and *Concrete Savior*

"With fire and white-hot energy, Barlow draws us into *Peak* at a dead run. Fans of Jack know that the Harperverse is a place where dark fears and searing pain morph suddenly into revelation. For Jack Harper, time is running out as she takes on her deadliest enemies yet. If anyone can leverage a snowball's chance in Hell, it's the resourceful Jack, as unpredictable as she is relentless. We readers are in most capable hands."
—Frederic S. Durbin, author of the Realm Award-winning *A Green and Ancient Light* and *The Bone Man*

"Whether you're new to the Jack Harper series or a returning fan, your heart will be racing as you read *Peak* at the edge of your seat. Every word is both chilling and delightful in Barlow's latest fantastical thriller that blurs the lines between good and evil."
—Rena Mason, three-time Bram Stoker Award winning author of *The Evolutionist* and "The Devil's Throat"

"Roarin' action and redemption: In this gripping closure to the Jack Harper trilogy, author L.C. Barlow blazes new trails in the eternal war of good versus evil with magic, gunplay, and an assassin who has the power to bring back the dead she kills. Recommended for all who love suspense with the supernatural, or else just a well-crafted story of heroism and the divine."
—**Eric J. Guignard, award-winning author and editor, including *That Which Grows Wild* and *Doorways to the Deadeye***

"L.C. Barlow has created a fiercely imagined world for her dark and daring thrillers. The pages will turn themselves, but be advised to keep the nightlight on!"
—**Rodman Philbrick, author of *Freak the Mighty***

PRAISE FOR PERISH: BOOK TWO OF THE JACK HARPER TRILOGY

"In *Perish,* Barlow sings the siren song of anger and revenge, expanding the universe of the terrible, and introducing us to even greater threats as she builds a world of the awful."
—**Weston Ochse, Bram Stoker Award Winning author of *Bone Chase* and *Burning Sky***

PRAISE FOR PIVOT: BOOK ONE OF THE JACK HARPER TRILOGY

"Impressive and arresting prose drives this vivid debut. (...) Barlow's gorgeous writing will easily propel readers through the rest of the series."
—**Publishers Weekly**

PEAK

PEAK

BOOK THREE OF THE JACK HARPER TRILOGY

L.C. BARLOW

A California Coldblood Book
Los Angeles, Calif.

THIS IS A GENUINE CALIFORNIA COLDBLOOD BOOK
A California Coldblood Book
Los Angeles, Calif.
californiacoldblood.com

ISBNs:
Paperback: 978-1-955085-21-2
Ebook: 978-1-955085-22-9

Set in Minion
Cover design by James T. Egan of Bookfly Design LLC
Typesetting by Sarcopress

Printed in the United States
Distributed by Publishers Group West

Publisher's Cataloging-in-Publication data

Title: Peak / L.C. Barlow.

Series: The Jack Harper Trilogy.

Los Angeles, CA: California Coldblood Books, 2023.

Identifiers: ISBN 978-1-955085-21-2

Subjects: LCSH Cults—Fiction. | Magic—Fiction. | Brainwashing—Fiction.

Paranormal fiction. | Horror

fiction. | BISAC FICTION / Occult & Supernatural | FICTION / Horror

Classification: LCC PS3602.A77561 P43 2021 | DDC 813.6—dc23

Dedication

For Mom, Dad, Sebron, and Adam. It's always for you.

CHAPTER 1
MICO

Jack

VISIBLE FIRE COURSED THROUGHOUT LUTIN'S body, shimmering through the lines that crawled like vines across his limbs and torso. His opalescent skin glowed like a pearl, except where dark lines circled his eyes, dipped below his cheekbones and clavicles, exposed by a cream boatneck shirt. Power emanated from him like bottled lightning, power to frighten away all except what was worthy—love, goodness, compassion. Lutin slid his hands on top of mine and squeezed, his warmth filling me till I felt fresh, new, revitalized. He leaned down and kissed my head. I breathed him in, relishing the scent of cinnamon and chimney. His lips curved into a smile, and face muscles relaxed, like he'd tasted something sweet.

My breath caught. The brilliant lines across his body wavered, the embers stifled. Various portions of his body dimmed and brightened, wobbling and shivering. Wrinkles etched themselves at the corners of Lutin's eyes, aging him. He suddenly seemed a thousand years old, and frail. As quickly as they arrived, the wrinkles disappeared. My heart fluttered. I opened my mouth to ask what had happened, if he was all right.

Before I could speak, a reverberation growled through the air. The snarl wavered across the mansion. Wooden floors and doors creaked, chandeliers jingled, and a pan in a distant part of the house fell, swiveling like a top, clattering like a cymbal, crescendoing before, at last, the symphony stopped. My eyes swept to the ceiling of the entryway of Cyrus's mansion.

"Thunder?" I asked. "I wasn't aware of a storm."

Lutin's dark eyes lingered on a panel above us, as though memorizing the knots in the squares of wood partitioned in aesthetically pleasing geometry, before they dropped to mine. He smiled and then winced, as though in apology. "Evil is being committed nearby."

I turned to the door. An image of a shining white monster flashed in my mind's eye, the body glossy and malleable like molten plastic. No eyes, nose, or mouth. Nothing human in him, just a walking doll that shaped itself into whatever it needed to be. The creature who had, behind a vast variety of facades, haunted me since I was six years old. "The Builder?" I asked. I broke away from Lutin and walked to the door, reaching for my gun. My hand quickly surrounded cold metal.

"No, Jack." Lutin caught up with me, his hand firm on my shoulder. "No, no. Not the Builder. I'm surprised you heard the echo." His black eyes pierced the door. "There are people not too far from here. They're…" He sought the right words. "They're committing a crime."

My heart slowed. Once again, words abandoned me.

He patted my shoulder as though asking if I were okay. "More and more, you're becoming one of us."

"Who are they? What kind of crime are they committing?"

He inhaled deeply. "I don't know, but we don't have the time to find out. We have to—"

Rage burned in my throat and exploded. I turned from him and grabbed the handle of the front door. I twisted it and marched onto the porch. "Where?" I demanded. But I could already feel it. A certain tension crawled throughout my body, raising the hairs on the back of my neck. The air trembled and tugged at me, urging me to travel the dark road to my left.

I stepped off the porch and tracked the reverberations, my gun ready.

Lutin followed, barefoot in the grass. With each step we took, the dry grass greened beneath us, healed by our ferric bodies. Although it had been nearly six months since Lutin gave me the power to resurrect, that power had only recently been realized. Never had I seen the world around me heal and ripen as it now did in Lutin's presence. It was as though I carried an invisible leviathan, as apart from it as I was part of it.

Lutin appeared in front of me, suddenly barring my path.

I looked him up and down, glancing back at the place where he had just been. "How'd you do that?" I asked.

"I'm sorry, Jack. We don't have time for this. My brothers are coming."

I peered down the road toward the continuing rumbles, toward something as equally immense as us. The electricity in the air tugged at me like a wave about to carry me to a deeper sea. "They can wait."

"They shouldn't have to. Remember—we have something important to do." He frowned. "You can't stop all the evil, Jack," he said. "Not tonight. Not ever. My kind have devoted our lives to it. Trust me. It never ends. We must, for the moment, look at the big picture, not the small one."

A thick reverberation, heavier than before, rolled along the grass and trees, transforming the earth into a rocking ocean. The sensation—sticky, ugly energy, slathered with fear—appalled me.

"You don't know me very well if you think I'm going to let this go," I said. "I can't stand the feel of it." I charged past him, following my yearning.

Lutin caught up with me again. "I can get us there quicker." He grabbed my arm.

The grass and trees, partially lit by Cyrus's porch lights, swirled with the black sky and stars, until everything spiraled, appearing as a galaxy. The road and woods disappeared like ink in black water. Lutin and I stood in the black, suspended on nothing. Beneath our feet, roots and ivy emerged, fleshing out a forest floor. Dead leaves speckled the dirt. Trees towered above us, and branches creaked. The rest of the land rolled out like an unfurled carpet. Twenty feet away, a gravel road appeared, a rusted red truck traveling on that road, headlights piercing the night.

"What was that?" I asked, breathless, spinning. I anchored my hand against the bark of a tree to steady myself.

"I translocated us to them."

I bent over and clutched my stomach, suppressing a wave of nausea.

"Are you all right?" Lutin whispered, one of his eyes reflecting the truck lights.

I breathed in, nodded, and straightened my knees. "Yes. Just…warn me next time."

I braved a step and broke through the foliage and trees. The red truck traveled down the road, its tires grinding gravel against the earth. Rust speckled the truck's body like age spots. Its headlights illuminated the empty road beyond. Behind it, something twisted in the dirt. I narrowed my eyes, making out a chain jerking behind the back fender. I followed its links to their end. The thick chain bound the neck of a dog. The truck shot along at tremendous speed, dragging the dog along the gravel. She jerked over the stones. The copper scent of blood filled my nose. Under the crunch of gravel, her yelps popped.

I aimed the gun and fired five bullets into the cab. The truck swerved to the right, off the road, and slammed into a tree. The sound of gravel crunching abruptly ended. Dust clouds disappeared behind the taillights. The dog's body spun and skipped across the road, landing behind the tires.

I stormed forward, breaking from the line of trees.

The driver side door groaned as it slammed open. A man in a blue baseball cap and red t-shirt jumped out of the driver's side, a cigarette wedged between his lips. The scent of alcohol bloomed in the air.

"Did you just fucking shoot at us?" he yelled, eyes wide, face red.

The headlights illuminated me, and his eyes widened before he shrank back against the cab. A woman shot from the passenger door, screaming something unintelligible. Then she noticed me and froze, suddenly silent.

I looked between them, smelling the bitter fragrance of their fear. I observed the fiery lines in my arms. I was something beyond now. I didn't match expectations anymore, especially on a dark road at night. I turned away from them and hurried to the back of the truck, where the dog lay. Lutin was on his knees, spotlighted by the truck's back lights. Clouds of dirt washed over him. He held the black Lab in his arms. Her ripped skin and torn muscles knitted together. Quickly, the raw skin pinkened, the fur thickened. Gravel embedded in her road-rash wounds plinked to the ground. The dog quietly peered up at Lutin. She licked his chin.

He spoke to her in the ferric tongue, a language I didn't understand. The sound was feathery, soothing. The dog regarded him as though it understood.

Lutin looked up at me. The enormity of his gaze made me feel as though I'd momentarily dipped into another world, entirely apart from this torturous spectacle. It seemed impossible that his world and this world could exist at the same time.

I shook my head and abruptly returned to the scene—the gravel, the scent of blood, dirt, and trees. I strode back to the two individuals and pinned the man against the cab of his truck, gripping his throat. "Why?" I said.

"Shh-sh-sh-sh—" he stuttered, spittle dribbling out of his mouth. His eyes widened and stared into mine, like he was looking into a void. "Wh-wh-what are y-you?"

I jerked him forward and slammed him back against his truck. "*Why*?" I growled louder. My voice boomed across the land like tumbling boulders.

He squeezed his eyes tight, his sweat-soaked face scarlet. "Sh-sh-she w-wouldn't sit," he said. "Sh-she w-wouldn't obey."

Fresh blood trickled down the driver side window of the cab, where his head had just smacked the glass. It dripped on his shoulder.

"I see," I said. With renewed rage, I squeezed his throat, shutting off his air. He clutched at my hand. I thought about killing him. Part of me asked, *Why not*? My conscience had reconciled far worse. It had been a long time since it'd had to reconcile anything at all.

I took a deep breath before I grunted and dropped my arm.

Coughing, he clutched his throat and bent forward, his mouth wide, tears tracking through dust and sweat.

My gaze shifted to the woman standing to my left. She stepped back blindly before she tripped and dropped to her hands and knees. "She just wouldn't sit. That's all," she whispered. "We were teaching her a lesson."

I stared back and forth between the two of them, frowning, wrapped in a strange sense of déjà vu. It was as though I'd always been on that road, had always known them. "You remind me of my brother," I said. "And my father."

Lutin's steps crunched behind me, and I turned. He carried the dog like a baby in his arms.

I clasped my hands together near my belly, my breath quieting, my anger shifting. I returned to myself. It was as though as soon as I had them figured out, everything in me settled. I knew what to do.

"So you believe it's important to discipline those who don't do what they're asked? Force them?"

The man and woman silently looked at me. The woman shut her eyes, and fresh tears poured down her face. "I don't know who you are, but… *please!*" she whimpered.

I bit my lip. "I ask because I tend to agree."

"Careful, Jack," Lutin said.

A wave of fresh anger coursed through me. "Are you not tired of this? You've experienced it far longer than I have."

"This is humanity," he said. "If I killed every person who harmed an animal, half of the human population wouldn't exist."

"Perhaps," I said. I frowned, and my blood slowed, no longer hot and quick. "But I know you can feel it in them, the same as I do. They're as likely to stop hurting animals as it is to snow tonight."

Lutin nodded and shifted the dog in his arms. "You can't stop it all."

"You're right. Not all. But I can stop this one."

I turned my back on the pair so they could not see what I was doing. I retrieved my gun and removed the empty shells, then refilled the cylinder. The gun now loaded, I turned to the man and woman. Before they could react, I shot them, killing them instantly. I put the gun back in my coat pocket and kneeled next to the corpses. I looked up at Lutin and, at the sight of his face, felt guilt. It disappeared quickly, though, as I remembered myself, apart from him. This was who I was. Death was part of my process.

I reached out and touched the man and the woman, one with each palm, as I summoned the power within me, letting it double and triple, until it ripened, rolled, fizzed—ready to detonate. It tingled in my core, crawled into my muscles, and danced along my fingertips. When I was ready, I shoved it toward the bodies. They jumped. Together, they gasped, resurrected. Life was also part of my process.

The two blinked and shifted, sitting up. The woman moaned. Waking as if from a dream rather than death, the man lifted to his knees. When the pair spotted me, they froze, their mouths slack.

"Do you know what I just did?" I asked. Their eyes widened, unblinking. They didn't react. "I took your life and gave it back." I glanced at Lutin. "There are many of us who can do so. But, you see, I am slightly different than the others. When I resurrect people—" I licked my lips "—I can control them. I have a singular power—the power to control those I bring back."

I rose to my feet, took the black Lab from Lutin's arms, and set her on the ground beside me. She panted, in perfect health.

"You have a leash on this dog, and *I* have a leash on *you*. Whatever I command, you are forced to do. I command you to never hurt this animal, or any other animal, again. You will love this dog like you love yourselves, and you will treat her as if she is greater than you. You will take care of her as though she is the most precious being to ever walk the earth. You will *never* hurt her or cause any other animal, or child, harm. *Ever*. Do you understand?"

They each nodded.

"And you will never speak to anyone about what happened here, about who you saw in the woods or what I did or said."

They nodded again.

I bent to the dog and kissed her next to her ear. I scratched her head. "You'd better be careful," I warned, "in the future. You never know who you might meet along these dark Louisiana roads at night. And you never know when I might come to check up on you."

I stood and said goodbye to the dog. I gave the trembling man and woman one more long, hard look. At last, I strode away from them, Lutin beside me. When we were well out of sight, he said, "That dog is going to have golden pillows and treats every day."

"Just as she deserves."

Lutin smirked. "You said you wanted a warning the next time I translocated. Here it is." The dark around us abruptly melded, tree branches, grass, road, and red truck swirling together. I braced myself, trying to let the sense of gravity shield me from the sense of seasickness. We would be at Cyrus's in seconds.

"I know you worry about what I think of you," he said, "when you do these things."

My heart trembled as the darkness whirled. Once again, guilt crawled along my spine and latched on my shoulders, unwilling to be shrugged off.

"But I will always love you," he added, the stars spiraling around us, reflected in his eyes.

My tongue became dry. "Oh? I thought you were trying to convince me out of it."

"Well, you're right about that."

The corner of my mouth lifted.

"But I'm primarily trying to help you to *see*."

I shook my head, not understanding. "See what?"

He blinked like a cat after a long sleep. "The space around all of it. The way that we and all other living things exist outside of these terrible atrocities, even when we experience them.

"But, even so, after seeing you do this, I think..." He nodded. "This plan is right. The plan to kill the Builder and have you resurrect him, control him, just like you did with those two individuals back there... It's solid."

"I know it is," I said. "I can feel it in my heart."

He tilted his head. "Our heart." He pressed his hand against his chest.

"Yes," I said, thinking of how he had given me a part of himself.

Within our cocoon of darkness, the wooden porch of Cyrus's home appeared beneath our feet. The posts around the porch sprung up, the red front door exploded beside us, and the empty land stretched out into the night.

Lutin licked his lips. "You need to know, Jack. The other ferrics may not like you. My brothers may not like you. But what you're doing is worthy. And whatever happens, you should see it through. No matter the cost."

I couldn't help but laugh. "I will, Lutin. When I sense what is right, I follow through, no matter the obstacle. Do you not know me?"

He shook his head. "You never know what could happen between now and the end. So many things in my life I've had to do on my own. And giving you that piece of my heart, I did that on my own, with many railing against me, damning me for not taking it back. Worthy things, things that must be completed, we often have to do on our own, outside the bounds of what others expect, beyond the rules they've formed and demanded we follow. And this, this may be no different for you."

"I've lived my whole life on my own, outside the norm," I said.

"Yes, you have. That's why I think you're right for the job. I just said that because it's important to remember. Sometimes we can become alienated from ourselves."

A noise echoed. Someone cleared his throat. My eyes turned to the lawn, where a ferric stood. Lutin's brother, Osric, clasped his hands behind his back, as though at military rest.

He looked back and forth between us. "You smell like death and resurrection," he hissed.

CHAPTER 2
MALUM

Jack

MY HEART THRUMMED AT THE sight of Osric. It'd been half a year since I'd last seen him, and that wasn't long enough. I clenched my hands into fists, opened them, closed them. The rush of adrenaline surged through my muscles, making them ache. I trembled, despite myself.

"Best not tilt your hand yet," Lutin whispered near my ear. "Till we know how they'll respond."

I nodded, and Lutin stepped forward, his warmth disappearing. I inhaled deeply, taking in the night that blanketed the entire front lawn and the woods to the right in the distance along the road. No other structures existed near us, no evidence of civilization. The darkness stretched forever, thick and suffocating.

Bit by bit, as if they'd dissolved the darkness, four more ferrics appeared on the lawn, shimmering like Osric and Lutin, their brothers, in the night. Orange and red fire visible in their veins, they moved a bit nearer, their footsteps silent on the grass. With each step, the dry grass greened beneath them.

The porch light illuminated Osric, the leader of their group. He stood as tall as Lutin, but stockier, built like a football player. His wide jawline jutted squarely; his short black hair curved slightly on top. His gaze was distanced, cat-like and somehow reptilian. His icy expression lingered on me.

The other brothers stopped in the distance. Osric ascended the stairs, the tips of his fingers pressed together, his black cloak swaying in the light wind.

"You have made an enormous error," Osric said, his deep voice cutting the quiet.

He had to be speaking of the two people in the woods who were torturing their dog, I thought. Then, he nodded to my left, as though he could see through the window of the house. "Bringing that *monstrosity* in there back to life."

Behind me, within the house, the presence of the monstrosity he referred to loomed. Cyrus—my dark mentor who had taught me to murder, the cult leader who had abducted children and sent them to their deaths, the maniac who had tortured Lutin for ten years—waited within. I couldn't blame Osric for his rage, but there was something he didn't know, and that something was everything.

"I brought him back to rehabilitate him," I said. Like the two people on the road, I'd resurrected Cyrus from his death to cure him of his dark desires. Once I'd discovered I could control those I resurrected, I concluded Cyrus was no longer a threat, and I returned him to life.

Osric's chest rose and fell, his dark eyes flicking to Lutin and back to me, as though what I'd said was not only impossible but a lie. "Mm hm. And do you know why *I* came?" He tilted his head left and right.

Lutin and I exchanged glances.

"It wasn't just because you returned a man who manipulated and killed hundreds, including me and my brothers." He rocked forward and back on his left heel. "No. Not just that."

The air thickened, like whipped cream. I froze, unsure how to respond.

"Why *did* you come?" Lutin said, taking a step forward, his eyebrow cocked.

Osric's chin tilted up. "My appeal to learn Jack's fate finally came through."

Adrenaline rocketed through me. Deep within my heart, the part of me that had always remained a child under Cyrus's care heard her name called, as if for the first time, and looked up from her dark cell. "What are you talking about?" I asked. "My fate?"

"Where you will end up," Osric said. "In the end." He took a few steps to his right and swiveled toward me. "I put in a request to our council as soon as I left this house. The last time we spoke, Jack, I wasn't sure of you, wasn't keen on you retaining immortal powers, but Lutin wanted it desperately. So, when I returned home, I submitted a request to know *your* fate, so I could understand you better. Where you end up at last—Domum or the Beretrum. Heaven or hell. Because, after all, if you were to end up in Domum, I would know that it was all right, that immortal powers would end up where they belonged. And also that I could trust you with them."

Half of my mind urged me to stop him from speaking, to tell him what Lutin and I had planned, what had culminated in the past few days. Another part of me, however, demanded that I be quiet, that I listen to whatever Osric had to say.

Hadn't I already reached my fate? Fire coursed over my body in branches, just like theirs. I could resurrect and heal people. I could do even more than that. What "end" could he be speaking of?

"But I'm a ferric," I said.

"You're a hybrid," Osric hissed. He shook his head. "Even if you weren't, there have existed fallen ferrics, many over the centuries. They go down into the Beretrum, where the Builder is—the Satan of your mortal mythology. And the Builder *eats* them." His bottom teeth gleamed white as he emphasized the word "eats." The knowledge of my fate remained on the tip of his tongue, threatening to spill out.

I shivered, barely able to resist the temptation to demand what he knew.

"Osric," Lutin said, his voice a warning. He stepped forward, his bare feet padding on the porch's dark blue boards. "*Now isn't the time.* Jack and I have been discussing options. We have a strategy for stopping the Builder from ever hurting this world again."

Osric squinted at his brother dubiously, as though wondering if he had lost his mind. He threw his hands out wide. "There's no way to kill the Builder. Not permanently. You know this."

"Things have developed," Lutin said.

"He's right," I added, waking from my shock. I repeated the words to bring myself fully back. Whatever my fate, this was more important. This was everyone's fate. "Let me show you something," I said, patting the air in front of me, urging Osric to watch.

Osric frowned doubtfully, but he took a step back nevertheless and nodded. I inhaled, steadying myself.

"Cyrus," I called into the house. "Come here, please."

From within the house, Cyrus's footsteps plodded closer on the wooden floor that creaked familiarly. He arrived at the threshold, his silver hair gleaming in the porch light. His tall, regal stature bespoke a leader. His silver eyes flicked among us. When he recognized his audience, he shrank.

"You *dare* bring him in front of me? I will gut him," Osric growled, stepping forward.

Lutin lifted a hand. "Wait."

I commanded my mentor, the man I'd resurrected against all that was sane. "Cyrus, I want you to apologize to Lutin and his brothers for the destruction you caused, for the people you hurt and killed, for the evil you fostered. I want you to mean it."

Cyrus's cheeks flushed. Tears welled at the bottoms of his eyelids, and the skin around his eyes grew puffy. Normally cold, his gray eyes did not seem so in that moment. "I'm sorry," he said, "for all of the destruction that I've caused, for all the people I hurt and killed, for the evil I fostered."

"And tell them that it will never happen again," I said, looking to Osric to observe his reaction.

"It will never happen again," Cyrus whispered, like a child promising a parent. He was honest, though. His genuineness hung in the air, a vibration on the opposite end of the spectrum from the evil vibrations from the forest.

Osric's face relaxed. He no longer stood erect; he leaned, as though he'd thawed. His expression was no longer strained but dumbfounded.

"How?" he inquired. He took an intimidating step forward, staring hard at Cyrus, as if at any moment he might destroy him.

"Because of me," I said.

Osric paused.

"I can control those I resurrect. I discovered it when I was held captive in the basement of a man named Jonathon Roth. He headed a kill-for-hire organization in New York." I swallowed. "He doesn't anymore."

I searched Osric's face for recognition of the name, but there was none. At least, none that I could see. Perhaps the ferrics had not left me in Roth's basement to rot after all; perhaps they simply hadn't known. Roth had lined my cell with lead in the hope that it would block the ferrics from discovering me. Maybe it had worked.

"I aligned with Roth to destroy the rest of Cyrus's cult—the balance of Infinitum *you* left behind," I said, pressing Osric, "and one of his men shot and killed me. I was dead for seven days. And when I returned, I had black lines throughout my body. They didn't fluoresce with fire like yours until much later, when I tried to control Roth's men, like I'm doing with Cyrus, now. And when I did, I became fully…ferric, I guess. But different. Because I can control those I resurrect, whereas you cannot. But that's not all."

Osric tilted his head, waiting. I hoped, in his silence, he would hear me.

"When I was dead, I had a vision of the Builder. I saw him as he was, in his entirety—the great white being. As soon as I saw him, it changed everything, and I knew he was the one I needed to set my sights on. That's why I resurrected Cyrus…and Roland. I had to know the truth of the Builder, of what I'd seen. I sought knowledge from *Cyrus* because none of *you* were answering."

Osric appeared to weigh my words carefully. He crossed his arms. "We never heard you call."

"I figured. But I prayed for all of you while Roth held me captive. I prayed, especially, to Lutin. No one ever came. So I gave up. And when I escaped and resurrected Cyrus, Lutin arrived."

Lutin squeezed my shoulder, and my heart swelled.

"When Cyrus told me more about the Builder," I added, "an idea came to me about how I…we…could stop him, even though he can't be permanently killed."

Osric tipped his chin toward me.

This was the moment, I knew. If they didn't agree to go along with me, then I was going to have to resort to far less congenial methods, like those in the woods, and force them to do things my way. I was fine with either path, though I preferred the easier one.

"If we were to kill the Builder, and I were to bring him back, I could control him…just like I controlled Jonathon Roth and all one hundred and sixty of his men. Just like I can control Cyrus, and Roland, if I want." What I left out was that I could also control Osric. In fact, I could control all of Lutin's brothers. I had resurrected them in the center of Cyrus's home six months before, saved them. If need be, I could force them to serve as my small army.

Osric chuckled unexpectedly. The smile on his lips didn't reach his eyes, though, which remained clear and mean. "Are you serious? Did you really come up with this, or is it another one of Lutin's ridiculous schemes?"

"It's all mine," I said, deadpan.

He shook his head and stared at the porch floor. His smile fell away, and Osric slowly lifted his eyes to mine. His tone sobered. "You really think you can take on a being like that? *Control* a being like that?"

"I do."

Lutin stepped to my side. "It's more than worth trying."

Osric bit the corner of his lip. "Because you like her, Lutin. You've always liked her. I, however, do not."

"Because that's your personality," Lutin said. "To be unconvinced. To dislike anything 'impure.' For once, Osric, try thinking *outside* the box. Outside the lineage."

I realized it might be necessary to prove to Osric that I had control over him and his other brothers. I clasped my fingers and considered tugging on the tether of his soul, to urge him to scratch his nose or cough.

Lutin slipped his hand against my back and pressed, as though he realized what I was thinking. *Don't,* the pressure said.

"It's *more* than worth a shot," Lutin argued. "It's a better plan than any we've imagined. *Ever*. And *you know it*."

Emotion swept over Osric's face—an emotion I didn't expect. Not fear or anger but sadness. "And what about you, Lutin?"

A long silence blossomed. The conversation had shifted to a different direction, and I lost the tether. Osric's question confused me. I looked between the two brothers.

"What's he talking about?" I asked.

Lutin shrugged. "Something old. Something unimportant."

"Ah. So you haven't told her," Osric observed.

"There's nothing to tell. It's decided."

Osric's eyes didn't veer from Lutin's. Neither cared about roping me into the conversation. Lutin spoke to his brother in their ferric tongue, which I didn't understand. Words wafted through the air, liquid and flowery. His tone was hard, a warning.

Osric repeated his question. "And what about *you*? You should at least tell her."

"After," Lutin said. "After."

I opened my mouth, about to demand that Lutin tell me now, but I stopped. The energy between the brothers was palpable, and I hated to destroy it. Now wasn't the time. I would wait and choose my timing carefully.

Tears wet Osric's eyes. "You believe in her that much?"

"I do."

"Why?"

In the pause, my heart thudded hard.

"Because of how she became what she has become. I wouldn't trust anyone else."

I shivered in the warm embrace of Lutin's words. I would never, ever part from him. We understood each other. Two halves of the same heart.

Osric's hands clenched into fists. His eyes became distant, as though the answer had drained him. "Then perhaps we should take a vote," he said, tears gleaming. He motioned for his brothers to come forward.

The others walked to the bottom steps of the porch. The overhead lights reflected in their unblinking black eyes.

"Is this worth a try?" Osric asked, turning to them. Their faces looked pensive, as though they had already asked themselves the question as they had listened along. "Do we trust that Jack is capable of controlling such a massive being? If she is successful, do we trust that she will do the right thing, given the disposal of so much power?" His tone made it obvious he didn't believe it.

The silence seemed to last forever.

"Can you really control *all* of those you resurrect?" one of them asked at last. This one's hair stood in long, dark twists, like licorice. His cherubic lips pouted, and his gray shirt and pants hung loosely on him, reminding me of Greek robes. Like Lutin, he was barefoot.

"Yes," I said, the center of my back rigid.

"Is there a limit to how many you can control? Or how long?"

"Not that I've seen."

Another brother said something in the ferric tongue. His frame was triangular, his shoulders noticeably wide. His long hair, draped over his shoulders, tangled into loose dreadlocks, was pulled back with a tie. His dark eyes were large and owl-like. One of the fiery swirls of his skin swooped directly in the middle of his breastbone and glowed beneath the brown cloth of his shirt.

The four of them spoke quietly, their voices barely discernable in the darkness. Osric stared at me, as though unsure what to do and having a hell of a time trying to figure it out.

At last, one of the brothers said, "We've made our decisions."

Osric breathed deeply, worry etched into the corners of his eyes. "All right. Who is in favor of trying this plan?"

Three of the four brothers raised their hands. Whether or not Osric included Lutin in the vote, the majority vote was yes. I exhaled in relief, and the tightness in my chest relented. I wouldn't have to force them to do anything. At least, not yet.

A grim look crossed Osric's face, and he turned around. He pressed his hand to his forehead and then dropped it abruptly to his side. "So be it," he said. "But if we are going to do this, we must move quickly, before the Builder or other ferrics learn what Jack is capable of or of our plan.

In which case," he said, looking around at all of us, "we should enact this tonight. Now, if possible."

"Agreed," Lutin said.

"Yes," said the ferric with dreadlocks.

An explosion of excitement swept through me. The fire in my veins fluoresced, heating me.

Osric wiped tears from his cheeks and held out that hand to me. The droplets sparkled like crystals in his palm. "Come," he said. "We go quickly."

His skin was pale in the yellow light, and the red lines in his flesh looked like fresh embers shifting on top of flowing lava. His brothers had already turned from the house, heading back into the night—silent, like tigers in a tall, grassy field.

I stared at Osric's hand without touching it.

"Cyrus," I said. "Go inside and sit on the couch. Wait for Roland to return and tell him what has happened here. Do whatever he says."

Cyrus padded away, back into the house, to do as I bid him. The door behind me shut.

When Lutin stepped forward, Osric allowed his tear-stained hand to drop. He turned and led us into the night. The air was cool and damp, the current electric.

I looked back once more. The mansion, its interior alight, was no longer threatening, no longer dominant. I hoped that when Roland finally returned he would be okay, alone in the house with Cyrus. I wished he could come with us, but I didn't want to demand that we wait for him. It was a blessing we were even on our way.

As we left the property, the particles of light around me shifted, expanding and diminishing. The world became fluid. Osric lifted his hand and dragged his fingers across the top of the image of the road, land, and distant trees. The image swirled, its colors spinning, spiraling. Awe for this translocation swept over me, and I tried to touch the fleeting colors. They broke apart and darted into nothingness. The seven of us stood in the midst of a windless storm, and when I turned away from where the house had been, everything settled.

A tall and narrow decaying building loomed above us. More abandoned buildings, just as tall and narrow, stretched left and right, like moth-eaten books on a shelf. A deserted street with three parked cars spread beneath us. Lamp posts illuminated bugs swirling along the asphalt.

"Where are we?" I asked.

"Nowhere special," Lutin said with a glance. "But we're about to be."

The five ferrics walked toward the building. I began to follow, but Osric, who had stayed behind, placed a hand on my shoulder and squeezed hard. He waited, watching the others walk away, before he spoke.

"As for your fate," he whispered. His eyes pierced me like I was a butterfly pinned in a frame. "The Beretrum," he said. "You're fated to go to hell, Jack." Rage and pleasure flooded his face, amid the drying tears. "And there's nothing you can do at this point to change that. It is an eternal fate." He smiled and released me. "You take my brother from me. I take you from you." He strode ahead to join the others.

CHAPTER 3
CHRYSOS

Jack

Strength left me. The sensation of a gut punch bloomed deep in my stomach. My heart slowed and mind teetered. When dizziness washed over me, I reached out to reclaim my balance, but my fingers swiped through nothing, and I barely saved myself from falling. Not sure what I was doing or where I was going, I pressed my hand to my lips.

Osric met the others in front of the building. They all turned and looked back at me, their eyes wide and unblinking, like owls.

I hadn't wanted to know my fate. I hadn't wanted to know it from Osric. And I hadn't wanted to know it right then.

Lutin called my name.

Unable to resist the sound of his voice, I put on a blank face and turned. His eyebrows furrowed, and he tilted his head, his skin shimmering under the fluorescent lights. He walked toward me.

"Are you all right?"

"Of course. Yeah. I just need a moment. After the…" I made a swirling motion in the air. "Teleportation."

"Translocation." Lutin looked me up and down. "Are you sure?"

I nodded.

He put a hand on my back, and calm warmth and soothing energy sifted through me, like circulation returning. Lutin poured his healing energy over me, like he had ground up the moonlight and doused me with its balm. My breaths came easier, and an immense weight lifted.

"Better?" he asked.

I nodded.

He patted me and motioned with his chin. "We need to get going."

As I followed him to the building, Osric eyed us, waiting, it seemed, to see what might have been exchanged. I became a blank wall, betraying nothing, never blinking as I stared back at him. He glanced at Lutin nervously and straightened his shoulders.

He walked to the dilapidated building's peeling door. After he retrieved a gold knife from some secret pocket, or perhaps from thin air—I couldn't see any place to store a weapon—Osric dragged the blade across his palm, splitting the skin. Blood speckled with fiery embers streaked his palm. He placed that hand on the upper left corner of the door and dragged it to the right. Blood smeared across the wooden surface. Brilliant embers of light, like molten coins, glittered in the blood, as though spreading the light that danced within him. It fluoresced, sparkling on the surface, as he stroked his hand down to the bottom of the step, then across to the left, and then up. A perfect ruby, twinkling frame delineated the surface. He placed his hand on the middle of the door, just to its left, as though on its heart.

"*Patefacio tutor godsoul,*" Osric whispered.

The brilliant frame exploded, specks of light dancing, hot and fierce. The world behind us dimmed until Lutin, his brothers, and I stood on nothing, in vast darkness, awaiting the opening of the door. Osric grasped the handle and turned it. As he pushed, purple and gold flashed into view.

The brothers entered one at a time. Lutin pressed me forward, so that he was last. I stepped into a hallway lined with matte royal purple rock. It did not glisten or shine. The scents of moisture and petrichor filtered through the cave-like air. The odor was not old but vibrant and fresh, as though there had just been a shower in a rainforest and the plants rejoiced. The deeper we traveled between the royal purple walls, the fresher the air became. Eventually it seemed I was at the source of life itself—what made Lutin Lutin, what made all of us anything. Time had stopped, if the concept of time even existed there. Only now was before us.

The brothers parted, spreading themselves out beyond the hall. We entered a large square room with the same purple rock on either side. A giant shimmering gold wall broke into view straight ahead. Almost translucent in areas, the stone appeared sturdy despite being covered in holes and tiny rugged patches, as though the structure had been chipped into. It stretched up about twenty feet to cover the entire wall, reminding me of a healthy, living organ, like a breathing lung. Bits of it dripped and bled, molten gold puddled on the floor where pools of it solidified like cooled wax.

A short, frail old man appeared at my left, walking forward, away from the gold, toward a large gray marble island that stretched long across the majority of the room, separating us from the gold wall. The air around him reverberated.

His face round, his eyes like coins, the frail man had a large nose and ears, hair sprouting from them. Gold glimmered on his hands, coating them, as if he had not washed them for a thousand years. The gold coating stretched up his forearms, ending near his elbows. It seemed like gloves or armor. Specks of gold splattered his gray shirt and pants. Gold dust glistened in the lines of his face.

I sensed, deep in my core, that the gold protected him.

And he protected the gold.

Awe washed over and refreshed me. I drank in the image of the man with gold arms more deeply. There was something about this place, something that made me understand good in its unadulterated state. My eyes wandered over each of the ferrics in the room. I could suddenly understand, with utter clarity, Lutin and his brothers in a way that I never had before. They were pure, had been made so, had remained so.

I didn't belong here, not with them. I belonged somewhere far, far away, covered in earth, buried in the Beretrum—just like Osric said.

I shivered.

"Lutin," the man said, smiling. "Haven't seen you in ages." He winked. His voice dropped. "Heard you had a bit of trouble down on the mortal plane recently."

The left corner of Lutin's lips lifted. He nodded. "A little."

The old man's eyes narrowed, as though he knew what "a little" really meant—ten long years of being tortured in Cyrus's basement, bits of his soul cut away and fed to the red box that shielded Cyrus from being discovered. "I'm sorry to hear it." He patted Lutin's arm like a father would his son, leaving glowing gold on the cream of his shirt. "I would've expected you to come here after. Heal."

"I didn't want to waste your supply."

"*That* would have been no waste. You *should have* come." The man's words were kind but emphatic. He sighed and moved past me without a glance.

"Osric," he said soberly, straightening his spine and frowning. "How have you been?"

"Well," Osric said. His tone conveyed the truth was anything but.

Lutin leaned in toward me. "This," he whispered, gesturing toward the short, elderly man, "is the Guardian, and that," he said, pointing the tips of his fingers toward the wall, as his eyes searched for its topmost portion, "is godsoul."

Lutin's smile didn't reach his eyes and quickly fell. "It's our finite resource of pure immortal power. We use it to fashion weapons that are capable of killing and/or poisoning the Builder. If one of us has been harmed by him, it can heal him or her. There used to be a plentiful amount," he continued, "but this wall is the last of it. It expands when left alone, but we often need it. It's a battle between safety and purpose. We cannot, however, claim it all. Once it's gone, we will all die. There would be nothing left to stop the Builder."

The gold dripped and sounded like a clock ticking. No wonder most of the brothers were willing to try my theory out. The only other option was drawing closer and closer to inevitable death.

Lutin looked at me closely. "You sure you're okay, Jack?"

I nodded. "I'm fine. It's a lot to take in."

Another sad smile stretched across Lutin's face. "Osric said something to you, didn't he?"

The tip of my tongue touched my upper lip as I considered what to say.

I stared into Lutin's ebon eyes and imagined telling him the truth. But what would that accomplish? He couldn't erase my memory, and we didn't need the extra baggage as we sought to kill the Builder. I turned and allowed Osric to interrupt our conversation.

"We each need a capsule of godsoul," he said.

The Guardian stared at me. His brightness dimmed. "What for?" he asked. Osric began to answer, but the Guardian held up his hand. His stare never veered from my face.

I opened my mouth, wary of speaking, but nevertheless I tried. "We're going to stop the Builder."

The Guardian's eyes widened. He slowly took a step toward me. Then another. Another. "Oh? Are you? He is only going to come back."

"There may be a way—" Osric began, but the Guardian cleared his throat. Osric half-grunted, half-sighed, as though he knew what to expect, and shut his mouth.

The Guardian shifted his weight. Though he was shorter than I, I intuited that if he wanted, he could obliterate me at any moment. He scratched at an arm, and gold flecks floated to the floor.

"What are *you* doing here?" he asked.

"Guardian, this is Jack," Lutin began. "She is a hybrid that I…"

"I know who she is," the Guardian said, swatting his words away. "Everybody knows who she is."

I took a deep breath, suddenly dizzy, wishing that there were no specks of blood on my clothes from the couple I had recently killed and resurrected. Facing the man, I wanted to clean myself. I forced out an answer. "I'm trying to *help* you."

He pointed his finger at me. "*You* cannot help *me*." His voice boomed against the purple and gold walls. "You are an abomination to ferric lineage and a stain on immortal power."

I shut my mouth. My teeth clacked. Despite myself, my eyes widened. Nothing was left to say. I wouldn't be able to change his mind. I nodded and peered around at the others. I sucked on my teeth with a squeaking sound. "Well, all right."

"And this," he said, pointing at me but turning to Lutin, "makes me even more surprised you haven't visited, since…"

Lutin put a hand on the Guardian's arm and squeezed. "Please," he said. The Guardian stopped short. His hand slowly dropped, and he sent me a sideways glance. "Ah, I see. You haven't told her." He cocked his head and peered up at the wall of gold that stretched in front of us. He walked away, to the other side of the marble island that stood between us and the wall. "As though she needs protecting," he whispered.

Whatever the hell Lutin had kept from me needed to come out, the sooner the better. Everyone seemed to know but me, and I didn't want to be blindsided with another piece of information.

"What do you boys want?" the Guardian said. He placed his hands on the island between him and the gold, leaning over it. He sounded like a bartender calling for the last round.

"We need eight pieces of godsoul," Osric said. "One to lure the Builder out with. The others to protect ourselves."

"And how imperative is this?"

"*Very.*" Osric gave no wink or indication that he was against the plan. He was as serious as he could be.

The Guardian frowned and crossed his arms. "I'll give you and your brothers whatever you need, but that creature you've brought with you isn't getting anything. This is a divine place, Osric. Lutin." His eyes scanned our half circle. "Pepluv. Flutri. Semic. Inarin. You do not bring a murderer here, someone with so much blood on her hands. It's obscene."

"Under normal circumstances, I never would," Osric said. "But this is urgent."

The Guardian bit his bottom lip between his teeth and winced. "I ought to call the council and let them know she's here."

"Please," Lutin said, stepping forward. "We need this pass. I promise. It's *worthy.*" He placed a hand on the Guardian's arm. "We may actually rein in the Builder. Truly. Imagine the Builder being gone, your supplies no longer dwindling. Being able to grow this place beyond what it has ever been. Walls and walls of godsoul. You could save the world."

The Guardian swallowed, his eyes drifting to a corner of the cave. "Don't tempt me," he said. "It never works out."

"But we still fight, don't we?" Lutin replied. "Even if it fails. Even if it hurts and we die."

A guilty look crossed the Guardian's face, as though he suddenly realized that the ferrics were soldiers responsible for disarming the Builder's weapons and fighting him. Their lives were always on the line.

The Guardian nodded, at last. "Maybe this time will be different," he said, jutting his chin to the side as he chewed over the idea. "After all, it is rare the two of you can ever agree on something, Osric…Lutin. It has only happened once or twice every couple-hundred years, if my mental log is correct. And you, Osric, are nothing if not exacting. Careful, though, Lutin. That you don't fall off the edge with that one." He nodded at me. "Or God help us all."

I rocked uncomfortably on my heels.

Sighing like a father relenting to his children, the Guardian gave in. "Just this once. Once."

"Thank you," Lutin replied.

The other brothers echoed their gratitude.

The Guardian reached inside a cupboard in the gray marble island and retrieved seven small glass cylinders. He set all but one down on the counter. He retrieved a tiny hammer, no longer than my right index finger, and chipped off a piece of gold, which fell inside the vial with a *tink*. As the rock tumbled in, a few drops of the golden blood, like viscous mercury, also slipped inside.

I released a breath I didn't realize I was holding. I closed my eyes and mouthed *thank you* to Lutin.

The Guardian set the capsule down and retrieved an empty one to repeat the process.

Surveying the room, I looked to my right, past Osric and the others, and noticed for the first time another door. Around the frame, a fierce and beautiful light glistened like sugar on fire. I felt drawn to it by eyes and by heart.

"Domum," Lutin said when he noticed my focus.

My breath caught in my throat. I refused to blink or look away from it, lest the image abandon me.

"The ferrics' home. *Our* home." He placed a hand on my arm. "One day, you will go there. We will live there."

The light surrounding the door to Domum resonated in me, and it did not pass when I looked at Lutin. Osric's threat on the abandoned street, however, pecked at me.

"I've never seen anything so beautiful," I said.

Lutin nodded, his dark and fiery features appearing all the more real. He half-smiled and cupped a hand to my face, returning me to myself. "You okay?"

"Yes," I said. I searched for something to say to distract him. "Why doesn't the Builder just come here and take it all?"

Lutin took a deep breath and spoke as though he knew that wasn't what was on my mind. "The Creator crafted the Guardian such that no one who has ever killed someone can kill him. That bars all the ferrics and the Builder from harming him."

"And you," the Guardian piped up.

My head swiveled to face him. His back was turned to us, but he was nevertheless aware of me, of our quiet conversation.

"Yes. And you," Lutin responded, frowning. "Only he can retrieve the godsoul, and only he decides who and who doesn't get a piece of it. Without him, the supply would likely have been depleted to nothing long ago."

"Centuries ago," the Guardian corrected. He filled the last capsule and capped it, setting it beside the others.

Osric clasped them all in a fist, his breath heavy. "Thank you, Guardian."

The Guardian closed his eyes and nodded. He crossed his arms and turned to the wall, as though he could barely part with what he'd given us.

"Let's go," Osric said.

Osric led us back through the chamber, down the royal purple hall lined with rock showing the faintest hint of gold across its matte surface. I wondered if those areas had been mined of godsoul long before.

The entrance door opened, and we exited back onto the street of Basille, Louisiana's arts district.

I turned to catch one more glimpse of the purple and gold cave and the little man in the middle of it all who stared at me before the door shut. The light disappeared.

CHAPTER 4
FRATER

Jack

Lutin's hand grasped my shoulder. Our eyes met.

"Jack," he whispered.

"Yes?"

"I can tell something is on your mind. I won't press you. But I do feel the need to say that whatever it is, whatever happens…if you don't believe you can do this, don't. But if you do, you should see it through. No matter what happens to me, what happens to the others. Do whatever you can to see it through."

My heart thudded hard. "I will," I said. "Of course."

He looked down. His black eyelids made it seem as though his eyes had disappeared. "And ignore the Guardian. He's been in his cave far too long."

"I know."

"I know you do. Even so, sometimes people have a funny way of convincing us we're less than we are."

"Like Cyrus."

He smiled. "You know well. Not to listen. You know not to listen to *anyone*. You should be as deaf to the highest of the high as you are to Cyrus."

I bit my lip and nodded.

"Yes?" he asked.

"Yes."

Osric cleared his throat, and Lutin's hand left my shoulder. Before I could speak again, to reassure Lutin and thank him, I sensed the others' eyes on me. Instead, I returned to them.

"Take one," Osric said. He handed out the godsoul capsules to his brothers and, finally, to me. I held mine up to the light of the nearby streetlamp. Golden drops slid down the sides of the glass, glowing. My mouth watered.

Soul blood. The Creator's soul.

The others slipped the vials into their pockets, and I did the same. We formed a circle. I stood between Lutin and Pepluv, the ferric with black dreadlocks—the only one who had voted against my plan.

"Do you understand what is about to happen?" Osric said. I lifted my eyes to him. He seemed to be weighing my intelligence.

I turned the capsule in my pocket. The gold inside clinked. "What?"

"We are about to go where the Builder is. To the edge of his cave. And I must warn you. Funny things happen to a person's mind at the edge of the Beretrum. Some behave unlike themselves. We are accustomed to it. You? I have no idea what effect it will have on you."

He and I both understood this was the second time he'd spoken of the Beretrum. Nothing in his expression betrayed that, though, or that he had told me my fate was hell. I tried to put what he'd said behind me. There was no time or energy for it.

"What kinds of things?" I asked.

"Some experience nausea and vertigo," Lutin said, "as though they are standing on a ceiling upside down. Others, receive a constant stream of thoughts and madness. Still others, a lust for a myriad of evil." Lutin's face betrayed nothing of what he expected from me. "But you might not need to worry about the latter."

Osric cleared his throat. "Or she might need to worry the most."

"I'll keep it in mind," I said.

"No pure ferric can willingly enter the Beretrum," Osric added, holding up a large piece of gold rock, the godsoul. It glowed in the night. "That's why we are going to lure the Builder out with this."

We all stared at the glowing gold.

"The Builder hungers for it, unable to control his appetite. That's why he eats the innocent," Osric said. "Because every innocent carries the tiniest bit of godsoul within. It's his way of mining it out of the world."

An image of Cyrus's red velvet box filled my mind and the memories of the men and women he had killed using it in his mansion. The shining, brassy gramophone I'd encountered in New York replaced those images, then the memory of being dragged across cement into a Victorian house, my clothes bleaching to white, the white goo that poured out of the bell nearly killing me. Other *arcas* flashed in my mind, as well as the whole of Infinitum, the faces of the children I'd saved, and Cyrus's planned bombing. Now I understood why the Builder coerced people to murder—he got something out of it, more than just the devolution of good. It was power, food. He could not get godsoul through the Guardian, so he'd found a different path.

"The *arcas* eat souls," I said, realizing what I'd already known, but in a much more comprehensive way.

"Yes," Osric sighed. "They are versatile tools he uses to coerce people, like your father, to murder again and again. Then he can absorb more and more."

"What happens if the Builder gets hold of that godsoul?" I said, pointing to the piece Osric held in his hand.

Osric glanced at Lutin. "His power increases," he said. "He grows, becomes able to create large-scale catastrophes—violence, death, and horror beyond measure. The balance of good and evil tips hard toward evil. If we don't tip it back, everyone dies."

I shivered. "What would happen if he were to acquire a larger piece of godsoul?"

"The end," Osric answered.

He nodded to the group. "We will drink the godsoul for protection. Then we will lure the Builder out and kill him," Osric said, pointedly staring at me. "And then you will *resurrect* him…if you can."

"Are you certain you want this?" Pepluv asked, tilting his chin up. His dreadlocks swayed behind him.

I searched inside myself for the answer. It wasn't about what I wanted. It was about what I needed, what the world needed—for the chaos to end, for there to be final, blessed stillness and, out of that stillness, something better. No more Cyruses, no more Roths, no more Alexes. Lutin had gifted me with a power beyond anything he or I could have expected, a power none of the others had. There was a reason for that. I was meant to use it.

It didn't matter that I was going to hell. There was already so much hell.

"Yes," I said. "More than anything."

The ferrics exchanged looks.

"All right," Osric whispered, an edge to his voice. He seemed vulnerable for the first time. He blinked slowly, and the world around us broke into particles. The colors blended like pieces of a puzzle, spiraling and spinning. Lutin, his brothers, and I stood in the midst of a reality that shifted like sand. Then the sand sank.

A cloudy sky showing the faintest edge of morning materialized above us. Cold air blew my hair back from my face. A wall of gray, blue, and white rock dropped down from the clouds. Snow emerged beneath our feet, and we sank deeply into it. Behind us, a cliff appeared, and beyond that, in the great distance, sprouted mountain upon mountain. A frigid wind caught us, but I didn't freeze. The fire within me remained impermeable. My feet and hands never threatened to go numb. I grasped the snow, noticing it melted in my hand without ever cooling it.

To our left, a circular chasm opened to reveal a cave far below. Around this circle, all the snow had disappeared. Deep claw marks sliced into white rock.

"Where are we?" I asked.

"The Appalachian Mountains," Lutin said, puffing moisture into the air like exhaled smoke. His black eyes mirrored the blue rock, momentarily humanizing him. The dawn gave his skin a human quality.

A frisson ran through me. It was one thing to move from Cyrus's house to the nearby Basille Arts District. It was another thing to travel across the country in mere seconds.

Lutin's dark pink lips spread. "You know, you can most likely translocate too."

"How?"

"Probably the same way that you learned to control others. You have to really want it. Think of a place and urge yourself there."

I considered his words and searched inside myself, poking and prodding for such a power. I pictured Jonathon Roth's office in Manhattan, where it was warm and rich and I controlled it all. I closed my eyes, drunk with the idea that I could will myself there. I decided to try. If it worked, I could then bring myself back to Lutin.

I gripped my hands into fists and squeezed my eyes tight. I envisioned Purdom with as much detail as I could—the marble floors, the lower-level parking garage with its fluorescent lights, the basement cell lined with lead where I'd been imprisoned for months, Jonathon Roth's office on the fourteenth floor with its dark wooden floors, open windows, and mint curtains twirling in the warm New York breeze. Yet cold air continued to creep along my skin. Nothing happened. I released a breath and relaxed my muscles.

"You don't really want it," Lutin said. "Not with this task ahead. You should try when we're through."

He was right. I didn't want it. Not really. More than anything, I was ready to end it.

Lutin placed his hand on my back, and we trudged through the snow.

Our group reached the edge of where the ice ended, fifteen feet from a pure white tunnel that led straight down into darkness. I waited for a sense of vertigo, of nausea, but all I sensed was the cool wind, the scent of the fresh air, the ice, and the warmth of the ferrics near me.

Flutri shook his head back and forth. Inarin pressed his hand to his mouth and lurched as if he might vomit. I leaned back, wary of splatter. None arrived. I listened to my body, waiting for a headache, a paranoid thought, a desire for death.

"Feeling anything?" Osric asked.

"No," I said, my eyes flicking to his. He remained expressionless. I knew what he was thinking—that it made sense I was unaffected. I was as impure as the Beretrum. That's why I was destined to belong there.

I stared back at him and cocked my head. *What of it?*

His gaze shifted to the group. He retrieved his vial from his pocket. I did the same.

I held the warm, glowing bit of soul in my hand, wondering what it would taste like. The others popped the caps free. Without thinking twice, I uncorked the glass and opened my mouth. I downed the contents.

The plasma and rock on my tongue tasted of sweet char—metallic, but honeyed. The solid pieces crushed easily between my teeth and melded with the liquid. It rolled down my throat. Inside, a firework exploded. The embers filtered out to my limbs, warming all of me, making me feel whole and part of every living thing that had ever existed or would exist—not just the ferrics but the Builder himself—as though all of life were one miraculous piece. All of us lived and died, warred and healed in beautiful, synchronistic symphony, each a specific and necessary cog.

I grinned, enlivened, powerful, and protected. I wanted to grab Lutin and hug him. A singular joy, one perfect moment, embraced me.

I reached out to Lutin.

My fingers glided through the air. Halfway there, something in my gut dropped, curdled. The beautiful thing inside me shifted.

I collapsed to my knees in the soft, cold powder.

"Jack," Lutin said. He dropped beside me. "What's wrong?"

I opened my mouth to say something, but I couldn't manage a word. Something lodged in my throat. My stomach convulsed, and I vomited bright red liquid across the snow. The heat turned ice to steam.

"Shit. *What happened?*"

I tried to answer Lutin, tell him I didn't know. I believed that my body was reacting to the godsoul, that something in me was rejecting it. But I couldn't speak. I trembled. The warmth that filtered out to my limbs numbed them. I couldn't feel the ice or wind or my own clothing.

Something neon red, as bright as fire, flashed nearby. I lifted my head. Lutin no longer knelt beside me. Some feet away, I found him standing in the middle of his four brothers. With a bright red rope, like a string of lava, they bound his hands in front of him. Osric said something. Lutin shoved him.

What was happening? Was the Beretrum creating this vision? Had it caused them to attack each other? I pressed my head against the ice, trying to steady myself. A wave of dizziness hit me, and I collapsed on my side. Too weak to pull myself back up, I could only watch.

"You're dying!" Osric yelled. "You've got to reclaim the piece of your heart!"

"I won't let you kill her!" Lutin growled.

"I won't let *you* die!"

As he lunged toward Osric again, three brothers grabbed Lutin and pulled him back. He floated for a moment and fell back to the snow under the weight.

"*You heard her!*" Osric called, cutting Lutin off. "She can control who she resurrects, and she resurrected *us*! She could use us to get the godsoul, and she would be unstoppable. If she has control of the Builder, there's no knowing what she would do. I can't allow this."

The brothers dragged Lutin down into the snow, jerking his arms and pinning him as he shouted. One brought out a knife and lifted Lutin's shirt.

An image of Cyrus's basement door flashed in my mind, my child's hand pushing it open, hearing Lutin's screams as Cyrus carved away his soul for the red box. "*No,*" I mumbled. Not again.

"For all you know," Osric said, "when that piece of your heart is back inside your chest, you will retain her power and enslave the Builder yourself. All we can do is hope."

Flutri sliced into Lutin.

I tried to scream but couldn't. Black dots flooded my vision.

Flutri cut a long line into Lutin's chest and stomach. He lay the bloody knife on the snow, and Osric walked to me, his dark coat flapping in the wind. The toe of his boot connected with my chest. I toppled onto my back.

He flourished a knife.

"Don't hurt him," I whispered.

He squinted at me. "Lutin? Wouldn't dream of it." He removed his coat and rolled up his black shirt sleeves. "After all, you're the one who's killing him. Without that bit of his heart he gave you, he has a limited time. A few months left, perhaps. And I'm not going to let his death happen."

Was that true? It couldn't be.

Osric dropped on his knees, sinking deep into the snow.

"No," I managed. "He would've told me."

"You don't know him very well. He loves you, and he has every intention of sacrificing himself for you. But we won't allow it. Not for someone bound for hell."

My mind reeled, and tears filled my eyes.

Osric spread the flaps of my coat wide and lifted my shirt. He raised the knife and brought it down.

"Don't," I snarled. The power in me commanded him.

The knife stopped an inch from my belly, the same place where Lutin had once sliced me to insert a piece of his heart. Osric struggled, trying to push his hand forward, to press the blade into my skin. The tip brushed my stomach, and I shut my eyes tight, pursing my lips, willing Osric to stop with all of my remaining energy. He struggled, thwarted by an invisible force that prevented him from cutting me. The tip of the blade shook against my skin.

The blade lifted, and Osric gritted his teeth, his eyes growing wide at his disobeying hand. He jammed the knife into the snow. "Shit."

I gasped, sweating. "Looks like I *can* control immortals as well as humans," I whispered through brain fog.

He shook his head. "Doesn't matter. I can wait for you to finish dying and claim the piece of his heart from you then."

"What did you do to me?"

"I weaponized your godsoul," he panted, "combining it with *actaea pachypoda*—a poisonous berry."

This wasn't the first time I'd heard of the plant. It wasn't the first time it had been used on me. Cyrus tried to poison me with it when I was a child, using it to choose which children he did and didn't take in, a kind of Russian roulette. I'd been fortunate to survive. Did Osric know? He had to, my gut told me. The attempt was too much of a coincidence not to have been planned.

"And you say you hate Cyrus," I said.

"Within the hour, you will die," Osric replied. "When you do, your power over us will end, I'll carve out that piece of your heart that's Lutin's, and I'll return it to my brother."

Tears slipped from my eyes. Why had I gone with them, ignoring that my gut had warned me in their presence? Why had I believed that they would help me?

"Either way, you lose," he said, "and either way, Lutin lives. So give up, Jack."

I lay helpless, as did Lutin across the snow, his stomach cut open. I sensed the poison at work, spreading throughout my limbs. "I didn't know he was dying," I said. "I'm sorry."

Osric bent low, his hands on his thighs. "He didn't want to tell you. He wants you to live. He believes in you." He leaned over me, and rage bloomed in his face. "I don't. I believe in Lutin.

"So, Jack, are you going to make him wait for his heart, bleed for the hour until you die? Or are you going to let me get on with it? I promise if you do, you won't feel a thing."

I should have taken control of all of them from the very beginning. They had tricked me, led me to think that they believed in me. Of course, they'd had to.

Lutin yelled in their language that I could not decipher—the liquid, florid language.

I let my eyes drift to the sky, the clouds slowly brightening in the sun.

I shut my eyes and willed the brothers to release him and me. I looked into Osric's eyes and demanded, "Help me. Cure me of what you poisoned me with."

Osric straightened his back and clenched his jaw. His body jerked. His hand retrieved from his jacket in the snow a larger piece of godsoul—the bait for the Builder. Holding it between two fingers, he brought it near my mouth. Specks of drifting snow landed on the gold.

I opened my mouth, ready for the antidote—pure, unadulterated godsoul.

A vein on Osric's face popped, and his white skin was tinted red. He shook, as though trying with all his might not to drop the godsoul in my mouth. His hand slowly descended.

Dots speckled my vision, and I urged him to hurry.

Boom.

The ground shook. Snow collapsed and tumbled. Balls of ice spilled across me.

A shadow loomed above Osric. In the distance, his brothers hollered.

A giant white hand, stretched like putty, hooked around Osric's body. His face revealed his horror as he was jerked away from me, the godsoul with him. The white hand dragged Osric toward the opening in the mountain. The godsoul dropped into the snow, far from me, landing like a tiny asteroid, forming a dot in the ice, quickly vanishing. I struggled to move toward it and managed a few inches before I lost power to the poison.

A creature, pure white, towered on the edge of the Beretrum, multiple arms protruding from its core, each looped around an unconscious ferric. Lutin lolled, his sliced stomach bleeding on the slimy white skin of the Builder. The blood blanched when it contacted the creature.

A second figure appeared, equally as white but a different shape, near the edge of the Beretrum. It was close to the ground, much shorter—a man. It walked toward me, stopping where the godsoul had landed to kneel. Fingertips and nails pierced the ice. A white sleeve met a white wrist. My eyes stretched up his form, barely able to make him out against the snow. White sleeves met a white collar, which met an equally white neck and face. I had never seen any person so white. It was as though he had been dipped in paint. His hair sprouted like ice crystals from his head.

He grimaced as he dug for the gold, and the face became familiar, like an illusionary piece of art finally becoming clear.

Alex.

He glanced without emotion in my direction as he pulled his fist free of the ice, opening it to reveal the chunk of gold in the palm of his hand. His eyes were entirely white, including his pupils. He regarded me as though I were just another person, part of the landscape, not the sister he despised. My brother, whatever he used to be, had been erased.

Alex's mouth widened, and he popped the godsoul in.

"*No!*" I yelled.

He swallowed, his white Adam's apple bobbing up and down. A powerful sonic boom filled the air. It reverberated, shaking the snow around me, beneath me, Alex at its center. A cold terror filled me. My body went numb.

Beyond him, a new limb formed on the white core of the Builder and dove into the snow, slithering over the ice like a snake. It reached for me.

I turned, shut my eyes, and whispered, yearning for the first place, the first person, I could think of.

"Patrick."

CHAPTER 5
CICATRIX

Jack

THE BUILDER, THE ICE, SNOW, and mountain all disintegrated. Blue, white, gray, and black swirled around me, blending, until there were no distinct images, no more colors. I was laying on blackness. I couldn't tell if I'd simply lost consciousness or if I'd become stuck in the dark, unable to fully translocate.

A blessed light bloomed around me. Warmth replaced ice. The scent of a fireplace infused the air. A voice spoke.

"Holy shit."

I opened my eyes.

I lay on a dark green carpet facing a vast floor, at the end of which a large, dark cherrywood desk gleamed against firelight. Behind the desk, three tall windows stretched like a cathedral, open to the night. Golden curtains framed them. To the left, a silver cart supported a large array of brown liquid in bottles. On either side of it were two closed doors. Flames reflected against the silver cart from a fireplace at my right. A figure moved from behind the desk, and a speck of red…or orange…broke into view.

"Who the fuck are…" The thin Irish accent stopped.

Shoes padded toward me across the carpeted floor. Someone sat beside me. I looked up.

Patrick.

He looked different than I remembered. His hair was more orderly, trim, although the back was messy, like he'd fallen asleep in a chair. His face was thinner, and he'd lost any remaining baby fat. The freckles on his cheeks were more pronounced, like he'd been in the sun. He wore black slacks and a white shirt.

His green eyes darted over me wildly. His hands reached out and then retreated, again and again, not daring to touch me but at the same time demanding to.

"Jack?" he whispered, squinting, his red eyebrows arched. He trembled, as if he were cold.

"It's me."

"What…what the hell happened? What the hell are you? How did you…What did…What are…" The half-formed questions kept coming, and he looked around the room and back at me as if for answers or someone who might be lurking and could explain everything.

I swallowed, feeling both safe and exposed at the same time. The white monster no longer loomed, threatening to kill me and pull me down into his cave. I had momentarily evaded hell. But Lutin was gone, his brothers were gone, and I was losing consciousness.

"I'm sick," I said.

"What happened to you? What…what's on your skin? You don't look like you."

"I'm not," I said, and I struggled to breathe. My chest hurt. "I've been poisoned."

Relief flooded his face. "Right. I'll call an ambulance. I'll get you to a hospital." He hopped to his feet.

"No, no!" My voice boomed against the walls. Patrick jumped at the sound and froze. "Don't call anyone. Come here." I held my hand out toward him. He winced, hesitated, but at last clasped my palm.

"You can't call anyone or tell anyone about me," I said. "No doctor can help me."

Patrick swallowed. "All right," he said uncertainly. "So what do I do?"

"I need to tell you something."

He leaned near, so near I could feel his breath on my face.

"There's something out there, Patrick. It's larger than any of us." I searched for words to explain it, but I didn't have the energy, and so I chose the fewest that would suffice. "Heaven. Hell. It's there. It's real. And I'm…"

"What?" he asked.

"I'm not of this world. I've been poisoned by something not of this world."

Patrick pulled back, nodding, though his eyes betrayed belief, disbelief, wonder, excitement, fear. "Okay, okay, okay," he whispered, more to himself than to me. He wiped his sweaty forehead. "I believe you, Jack. You're just…you don't look so good, and it's scaring me."

"I'm not," I said. "I'm dying."

A muscle in Patrick's jaw popped. "Okay. So…tell me what I need to *do*. Tell me what to do to get you better."

He didn't understand. "There is no getting better. I can't get better. That's what I'm trying to tell you."

He grunted and jumped to his feet. "What do you mean?" He laughed without humor. "You're just…you're just laying here and dying? How did you even get in here? Is there someone I can get for you? Isn't there…? I mean, there has to be someone I can call."

My mind shifted to Osric, Flutri, Pepluv, and the others. The image of the white creature grabbing them all. The last bit of godsoul—my last hope—dropping into the snow. Alex claiming it, eating it. Rage bloomed.

The godsoul.

Godsoul.

That was what I needed. Osric had almost held the antidote to my lips, as I'd commanded. But the Builder grabbed him, and he'd dropped it. Alex had found it and eaten it. There was no more godsoul available. I squeezed my eyes shut, tears slipping down my cheeks.

Another image came to me. An old, frail man with a large nose and hairy ears frowning at me, rageful, gold covering his arms like gloves.

Lutin's words echoed in my head. *The Creator crafted the Guardian such that no one who has ever killed someone can kill him.* My gaze lifted to Patrick.

Patrick stared at me, wide-eyed, like an innocent lamb. His supple lips and freckled skin, his red hair all lustrous and charming. The idea that came to me was so horrible that I cringed and rolled away from him.

"Patrick, get away from me," I warned.

He knelt down. Once again, his breath fell on my face.

"What are you talking about?" he said. "Tell me who to call."

I shook my head. "You couldn't possibly…"

"What?" he asked, suddenly vulnerable. Moments passed before he repeated the question.

"…be capable of what I would need from you," I finished. I brought my knees to my chest.

I shouldn't have called out for him, shouldn't have translocated to him. I should have gone to Jasper instead. Jasper had worked with a kill-for-hire organization for years, had seen people die—he could withstand it. As weak as I now was, I doubted I could get to him. All I could do was lay on the floor and breathe.

Patrick crawled around to face me and pressed a palm to mine. I looked down and saw that all the light in my body had extinguished. The lines in my skin had blackened. Dust or char replaced the brilliant, fiery strikes in my flesh. It marked the green carpet.

Tears slipped down my cheeks and dropped to the floor.

Patrick whispered, as though something beyond him was speaking through him. "I cannot sit here and watch you die. I'm capable of whatever you need from me. Tell me what to do."

I stared into his face, tears burning my eyes. My throat refused to swallow. He had no idea what damage I'd done to him a month and a half ago. He had no idea what I truly was. I couldn't ask him to help me.

More importantly, what was the point? I had been rejected by those most like me. All the ferrics I could control had tried to kill me and then been abducted, likely killed. Lutin included. It wrecked me to even think about it. And more, according to Osric no matter what I did or chose, I was bound for hell. Permanently. I was permanently unclean. And I wasn't about to spread myself like a virus.

"I'm not worth you losing yourself," I told Patrick, resting my head more solidly on the floor.

"Jack." He shook my arm. "Jack, I know you. And you are...you are worth *everything*. Just tell me what to *do*." He pressed a hand to my face and trembled. "Tell me what to do, and I will *do it*," he implored.

I swallowed bile and thought about what the consequences of my death there in his office might be. What would Patrick do with my body? What would happen to Cyrus? And Roth? And the one hundred and sixty individuals I had been forced to resurrect? Free from my control, would they go back to their former behavior—murder, building a cult, killing for hire? What would happen to the Builder?

Lutin's voice arrived, as though he were at my ear. *Do whatever you can to see it through.*

I groaned. My cheeks flushed, and I momentarily felt warmth in my skin.

"But you are so innocent," I said, looking up into Patrick's face.

Through Patrick's fog of fear, a wicked grin broke free. Sweat dribbled down one cheek as he laughed. "Come on, Jack. Who do you think you're talking to?"

I swallowed, guilt and exhaustion pressing upon me. My eyes became heavy.

"No one's innocent here," he said.

I shuddered. It was a nice thought, but it was the thought of a naive summer child. Sure, Patrick had been a drug addict for most of his life, but there were vast differences between drug use and murder, manipulation, and loss of soul.

My breath wheezed; my chest rattled. If I was going to make a choice, I had to do it soon.

Despairing internally at what I was about to say, I formed my hands into fists. I needed to survive. Not for me. But for the world. If I fell like Lutin and his brothers, chaos and evil would inevitably gain footholds. Ferrics were the dam that held them back. Besides, Lutin might not truly be dead.

"Fuck," I whispered at last. "I have a gun in my jacket pocket, Patrick. Take it."

I felt him rustle in my coat. He retrieved the gun and held it in his hand, tip to the floor. "All right," he said.

"Now, I need you to tell me the truth." I peered up at him, locking onto his eyes. "Have you ever killed anyone?"

His forehead creased, and he slowly shook his head. "Of course not."

Relief and fear flooded me at the same time. "Swear to me."

"I swear. I've never killed anyone." He laughed. "What does it matter?"

I sighed and shivered as a new wave of fever broke out across my skin. "I believe you. I believe you." I took a deep breath. "Now, listen. I might lose consciousness, and if I do, I need you to wake me. But I'm going to tell you what to do. I need you to get a knife. Cut me somewhere. My palm, my arm, it doesn't matter. I need you to collect my blood in a bowl. Can you do that?"

He grimaced and nodded.

"Quick."

He stood and then left the room. I lay on the floor, feeling the slow, languid beating of my heart, until he returned. I had begun to feel death itself invading me, and I was thankful that I wasn't alone, whatever we were doing, even if I was leading Patrick to hell's ledge, if not simply pushing him over. I felt my hand being lifted and then the slicing of my skin. After a moment, Patrick said, "Is this enough blood?"

I peered into a hammered golden bowl, a meditation bowl. It was about half full of my blood.

"You did good," I said. I lifted my bloody hand and pointed toward a door to the right of the silver liquor cart. "Use the blood to outline the door, from jamb to floor. Create a frame."

Appearing dubious, as though for the first time wondering whether this was just some strange hallucination that might harm us if he continued, Patrick walked to the door. He dipped his hand in my blood, which had turned black, and drew the outline, just as I asked.

He peered back at me expectantly.

"Now, I need you to lift me," I said.

Without question, he set the now-empty bowl down on the wooden desk and came over. He tried lifting me, but it was a struggle. I was barely able to balance on my own two feet. At last, I found a way to stay upright, and he walked me toward the door. There, I nearly collapsed.

I leaned against the wall and pressed the hand Patrick had cut to the right of the door's center and mumbled the words that I remembered Osric saying. "*Patefacio tutor godsoul.*"

My blood glowed hot around the door frame, as though embers had ignited in it. Wavering light shone from beneath the door. Patrick gasped and nearly dropped me.

"Sorry," he muttered.

"It's okay. Set me down."

He did. All around us the room dimmed, and his attention veered this way and that as he watched reality disintegrate. All that remained was the door. Dots speckled my vision, and I felt like vomiting.

"Do you have the gun?" I mumbled, my mouth dry, the words sticking.

"Yes," he said, wiping sweat from his jaw with the back of his forearm. He stared at the doorway, wide-eyed, mouth open, as though he surveyed the edge of a miracle. He wasn't ready for what I needed.

"Good," I said. I used the little strength left in me to keep from collapsing. "I apologize for what I'm about to ask of you. I can't demand it. It's something you need to choose for yourself."

Patrick nodded.

"The only way I can heal is if you open that door and kill the person on the other side. He guards what looks like golden rock. I need a piece of that rock. That's the antidote to this poison. I need you to take a piece from him.

"But you have to kill him, Patrick. He won't just give it to you. If he learns it's for me, he'll likely kill me, and maybe you too. And, to tell you the truth, I'm not entirely sure a gun will work on him. But it's the only thing I can think of right now. And you're the only one who can do it.

"Look at me," I pleaded.

The shimmering light from under the door played on half of Patrick's panic-stricken face, an emerald eye, his crimson hair. The other half stayed in shadow.

"I know that what I'm asking of you is terrible, and I can't demand it. I'm about to lose consciousness. When I do, if I die, I die. I don't hold that against you. You shouldn't either. Do you understand?"

Patrick bit his lip and nodded. He stared at the door and the shining light beyond it.

"I always loved you," I said. "In the way I knew how."

Darkness flooded my vision, and my head met the floor. All was silent and still.

CHAPTER 6
PEPERIT

Patrick

JACK LAY UNCONSCIOUS, HER BODY cold, black in places it'd never been black before, like bruises. A dark, rough substance sloughed off from a black line on her clavicle. It resembled dried tar. Whatever flowed in her wasn't black in just color. It seemed to draw all the energy from the air and from me. The green carpet of my father's office became yellow around her, then white. *Impossible.*

A warm gust of air approached to my right. I turned. My heart rushed to the base of my throat, climbing up and out, apparently ready to abandon me. Just before the last time I'd felt like this, ten lines of coke on a small mirror beckoned. I'd snorted the electricity quick while Donovan and Carina made out on the pink velvet sofa in Carina's apartment. That was over four months ago.

Gold dust tumbled through the crack below the door. A speck landed on Jack's revolver. My hand shook. The adrenaline crackling down my spine insisted that it was impossible I was holding a gun, but I needed to use it, and I needed to hurry.

Reality hit me in waves. Jack both was and wasn't on the floor of my father's office. She both was and wasn't a creature unlike anything I'd ever seen. I both had and hadn't been pulled away from reviewing costs to rebuild the four destroyed Lucient Laboratories buildings. I didn't know where I was anymore. I didn't understand what reality was anymore. A woman I hadn't seen in two months appeared on my floor, and soon she told me that if I didn't kill someone and steal something she would die. It was a sick joke, and I wished it would end, that someone holding a camera would open the door and tell me it was all a prank.

No one was coming though.

I pushed myself up to my knees, rose to my feet, and walked toward the door. Golden light wavered on the tips of my shoes. My teeth clacked like marbles and earthquakes, grinding together. It was a wonder they didn't break.

I held the gun in my hand.

I didn't want to go through, but Jack was dying.

Jack was dying.

And Jack had always been good to me.

I took a good look at the revolver. There might be a safety, but I couldn't find any semblance of one. Jack had held this gun, and I tried to take comfort in that. I tried to take comfort in the gold velvet curtains on the other side of the room, in the fact that I could start using again after this if I wanted. I could do whatever I desired. I gave myself permission to go wild. I just had to go do this one thing, and then I'd be forever free from doing it, or anything else, again.

I grasped the warm door handle and pulled. The door groaned open.

A purple rock hallway lined with shimmering gold stripes like spider's web and honeycombs reached high on either side of me. I didn't have the time to gape, but I couldn't help it. Through the miraculous hallway, at the very end, shone pure, endless gold. It stretched impossibly tall, like a frozen wave, and shimmered with energy. A small gray and white counter stood in front of it. Only the sound of dripping met me. I waited.

Someone shuffled inside the room that opened up beyond the hall.

My body broke out in sweat. I wasn't hot though. If anything, I was cold. Had I caught whatever it was Jack had? I wanted to climb the walls and take a bite, swallow the gold —all of it. I wanted to chisel the gold into powder and go back to the apartment with Donovan and Carina and snort gold lines until my eyes turned gold.

My footsteps echoed far above me, as though I were a giant following myself. I sensed several other versions of me trailing behind, all of us Patricks dressed for business and knowing not at all how to conduct it. God, I needed a drink. And a snort. And a laugh. And a cry. And a fuck. And I needed them all at once or I was going to explode.

I reached the end of the hall.

"Son," someone said. I turned to the man at my left. My gaze met his golden eyes, and it felt as though the room itself were watching us, waiting to see what happened. I hesitated, afraid he'd launch himself at me before I could lift the gun, as though he were a creature with impossible powers, like Jack turned out to be. I had a feeling impossible powers were the rule on this side of the door.

I gasped and tried to swallow. There was no saliva left.

Could he see the gun?

I leaned against the island in the center of the room, as though I were a man looking at jewelry in a case, choosing a piece for his lover. I bit my bottom lip, met the man's eyes again. He wore a gold-splattered apron, as though he'd been painting with it or killing it. Gold stretched up his arms like gloves and glistened as bright as the wall behind him, like he was part of the wall, like the wall was stretching out toward me, looking at me through this man's eyes. His gray hair spiked up, gold on the tips, like a halo. He was not a tall man, but the energy coming off him was hot and fierce.

Was this the moment that would destroy me or was I already destroyed?

The man smiled a knowing smile, like he'd foreseen what was coming and he knew how to stop me. I might have been a fly he could swat without trouble. *Come on*, his expression seemed to say. *This is nothing compared to what I've seen.*

I raised the gun, and I aimed, breathing out, careful not to hold my hand rigid. I didn't squeeze the grip as I pulled the trigger. I allowed the gun to do its job without interference. An explosion echoed around the walls, the ceiling. I pulled the trigger four more times, and four more explosions followed. The man dropped to the floor, face first, blood coursing along the floor.

I backed away and stumbled, still pulling the trigger. Two clicks sounded before I stopped. A moan curled itself in my throat before I bolted down the hallway, away from the man and the blood. I dove into my father's office, dropped the gun, and scooped up the bowl that had held Jack's blood.

I pressed my hand to my mouth as my stomach roiled.

Nearly done, I told myself. *Just one more thing.*

Bowl in hand, I steeled my resolve, stood upright, and returned to the hall. A high as extreme as I ever felt washed over me. Was this why people murdered—the high? Did the high tell them that they're gods, powerful and impenetrable? It probably told them the same lies the high had always told me, whether coke, meth, or heroin. None of that omnipotence was real. It was just pretty. I was glad I'd stopped believing in pretty.

Rounding the island, I faced the wall of gold. The fragments that jutted out dripped, coating the floor beneath in a hard layer, flooding the stone floor beyond the marble counter island as though the wall had been weeping for millennia. I touched the rock, testing. Perhaps it wasn't as tough as I suspected. Maybe I could press my fingers into the surface and claim the material, simply drop it in the bowl.

But that attempt failed. The rock was too rough, hard. I scraped my knuckles against the surface. As quickly as blood began to seep, it stopped. The red slices healed over, no evidence they'd existed. The miniscule pain disappeared.

I inhaled and sighed it out. Jack wasn't lying. If this were a hallucination, logic controlled it, which meant it probably wasn't hallucination.

I scanned the area around me and noticed the doors along the island behind me. I stooped and opened them, one at a time, discovering a variety of clear bottles of varying sizes. Inside the set of doors to the right rested scissors, chisels, prongs, and saws. I grabbed a set of prongs and returned to the shining wall.

I walked to an area of jutting rock and held the bowl underneath. I clasped a lump with the prongs as hard as I could. Gold oozed over the tool, and I jerked the handles, breaking the chunk off. Thick, golden plasma flooded the bowl as if it were being pumped by a heart in the wall. It slowed. I dropped the piece of gold into the bowl and tossed the prongs into the cupboard.

Careful not to spill the full container, I circled to the other side of the island so I didn't have to see the body. Back inside my father's office, I sank to my knees beside Jack. I lifted her head and pressed the bowl to her pale lips.

"Drink," I whispered. "For the love of God, drink."

CHAPTER 7
MEDICOR

Jack

SOMETHING COOL MET MY LIPS, and a sweet, metallic flavor, not unlike blood, flooded my mouth. The familiar honey char was weighty but cleansing, and it slid down my throat as though it had purpose. I barely needed to swallow.

The fluid moved discernibly inside me, filtering into my organs, cleaning out the numbness and darkness with finesse. I opened my eyes and saw the bowl that had held my blood full of glowing gold in Patrick's hand. It held twenty times the amount that Osric had taken.

Wrong. Too much.

How could Patrick know better? He'd done as I asked. He'd won me my cure.

That meant he must have killed the Guardian. I shivered, and guilt expanded in the wake of relief.

I pushed the bowl away.

The beautiful, familiar wholeness, the sensation of life, of oneness with all, swept through me. I gasped, and pleasure erupted across my cells. I shuddered in delight.

Patrick sat there, bowl in hand. I saw him more and more clearly, smelled him, felt his presence, his gorgeous being.

He jumped back.

"What?" I said.

"Dear God. Your body."

I looked down. Fire flowed through the black lines in my skin. Sensation returned to my limbs, and I felt warm again.

"It's okay," I said. "It's supposed to be like that. You saved me, Patrick. Thank you. You saved me."

I noticed the purple rock hallway visible through the half-open door to my left. I couldn't see any farther.

I turned back to Patrick and thanked him again.

His face blank, he set the bowl down on the carpet and slumped with a deep sigh, as if released from a heavy weight. He scanned me with narrow eyes, appearing mesmerized by the fire under my skin. He leaned against the front of the desk and rubbed his face. Specks of blood dotted his white shirt.

"What...are you?" He peered at me, his fingers tented against his cheeks.

I recalled the words Lutin used to describe himself: *Noir étoile. Fear réiltín.* Blazing man. Ferric. Patrick wouldn't understand those terms.

He searched my eyes, waiting.

"I'm on the side of the good guys."

"That doesn't answer my question."

I rolled my upper lip between my teeth.

"Tell me." His determined voice had an edge. He didn't sound like Patrick. If he'd killed the Guardian, he probably wasn't exactly Patrick anymore.

I shouldn't tell him, but I wanted to. To my surprise, I yearned for confession. The words left my lips before I could stop them. "When I was seven years old, I was adopted by a man. His name was Cyrus Harper."

Patrick furrowed his eyebrows. "I know that name."

"That doesn't surprise me."

He squinted. "He's that cult leader, right? The one they never found?"

"Yes," I said. "And when I was a child, he adopted me, and he taught me how to kill."

Patrick searched my face. He opened his mouth but then shut it.

"If you want to know why, it was just who he was. He wanted to instigate the devolution of everyone he came in contact with, including me, including his son. He went about it in far different ways with each individual he encountered. I was useful because I killed those who blasphemed against him." The term "blaspheme" brought back old memories and sensations that I didn't care for of rituals. Blood. Sacrifice.

"And Cyrus, well…he was the real deal. He truly had…" I searched for the right word. "Magic."

Patrick's expression became alert, focused on what I was explaining.

"But the magic came from a creature locked in his basement. He siphoned blood and soul from it. He fed that creature's soul to a device that would identify traitors as soon as they turned against him. It also shielded us from ever being discovered. He used blood from that creature to resurrect people." I quailed at the memories. So much chaos, so much disorder—I was tired of the unnecessary horror.

"When I was seventeen I went down to the basement and met this being for the first time. And when I met him…"

I pictured Lutin lolling in the frayed and worn chair, a moth-eaten blanket covering his fiery body. As I smiled inwardly, tears filled my eyes.

"Well," I resumed, "he looked like I look now. I was fascinated, to say the least. Then…he did something no one else had done for me."

"What?"

"He gave me a piece of his heart. Slid it through my abdomen and up into my chest, placing it next to my heart. It didn't hurt. There was no pain. And then the wound immediately healed, just like an incision had never happened. It transformed me. I was able to resurrect the dead. The very first thing I resurrected was a rose." I smiled. "After that, a dog. After that, three girls Cyrus had poisoned."

"And then you escaped?" Patrick asked.

I shook my head. "No. No, that is what a normal person would have done. I'm not normal. We killed Cyrus. The other ferrics and I."

Patrick shivered.

As I continued my tale, the room around me came into focus, my hearing fully returned, and my heart rate slowed. I could breathe without pain, and my awakening limbs sensed my clothes and the soft, green carpet beneath me.

"Cyrus worked for the Builder—the enemy of the ferrics, which are creatures like me, like the being he imprisoned in his basement. The Builder is, essentially, the devil. He creates devices that he places around the world to beget murder. He convinced Cyrus to send thousands of children to schools and churches to bomb them. The night of one bombing, I discovered Lutin's brothers in an isolated part of the house and resurrected them. They helped Lutin and me escape. The brothers stopped the bombing, and Lutin killed Cyrus."

"Lutin was the creature?" Patrick asked.

"Yes." I nodded. "The ferrics abandoned me that night. For multiple reasons, I think... So I drove to New York in Cyrus's car."

Patrick lifted his eyes and tilted his head, as though weighing everything I'd told him. He scratched the red stubble on his chin. "What about the fire...in your skin?"

I glanced down, acknowledging the lightning strikes. "This is part of being a ferric."

"I didn't notice it when we were together last time."

Of course. I was not yet thinking clearly. "I was forced to help a man when I came to New York—one of his employees killed me. I was dead for seven days but I came back to life. When I did, my body had black marks, like vines, across it. Later..." I paused, on the verge of explaining that I could control those I resurrected. I realized I shouldn't. Not with the doorway to the ferrics' realm so near. Not for Patrick's safety. "When I fully realized my power, the fire entered my body. And now I look like any ferric."

Patrick slipped his hand through his hair and tugged a hunk of it hard; his forehead went white.

"So you can resurrect the dead...and you are fighting what is essentially the devil."

I considered his words. "Yes."

"Then you are an angel," he said.

I thought about Osric defining my fate, and that he had poisoned me. "There are no angels here."

Patrick rose from the floor and headed to the silver cart, where he lifted a decanter. He poured himself a glass of brown liquor and leaned against the desk. I recalled my last phone conversation with Patrick, when I was still trapped with Roth. He'd said he had voluntarily gone to rehab to get clean. But I couldn't blame him, sober or not, for drinking after a night like this. He might drink every night. I just hoped he would be able to live with himself.

"How did you end up here, in my father's office?" he asked. "And what happened to you?"

I studied the room, taking it fully in for the first time. So this was Bryan Flannigan's office. The last time I saw Flannigan, Roth had killed him. Patrick didn't know that, and I wasn't about to tell him.

"I was poisoned. The Builder surprised us all when we arrived at the entrance to the Beretrum—that is, the entrance to his dwelling—and took Osric, the ferric who tried to kill me, along with several others. I escaped by translocating to the first place I could think of in detail. My power brought me here."

I understood now that Patrick had indeed killed the Guardian of the godsoul. Guilt, fear, and exhuastion emanated from him.

"I'm so sorry, Patrick," I said. "I'm sorry I asked that of you."

He closed his eyes, shook his head, and gulped a large swallow from the glass. "What's done is done, and you're alive. You didn't force me. I chose it. Just like you said." He studied me from behind his glass. "Who, though, did I just kill?"

"A man who wouldn't have let you save me. He controlled what's left of the godsoul."

"Godsoul," Patrick said, trying the word out. The meditation bowl gleamed beside us, empty of my blood, now a little less than half full of the liquid rock. "What is it?"

"I think…It may be the essence of a creature that created the world…"

Patrick swilled the rest of his drink. "Does that mean God?" There was tenderness in his voice, fear and sensitivity.

"I don't know."

Patrick's green eyes flashed. He moved from the desk and came to sit beside me. "Killing the Guardian of what's left of God was not good for a Catholic." He pressed two fingers to the outer corners of his eyes.

I winced. "No."

He exhaled with a gasp. "I'm glad you're okay," he whispered. "Don't get me wrong. But I don't know if I am."

I touched his back, releasing a little of my healing power toward him, doing my best to heal his soul. How he had blindly killed someone for my sake, I would never know. Had he done it because he trusted me? Or because the choice had been quickly forced on him? Maybe he couldn't let me go?

There was a philosophical conundrum along those lines about a train on a set of tracks that would diverge. One set of tracks led to five strangers; if the train went that way, it would kill them. The other set of tracks led to your sister or mother or best friend. Which set of tracks do you choose?

Patrick had made his choice.

His eyes traced the contours of the fire in my body. He pressed a hand to my clavicle. "You're so warm." He blinked. "I want you to tell me the truth."

I tensed, and I tried not to show it.

"All right."

"Do you think you're going to win?"

"Win?"

"Against the Builder."

I searched for the right words. "I hope so."

He brushed his hand against his cheek, and I couldn't tell if he was wiping away a tear. "If you don't, what will happen?"

"From what I understand, we'll all die."

"But you're not going to let that happen, right?"

I took a deep breath. It wasn't as simple as that, but I'd let it seem that way. For now. "Right."

Patrick slipped his arms around me, hugged me firmly, and I pressed him close, thankful we were both alive.

In my weakened state, so close to death and then saved by him, I seemed to feel love for Patrick more acutely than before.

At last, I released him and rose to my knees, then feet. I walked to the door that led to the Guardian of the godsoul. I pushed the open door wider and observed the pools of blood below the purple and gold. A body lay at the end of the hall.

All was quiet. No ferrics had yet arrived. It might be possible that no one knew the Guardian was dead or who killed him.

"Why don't you make us something to eat?" I said.

"I'm not hungry," Patrick replied.

Our eyes locked. "Even so."

His lips parted. "Oh." He shivered.

He pushed himself to his feet, grabbed the bottle of liquor off the cart, and left the room, shutting the door firmly behind him.

CHAPTER 8
ANIMUM

Jack

I RUSHED INTO THE PURPLE hall, toward the golden wall and the corpse of the Guardian. I peered down at his body, observed again the gold speckles on his clothes and the coat covering his hands and arms. He lay on his stomach, his face in profile. His eyes were empty, and he didn't breathe. I turned him over, pressing my fingers to his throat to test for a pulse, if he'd had one before. Blood coated the right side of his body. Blood seeped from a bullet hole in his cheek and from several in his chest, stomach, and pelvis. Patrick had unloaded on him.

No pulse. As far as I could tell, he was dead.

I wondered what the Guardian had thought when Patrick arrived, whether he'd said anything.

"I'm sorry," I said to his body.

I bent and grabbed the Guardian by his hands. I dragged him away from the godsoul, down the hall to the threshold that led to Patrick's father's office. His dead weight was heavy, but I was quickly returning to myself, my strength greater than any human's.

A red streak trailed behind on the marble floor. If I pulled him onto the green office carpet, the stain would be an eternal reminder of Patrick's act.

I searched Bryan Flannigan's office for something I could put under the body. My eyes settled on the gold velvet curtains behind the desk. They were long—the windows extraordinarily tall—and could be folded double or triple. I left the body and jerked one panel down. The rod popped off the wall, and I caught it, gripping it in my fist like a spear. I'd barely made a sound.

I removed the rod and folded the curtain in half before I rolled the corpse onto it and dragged the curtain and body across the carpet. Again leaving the body, I opened the door on the opposite side of the silver cart and flicked the light on to illuminate a white-tiled bathroom with a toilet, large marble sink, and bath tub. It would do. I pulled the Guardian into the bathroom, then heaved him into the tub. I gently lowered the Guardian's head and spotted four green towels to the left. I grabbed them. Next, I carried the towels to the godsoul room and pressed the towels to the floor hard, moving them forward slowly to make sure the cotton had a chance to absorb the blood. I kept an eye on the door to Domum, in case it opened.

The amount of blood was excessive for the soaked towels. I carried them back to the bathtub and then jerked down a second curtain panel.

I returned to the godsoul room and dropped the curtain to the floor to absorb the remaining blood. I wiped splatters from the cabinets with a washrag and sighed in relief that now no blood was noticeable. It was rushed work, but it would have to do.

I collected the bloodied curtains and washrag and carried them to Bryan Flannigan's office. After one last look down the hall, I firmly shut the door to the ethereal chamber. The darkness evaporated from the office as LED lights revealed the desk, green carpet, bottles of liquor, and sitting area. The frame around the portal faded away. I shuddered, and a heavy breath escaped me.

Dropping the curtains and rag on top of the body, next I scrubbed my hands at the sink, careful to eliminate blood from under my nails, and I observed myself in the mirror that stretched across the entirety of the double-sink counter. Tinges of illness were present in my face, almost like allergic shiners, but had nearly disappeared. My skin was pale, like tea mixed with cream, except my eyelids and near my clavicles, which were dark, as though coal had been drawn there, much like Lutin's. The fire in the lines that crawled like vines on my limbs burned hot and bright, shining through my clothes. My hair, so black it was almost blue, was badly tangled, and I ran my hands through it, separating the strands as well as I could. I splashed water on my face and dried it with a clean hand towel. A speck of blood dotted the sink, and I stared at it a long moment.

What should I do with the Guardian's body? My stomach churned.

It wasn't the poison. It was an overdose of sadness, weariness, yearning. Images of Lutin's body slack in the grip of a great white creature flashed through my mind. I leaned against the sink and dropped my head in my hands.

Lutin might not be dead, but he was gone, as were the others. I was entirely alone. There were other ferrics in the world, sure, but I didn't want to meet them. For all I knew, they would only impose additional impediments between me and my goal or try to kill me, like Osric. I had no idea what to do.

And was I truly doomed to the Beretrum? If, no matter what I did, that was my end, there might not be a point to any action anymore. I stood and turned away from the mirror and leaned against the sink.

If hell was my future, did that mean I would fail to stop the Builder, or perhaps succumb to temptation once I had control over him? I clacked my molars together. Did I have more wherewithal, more self-control, than that? Or was my fate inexorably tied to my past actions, rather than future ones? I had admittedly killed an unknowable number of individuals under Cyrus's direction. I had also forced Roth's kill-for-hire group to slaughter the last remnants of Cyrus's cult, Infinitum. There was blood upon blood on my hands, as thick as paint on a canvas. How could I be allowed in Domum?

It made sense to me that I wouldn't. People like me, people so deep in moral muck, were not allowed there. The only question now was would I nevertheless help the world, even though I was doomed? Would I try to help Lutin, even though he was probably dead? Would I try to kill the Builder, even though I would likely die?

Yes.

Of course. Yes.

There was no other answer. Patrick had sacrificed his soul for me. I could swallow whatever I had to.

Fresh determination seized me. Nausea receded. Even at my lowest, I had limitless freedom.

The blood-soaked towels and the Guardian's corpse remained to be dealt with. I took a deep breath and approached him.

With my hand on the Guardian's chest through the towels and curtains covering him, I closed my eyes and tried something new. I concentrated and willed myself and everything I touched to Cyrus's basement. Would everything arrive?

The bathroom's colors—cream, green, and white—swirled and blended into blackness. Abruptly I found myself standing on dark concrete in a musty room scented with smoke, in front of an incinerator, pulsing with heat. To my left stretched a hall that led to a set of stairs out of the basement. To my right, the hall veered sharply to the right and empty rooms. The loading doors of the incinerator were part open. A hot fire that had obviously been building for hours lit the chamber.

Who had filled the incinerator, started the fire? Certainly not Cyrus or Roland. My heart skipped. It was like the house had guessed what I wanted and was giving it to me.

I took a deep breath and opened the black grated door. Though the hot metal stung my fingers, it didn't burn me. I was too remote from my humanness for that.

I lifted the Guardian's body, finding that easier than expected. I realized I didn't know my own strength. I easily pushed the corpse inside. The curtains and towels I piled on top. The flames pulsed higher, thicker. I nimbly stepped back, sealing the door.

Beyond the vertically-sliced holes in the doors, red flames in the furnace turned blue, and the body caught. The skin blistered, blackened, and peeled. Sloughs of fabric and skin dropped through the grate.

After a final glance, I looked down the hall that led to the stairs to the first floor. Cyrus and Roland were up there, and I desperately wanted to check on them, but Patrick needed me. I had to see how he was handling things. I steeled myself and wished the two of them well. I translocated myself back to Flannigan's office bathroom.

I rinsed the bathtub clear of blood. No spatters polluted the tile floor, and I was thankful for that. Everything looked as it should, aside from the missing bathroom towels and office curtains.

Inhaling, I felt a weight drop from my chest, enough so I could momentarily relax. I extinguished the bathroom light, left the office, and made my way downstairs to find Patrick.

CHAPTER 9
HÆREDITATEM

Jack

I TOOK SEVERAL WRONG TURNS in the dark house, but I finally located the kitchen, where Patrick sat at a shiplap table beside the bottle of liquor from upstairs. The kitchen lights were on, and I stood at the threshold. It felt as though we were floating on an island together.

The kitchen stretched long, the floor covered in ombre wood planks that varied from golden to dark brown. Tall black cupboards formed a square around a kitchen island topped with brown marble. Above the island hung copper pans of varying sizes that gleamed beneath recessed lighting. On the back left, the glass cupboard doors were etched with a trellis design. Beyond the glass, lights inside illuminated stacked white plates, cups, and saucers. A copper tea kettle sat on the back-left burner of the bright red Bertazzoni stove. Plaid bar stools waited at the island. A brass chandelier illuminated the kitchen table where Patrick sat.

"Hi," I said.

"Hi."

His red eyes were aware, and the liquor bottle was capped. He seemed contemplative. He brushed tear stains from his cheeks with the back of his hand.

I opened my mouth to ask how he was doing, but a ringing tone pierced the air, echoing around the empty kitchen before it ended abruptly and repeated. I jumped. We both looked down at the table, where Patrick's phone buzzed across the surface, face down. Had he called someone, told somebody about me and what had happened? I battled the urge to grab the phone before he could answer.

"Who is it?" I asked.

Patrick shrugged. "Let's find out." He flipped the phone over and answered. "Yeah."

A deep voice responded with indistinguishable words. Patrick tapped his palm on the table and closed his eyes. "Thank you for letting me know. I need to call you back."

More low chatter followed.

"Right. I will. I'll call as soon as I can. Mm hm. Bye."

Patrick set the phone on the table. He ran both hands back and forth through his red hair.

"Who was that?"

"Hank," he said, rubbing his face. He offered nothing more.

"Who is he? What did he want?"

Patrick shook his head. "The VP of Lucient. He wants me to turn on the news."

"Why?"

"I don't know."

The hairs on the back of my neck prickled. I looked around the kitchen. No television revealed itself. Part of me wanted to ask Patrick where one was located, but another part of me knew I needed to be on my way.

Patrick scratched his arm. "How about breakfast?"

Breakfast? I blinked. Wouldn't that take a while? An urge to find Lutin, to do what I could to help him, haunted me. I needed to form a plan for what I should do next, and I needed to call Jasper and ask him to get Jonathon Roth and his men ready. I had to get to Roland, explain what'd happened. I suddenly realized that I needed to destroy what was in the trunk of Roth's car, which I had driven from New York to Basille, Louisiana. As I thought about it, I felt less and less safe with the vehicle parked outside Cyrus's house. So many things to do, and the clock was ticking.

Patrick's emerald eyes pleaded with me. The quiet kitchen and the awkwardness between us required movement—something normal. I shoved down the urge to leave. "I'd like that," I said. I swore to myself I wouldn't stay long.

Patrick nodded and rose from the table. "How do you want your eggs?"

"Surprise me." I slipped into the chair opposite his at the table.

He retrieved a frying pan from above the island and several eggs from the fridge. He turned the burner on, cracked the eggs over the pan, and threw away the shells. He tinkered with the coffee machine, and it hissed and hummed. I inspected the wooden floors, brown marble countertops, and black cupboards and then redirected my attention to a dark room beyond the kitchen, where a black television hung on a wall above what seemed to be a sitting area. A TV had been behind me the whole time.

"How are you feeling?" I asked, eyeing the dark screen.

Patrick scraped the eggs with a whisk. "Strangely...nothing." He glanced at me as though to see what I thought.

"You might be in shock."

"Maybe." He bit his lip. "He, uh, said something—the Guardian, I mean—before I shot him. In a language I didn't understand. And then, right when I...did it, he smirked at me, like the...the joke was on me." Patrick looked at me over his right shoulder.

I didn't know what to make of it, but I needed to be reassuring. The last thing I wanted was for my friend to have a mental breakdown. "It was the ferric language," I said. "And...he was an odd man. He'd been in his cave too long." I didn't say what I was actually thinking—that he likely expected Patrick would fail, because only someone who had never killed anyone before could kill him. That important fact about the Guardian was what Lutin had told me in the Guardian's lair; it wasn't something I was going to forget. It was also why Patrick had been perfect for the job.

"I know," Patrick said. "Still. Odd."

It was all odd. There was no more normality. Everything had broken apart. Elbow on the table, I rested my head on my palm. I stuttered out a breath before a weariness took hold, as though poison remained in my system.

"Are *you* okay?" Patrick asked.

It seemed to be my turn to say that I, too, felt nothing. Was that what our adulthood was to become—both of us saying to each other that we were supposed to feel something but couldn't? There was too much shock.

"Yes. Of course."

He frowned and raised a red eyebrow. "We don't have to talk about what I just did. In fact, it'd help me if we didn't. Not now. I just can't… process it. Tell me what's going on with you."

My lungs released another shaky breath. It felt selfish to mention anything beyond what Patrick was feeling and dealing with.

"Please," he said.

I winced. "It's just…"

The eggs hissed, and he ran his spatula through them. "What?"

"I guess I'm trying to do the right thing, but for the life of me, I don't know if I am. Everything feels disjointed, as though nothing's fitting into place like it used to."

Patrick set the spatula down on the edge of the pan and uncorked the bottle of liquor, which swirled inside. He put it in my hand. I looked at the bottle, at how the liquor's tears clung to the glass, and doubted I would feel anything. Still, I drank. Only then did Patrick go back to the eggs.

"I…I dragged you into this mess," I said. "I used you to save myself. Before that, the other ferrics turned against me. Things heated to a boiling point, and that's how I ended up here. One of them poisoned me."

Patrick opened a cupboard, grabbed two plates, and set them on the counter. He emptied the cooked eggs on top of them, shut the burner off, and placed the frying pan on a back burner. He crossed his arms.

"What are you worried about? Give it to me straight. No dancing around. Or I've got a blue bottle upstairs with your name on it that will release the answer."

"I don't think drugs work on me anymore. I don't know if they ever worked."

"Drugs *always* work." He tapped his chest. "Out with it."

I circled my thumb around the lip of the bottle. "I've got this nagging fear that whatever I do, it's wrong. That I'm at the core of everything going wrong, and there's no way to change it. I mean, ruthless people believe in themselves to their graves, dragging everyone and everything down with them." Like Cyrus. "How do I know that isn't me? How do I know I'm doing what's right, when everyone tells me I'm wrong? When there's no sign it's the right thing. When I'm winging it?"

Patrick quirked his lips. He brushed his nose with the back of his hand. "You know, that may not be what this is about."

I lost my momentum. My mind whirred. "What do you mean?"

He shrugged. "With the other ferrics. You know, it may not actually be that they don't believe in you. It may be something else entirely."

"Trying to kill me says they don't want anything to do with me."

Patrick leaned forward. "Maybe my friendliness has spoiled you, and you haven't realized they're just not the approachable, outgoing sorts." He winked. "You know, a few weeks ago, I met with the lawyer handling my father's estate. Roger's his name. For the past twenty years, he handled everything for my father and was sort of trying to sell himself and his company to me, to ensure he got my business too. He laid out everything necessary for me to take over. We talked about investments, about what was going to be transferred to my name."

My back tingled at the mention of Patrick's father, and I shut the guilt away as best I could, trying to remain in the moment.

Patrick smiled. "It's funny. I'd always wondered if he'd written me out of the will, what with our history. But, this time at least, family came through." He bobbed his head side to side. "Or maybe he just didn't get around to changing the will.

"In any case, Roger said something at the end of our meeting that kind of stuck with me. He said, 'The hardest thing about having money is not spending it.'"

Patrick's emerald eyes flicked to mine. "I thought he was just telling me that because he knew about my colorful past. Looking back on it, though, I think he tells that to all his clients who inherit money, and he has good reason. If they don't keep their money, he doesn't keep his job." He nodded at me. "In a way, you inherited something, didn't you? Something you didn't expect, that perhaps no one expected you to get. Because you weren't the blood of the ferric who chose you?"

I scanned the table. "I guess. Yes."

Patrick shrugged and pressed his thumb in one of the table's divots. "Maybe this trouble with others of your kind is just like my family worrying about whether I'm going to blow all my father's money on drugs, clothes, women, and cars. Only, your 'drugs,' 'clothes,' 'women,' and 'cars' carry a higher consequence. They could potentially end the world."

I leaned back in my chair, fingers pressed to my lips. "Maybe."

Patrick stood. He walked back to the kitchen counter, past the plates of eggs, and grabbed the pitcher of coffee, which had finished percolating. He seized two glass mugs from beside the machine and brought them over. He filled each of the cups and collapsed back into his seat, staring at me and sipping.

"I'm thinking about my own father now," I said, grabbing the other mug. "I mean, the man who raised me—Cyrus. He taught me so many lessons about money when I was young. When I was about seventeen, he started paying me for my…assignments." I looked at Patrick. "But before that happened, we had hundreds of lessons about money. A thousand, perhaps. Maybe all fathers worry about their children and their money."

Patrick nodded. "Partially for the money's sake. Partially for the children's sake. You have to nurture both so they'll grow."

I bit my lip, the taste bitter now. "How do you think that happens? How do people who inherit money end up blowing it all on meaningless things? Especially if they know better?"

"I've thought about that," Patrick said. Coffee steam swirled in front of his freckles and emerald eyes, making him look enchanted. "I think what it comes down to is, money makes them feel safe. The night that I learned all the funds had transferred to my name," he shook his head, "was the best night I ever slept. I dozed straight through my alarm and nearly missed my first meeting at Lucient. People enjoy prosperity, I think. They want to relax, want to sleep, and I think they find more ways to remain unconscious once they have more funds. First, they rest. Then, they escape. And money can provide *quite* the escape. The more money there is, the more escapes are open to you, the more likely you are to become addicted. To flee and flee and flee whatever discomforts you. You get to where you don't want to wake up, and so you don't. Till the money runs out. Till you have to wake up because there's nothing left to help you bury yourself."

I nodded. "Why don't people realize what they're doing?"

"Because they really and truly believe money's their answer. They're tricked into thinking that they finally possess the cure to their pain."

"What's the actual cure?"

Patrick grinned. "When I find out, I'll tell you. But money, my friend, isn't it."

I smiled halfheartedly. I recalled Cyrus's operations—a good portion had always concerned the mystical, the magical beyond the human. The other part, though, had dealt with money, and Cyrus had been very careful, very strategic with it. His style mimicked Jonathon Roth's maneuvering and manipulating his kill-for-hire organization. And it reminded me of the ferrics' preservation of their own blood, heart, and powers.

"Maybe you're right," I whispered.

"Of course, I am. It's not really about you failing. I mean, it is, but it isn't. It's about them not knowing if you're going to use your powers to sleep through the pain, to think you have the key when you don't, to exclude them from the process of ensuring that the world keeps on spinning as it has. They fear you, Jack, because you're an heiress, and new blood in the system doesn't always work out so well." He shrugged. "Think about the Medicis. That family poisoned and stabbed and killed everyone they had to, did everything they had to, to keep their power. You think you're immune to that, just because you're one of them now?" He shook his head. "You'll never be one of them. They'll never accept you. You just have to roll with it."

I leaned forward and clasped my hands on the table. "Let's say you're right about all of this. That you've just inherited your money, and I've just inherited these powers. And our families fear that we're going to exploit them, to become unconscious and cause utter destruction using the gifts we've been given. How do we not let that happen? Not let them be correct about us?"

Patrick scratched the side of his head and pressed his hand through the shining red bristles on his jaws that sparkled like needles in the light.

"I mean," I added, "if we think we've found the 'cure,' and it's not, how do we step away and see it for what it is—a lie? And how do we know if we've found the truth or if we've settled for a fantasy?"

Patrick swallowed, and his throat clicked. "I don't know," he said. "This is why families lose fortunes, why people go bankrupt, create Ponzi schemes. Far better people than us have fallen." He pursed his lips. "But if I had to bet on one of us succeeding, on seeing past the lie, even if we fall for it the first time, I would bet on you." He pointed in my direction. "Not me. Despite all my lawyers." He winked.

"Why?"

He leaned forward so our faces nearly touched. "That *gravitas* you have." He touched his chest, above his heart. "That's trustworthy. It's why I did what I did for you. I can sense I can trust you. I suspect your... friend...father...converter—whoever he is—Lutin feels the same way."

I covered his hand with mine. "No pressure there," I said.

"No pressure you can't handle." He shrugged. "That's all you need though. And, I mean, if you fuck up, at the end of the day, you haven't done anything worse than what anyone else has done. It's not as though you have any other choice but to go your own way."

"My own way?"

He looked at me as though what he meant was obvious. "Trusting others to get the job done for you is just another way of sleeping through life. It's how you end up dead. Or worse. Married. Everyone around you is always waiting for you to slip, because they, too, want power. They probably don't even care about the world like you do. They're fine watching it burn, as long as they get to keep what you have."

An image of Osric shot to mind, the smile on his face when he told me I was doomed to the Beretrum, the sound of his voice when he said he'd poisoned me with the same berry Cyrus had nearly killed me with when I was seven. It'd been stupid of Osric to try to transfer the piece of my heart back to Lutin at the edge of the Beretrum. He carried the godsoul with him, and he knew it would lure the Builder out. A transfer was beyond dangerous. Now, all of them were in hell, and I'd barely escaped. Osric was a ferric that lived in Domum, and even *he* had made a choice that failed. He'd brought everything to a halt, had caused the death of Lutin.

Tears threatened to break free, and I held them back as best I could.

"I have to follow what I believe is right," I said, "even though I have so little experience fighting on this side of the line."

Patrick nodded, his face pensive. "Yes. And you can't count on another to replace you. You can't sleep while someone takes over the controls. That's when things go even more awry."

"And if I do something unforgivable?"

Patrick shrugged. "I'll kick your ass."

I laughed, first low, a chuckle, and then I laughed at my own amusement, until the laughing tripled and I was all laughter. Pressure released from my chest for the first time in a long while, and I relished it. When I finally stopped, the tears had evaporated, and Patrick was smiling.

He placed his hand on top of mine. "I believe in you, Jack. Believe in me who believes in you."

"You're not so bad yourself."

Patrick pointed toward his chest. "I *am* the best."

We smiled at each other in the stillness, in the quiet.

"Can I ask… How'd you do it? How'd you kill someone you didn't know to save me?"

Patrick pressed his lips together and released them, suddenly looking away. "Wouldn't you have done it for me?"

"Unquestionably."

"That's how."

He released his mug and reached toward a small table to his left and grabbed a large device that looked like a tablet.

"Do you mind?" he asked.

I nodded, not knowing what he was asking. He pointed the tablet at something behind me. I turned. The television that spanned the wall in the room behind me brightened. Apparently it was a remote.

"I just need to check this real quick."

A woman in a bright red pantsuit stood in front of a Methodist hospital. Long black hair trailed in perfect waves over her blazer. She held a microphone to her lips, her red lipstick shining like candy. It was a night scene behind her, but she seemed wide awake, gripped by the story she delivered.

"The CDC has yet to say what kind of virus we may be dealing with, if it *is* a virus, or whether they have ever seen or heard of this disease before. What we do know is that doctors have started testing experimental new antibiotics on the disease. In addition, we have testimony from one of the participants at the meditation retreat who witnessed the frighteningly quick transformation that the attendee experienced. Watch Lisa Perelli's account here."

The reporter paused, and the image switched to an impromptu interview being conducted on a dark, empty street. A woman with long brown hair wore an oversized cream jacket, which she hugged tightly around herself. Her eyes were large and wide in a thin face.

"We were all just meditating, and then Jeremy started yelling. I was in the back and couldn't see him real good. But then everyone jumped up. People screamed. Everyone was running out the door. I started to run, too, and looked back at Jeremy, and he didn't look like himself anymore. He was twisting, like everywhere hurt him. And his skin…he looked so pale."

A man's voice broke in. "Why did everyone run?"

The woman's face went blank. Her mouth dropped open and then shut again, as though she didn't want to say. The ensuing silence, and the camera, seemed to force words out of her. She stared directly into the camera. "Because he didn't sound like Jeremy anymore. And he said… he said… I mean, I don't know what he said. He was hallucinating or something. Just insane."

My back tingled with chills. I glanced at Patrick, his green eyes locked on the television. The video ended, and the image switched back to the reporter standing in front of the hospital.

"After Jeremy Porter became infected, he threatened to kill others at the retreat. He attacked an attendee, putting him in critical condition. That man's name has not yet been released. What concerns the CDC is not only the fact that doctors have not been able to adequately diagnose

Jeremy Porter, but that it is beginning to appear the man he attacked may have begun to exhibit the same symptoms. Considering it has only been six hours from the original incident, the speed of this virus, or whatever it is, is unparalleled, causing concern for doctors, nurses, and the public."

"I guess that's why Hank called me so early. It's an emergency," Patrick said, drawing my attention away from the report. "Lucient mixes a lot of experimental antibiotics."

My eyes narrowed as I chewed over the scant information. "It sounds like whatever they have at the hospital isn't working."

"No. But if they find something that does, and if this thing moves fast, they're going to need product as fast as we can make it. They might want to speed up the production of other experimental drugs."

I took a deep breath and glanced at the television screen, which Patrick muted. The chaos never ended.

"Promise me you'll stay away from all this," I said.

Patrick's green eyes met mine. "The disease?"

"Yes."

"Of course." He tilted his head inquisitively. "But I'm not free of Lucient, or responsibility, yet. I plan to hand it over to the VP as soon as I'm legally able…assuming my father never returns."

"You don't want to keep the company?"

"I don't think so. No. I don't know that it's good for my sobriety to have access to so many free pharmaceuticals. I'm not that strong."

I winced in sympathy. "I think you're stronger than you think you are."

"Thank you. But, trust me. I know my limits." Patrick tilted his head back, his lips parting, as though an idea had come to him. A familiar twinkle returned to his eye.

"What?" I asked.

"Could you heal them? These infected people?"

I looked back at the television and pressed my hand to the cool surface of the table. "Yes."

He chuckled.

"What?"

"You could put Lucient out of business, Jack. Yet another reason to quit. You are my greatest competition."

The slightest tinge of lemony light broke into the kitchen and eliminated the darkness that had surrounded us. It woke me, as though our time in the kitchen had all been a dream. It was time to move, to save Lutin, if that was possible.

"I have a few more pressing things to deal with," I said, rising from the table.

"I know," Patrick replied. He cupped his mug between both hands, looking far more mature than he ever had before. It wasn't just that he'd aged in the preceding months. It was as though his father's death had done something to him, something that the rest of life hadn't. "You've never failed before, have you?" he asked.

I paused, thinking, and realized that he was right. "No," I said, more to myself than him.

"That's what I thought."

CHAPTER 10
RUBRUM

Jack

THE RED AND ORANGE OF Patrick's hair melded with the various browns in the marble countertops, the black kitchen appliances, and the bright red Bertazzoni oven. The colors swirled and mixed like ground chalk tossed into a wind. They evaporated, revealing blackness. A brown desk came into view, then green carpet, one set of golden curtains, a silver cart full of liquor. A fire burned low. I tiptoed across Bryan Flannigan's office, careful not to make a sound to clue Patrick that I hadn't yet left the house.

I squatted down and picked up the gold meditation bowl containing the plentiful amount of godsoul—far more than I had needed to wipe my blood clean of the poison. It glistened in the overhead lights. I cupped it and held it to my chest. Taking a deep breath, I remained as still as I could as I translocated again. In the place of green carpet, open windows, liquor bottles, and the large ornate wooden desk, darkness converged. As the world swept, spun, and disappeared around me, my heart thrummed. I was ready to move.

Cyrus's mansion spread out before me, tall and wide—far less modern than Flannigan's manor—and remarkable. Over its center, black smoke filled the air from the incinerator where the Guardian's body apparently still burned.

Grass appeared beneath me, and I began to walk before the sky had materialized. I approached the black car parked in front of the garage—Roth's car, which I had driven down to Basille, Louisiana, from New York City.

It was still dark outside—not yet morning as it had been in New York—so the waxed surface of the black car reflected the garage light. I set the meditation bowl full of godsoul on the car roof and retrieved my phone and keys. I called Jasper.

He picked up on the third ring. "Yes," he said, his voice low and gritty. I pictured his flat face, like a mutt's, and imagined I heard the squeak of his black leather jacket.

"Jasper, I need you to do something for me."

"We're just wrapping up here now. Should be done with the sale of Purdom soon. Then the men and I will head down to Basille. I have to say, it's odd being around them now, what with you in control. One hundred and sixty men. Complete silence. I'll never get used to it."

I smiled inwardly. "That's what happens when people use me."

"I won't forget it," he said, a humorous lilt in his voice. "None of us will."

I looked around the dark yard. "In any case, don't worry about selling Purdom just yet," I said. "This is more urgent."

He paused. "*More* urgent? Infinitum isn't back, is it?"

That made me chuckle. What he spoke of—my using Roth's army of one hundred and sixty individuals to entirely destroy Cyrus's cult—seemed hundreds of years ago. Things had come so far in just twenty-four hours. He had no idea.

"No," I said. "Much worse than that."

"Oh joy."

"Instead of coming to Basille, I need you to have Roth and the others prepare the weapons and body armor. Just like they did when taking down Infinitum."

"What's happened?"

I pressed a button on the car key, and the trunk popped open, revealing four black duffel bags. Beside them was a backpack. When I unzipped it, the lip of a bright, shiny gramophone bell reflected my distorted image back at me. I rezipped the bag and slung it over my shoulder.

"I don't feel safe telling you over the phone. I'll tell you when I get there."

"And when will that be?"

"Today," I said. "Soon. Just make sure they're prepared."

"Sure thing."

I paused, testing the weight of the gramophone on my shoulder. I didn't like having one of the Builder's *arcas* at my back. It was too close. "Jasper…"

"Yeah?"

"Am I…" I sighed and looked up at the stars, trying to determine if the question was worth the trouble.

"What?"

"Am I a terrible person?"

Silence on the other end of the line.

"For controlling Roth and his men," I added, "for taking away their freedom and making them destroy Infinitum. I had them kill thousands and thousands," I said, realizing it differently this time—harder.

"Why do you ask?"

I shook my head. Tears irritated my nose. I pressed the back of sleeve to my eyes. "I just want to know if I'm monstrous."

He laughed. The laughter slowly shrank to a sigh. "I'll tell you what I told you the first time we met."

"You mean when you kidnapped me?"

"I was hoping we could let that slide." He cleared his throat.

I smirked.

"I told you I knew the kind of person you were. The kind who liked to sit by the apple tree and listen to the snake talk. You enjoyed the attempt at temptation, but you were never tempted. As for me and Roth and the others, we were. We ate. Heartily. What I mean to say is, if you're monstrous, Jack, then I'm fucking Stalin. We all are. You could have turned out like your brother, but you didn't. Yes, you have blood on your hands, but you're not Alex. You've done what you thought was right, and I commend you for it. I commend you for surviving. Anyone who endured a childhood like yours, I suspect the best they could do was just survive it. You did more. And you saved a lot of children at the same time."

I chewed at my lip. "Thanks, Jasper."

"Of course." He paused. "One of your kind say otherwise?"

He was good. "I guess you know how it works."

"Things don't change, even when they change."

I smiled. "I have to go."

"Talk to me. When you have time."

"See you later today."

We both hung up. I slipped my phone in my pocket and tightly secured the backpack. I breathed deeply and surveyed the night. All was quiet, so silent it was as though nothing else I'd ever experienced had existed. I wondered for a moment why the world had to pick up where it left off, why it couldn't just suddenly shift in an entirely new direction. I desperately wanted to close a door on all of it.

I shut the trunk and carefully picked up the meditation bowl of godsoul, cradling it against me, and walked to the front door of the house. I slipped inside.

The door shut behind me; the house was even quieter than the outside had been.

To my right, the living room was empty, as was the den to my left. I called for Roland. No answer arrived.

I walked down the hallway, checking each of the rooms as I continued. With each one, déjà vu set in. The small room on my left always hosted a Christmas tree in the winter. I'd click my nails against the red and gold ornaments, imagining myself able to climb the limbs and arrive at a strange new land. Odd, now that I thought about it, that Cyrus would even have a Christmas tree. The familiar tradition must have been useful for manipulating people, convincing them to stay.

I passed the second room on the left, glancing inside. It featured a conference desk and twelve chairs. Cyrus held many meetings in this room.

Straight in front of me, about twenty-five feet away, was a room where everything had turned white. In that room, I had first seen Cyrus use the red box on a man to suck the soul right out of him and the color from everything in the room. I walked toward it.

To my surprise, Roland sat inside on a couch. He wore a red shirt that appeared velvety in the light, and cream linen pants. Cyrus sat near him, dressed in black and gray.

Behind them, through the windows, the slightest tinges of pink filtered across the sky. Morning was about to arrive in Basille.

"I'm surprised you aren't asleep," I said to Roland as I broached the threshold.

"Haven't felt tired," Roland said, rising from the couch. We stared at one another thoughtfully as his words lingered. It was the first time we'd seen each other since he had left to get food for the house in his car.

"Did Cyrus update you on everything?"

"He said you and the ferrics left to go and kill the Builder."

I nodded. The need, the desire, to tell him what happened pecked at me. I studied Roland, his posture, how he radiated kindness. I was quite lucky, I realized, that he was speaking to me. Perhaps he appreciated resurrection, his return to life, more than I expected. I had no idea what to assume, but Roland had been brought back hundreds of times in his life, after each of Cyrus's lessons in killing. I suspected anyone would tire of death—and life—eventually.

"How did things go?" he asked.

My eyes flicked to Cyrus, who remained quietly on the couch. "Not well."

"How so?"

I sighed, exhausted, suddenly too tired to form the words. "The Builder got all the ferrics, including Lutin. I barely managed to escape."

"Jesus."

I nodded. "There's something I need to show you."

He followed me out of the room; Cyrus remained, still as a statue. When Roland walked past me, I shut the door.

"How's he doing?" I asked low, nodding to the door.

"Been fine. Hasn't said much of anything, aside from updating me on what happened here. Hasn't really even moved."

I bit my lip. "There's no telling how much of him has remained, how much of him might have actually changed, if anything."

"No. I don't think there will ever be a way to know that. He'll remain quiet, and you'll always be second guessing."

I nodded. "Not always second guessing, though. I can force him to tell me what he thinks."

His expression made it clear Roland hadn't considered that. "True."

"Look." I sighed and rubbed my left eyebrow with the back of my thumb. "If you're up for it, if it's not too much for you, I need you to see what you can do with this." I lifted the meditation bowl. Bleeding bits of gold pulsed and glowed inside. Half of it solid, half liquid, the blood and tissue of the immortal of all immortals shimmered. Roland's eyes widened, and his lips parted.

"Nothing's too much for me. You know that I'd do anything for you. What is it?"

Relief and love flowed in me, and I smiled at him. Maybe he didn't hate me for bringing him back after all.

Within the sense of the unconditional love I felt for him, a tingling sensation crawled across my back. Sensing I was being watched, I glanced toward the door I'd just closed and pulled it open. Cyrus stood three feet from me, just beyond the threshold.

A shiver rolled down my spine.

The right corner of his lips turned upwards.

"Go back to the couch and sit down. Don't move from that spot, and don't say anything," I ordered.

He turned from me robotically and walked back to his original spot. He turned and sat. His eyes sparkled and seemed to betray his satisfaction in frightening me.

I shut the door again, and Roland and I started down the hall.

"Scared me half to death," he said.

"I know."

"Might it not be best to just…get rid of him?" Roland asked. "You have what you need. You don't like him, and neither do I. Is he not just a ticking bomb?"

I bit my cheek. I'd considered what Roland suggested. "If you desperately want that, I will. But I don't know," I said. "I'm still thinking."

Roland nodded. "It can wait."

We entered the living room at the front of the house, and I set the bowl of godsoul on the coffee table. Pierced by the expanding morning sunlight, it seemed almost translucent, multicolored—specks of brilliant blues, reds, whites shining throughout the gold.

"The ferrics call it godsoul," I said. "It seems to be some sort of pure power left over from the Creator, who has disappeared. Maybe part of his body? There's a finite amount of it, and a little bit more disappears every time the ferrics need to battle the Builder. It's how they protect themselves from death."

"And what, exactly, do you want me to do with it?"

"I want you to see if you can meld it with metal. Knives…bullets.

Roland's eyes scanned it, and his fingers hovered near it. "May I?"

I nodded.

Roland's pointer finger touched the tip of a jutting piece of rock. He pressed the finger to his tongue and tasted it.

"Hm," he said. He swallowed. "That is…" He shook his head, perhaps not knowing how to end the sentence. "How do you know that it can even be melded with metal?"

"That's what the ferrics do when they attack the Builder. They have weapons built with it, at least according to Osric. It seems that it takes whatever weapon it's added to to a paranormal height. Even poison."

Roland slipped to his knees. He peered into the translucent gold.

"Will anyone come looking for this?"

"Maybe."

"What happens if the Builder gets hold of it?"

"He consumes it and grows more powerful, is my understanding. It gives him power."

Roland peered at me, unblinking. "Keeping it here may not be safe."

"It is if we work quickly. It won't stay long. I need to get to the Beretrum, to see if Lutin's alive. His brothers too." I sighed. "And I need to do so as soon as possible."

Roland furrowed his eyebrows. "I thought you said they're dead."

"They might be. I don't know. I need to find out for sure."

"Where are they?"

"In some world beyond here. The Builder's world, I think. The Beretrum. It is a veritable hell, as I understand it."

Roland shook his head and pressed a hand to his skull. "Jack, you can't go there. And you certainly can't go alone."

"I'm not," I said. "I'm taking Roth's men with me."

"Roth?"

I sighed and considered explaining about my time in New York City. How I had been forced to team with a man responsible for a kill-for-hire group, that I had aligned myself with him to take down Infinitum, but he had turned on me, required me to resurrect his dead colleagues. I very nearly died in the basement of his Manhattan building, but I'd figured out at the last second that I was able to control every person I resurrected. "It's a long story," I said. "But I have about a hundred and sixty individuals at my disposal. I control them like I control Cyrus. And that means I have one hundred and sixty people armed with guns who can shoot whatever bullets you make here, can slice with whatever knives you make."

Roland chewed the inside of his cheek. "They aren't ferrics?"

"No. But they're something."

His gaze, which had been distanced, refocused on the matter in front of us. He seemed to reach a decision.

He lifted the bowl. "I'll see what I can do."

"That's all I ask."

We walked upstairs to the armory, and Roland flicked on the lights. I paused. I'd forgotten how beautiful the room was. Picture-frame wood molding decorated the walls, giving the massive area warmth. High above, wooden beams separated the ceiling into small geometrical squares with a yellow ceiling tile inside each. Four metal pillars, rough texture stretching up halfway and a kind of hexagonal pattern taking over midway to the ceiling, stood at each third of the room, connecting the floor to the ceiling.

Lanterns with ornate clover-shaped swirls hung from the pillars. Wooden slats divided the floor in the center of the room into squares about a foot by a foot. These squares were laid out to alternate between horizontal and vertical. Beyond, in the perimeter, the wooden slats were in a chevron design. At the opposite end from the doorway, a giant fireplace took up half the wall, framed by a brilliant aqua tile mosaic. Above the fireplace, an image of an eagle facing a screaming snake lashing out of water was carved into the wood.

Around us on every wall hung rows and rows of weapons. Handguns, shotguns, rifles, sniper rifles, semiautomatics, and automatics. Identical decorative nineteenth-century cavalry sabers and cutlasses crisscrossed in rows, making the room seem regal—something always important to Cyrus. Pressed against the walls were work tables holding various tools.

Roland gathered everything he needed—files, clamps, sharpening stones, a hacksaw, bench vise, drill, Dremel, and belt grinder—for the knives, plus the cartridge case cleaner, reloading press, die set, powder scale, calipers, and case trimmer for the bullets. I walked diagonally across the wooden floor and said what was on my mind.

"My plan is to kill and resurrect the Builder."

Roland turned around, looked at me, and turned back. "I know."

"Do you think it's smart?"

"I think it's an excellent strategy."

I frowned, tinkering with an empty bullet cartridge on a table. "I mean, do you think I'll be able to remain myself if I'm able to control him?"

A tendon in Roland's jaw quivered, and he set down a caliper. "You're afraid of losing yourself, of him turning you evil?"

I scanned the weapons surrounding us. The number of rifles on the wall was insane—far too many, more than any one person might ever need. Unless, of course, they were arming an army.

"If thirst doesn't make a woman drink, a thirsty man will," I said. "It crossed my mind."

Roland frowned, and a variety of expressions crossed his face before he seemed to finally settle on one. "You have quite a bit of power already, and you haven't used it for evil."

Oh, how he was wrong about that.

"And it seems to me that you could have, at any time, joined forces with the Builder."

That was true.

"I think you lived your whole life deceived by Cyrus…and I helped some with that. I regret it *eternally*. But the most important thing, I think, is that you're tired of being deceived. I don't think you'll ever go back to it. And neither do I see you tolerating the abuse you experienced in your childhood." Roland's eyes wandered over the table. "Or recreating it. No. I don't think you will be swayed by him."

Relief flooded me as soon as he said the words. "Not ever?"

"No. Even if you were," he said, toying with the caliper, "someone would come along and stop you."

"Who could?"

He shrugged. "I'm sure before now even the idea of stopping the Builder was impossible. And then you appeared. Maybe all that's necessary is another you. Another you would come along and ensure that you were gone."

I considered that. "I wouldn't let it get that far."

"I know." He smiled. "And you know it too."

My heart swelled. I walked up to Roland and hugged him, breathing him in and relaxing against him. He returned the embrace. "I missed you," I whispered.

"I missed you too. I couldn't say it before because there was so much going on, but I have. And you've changed *so much*. It's wonderful."

My eyes burned with tears. I was tired of tears, but not this kind. "I'm so sorry Cyrus killed you. Life would have been so much better if you'd been there."

"But I wasn't supposed to be. Not for your whole life. Otherwise—"

"Otherwise I wouldn't have become who I'm supposed to be."

Roland nodded. I inhaled shakily. "What did you see? When you were dead… Did you change at all?"

He shook his head. "I don't remember anything. I know I went somewhere. But that's all."

"I wish we had enough time so I could share everything that's happened, but we don't."

Roland hugged me tighter and then let me go. "Someday, when the world isn't going to hell." He winked.

I laughed. We separated, and I walked to the armory door and lifted the backpack.

"What's that?" he asked.

"Nothing," I said, wiping a tear. "Just something I need to do real quick."

I left.

⌒

I SLIPPED DOWNSTAIRS AND HEADED to the back door of Cyrus's home. I unlocked it and walked out to the back of Cyrus's property, what would have been the backyard if there had been any sort of fence. Instead, yellow grass stretched to a tree line, beyond which was a forest. There was no porch, no anything, save for a large rectangle of concrete patio with grass sprouting through the cracks. Black marks rolled over it in billows— remnants of when Cyrus's mansion had burned.

I sighed and set the backpack down on the patio and unzipped it. Inside was the shining gramophone. I lifted it free and set it on the concrete. It was quiet, still, but nevertheless I could hear the big band tune, as if echoing from the depths that stretched down and down into the bell, impossibly far, straight to hell.

I looked inside, and I cocked my head. A memory appeared. Six months before, when I'd resurrected Lutin's brothers both to save them and destroy Cyrus, Osric had held Cyrus's red velvet box, one of the Builder's *arcas*, in his hand and sent it bursting into flames. It was a power, like the power to translocate, or heal, or resurrect, that the ferrics seemed to have, and it made me wonder if I, too, had it. If so, could I not perhaps use that power against the Builder himself?

It was important to find out. I pressed my hand on the bell and took a blind shot at willing whatever power was within me to destroy it. I had the ability to translocate, and I hoped that the ability to disintegrate one of the Builder's creations had also transferred to me.

Nothing happened.

The gramophone remained there, reflecting sunlight at me. I took a deep breath and again pressed my hand on it. I closed my eyes and urged a ball of rage to boil within me—rage at its threat, at its being used against me, at the fact I'd nearly died because of its existence, at the way it terrorized the children raised in Infinitum. Rage at being cursed, half because of Cyrus, half because of me, to hell blended with my memories. I let that ball fold in on itself, do somersaults, until I was trembling and my brain was on fire. I sent the ball of energy down into the gramophone and opened my eyes.

The bell expanded, widened like a flower opening to the sun. It shifted up, and the black center of it moved, as though it looked at me. I toppled backward and suppressed a violent urge to rush to the door. My heart jackhammered, and my skin broke out in a cold sweat. My hands tremored in front of me. My mouth unbearably dry, I tried to swallow and couldn't.

It had *grown* instead of self-destructing. Was it mocking me?

I squatted on the concrete and released a shuddering breath. I rubbed my sweaty cheek. My heart slowed. I trembled, but less intensely.

Looking into the tops of the nearby trees, my focus slipped to the blue sky. What was I doing wrong?

As though in response, the tops of the trees moved, swaying in a breeze that arrived belatedly, blowing my hair from my face. The sound of leaves rustling in the wind was a gentle white noise that expanded and decreased like waves in the ocean.

I thought I heard something rustle nearby. My eyes searched the yard before me. Was someone else there?

"Lutin?" I whispered, not knowing why his name slipped from my lips. It couldn't be Lutin. Lutin was down in the Beretrum. I pressed my lips together and waited.

No response.

I frowned and leaned forward, wrapping my hands around my shins. I looked down at the gramophone and tilted my head.

My lips parted with a sigh.

I sat up on my knees and crawled closer to the instrument. It seemed to lean away from me and shrink. Bravely, I pressed my hand to its surface and closed my eyes again. This time, I sent myself down into my core, away from thoughts of all the negative things circling me and my life. I pushed myself further into the present moment, as though it was the only true moment. The wind and the trees and the warm patio and my breath were all there was.

I allowed one thought as I focused on my breath entering and leaving my body.

I abolish you.

A brilliant light fluoresced. I opened my eyes and pulled my hand back as red and orange flames encompassed the base, stylus, and bell of the gramophone, growing hot and tall. The gramophone was reduced to a puddle on the patio in a matter of seconds, just as the red box had disintegrated in Osric's hands. Lava-like liquid slipped between the cement cracks, covering the grass that had sprouted.

I inhaled deeply and realized that I'd barely pushed any energy out at all. Instead, it seemed I'd retained my energy and simply told the box what it was to do. Power to destroy it hadn't come from hatred. It'd come from calm, from staying centered.

I blinked and dipped my finger in the melted material, wondering if I could practice on a few more objects before going down into the Beretrum. If I could improve the focus of my power, I would feel more confident I had a reliable force when I faced the Builder. I wondered what I should burn next.

A noise reached me I couldn't ignore.

I looked up and rocketed to my feet. I reached inside my black coat for my gun.

Something red waited at the edge of the forest. I gritted my teeth. A shiver rolled down my spine.

It was a man. He wore red pants and a double-breasted red trench coat, its sleeves pulled up to reveal his arms.

My muscles tensed. "Who are you?" I said, too low for him to possibly hear. I felt a desire to crouch, but I remained standing, hand on my pistol, trying to figure out what to do.

"My name is Ven," the man in red responded. He *had* heard me.

Even from a distance, he seemed ethereal, like he might be a ferric. An aura, hot and spiky, emanated from him. Perhaps he worked for the Builder.

He was clearly trouble. I didn't have the time or energy for any more moguls.

"What do you want?"

"To talk."

Yeah. Right.

But I knew how the game had to go. He wasn't about to leave. I beckoned him forward, remaining where I was.

He took a step, then another, and then seemed to glide over the top of the grass. As he approached, the lightning strikes in his flesh burned like rivers of fire. So he was a ferric. His hands, though, unlike the other ferrics I knew, were black, the same as his hair and the rims of his eyes and his pupils. It was almost as though he had sunk his hands in the ashes of a long-extinguished fire. He wore no shoes, and his feet were covered in black, the same as his hands. The lower legs of his pants, near his ankles, were in tatters.

He approached with a smile on his face. His lips were wide, his face thin, cheekbones high. The closer he came, the stronger the smell of pennies in sugar became—blood. I eyed the red in his clothes again. When he was twenty or so feet from me, I gestured for him to stop.

His bare feet came to rest alongside each other. He bowed shallowly. "It's a pleasure to meet you, Jack Harper. At last."

I waited for more. "I'll ask again. What do you want?"

He rubbed his black fingertips together, as if in prayer, seemingly enjoying the sensation of whatever coated them. "You."

"Why?"

He rolled his eyes. His voice floated to me, soft, low, and grave. "For the disappearance of Semic, Pepluv, Inarin, Flutri, Osric, and Lutin. For the death of the Guardian of the godsoul. For all the individuals you've killed. And for the godless disease that you and your family have distributed across this world."

I narrowed my eyes. I didn't get the sense that Ven existed to heal and right wrongs. Lines fanned from the corners of his eyes; his clothes were speckled with holes. Ferrics could heal what they came in contact with, and their clothes always appeared pristine. I remembered Osric and his brothers, the way the moth-eaten holes of their clothes filled in. Why didn't Ven radiate that healing energy?

"I don't know what you're talking about," I tried.

Ven half-smirked. "Is that not the Guardian's body burning in your basement? Hm?"

My heart fell, and I swallowed, trying not to react.

His lips firmed. His eyes looked like a predator's. "I can smell him."

I clenched my teeth. *Who is this guy?* "You know about that, huh?"

He nodded. "I know a lot of things. I've been ready to take you out ever since I heard Lutin made you. Didn't get the okay until today."

I grinned. "Well…congratulations."

He didn't respond but continued to press his dark fingers against one another.

I took a deep breath. "I think this goes without saying, but I'm not going with you."

"You are. I'm taking you back to our world, to trial, for justice."

I shook my head. "You say I'm responsible for Osric and the others, but do you really know what happened on that mountain?" I narrowed my eyes and shot the rageful energy that had intensified within me his way. "Osric poisoned me."

Ven continued to rub his hands as though I hadn't said anything. "And then you made him disappear," he said point blank.

"I didn't. The Builder did."

"I'm not here for the Builder. I'm here for you."

"Look. I have things I need to do. I don't have time for this. And if you were half as intelligent as you think you are, you'd let me be."

His eyes narrowed. "Oh? Why would I let someone who was raised to kill, assisted in thousands of deaths across the world, enslaved a group who kill for money, caused the death of the only Guardian of the godsoul, *blocked us* from reaching the godsoul, and made five of our kind disappear, go free? Not to mention, you resurrected a man who tortured men,

women, and children, a man you yourself previously sought to destroy—
Cyrus." He shook his head. "You've gone mad. It might be that immortal
fabric in you. It's starting to convince you that you are more than you are."

I took a deep breath. "I'm doing these things because I'm trying to
help you. Believe it or not, I am trying."

He laughed. "You are failing. At everything. Did Osric not tell you?
About your fate?"

My heart thrummed, and a crawling sensation started at my shoulder
blades and spread to my neck. "He told me."

"So then. You know. The report is that you are bound for hell, and
there's no way to get out of it." He nodded. "The world has enough hell-
bound people, I think."

"It does. If that's my fate, that's my fate. So be it. But before I get there,
there's something I have to do. I can't make you understand, but I'll say it
anyway. I have no intention of destroying the ferrics, of taking over the
world, or of joining the Builder."

"That's nice, Jack, but it seems we're both short on time. I'm not here
for a discussion. I'm here to take you in before you cause more damage.
You have been nothing but a black spot on this world, and I have every
intention of getting rid of you. I have been asking to do so for the past half
year, and the council has *finally* listened.

"I just…wonder," he added, tilting his head. "Do you regret any of it?
What you or your family has done? Any of your actions? Or the fact that
your brother has introduced something into this world that none of us
have seen before?"

My eyes searched his face for meaning. "What are you talking about?"

He grinned with maniacal energy. "That's right. It's just as frightening
as it sounds. There's something here now. We don't know what it is, but it
is *fierce*." Ven threw the word toward me.

My hand tightened into a fist. "What did he do this time?"

Ven pursed his lips. "Perhaps you've heard of the new disease that's
sporadically popping up across the country? Well, it's not a *just* a disease.
Alex created it. Alex spread it. Alex *is* it. And it's wiping people out." Ven
exhaled a low whistle. "He is so fast. He is sickening people all over. It's a

new weapon, born of the Builder's blood." He pointed at me. "This was only possible if the Builder claimed a piece of the godsoul."

An image of a chunk of gold falling into the snow and a white hand reaching down into the ice to retrieve it replayed in my mind's eye.

"Shit," I said. I pressed my hands to my forehead.

"Several people here in Basille have the infection. Alex made sure his hometown was affected. From what I've heard, that includes a friend of yours."

I looked up at him. "A friend? I don't have any friends in Basille."

Ven tilted his head and shrugged. "It's what I've been told. Don't worry. You'll have plenty of time to figure out who it is. On our way to Domum. For your trial."

He reached inside his coat and retrieved what appeared to be neon red fire circling in two loops. I'd seen something like it once before. Lutin's brothers had used it to bind his hands together when we were in the mountains. It had weakened him, perhaps, I realized, stopping him from translocating.

I shook my head, backing up, staring at the loops. "If Osric hadn't tried to poison me, none of this would've happened."

"This isn't Osric's fault."

"*It is*," I yelled. "Look. I'll…I'll find Alex, and I'll stop him."

"Oh?" Ven said. "Like you have for the past how many years?"

In a blink, Ven stood in front of me, his crimson form blotting out the sun. I pulled my gun up and shot him repeatedly, not stopping until all the bullets had filled his chest.

He looked down at his torso. Embered blood soaked into his clothes, making them look like they were on fire. Slowly, the wounds stopped bleeding, and the holes in his coat partially filled, until they were as small as the other holes there.

Ven grabbed my firing arm, jerking me toward him. I grasped the knife from my other pocket with my free hand and stabbed his forearm. He grunted, as though merely annoyed, and released me. He jerked the blade out of his skin and threw the knife to the ground.

"You *will* come with me."

I shook my head. I threw a right punch, but he was faster than I expected. He jerked my arm in the direction of my punch and slipped his arm around my throat. He tugged me back against his chest, dropped his other arm to the back of my neck, and squeezed. He lifted me off my feet. I couldn't breathe or scream. Black dots flooded my vision.

I urged the world around me to help me. Something, anything. A mad scramble of power burst free from me, rolling in waves across the grass, which brightened, greener than it'd ever been. The green swept across the entire backyard to the edge of the forest, where leaves on trees thickened and grew.

"This is futile, Jack," Ven huffed.

More waves of power shot from me, charging through the landscape around us. I tried to focus, to urge Ven to burn, like the gramophone, with no result. Waves of power flowed from me, undirected.

Ven's arms pressed harder against my neck, and the black dots filling my vision swarmed like frantic bees. I kicked and clawed his arms.

At last, Ven's grip relented. "What the—"

Big band swing—a cacophony of trombones, saxophones, trumpets, and clarinets—thundered in the air.

He dropped me.

I slammed to the ground. Something white slithered beside me, and I scrambled to my knees. The gramophone poured music at full volume on the blackened cement, the record spinning, the bell widening, white goo dribbling from the center.

Ven bolted, but it was as though an invisible wind gripped him and held him back. He fell to his hands and knees and attempted to crawl away. The fire in his veins dimmed, his red clothes faded to pink.

I scrambled backward, open-mouthed. He turned to me, his face becoming paler by the second.

The rage on his face declared that he would have killed me right then if he could have. He opened his mouth wide, as if he might bite me.

"Domum," he said before he closed his eyes.

I expected him to vanish for parts unknown, but he remained on the patio. His eyes bulged. The fiery veins cooled to a dark gray. His bleached-out clothes faded to white. If the gramophone didn't stop, it seemed clear he would die.

"*Domum*," he yelled. But he didn't translocate.

Was I going to let him die? Like this?

I gritted my teeth, unable to bear it. For too many years, I'd battled Cyrus's red box, then the gramophone, then the other *arcas* that Roth's group had collected as they brought Infinitum down. Ven wanted to kill me, and I hated him, but I couldn't stand the idea of letting a ferric, any ferric, die in the clutches of one of the Builder's machines.

"Promise me you won't take me in, and I'll stop the gramophone," I told him.

His eyes locked on mine. His cheeks were gaunt and hollow, the pale skin stretched tight against bone.

"Promise me," I said, "and I'll turn the gramophone off."

He glared at me. "What kind of monster brings one of these back?" He heaved, his entire body jackknifing, and then his head dropped to the concrete. His eyes became empty, blank.

Certain that Ven was dead, I scrambled away from the gramophone. Surely the Builder's *arca* would suck me toward it and kill me, exactly as it had tried to do at 405 Brimmer. I clenched my teeth and prepared for an attack.

The goo that encompassed Ven paused and then reversed. Tendrils lifted from the fibers of Ven's now-white coat and pants. All evidence of the plasma soon disappeared back into the gramophone bell. The record stopped spinning, and the stylus lifted and returned to its original place. The enlarged bell shrank to normal size, the air again silent.

I closed my eyes and drooped to the ground, pressing my hands against my neck where Ven had squeezed. I coughed until the ache in my throat went away. Each new breath came easier.

When the pain relented, I clambered back to my feet and gazed down at the gramophone. Why hadn't it killed me? Why hadn't it remained melted?

Ven's voice came to me. "What kind of monster brings one of these back?"

Back.

I looked around me in Cyrus's backyard. Beyond the mansion, the grass was no longer yellow but emerald. When Ven was throttling me and I'd called on the universe for help, the waves of my power had flowed across the grass and trees, turning everything green, reviving everything around me. My regenerative power had apparently included the *arca*. It hadn't tried to kill me—it had saved me.

It was like everything I'd ever brought back.

Mine.

It was protecting me.

I lifted my hand toward it. Slowly, the arm of the gramophone lifted, as though reaching toward me. I shivered.

The gramophone was under my control.

I bent my head and pressed my hands to my face.

It was completely restored, as though it'd never been melted in the first place. It shined spectacularly in the sunlight, quiet and ominous beside Ven's body.

My mind shifted toward a recent memory—the flames in Cyrus's incinerator rising to meet the Guardian's body as I had requested. The things I restored—not just people—listened to me, obeyed my commands.

I lifted my head from my hands and spoke to the gramophone.

"Look at me," I said.

The bell shifted up, turning to me. The golden brass fluttered.

"My God."

CHAPTER 11
SOMNUM

Patrick

I BLINKED. JACK DISAPPEARED. HER black hair and dark eyes and the fluorescent lines in her skin that dartled through her clothes all vanished. She left me sitting at the kitchen table alone by the Folgers and Chivas on the scarred and pockmarked shiplap, wondering if I'd lost my mind for the third time that year.

My coffee mug read, "Fuck this shit. And fuck that other shit as well." I gripped it hard and pushed it away. I rested my head on my forearms, rubbing my forehead against them.

That's it. Just one moment at a time. I'm not crazy right now, and that's all that matters.

But I could feel it edging in—rotten and abysmal anxiety and, on the back of that anxiety, a mysterious darkness. It threatened to suck me up into it. I jerked my head up and looked around the kitchen. I wished for my mother. And, to my surprise, my father, too, as wretched as he was. Wolf or lamb, it didn't matter. Anyone, really, would do to not be alone.

I clenched my hands into fists. I loved Jack. Sure. But I feared her, and I didn't mind admitting that. I feared anything that had a spell on me because I couldn't resist bewitching. Cocaine, meth, or Jack, it was all the same. I'd loved her since the first time I saw her standing outside of that ramshackle building with a cigarette in her mouth, her black hair almost blue beneath the yellow fluorescent light. She could take care of herself. She didn't need me. As I sensed her independence, my mind urged me to approach her, know the kind of person who didn't give a damn about the lullaby of money and cars and trinkets and clothes.

Yet my heart had been disfigured in the last hour. She was the one who'd disfigured it. I felt betrayed.

I looked at my shaking hands. They'd killed a man—no, a creature beyond anything remotely possible. I didn't recognize them. These were somebody else's hands; my heartbeat belonged to someone else.

Whatever I'd been had bled out, alongside the blood of the golden man.

I stood and ran my fingers through my hair, gripping the roots. How could love do this to me? How long would I bleed?

No matter. I knew how to numb myself.

I snatched my iPhone and swept my thumb across its cracked glass cover. I selected my contacts, then voicemail, and finally the messages I'd deleted. I eyed the only message I hadn't yet wiped entirely—a number without a name because I'd deleted the name. I pressed the number and held the phone to my ear. The ring repeated. My pulse thrummed.

Please, for the love of God, pick up.

The line clicked. A man cleared his throat, followed by a long pause. "Patrick. It's been a while." People chatted in the background. Two girls laughed. A party, somewhere, continuing into the early morning.

"Where are you?" I asked.

Donovan chuckled. "You sure you want to know?"

"I...I... Something happened." I pressed my thumbnail hard into the bottom of my lip. *Don't say anything more.* "I need you to tell me where you are."

"Hm," he said, his voice wistful. "You realize the last time we spoke, you said that if you ever called me again, I should hang up?"

I leaned my forehead against a cabinet and dropped it slowly. The wood scraped against skin. "I didn't know that this would…" I couldn't finish. "You'd be right to hang up on any other day. But not today."

His silence on the other end was moderated with gentle tinkling laughter from people far from my reality. My insides itched as though living insects crawled in my organs. I dragged my fingernails across my stomach.

"That's all I need to know," he said. "Why don't I come to you?"

"No," I said. "I've got to get out of here."

"Well, I don't know if Jesse'll like that." He sighed. "Give me a second."

Donovan set the phone down. I focused on my breath while he was gone. *Breathe*, two, three, four. *Hold*, two, three, four. *Out*, two, three, four. *Wait*, two, three, four. I repeated this incantation several times. Sound rose from the other end of the line. Donovan cleared his throat. "We were all about to head to S9."

Thank God their party was continuing.

"I'll see you there."

I clutched my keys and headed out the door to my car. The sun was just above the horizon, which meant it was around six in the morning. Halfway to S9, I realized I'd forgotten my phone. I didn't go back for it.

When I got to the club, hardly any cars speckled the parking lot. I'd been to S9 before and remembered people lingering outside, the queue circling the establishment, a girl at the door with bright green hair, ink-stamping hands, but it was early morning, and everyone else had gone home. Donovan and his party had free rein.

I opened the door. Music thumped softly in the background. Beyond a part in the beaded curtains, ten or so people lounged on purple velvet cushions. Lemon and lime wedges and glittering broken glass sprinkled the floor. A phone rang. Two girls took a selfie beside shots lined up on the bar. The scent of old cologne, vomit, hairspray, and body odor mixed with the fresh air from outside, making it stale. The after-scent of overheated electronics wafted through the room. Any other day, I would've passed through the curtains, not caring what those inside thought of me. But a very dark mirror had just been held up to me in the hour before. I took several steps back.

Donovan waited in a corner of the entryway, alone, a cigarette in his mouth. I hadn't seen him.

I leaned against the closed outer door, nervous, my mouth dry. Somehow, I'd made it. I barely remembered the drive there.

Donovan's thick brown eyebrows furrowed. He walked up to me and tapped his hand on my cheek. "You all right?" My knees collapsed, and he grabbed me, stopping me from falling straight to the floor. The music grew louder, and someone whistled. Champagne popped, hissed, and splattered.

"What happened to you?" he said. The cigarette wobbled against his lips.

I wiped the sweat from my face. "You've got something, right?"

Donovan reached into his pocket. He grunted in assent and retrieved a bag of white powder. He licked his lips. "You're not going to die on me, are you?"

I plucked the bag from his fingers. "It's not like that. I've just had…a rough day."

He cocked an eyebrow.

"I didn't bring anything with me," I admitted.

He nodded. "You're shaking. I'll be right back. Stay here."

Donovan returned with a syringe, spoon, lighter, half-empty water bottle, cotton ball, and tourniquet. I removed my blazer and rolled up my shirt sleeve.

"Maybe you should lay down," he said.

Not a bad idea. I sat and then slid down, my back against the greasy cement floor. I pressed my left hand to my eyes, leaving my right arm to Donovan. He tied the band around my bicep, and I felt the familiar swelling sensation. He tapped my vein. "You sure you want to do this, Flannigan?"

"Quit asking me that." I lifted my hand from my eyes to glare at him.

He frowned. "I have a feeling you're going to be pissed when you wake up."

"I've just got to get out of my head."

"Mm. Don't we all?"

Donovan heated the contents in the spoon. Eventually, the needle bit, and I held my breath, waiting for it.

"What happened?" he asked as he pressed the plunger. "I've never seen you like this before."

Relief flooded my body, like returning equilibrium, a sensation I'd nearly forgotten. My body felt like a crumpled sheet of paper being straightened again. On the back of that was pure bliss. I pushed my feet back and forth over the concrete. God, oh God, why had I ever quit?

My breath evened out. I closed my eyes, feeling more serene than I'd felt in what seemed like millennia. The ecstasy budded spectacularly.

"Come on," Donovan said. He grabbed my hand and pulled.

I found myself standing, being led down the entryway, to the left. We passed by several entrances to the main floor, where electric lights shined, music pulsed, and Donovan's friends sang, hooted, and laughed wildly.

He escorted me past the party to the end of the hall, to the left, to the right, at last leading me into an empty room, flooded in purple lights. I stepped on a half-melted ice cube, which skittered from under my foot and hit the edge of the wall with a *clack*. Inside, the scent of smoke and pot, fruity drinks and beer, was thick. Sweat trickled down the back of my neck, and I swooned, lightheaded. I barely made it to one of the velvet cushions against the wall before I collapsed onto it, face down, and rubbed my cheek against the fabric. It felt delicious. At the same time, the drugs seemed like they'd seeped down into my bones, and they made me ache familiarly, hard on my body like a sickness. A little bit of bliss wore away.

Donovan sighed, puffed on his cigarette, and pushed the door shut. Above his head, a red exit sign glowed. He crossed his arms and leaned against the wall. "Are the police going to come looking for you?"

I shook my head and rubbed my hands against my face. Everything tingled. "It's not like that."

"Then what's it like?" In the purple light, his gaze was cold and steely.

My mind clicked to the gun in my hand as it went off, the spraying blood, the man with golden arms collapsing, dropping. My stomach seized, and I wrapped my arms around my middle before I turned over. Why hadn't the heroin erased this harsh memory?

I pulled my knees up into a fetal position and squeezed my eyes tight.

The cushion beside me shifted, and then Donovan was sitting there, staring down at me.

"What?" I asked.

"You're not so sure you should tell me, and I'm not so sure I should tell you." He cocked an eyebrow and lifted the corner of his mouth.

I breathed deeply, pretty sure I knew what he was about to tell me. Another part of me, though, had been blindsided by the day and wouldn't let anything remain in the dark.

Dig it up.

"Tell me."

He sighed, reached in the opposite inner pocket of his black blazer, and held up a small vial of powder. "If what you're going through is *really* that bad, I recommend this."

My whole body pulsed. "What is it?"

"It's something that's come out since you quit. People call it mega." Or did he say mecca? I couldn't tell.

I licked my lips, barely having enough spit to moisten them. Why hadn't he offered it to me before the heroin? I rested my head back on the cushion and closed my eyes. Images of blood and a falling body played on the screen behind them. I could still picture the murdering. I didn't want to be able to picture anything.

I nodded.

Donovan unscrewed the tiny cap and helped me sit up. He tapped a tiny bit of the powder into the cap and held it under my nose. I pressed on one nostril and inhaled quickly.

Fireworks exploded. I couldn't see, couldn't hear, couldn't breathe. The drug glittered throughout my body, settling throughout me, smothering all thoughts like ash muffling the coals of a fire.

Thank God.

⌒

I walked down a purple hallway lined with cobwebs of gold toward a wall dripping with it. A man stood across from a work island, a smile on his face, his arms spread, as though he hoped to sell something. Gold coated his arms like armor and splashed across his cream apron, the edges tattered. His gray hair stood about his head at all angles, and on the tips of the strands gold sparkled.

"You're just the man I've been wanting to see," he said, beaming.

I tried to run, but he beckoned with his hand, and I could only march forward, closer to him, as though he controlled me. I approached, and blood appeared across his body and the floor—his blood.

"What do you think you're doing?" he said.

"I'm trying to get away from you."

He shook his head. "That's not what I mean. I mean, why did you go to Donovan? Why did you drug yourself?" I gaped. How did he know? The way he asked made it seem like taking drugs was inconceivable for a person of my caliber, of *our* caliber. He made me feel pure and damaged. Guilt crawled up my spine, and comfort washed over me. He cared about me, and that said maybe I should care about me too.

I repeated, "I'm trying to get away from you. I killed you, and I can't stand it." Inside my chest, a wail took form like a wave in the ocean. I tried my best to tamp it down.

The small man tilted his head. His wild gray hair gleamed in the light. "Maybe you did. Maybe I let you," he said quietly. "Maybe both happened at the same time." His voice, coated in benevolence and seriousness, filtered from my ears down into my soul.

"Why would you do that?"

The Guardian turned from me. He walked to the wall and placed his hand upon the rock. He gripped it and broke a piece off, rolling it between his hands as if it were a mixture of clay and dirt. He returned to me and held his palm up under his chin.

"Because you need this more than I do," he said.

He took a deep breath. "Patrick," he said, like he pitied me, like I was supposed to know what he meant. "It's time to wake up. You have work to do." He blew.

Gold dusted my face.

MY EYES SHOT OPEN. I stared across at an empty room. The sensation of lips and hot breath on my neck brought me to, fully. A tongue glided across the skin beneath my chin. I shoved myself upright. Donovan lay on the purple velvet cushion beside me, staring up at me. He frowned.

"What the fuck are you doing?" I asked. I pushed myself off the cushion, stepped back. I slapped my neck, felt his saliva beneath my hand, grimaced, and jerked it away. Rage bloomed hot within me, boiling away all other sensations.

Donovan chuckled. He studied me, his face sober, his mouth twisted as though he tasted something bitter. In the purple light, half his face was shadowed, but his eye shone. "How are you even awake?" he asked. He glanced at the vial of powder in his hand. The lid was unscrewed.

I pressed my hand to my nose and wiped away white powder. Within the powder, specks of gold glittered, untouched by the dark purple lighting, shining like tiny diamonds. My teeth clacked together. Was it not all a dream?

"Have you had this before?" Donovan asked, screwing the cap back on. "Your tolerance is…" he laughed, "phenomenal."

I reached down and clasped his shirt. I dragged him upright and then shoved him back down. I pulled my right fist back and launched it at him. Pain exploded in my knuckles as they connected with his cheek bone.

Donovan tumbled over the cushion onto the floor. I rubbed my fist and backed toward the door. "What the fuck is wrong with you?"

I looked around the dingy, stinking room. What the hell was I doing there? Mold, vomit, and cold air permeated my clothes. The overbearing presence of unconscious and drugged people awaited in the other room. I couldn't breathe, felt trapped and claustrophobic. I had to get out of there.

Donovan yelped and held a hand to his cheek.

The door behind me was locked. I spun the bolt, jerked the door open, and launched myself down the hall. Two individuals entered from the main floor, chuckling, but leaped back as I marched past.

"Patrick?" one of them said.

"No," I told her.

I shoved the main door open and stalked out into the light. The music muted behind me as the door swung shut, and all that was left was the early morning—the honks and smell of cars, the brilliant light of the sun.

I inhaled deeply, willing the fresh wind to wash S9 away. I could still feel Donovan's saliva on my skin, and my stomach churned. More strongly, though, I remembered the healing purple and gold presence, heard the voice of the man on the other side, the one I'd killed, as though he were still present.

I searched my pocket for my car key. When I found it, I sent a little prayer, thanking God that someone, something, had woken me.

I got in my car and pulled onto the road, headed home, my heart inexplicably calm, my head centered.

I thought of Hank's call, the images on the television. Lucient needed me. Moreso, I needed to find out what was going on, find out what Jack was, what she required of me.

I wasn't ready to go back to my father's house. Not yet. I was reluctant to be alone, especially in the room where I'd witnessed Jack, poisoned and dying, on the floor. It was all too real just now. My mind quickly flashed on a place I could go. I followed its demand without question.

I lifted the blinker and took a right instead.

CHAPTER 12
TANDEM

Patrick

ST. CHRISTOPHER'S CATHEDRAL STRETCHED HIGH above me, its moldings and tracery, pilasters and cornices, arcading and finials all familiar and comforting. Golden dots interspersed the cobalt blue ceiling like stars. It was the best of both night and day. Gray marble columns supported the ceiling, golden wood archways between them. A second-floor balcony was separated from the rest of the room by a marble rail so ornate it resembled decoration on a wedding cake. A hundred pews lined up like soldiers before the chancel.

I walked to the right and dipped my fingers in the holy water. I tapped them to my forehead, abdomen, left and right shoulders, whispering the familiar words that I'd left and rejoined, left and rejoined over the years. Father Anderson didn't know it, but I'd been baptized seventeen times over the past five years. After each drug binge, the guilt would deluge me, and I'd seek out a new church, any church, to clean me, hoping it would take this time. I hadn't told anyone. Too many addictions to share.

"In the name of the Father, and of the Son, and of the Holy Spirit. Amen."

No flames. Thank God.

My shoes clacked against the cream and white tile. I approached the front and stopped at the third row. I dipped my right knee to the ground toward the tabernacle and then slipped into the pew. The wood groaned beneath me, as though I'd made it ache.

I rested my head in my hands. I collected myself and pulled the blue cushioned kneeler down. I knelt on it and licked my dry lips.

"Dear Lord, I…" I sought what I wanted to say. "I'm out of my mind. I don't even have the words for today.

"Don't know what I'm doing. Never have. But I especially don't know what I'm doing now or who I am. I would never murder anyone, Lord. But Jack appeared in my father's office. She was dying. I admit I wondered if she was yours, if you sent her to me for help.

"But when I saw the blood explode out of him, I realized…what I'd done, what I was doing. It made me question everything. If Jack is not an angel, but instead some devil. Is it possible you intended violence?" Tears rose. I let them remain unshed. Emotion welled in my chest and threatened to choke me. "I wasn't ready for that, and that's why I called Donovan. I couldn't handle what I saw, what I did. But then…" My eyes opened briefly. "I dreamt of the man I killed, and he spoke to me, hinted that I was supposed to kill him. This doesn't excuse me murdering him, but I wonder, Lord.

"He said he let me kill him. Did he?

"Either way, he blew the gold into my face, and when I woke, I wasn't high anymore. What could do that? It was a miracle. And that makes me wonder—was it you? Is Jack yours? Was I supposed to murder that man? Did you clean the heroin and mega from my blood? So I could wake and do what I'm supposed to do?"

What am I supposed to do?

Silence filled the chamber. I gripped my hands harder together.

"Maybe all murderers speak these thoughts to you. I can't decide if I'm going insane. If Jack would only return, it might convince me that this is all as it should be, but nothing ever has been as it should be, not with my mother, not with my father, not with me. So how can it be now?"

I pressed my bottom lip between my teeth. "Have I committed a mortal sin? Is this the moment I give up?"

Tears dropped on the backs of my hands. I pressed my thumbs to my eyes and wiped at the liquid.

"As if I don't know the answer. As if I didn't know I was always headed here. To failure and rot, the hopelessness, the emptiness. We both know I've never chosen stability. I'm rash. My religion is half Catholicism, half vanitarianism. But I didn't see this particular atrocity coming. I didn't think this was how I'd burn out."

I looked up at the cross and scratched at my bottom lip with the back of my thumb. "Thank you for the sobriety."

To end my prayer, I repeated the sign of the cross and rose from the kneeler.

I turned to leave the pew. Father Anderson, brown hair, blue eyes, dimpled chin, a small scar just above his left cheek, lingered at the back of the cathedral, hands clasped behind his back. He smiled kindly.

My heart lurched. I walked toward him.

"Good morning, Patrick," he said as I approached.

I nodded. "Good morning, Father."

"Are you okay?" he asked, tilting his round face up beneath the circular and kaleidoscopic stained-glass window. The blue and red light bounced off his eyebrows, making him look particularly inquiring.

Hours before, I hadn't been able to stop shaking, sweating. My heart had raced, and my breath was hot and quick. Now, I felt wilted and tired. Sober. The dream of the Guardian was a vision that obliterated the blissful drugs in my system and the torment of adrenaline.

"I am," I said.

Father Anderson patted me on the arm. He began to walk past me.

"Father," I said.

He turned.

"How do you know when you've experienced a miracle from God?"

The man's bushy eyebrows furrowed. His normally open and clear expression became considerate. "Well," he said, "I suppose it depends on what you're calling a miracle. Miracle might refer to the slim likelihood of something occurring or an event that's unexplainable according to science or natural law. God works through nature, natural laws, and science, of course, but when He works beyond them, that is what we consider miraculous."

"But how do you know it's God?" I asked. "And not…"

"And not the Devil?"

"Yes."

Father Anderson's lips twitched. "I suppose it entirely depends on the experience. What did you see happen?"

"Rather not say."

"You won't tell me, Patrick? How long have we known each other?"

"A long time," I admitted.

Father Anderson waited, but I didn't relent, except to add, "I've been spared from something terrible, and I didn't deserve it. It's making me reevaluate the things I've done, and I wonder…if they're not all part of something more. Something entwined."

My gaze slipped up to the stained glass.

Father Anderson tilted his chin. "There are many threads in the tapestry, some of them interlocking and interlocked. You may never know for sure. That is the nature of things beyond our understanding. But you can pray, give yourself over fully to God, and, if you believe you have been spared, thank Him. That does sound to me like the work of the Almighty."

"And if I'm wrong?"

He placed a hand on my shoulder. "All is temporary but God. Pursue Him to the end, and all else perishes."

I couldn't decide whether his words helped or not. "Thank you."

"You're welcome. If you ever need anything, please let me know."

I nodded, bid him goodbye, and headed out to my car.

I drove back to my father's estate and pulled into the drive. Sunlight beamed down on the green lawn and white driveway, bounced off the red hood of the Maserati. I shut the engine off. Whooshing wind filled my ears. The trees beyond the house swayed softly in the breeze. A cloud passed over the sun, dampening the brilliance. In the shadow of the cloud, my body slumped with exhaustion. I was clear-headed, but tired and ready for sleep.

I went in the house and shut and locked the door behind me. I found my iPhone in the kitchen by the dry, stale scrambled eggs in the Le Creuset frying pan. I climbed the stairs one at a time and entered my room, not bothering to brush my teeth or change my clothes. I collapsed on my bed, feeling very aged and younger at the same time.

I peered at the clock on the nightstand to check the time. My heart lurched.

My mother's rosary rested in front of the picture of her wearing a green dress and gray felt hat, but a quarter of its opal beads dangled off the edge of the nightstand. Wrong. Different. Shifted. I sat up. *Am I losing my mind?* I shook myself free of the notion. No. I always placed my mother's rosary in a spiral in front of her picture. It'd been moved.

I scanned the room and listened. Nothing. I got up and checked the bathroom, flicking the light on as my pulse pounded in my ears. My eyes bounced from the black-and-white mosaic tile to the shower, toilet, and sink. Empty. I checked several more rooms of the house, but it was pointless. The mansion was too big to clear. A person could hide away and live there forever, if he wanted.

I wished my father had set up security cameras in the house. He never had. *I should get that done as soon as possible.* Until then, what? I was so exhausted. The answer came to me almost immediately, my mind urging me to rest.

The car.

I made my way to the front of the house, walked outside, and returned to my car in the drive. I climbed in, locked the door, reclined the seat, and instantly fell asleep.

CHAPTER 13
AMICA

Jack

I slipped the gramophone into the black backpack, zipped it, and slung it over my shoulder. I dragged Ven's body across the patio and through the back door of Cyrus's mansion. In such close proximity to my power, his clothes slowly darkened from pink back to red, and the holes filled in. After I dropped Ven's heavy body just past the threshold, I shut the door, locked it, and took a deep breath.

Leaving Ven's body where it lay, I walked up the stairs to the armory where Roland worked. In there, he wouldn't have been able to hear the gunshots from outside. That's why he hadn't come running. I took a steadying breath and analyzed my clothes for signs of the altercation. An oval mirror hung to the left of the door, and I examined my neck in the reflection. I noticed no red marks or bruises. I'd healed quickly.

I passed through the large, castle-like door into the armory and cleared my throat. "I need to talk to you."

Roland sat at a work table and held a speck of the godsoul with a set of tweezers, analyzing it beneath a bright lamp.

He straightened. "Jack," he said, barely looking up. "Come here."

I sighed, set the backpack down, and walked to him. He placed a bullet in my palm and pressed the godsoul secured by the tweezers to the tip of the bullet. The gold slowly seemed to melt into the tip, until a mixture of gold and steel shaped the cartridge.

"Whoa," I said.

"I'm not going to need to build bullets for you. They can build themselves. Somehow, the godsoul knows what to do. No heat or melding necessary."

He paused and turned his shoulders toward me. "What's wrong?"

I sucked my bottom lip between my teeth. "A ferric attacked me."

"Just now?" he asked, jumping to his feet. He dropped the bullet and retrieved a handgun. He jerked the slider back.

"He's already dead," I said, putting a hand on Roland's arm. "His body is by the back door."

Roland took two strides before I pulled him back. "It's okay. Really."

His eyes narrowed, and his voice dropped low. "What'd he want?"

"To take me in for the disappearance of the ferrics, of Lutin. And… there's something else. He said people out in the world are infected with some sickness, that Alex created it. They don't know what it is."

His jaw muscle jumped as he gritted his teeth. "What kind of sickness?"

"I don't know, but when I was at Patrick's, there was something on the news about an illness. It sounded like doctors weren't sure what it was or how to cure it. They seemed concerned it could be contagious. The ferric who just attacked me said Alex has been hopping all around the country, distributing it."

Roland put the gun down on the table and slumped back on his stool.

"I didn't hear a thing," he said. "If I had, I would've helped you."

"I know. But it turned out for the best that you didn't try."

"Why?"

I recalled the backpack with the gramophone inside. "I killed him with one of the Builder's *arcas*." I didn't explain the rest—that I had destroyed the *arca* before Ven arrived, then resurrected it. That I had used it against him, controlling it. "If you'd been there, it might've killed you too."

"You kept it?"

"I was about to destroy it," I said, thinking quickly, "before a ferric dressed all in red showed up. He said his name was Ven." I wasn't sure why I wasn't telling Roland the whole truth. After all, I trusted him with my life. I searched deep down and found that I suspected not revealing my secret might protect him.

Roland winced. "They're not going to like that."

"Nope. You need to keep some of those bullets here, in case they come."

Roland released a breath and nodded.

I looked over at a table where open ammo boxes containing several sizes of ammunition sat. All the dark gray bullets featured striations of the luminescent gold.

"I…" I began, not knowing exactly what to say next. "I'm impressed with what you've done here. Have you tried it on a knife, yet?"

"No." He turned to the wall and eyed one of the larger buck knives.

"Try it on this." I retrieved a knife from my back pocket and handed it to him. He flicked it open and tweezed another piece of the godsoul from a petri dish beside the ammo boxes. He dropped it on the metal. It melted into the surface, expanding as through molten metal. It quickly solidified.

I turned the knife over. The striations in the blade were visible on both sides.

A weight in the center of my chest released.

"You understand the Builder might come here. And the ferrics might come too," I said, meeting his eyes. "Or Alex."

"I know."

I nodded. "Maybe keep several boxes of ammunition." I turned to leave.

"Where are you going?"

"There are some things I need to take care of. I'll come back when I'm finished."

Roland shifted on the stool. "Are you sure that's safe? Going alone?"

"If that deterred me, I'd never get anywhere."

"I could come with you."

"I'd prefer you didn't. I want you safe."

Roland opened his mouth, but I shook my head. "Trust me. It's okay."

I turned and left.

———

I WENT DOWNSTAIRS TO WHERE the ferric wearing red lay. I grabbed the neck of Ven's coat and dragged his body down the hall, into a room on the right with a door to the basement. I opened the heavy wooden door and peered down a set of dirty stairs that ended on dark, buffed concrete. Deep within, the incinerator hummed, but that wasn't where I was taking him. I secured my hands beneath Ven's arms, moved down a couple of steps, and pulled him down the stairs and to the left to a circular wine room with bottles stacked from floor to ceiling. I'd been in this wine room many times. It was an area I'd had to pass on my way to visit Lutin.

An island stood in the middle of the room, and I dragged Ven's body around it, to a large metal door that resembled a bank vault. I noticed the key card scanner next to the large handle and realized the key card was likely upstairs, perhaps on Cyrus's bookshelf. I sighed and released Ven. As he dropped to the floor, a hiss of releasing pressure hit the air. Behind me, the vast metal door opened. My skin prickled with goosebumps.

The house had once again acted according to my wishes, without my even thinking about it. I felt it down in my bones, as if the two of us were connected. Was I getting stronger? Or was I only just now realizing my strength?

With no time to question it further, I pulled the door open and grabbed Ven by his reddening collar, trying my best not to touch his skin. It seemed possible my power might automatically bring him back if I merely touched his skin or was too near. I didn't want him alive again, even though I'd be in control of him. The fewer ferrics I dealt with, the fewer clues about what I was capable of I gave them. Besides, the only help I might need from Ven involved the Beretrum, and ferrics couldn't be near the place without ill effects—forget going inside. I'd secure his corpse until I returned and decide what to do with it then.

I dragged Ven past the vault door and followed a brick hallway, which curved to the right, heaving Ven's body to the second door that met me. I turned the doorknob shaped like a large diamond and opened the door. The small area had a fireplace on the right side—the mirror image of Lutin's former prison next door. He'd suffered in that prison for ten years. I'd suspected when I was imprisoned in Roth's basement that Cyrus had lined the room with lead—the same substance Roth had lined my own prison cell with. When I was in that cell, Lutin couldn't hear my prayers. When Lutin was in Cyrus's cell, he couldn't escape or be seen by his brothers.

As I looked around, hope wilted. I realized how stupid bringing Ven down there was. There was no hiding anything in this house from ferrics. They'd already been here, had seen the inside, and had likely told everyone in Domum about it. When Ven went missing, this would be the first place they looked. No. He couldn't remain in Cyrus's home. These cells were now useless.

I looked down at Ven's body and wondered what I should do. Ferrics' bodies, according to Lutin, couldn't be destroyed. That's why Cyrus had shut Lutin's brothers' bodies away in his upstairs office instead of burning them.

I was going to have to put Ven somewhere, anywhere, else. I closed my eyes, considering where I could possibly take him. The answer arrived quickly, as if my subconscious mind had already been working on the problem. One other place like Lutin's cell existed—mine, in the lower levels of Jonathon Roth's building. I would be going there soon to meet Jasper.

Ven's body could wait here during the brief time Roland needed to finish the bullets. I dropped him inside the cell and shut the door. Then I followed the red-brick hallway, closed the giant metal door, passed through the wine room, traveled up the stairs, and shut the door to the basement behind me.

I sighed and reached inside my jacket, retrieving a pack of cigarettes and a lighter. I lit a cigarette and pressed it to my lips, inhaling deeply, inviting the nicotine to drown my brain in delicious chemicals. The slightest swoon rocked me before it was gone again, as though it had never been there. Being immortal had its downsides.

Something that Ven said when he listed all the terrible transgressions I and my "family" had committed made the center of my brain itch. He said that Alex had spread his disease to Basille, Louisiana, and that one of my "friends" was sick. I had no friends. Well, aside from Patrick, but Patrick was in New York City. Who could he have been referring to?

I puffed again on the cigarette perched firmly between my lips and exhaled the smoke. Part of me urged myself to return upstairs and help Roland and then get to the Beretrum as quickly as possible to rescue Lutin. Another part, however, demanded a quick detour—just a few minutes off the path—to discover who Ven could possibly have been speaking of.

I took a breath, closed my eyes, and pictured the same hospital where Meredith—one of the women in Cyrus's cult who I had sought vengeance for—had been many years ago. I pictured its medicinal-cream corridors, the smell of alcohol and bad health, the incessant beeping of monitors. I needed to go there. Just for a few minutes. Then I'd return to Cyrus's.

I closed my eyes and willed myself to the hospital lobby.

The dank reds of the brick hallway swirled and blended and then faded to nothing. Blackness surrounded me, an emptiness beyond the world. A pair of silver elevators stretched ahead, dipping their toes into the emptiness. I turned and recognized two more behind me, and a fake plant appeared off to the left, by a water fountain. Cream linoleum squares spread beneath my feet, stretching out ahead for twenty-five feet or so. Then a tall wall of windows appeared and beyond them a circular drive and parking lot. Warm air suddenly rushed through a set of sliding doors, the smells of sweet grass and gasoline fumes mingling with anesthetic, steel tools, and floor cleaner.

Two people passed me, both in turquoise scrubs, blue surgical masks pulled below beneath their chins. "They're strong," the one with dark hair, sweat rolling down his temples, was saying. "Like meth strong. They don't feel pain like they should."

"Aren't they worried it'll spread to others?" the second man asked. He had dirty blonde hair and blue eyes.

"They've quarantined them on the fourteenth floor. Should be safe."

The pair disappeared behind a column.

I saw no other people. I stepped forward and pressed the white "up" button to signal the elevators. The elevator dinged, and the doors jerked open. The stainless-steel walls and floor smelled strongly of synthetic lemon and chemicals. I stepped in. My hand wandered over the numbers on the right and pressed level 14. The button illuminated. The doors, however, remained open. The button went dark.

I frowned and pressed the button again, harder this time. The button illuminated, then went dark again, and the doors stayed open. I finally noticed a laser scanner beside the buttons.

Oh.

Only someone with clearance was allowed to select the quarantined fourteenth floor. I left the elevators and returned to the hallway, my shoes squeaking on the tile. I heard the doors slowly shut behind me.

I scanned the lobby's high white ceiling, its recessed lighting and multitudinous cobwebs, as though I could see through it, and wondered if I would be able to translocate up to the fourteenth floor, even though I'd never seen it before. It was worth a try. I willed myself upwards. "Fourteenth floor," I said to myself, not sure what to picture.

As I spoke, a little girl in a pink dress and pigtails ran around the corner and jerked to a stop. She stared at me.

The world swished away like sinking beads of sand, and the girl's mouth dropped into a perfect O before she vanished. An almost identical hall now replaced the lobby hall.

I grimaced. But no one would believe a child.

Screams echoed, as though I'd entered a cave. No natural light, just low-grade fluorescents. I stood in a blue hallway with twenty or more doors stretching down it. The screams continued, and I looked around, tingling with fear.

I pressed a hand against a wall and leaned against it. My eyes darted across every closed wooden door. The screams did not emanate from them. They were coming from behind me. I turned and discovered a nurses' station in the distance. Three people wore what looked like hazmat suits. Another person in the same attire arrived from a hall on the left.

I froze, hoping no one would see me.

The new arrival said something to the woman sitting at the station. She jumped up, and all four bolted in the direction of the screams. They disappeared down the second hall. I moved quickly toward the closest door. I peered up at the room number and, beside it, the plastic holder containing a clipboard with the patient's name.

Mark Hartfield.

The name made no impression on me. I continued to the next.

Stacy Whitaker.

I gave this name some thought, wondering if she might have once been a child abducted into Cyrus's cult. Perhaps that's what this was about? Was someone I'd saved in one of these rooms? That wasn't what Ven had said, though. He'd said a friend was here.

I took a deep breath and read several other names before crossing to the other side of the hall. I picked up the clipboard from the first room at the end.

Margaret Wilhelm.

My heart sped. I gasped and dropped the clipboard. I caught it before it hit the floor. I pressed my thumb to the name on the sheet, and a lump filled my throat. Margaret and I had only met once. Nevertheless, I did consider her a friend, perhaps holding her in higher regard than that. How had Ven known? It seemed as though the ferrics had reviewed my entire life.

I swallowed dryly and replaced the clipboard in its transparent slot. With a calming breath, I put my hand on the door latch. A large plastic sign hung at face level: *Quarantine*. I highly doubted that applied to me.

I pulled the latch, and the door opened. I slipped inside.

The room was dark, except for a lamp above a white hospital bed. Various tubes were hooked up to the woman with white hair beneath the sheets, including an IV and heart monitor. A blood pressure cuff began to inflate. The echoes of pressurizing air and beeping monitors were the only sounds in the room, which was large for just one person.

Wooden cupboards to the left and right, a chair pressed against the wall to my left, a doctor's stool to my right in front of a computer; the screensaver was a lagoon with fish swimming in it.

I approached the bed slowly, silently.

The woman lifted a hand to her face and scratched beside her nose. I took another silent step toward her. I made out her high cheekbones, her heart-shaped face, the cut of her hair, her small frame—it was Margaret.

But the hair color was wrong. It was white. Her hair had been burgundy the last time I saw her. And her complexion had paled.

Margaret opened her eyes. The blue was too pale, as though they were fading into nothing. Her lips parted, and her chin trembled.

I put a finger to my lips, gesturing for her to remain quiet. "Shhhhh."

"I…remember you," she whispered. "Jack."

I smiled and nodded, fondly recalling the memory. Six months before, I had awoken in a cemetery after the worst night of my life, and she'd lifted me out of the grave, with the help of several other people. They'd come from her niece's wedding, and she brought me back to the reception and fed me. We'd talked, and through our discussion I'd gained enough sense of self, enough resolve, to go back and finally put an end to Cyrus. She had illuminated the world for me and strengthened me. I owed much to Margaret.

Her eyes drank me in, and she pressed down on the hospital bed, lifting herself to rest against the pillow. "You're different. Is that…is that fire in your skin?" Her voice was drained, crackly. "Your eyes. They're so dark. It's you, but it's not."

"Yes." I thought back on our last conversation. "I took your advice. I took a step outside my home, and you were right. There were many glorious things in the world. I'm now one of them."

She put a hand to her face. "I thought this *disease* was supernatural. But you, you are simply…" She smiled, tears in the corners of her eyes. "Dazzling."

Her words filled my heart. Part of me wanted to collapse in her arms, to tell her everything, as though she were my mother. My heart yearned to do so, but she was not, and there was no such thing as collapsing into anyone's arms anymore. "I never thought that we'd meet again. And when I did imagine it, it certainly wasn't like this. You were strong. And I was weak. And now…I don't understand it."

She nodded. "Time has a way of reversing things." Her smile wilted. "What are you?"

I put my hand on the rail. She didn't shrink away; she stared at me with wide, unhesitating eyes. "I'm what they call a ferric now."

She shook her head. "I don't know what that is."

"No one does," I said. "I heal all the things in the world. I fill in the cracks. I make life worth living again."

"You weren't this way when we met."

"Not entirely, but I was on the path."

She searched my face. "What wondrous things you must've seen."

I smiled. "As wondrous as a healthy pink lung."

She chuckled. "And the glowing blood of a soul?"

A frisson traced my limbs, and I shivered. Not only had she remembered my answer to her question, "What could represent the soul?" at her niece's wedding reception, but she had just reminded me of my answer—glowing plasma. My mind returned to the dripping, glowing gold wall. Uncanny.

"You have no idea," I said.

"I bet." The corner of her lips twitched upward. The smile didn't quite reach her eyes, where tiredness remained.

I looked from her white hair to her feet, at the lines connecting her to monitors. "I'm going to heal you," I said. "I'm going to save you. Just like you saved me. That's what ferrics do."

I pressed my hands against her cool arm, calling the power within me to loop and loop again, winding and binding, mounting, until my blood was carbonated and felt ready to pop. The bubble expanded, growing. Margaret's eyes wandered over me, as if she could feel the power culminating. She drew back.

"It's okay," I whispered.

"Your eyes are glowing."

"Are they?" I'd never observed myself using my power before. "It's okay. Everything is going to be okay."

I shot the power out through my palms, down into her. But it ricocheted and slammed into my chest, knocking me off my feet. My back and head slammed against the cupboards. I dropped to the floor. Black dots flooded my vision. I looked up at Margaret's bed. Her face peeked over the edge, her expression fearful.

"Are you all right?"

"Yes," I whispered, but fear had edged its way into my heart. That'd never happened before. My power had always passed down into whatever

I healed or resurrected. Never had it been forced back on me, as if rebounding off an impenetrable surface.

I slowly lifted myself to my knees and pulled myself to my feet, leaning against the counter behind me. The pain in my back quickly disappeared, and my balance returned.

"We're going to try something else," I whispered, catching my breath.

I walked to the cabinets on the other side of the room and opened drawers until I found what I was looking for—a box of syringes. I withdrew one, ripping free the clear packaging that encased it, as well as a pale tourniquet that I tied tight around my left arm. I made a fist and found a vein just beneath the surface. Thankful for my preternatural sight in the dark room, I inserted the needle into my vein, as I'd done many other times when I was younger, using heroin to drown out the horrors of my life.

I pulled the plunger back, and blood filled the syringe. I released the tourniquet and went to Margaret's bedside.

"Do you trust me?"

She nodded. "Kill it. Whatever this thing is."

I pushed the needle into her IV and flooded her line with my blood. Her large eyes watched me and then searched the room as if waiting for a sensation. Her pale hand reached for mine, grasping it. She held on tightly. I stopped breathing.

The white clock above her bed ticked. Thirty seconds passed. A minute. It'd never taken this long. I trembled and exhaled with a sigh.

Margaret's eyes sought mine. She shook her head, a dribble of sweat sliding down her temple. Her hand shook in mine, and she squeezed her lips together, as though she was trying not to cry. She released my hand and patted it.

I pressed my fist to my mouth. "What is this thing?" I whispered. Was I failing because I was a hybrid?

"I want to tell you something," she said, "that I didn't tell the doctors." Again, her hand found mine; this time it was rigid, like a claw. I bent to her level and leaned in close, letting her squeeze my palm. Her eyes pleaded with me. "The night I became sick, I had a dream. A young man with white eyes, white skin, white hair appeared in my room. He crawled through the floorboards, and he came to my bed. I tried to scream but couldn't. I couldn't even move. I dreamed he poured his blood into my mouth. But it wasn't red. It was white. And it didn't taste like blood. It tasted like death." She licked her lips, looking guilty and scared. "I didn't tell anyone because I didn't think it was real. But seeing you…transformed makes me think it might have been."

My lips parted. I almost revealed to Margaret that the boy in her dream was indeed real— he was my brother. But I didn't have the heart to disturb or overwhelm her. I didn't want to alarm her.

"Thank you for telling me," I said. I frowned. "I'm going to get you healthy, if it's the last thing I do." I brushed her white hair from her forehead.

"Don't get me wrong, Jack. I've made my peace with my God about death. If He wants to take me, I go to Him joyfully. But the things I hear in this hospital…" She shook her head. "They sound like hell. Like God has nothing to do with it. He's far, far from here, isn't He?"

A shiver rippled down my spine. "I don't know," I said. "But *I* am here." I gripped her hand tightly. "And I will always be here. With you."

She nodded, and tears filled her eyes.

"But, listen. I'll be honest. I've never had my power fail to work before. And, really, there's only one option left that I can think of. You won't like it, but I've done it before."

Her large, saucer eyes searched mine, urging me to go on.

I sighed. "Before I came fully into my power, in order to heal people, I had to…kill them, then resurrect them, fully healed. I…" My throat closed, and I tensed. I couldn't say it.

A look similar to sorrow, but not, washed over Margaret's face. It was too knowing for sadness, too sober.

"Do whatever you have to do," she said.

I wondered if I should. Two attempts to heal her had already gone wrong. Was it likely this radical approach could succeed? What if I killed her and couldn't bring her back?

I glanced at the machines Margaret was hooked up to. If they detected an alteration in her heart rate for too long, the nurses would come running. Whatever I planned to do, I would have to do it quickly.

I swallowed. "I really don't want to."

"I know," she said. She smiled and nodded, though the smile didn't reach her eyes. "It's okay. I'm at the end, and at the end, everything is okay. Do it."

I did my best not to bite right through my bottom lip. "Close your eyes."

She did. Tears trickled down her cheeks.

I tightened my jaw, determined to finish quickly. I pulled the pistol from my coat pocket and retrieved a pillow from under her head. I pressed the pillow to her face, aimed the muzzle at her forehead beneath it, turned my head, and squeezed the trigger. When the shot resounded, my heart jumped. I couldn't believe I'd actually done it. Not this time.

I brought the pillow down, and white stuffing threatened to spill out of it. I sought the familiar chaotic ball of energy within myself and urged it to build, doubling it, then tripling it.

Margaret stared at me with wide, blinking eyes. Blood pooled and dripped from her forehead, but the blood was not red. It was light pink.

She blinked. "What happened?"

The machines to my right beeped, sounding an alarm. The screens flashed red. The heart rate monitor's formerly rhythmic line dropped, flattened.

"Shit," I said.

I'd shot her, yet she was perfectly alive. And her blood was nearly white.

Footsteps echoed in the hallway.

"I'm so sorry," I said, backing away, dropping the pillow. "I have to go. But I'll come back. I'll fix you. I'm so sorry."

Her eyebrows lifted. She reached a white hand up to her forehead and pressed the wound. "You shot me, didn't you? How am I still alive?"

The door opened behind me.

I willed myself away from her, and the dark yellow room swirled, melting into nothing.

CHAPTER 14
ALVARIUM

Jack

CYRUS'S HOUSE APPEARED BEFORE ME in broad daylight, a drastic contrast to Margaret's dark, claustrophobic hospital room. Pure rage enveloped me as I looked up into the bright sky. I saw my brother's white face—the catalyst of a war and a problem in my life for far too long. Though I'd killed him before I killed the rest of Infinitum, the Builder had inserted a piece of himself into my brother, and he'd come back to life, stronger and stranger. He was pouring his blood across the world, infecting people with something that stopped life and death. Why Margaret though? Had he realized that she and I knew each other? Or had she simply been caught in his web?

It didn't matter. It was time to end the problem a second time, and I *would* end it.

My rage expanding, I walked back inside Cyrus's mansion and translocated to the armory, where I found Roland placing ammunition into black bags.

"Where are you at?" I asked.

He jumped and nearly fell over. "You scared me," he said, clutching his chest.

"Are you almost done?" I asked, heading to the stack of bags.

He nodded. "I am. Are you…all right?"

"Fine. I need to get these to New York. Now." I jerked the bags toward me. "Don't leave the house if you don't need to."

"Why?"

I blinked. "Whatever Alex is spreading around, it's here in Basille, like Ven said. But it's far worse than I could've guessed."

"You saw it? Where?"

"The hospital."

"What is it? How is it worse?"

I shook my head. "I don't think ferrics can heal people from it."

Roland's eyebrows furrowed. "What are you talking about?"

"Look. I'd love to talk through this with you. Strategize. But I have to get the ammunition to New York."

"Jack, are you going to be okay?"

"Of course." I gave him my best reassuring look. I felt none of the confidence I exuded.

"I love you, Jack. Stay safe," Roland said, looking as if he knew he'd lost a battle.

"I love you too." My voice softened.

I sent myself to the basement room where I'd deposited Ven's body. Roland's kind, teary-eyed face dispersed beneath the lights, swirling among them. All the knives displayed on the walls melted, like dye in black milk, until nothing was intelligible, and I stood alone, surrounded by darkness. Slowly, four red-brick walls materialized around me. The black bags, my backpack, and I arrived on the dirty concrete beside Ven, his red clothes now covered by dust and dirt. The smell of mold permeated the air. I glared down at him and then urged everything around me to Purdom, Jonathon Roth's building in Manhattan. To Jasper.

The red bricks disintegrated, having barely formed. Blackness emerged. Then a room.

A large office that seemed to span an entire floor spread out before me. Wood slats creaked beneath my feet. Mint green curtains twisted in the fading daylight. Across the room stood a large desk and an empty chair—an empty throne, more like— with two empty chairs opposite them. To the left, several square columns separated the area from a conference table with a multitude of chairs. A television stretched across a long portion of the wall on the other side of the table. The television was on, muted. A woman in a blue suit, her black hair tucked behind one ear, stood outside a building. "EMERGENCY" glowed in red letters just above the building's glass door entrance.

"Back so soon?" a voice said behind me.

I turned.

Jasper stood there at parade rest, hands clasped together behind him. His face was lined, his eyes like two laser points. His stare was cold, but he smiled. He wore an unzipped black leather jacket and black shirt, dark blue jeans, and black boots. Four men stood behind him, motionless, appearing almost like soldiers. One was bald and broad-chested, another wiry, with gray hair. The remaining two were shorter than Jasper, both with buzz cuts. All looked like people I would never have wanted to meet. I'd seen these four others once before, but the only impression they'd made on me then was that I could sense, deep down in my bones, that I'd resurrected them.

"Sorry to disappoint you," I said.

"Like that could ever be true." He walked forward and looked down at the bags.

"Ammunition," I said.

"We have ammunition."

I shook my head. "Not this kind."

Jasper bent down and unzipped one of the black bags. He retrieved an ammunition box and from it a bullet. He held it up to the afternoon light. Gold striated the tip.

"It's special," I said. "The only sort of thing that can kill the Builder… or Alex."

Jasper cocked an eyebrow. "Alex is alive?"

"Oh yes." I pressed a hand to my jaw. "He's not himself anymore. But we're going to take care of him. Today."

Jasper tilted his head at Ven. "And this poor bastard? Is he one of your kind?"

"He is."

"Got on the wrong side of you, hm?"

I smiled. "I'm going to store him down in the lower levels, in the old cell where Roth hid me."

He nodded. "Why?"

"Their bodies can't be destroyed, and I can't keep him in Basille. I'll hide him here."

"Do you really think you'll be able to hide him anywhere?"

"Maybe. Cyrus did it for a decade. Roth did it for months."

Jasper nodded, and his narrowed eyes returned to the bullet. "How long did this take you to make?"

"Roland made it. And not very long."

"Roland…" Jasper frowned. Cogs turned in his head. "I don't recognize the name."

"You wouldn't." That was true. All evidence of Roland had long disappeared, and Jasper knew only what Infinitum and I had told him. They'd probably never mentioned Roland, and I knew I hadn't.

"Is he trustworthy?"

"More than you."

He chuckled. He placed the bullet back in the box and returned it to the bag. "Reminds me of *kintsukuroi*. And of your body."

"What?"

"The gold filling in the bullet like cracks."

My lips parted. He was right. It was reminiscent of my fiery cracks. And of the gold in the purple rock in the godsoul room. Striation upon striation connected like a spider's web across a uniform fabric from which all came.

"Where are the men?"

"They're downstairs in the garage," he said. "They're ready. The others…" Jasper motioned to the men behind him, and they walked forward.

"Take these bags down to the garage," he said to them. "Take this body down to the lower level, to the cell." They moved immediately, obeying his command.

As they loaded the elevator, I felt a sense of unease. I'd left them alone so long, my blood in their veins. Should I trust our connection? My control of them?

When they were finished and the elevator doors closed, the two of us were alone. Jasper said, "So what's the plan?"

I took a deep breath. "You're going to stay here. I'm taking the men, and we're going to the Beretrum."

"The…?" He tilted his head.

"Where Alex and the Builder are."

Jasper blinked. "And you think that I *shouldn't* go with you?"

"I'm fine with Roth dying and the others. I'm not fine with losing you. All those I care about remain on this side."

"And do what?"

"Stay inside. Don't go out. And guard yourself." I tilted my chin toward him. "You still have the jewelry box from the raid on Infinitum?"

The jewelry box was an *arca* that'd been taken from one of the houses. It would've killed the men if they hadn't had my blood in their veins. That was what saved them time and time again—they'd created inhalers that dosed them with my blood, making Roth's men invincible. They still had doses left in the insulin pumps they used. I wondered if they would be useful for immunizing them against Alex's blood. Too bad there was no time to test the theory.

Jasper nodded and proceeded toward a wall safe above a table in the entryway. He plugged in the necessary code, and the metal box clicked. He pulled it open.

Inside was a black lacquer box with a shell design on top. Duct tape wound around it in hasty, hurried loops. I went to it and tugged the tape free.

"What will happen if you die in the Beretrum?"

I eyed him as I removed the tape. "This has to be done."

"Oh, I know that," he said, as though it were the most obvious thing in the world. "It's just…is anyone going down there with you who's on your side? Where is your ferric friend—Lutin?"

At the sound of Lutin's name, my heart jumped. "That's one of the reasons I'm going," I said. "To save him. He's trapped down there."

"You mean some of your kind is already down there?"

I nodded.

"And you don't know what's inside…the Beretrum?"

"No."

He sighed out through his lips, as though whistling, but no whistle arrived. A sad, pitying look crossed his face. He caught himself and recovered. "You've done fine so far. You've always been good at improvising." He slapped me on the back. "You sure you don't want me there?"

"Positive."

I pressed my hand to the jewelry box's lid and closed my eyes. Jasper remained quiet as I worked.

I sent myself down into my core, away from all the negative truths circling my life—Alex, Margaret, the disease, the ferric in red who'd come to take me to trial, the loss of Lutin, my being fated to hell. I dismissed those things and entered into the moment as though it were the only true moment, as though all that existed were Jonathon Roth's empty office, the still air, Jasper, and my breath.

I allowed only one thought as I breathed.

I abolish you.

A brilliant light fluoresced. I opened my eyes and pulled my hand back as the jewelry box melted in red and orange flames.

It puddled on the table, reduced to nothing, just as the gramophone had melted on Cyrus's back porch. The stench of smoke and sulfur permeated the air.

I took a deep breath. I'd barely had to push any energy out at all. I had simply told the box what to do. The power to destroy it had come not from hatred. It had come from calmness, from staying within myself.

I dipped a finger in the ash. It scattered away from my hand, as though repelled by a magnet.

I spread my fingers wide, and I willed the energy within me—the energy that used to feel like I was returning to myself, that circulation was returning to my brain—and I pushed it out to the box. In the blink of an eye, it was again whole and complete.

I bent down near it and whispered, "You will protect Jasper."

"What did you just do?" Jasper asked.

"The Builder isn't the only problem anymore. You know that ferric that attacked me? I have no doubt there are more where he came from. You're going to use this to protect yourself," I said, sliding the jewelry box over to him. "It works for me now."

"How is that possible?"

"Everything I restore I can control, including the *arcas*. If a ferric comes for you, use this."

Jasper studied the box. "Are you sure you should be doing this?"

I picked up the black box and held it out to him. A long moment followed before he accepted it.

"You don't know how necessary this is yet. But it is. All the others are gone. It's just us now. Me, Roland, and you."

I slapped a hand to Jasper's chest. "Thanks for everything."

"Of course."

I walked toward the elevator. Jasper followed, and we descended from Roth's office to the garage. When the doors opened, row upon row of men were loading their weapons with the special golden ammunition. When I stepped away from the elevator doors, they stopped and stood upright, face forward, twenty feet away. It reminded me of when I'd first seen them down in the garage, after Roth had dug them up and forced me to resurrect them. Their bodies had been laid on blue tarps, dead roses in their pockets. Now they wore Kevlar vests and black boots.

I attempted to mentally prepare myself for whatever might be inside the Beretrum. Lutin and his brothers hadn't been able to tell me anything about it because, as they put it, the pure could not enter. I was guessing that wouldn't be a problem for me. Or for these men. I wasn't pure, and neither were they. I was betting we would make it through. But then what?

Was it possible we would be dropped into flames? Would there be demon creatures of some sort throughout the lair?

The last time a vision of the Builder had come to me, the entire space had been black, a void, as though nothing could exist in it. Whatever the Builder needed formed itself out of his white body, and he took on whatever shape he needed. His arm had turned into a knife to cut into my brother to place a piece of himself there.

I supposed if I were to meet a demon, it would be Alex, who wasn't my brother anymore.

I swallowed and gripped my backpack strap tightly.

"What's in there?" Jasper asked.

"Another *arca*."

I walked into the garage, faced the thirteen rows of men, and studied their faces. Jonathon Roth was in the middle of the front row. I looked straight into his dark eyes, at the lines just below his cheeks that reminded me of tribal scars. I wondered if this small army would be enough.

"I need to tell all of you," I said loudly, my eyes sweeping over every individual I controlled and could disperse at will, "about where we're going. It isn't anywhere you've ever been, and it isn't like anything you've ever seen. It's not on Earth. It's in a different world altogether. I have never visited there, but as I understand it, it's literal hell, where all the fallen souls go when they die. Where the devil resides. It is where my brother hides. It's called the Beretrum."

No reaction from them, but that was no surprise. They were under my control, and what my power commanded was to listen, to obey my commands—nothing more. It was impossible to allow them any freedom beyond that, especially since they now had bullets in their guns that could kill me.

"At the edge of the Beretrum, strange things happen to people's minds. That's what I've been told. I haven't experienced it yet, but I've heard that it can be nauseating, terrifying, can cause paranoid thoughts and delusions. I'm commanding you to, to the best of your ability, keep your wits about you. Stay sane as best you can. You've already got one person up there in your head—me. There's no knowing what will happen once we're in there."

None of them responded. Then again, they couldn't. They knew something terrible was about to happen to them, but they had no choice.

For a moment, I felt a pang of guilt. I had to remind myself that they had forced me into a cage to resurrect their blood brothers, to share my blood to make them near invincible. Roth had threatened to kill Patrick. My eyes shifted to him.

"I don't know exactly what we're going to face, but I can say this. There is a monster. He lives in a world far from here, and he builds contraptions—instruments that you yourselves faced at Lucient Laboratories and in the houses Infinitum owned. He disperses them into the world to beget murder. Not only that, but he has now dispersed an illness of some sort. We have to kill him. That's what the bullets in your guns can do. They can kill him. So if you see a large, shining, plastic-like white creature, do what your instincts tell you—shoot him.

"But he isn't the only one we're worried about.

"My brother, whom I stabbed and killed, was brought back to life. The Builder saved him by inserting a piece of himself into my brother, restoring him. He stole a piece of godsoul and consumed it, and since then, he has been able to sicken people by spreading his blood to them. I can't…heal them." My throat constricted as I thought of Margaret. "I've dealt with Alex for so long, but he's getting stronger. We have to eliminate him. Now is the time, even if we don't kill the Builder. Because I'm not sure there is a cure for those who are ill, and we can't allow Alex to spread this plague any further."

I swallowed, wishing that Lutin were here, that the bastard Osric were here, that all of them were. Instead, I was alone. There was an army in front of me, but it was like being alone when I was with them.

An emptiness washed over me, full of sadness and despair. I stared at my army, thinking that it would be easy enough to have them do away with me. All I needed was to command them to shoot me, and it'd all be over. I wouldn't survive a bullet melded with godsoul.

The fluorescent lights hummed sickly, and my gaze was drawn to them. A moth flew past, banging into a glass bulb—life at the edge of the synthetic.

Momentarily, the despair lifted. My wet eyes dried.

"Are you ready?" I asked, as if I were talking to myself. My voice had a vulnerable edge.

They nodded in unison.

"Then let's do it," I whispered.

CHAPTER 15
BERETRUM

Jack

I HAD THE MEN CONGREGATE as close as possible around me, so they would not be spread out across the side of the mountain when we arrived. The last thing I wanted was for them to go tumbling over the cliff after we translocated.

My hands trembling, I pictured the edge of the Beretrum, that black void, the white around it, and the giant claw marks in the rock, and I willed myself and the men there.

The dark cement garage floor and the fluorescent lights melted and swirled and darkened, vanishing into black. I looked into Jonathon Roth's eyes, surprised to find that they weren't vacant but piercing—fearful, even. The only other time I'd seen him look like that was when I'd shocked him and his men by resurrecting Julian in front of them, showing them what I could do for the first time. I knew what he was probably thinking—that it was pointless and idiotic to delve into hell, that I was taking his men somewhere far worse than he ever had, that I was a black magic, no longer efficient, that I needed to end. Roth was always about efficiency, about what I could provide, and I had long ago become more trouble than I was worth.

It didn't matter. I had control now.

A snowflake drifted between us and landed on the black fabric of his Kevlar vest. The need to apologize to all of them for what I was pulling us into seemed urgent, and I nearly opened my mouth to do so when the snow below our feet appeared. Wind whipped and pushed at us. Storm clouds formed above. The men crouched.

Roth placed his hand on my shoulder and pressed, urging me down. I stared into his eyes, not knowing whether he'd chosen to do that or if I had instinctively forced him.

"Thanks," I said.

The corner of his lips twitched upward, his wind-whipped black hair thrashing over his forehead and dark eyes.

I pointed toward the giant opening in the mountain. "There," I said. All the men looked in unison. We hunkered low in the snow and crawled toward it, me in the middle of the pack. When I reached the edge, I looked down into the pit, a black hole with no discernable bottom. Snow fell into it and disappeared. The claw marks in the rock around the entrance were smooth. My right arm fit snugly into one.

I sought the memory of the last time I was at the Beretrum's edge. I replayed the sight of the giant white creature scooping Osric away from me, clutching Lutin's bleeding and unconscious body in its shiny, plastic-looking paw, his head lolling. I shivered.

Would all the men survive the landing, whatever it was, wherever it was?

No matter my doubts, I had to try.

"On the count of three!" I yelled against the wind.

"One!"

"Two!"

I shut my eyes and sucked in a deep breath.

"Three!"

We thrust ourselves into the black pit.

GRAY.

The gray shifts to black.

Mist rises around me. I look for the others but I can't make out anything.

Nothing is beneath my feet. I drift, suspended.

Dead grass appears below me, rises quickly to meet me, and I brace myself. I land softly, barely sensing the thud against my feet. I find myself standing in a clearing. One at a time, the men around me land just as gently, as if gravity is different here.

Roth appears beside me. The lines, like tribal scars, in his face are barely visible. The mist rolls back, and a tree-speckled hill appears beyond. To the right is a dilapidated white building.

It seems like we are still on Earth, in our reality, except for the lack of scent, lack of sound, lack of wind, though magically the trees sway in the distance. Everything appears normal, but absence permeates the atmosphere. I sense the deficiency of something deeply important in my gut, though my eyes lie to me. The incongruence between what I see and what I can't sense makes my stomach roll with nausea.

A couple of Roth's men drop to the dry, dead grass clutching their stomachs.

A man with sandy brown buzz-cut hair vomits. Thick, oily fluid flops onto the grass, a mixture of yellow and green half-digested food. Rapidly, the dirt absorbs it, and it is as though the vomit was never there.

Hearing voices in the distance, I look up at the hill. Hundreds of individuals in matching white-and-black striped uniforms quietly face us. I shiver. Who are they? Were they there before?

I walk forward through the men until I arrive at the front of the group. "Do your best," I command my army. No need to yell because they can hear me in their minds. "You might feel sick. Don't attack one another. Don't attack me. Protect yourselves and me."

I take a few more steps toward the strangers on the hill. Buildings, decrepit and gray, appear around us, details filling in. Beyond them, a tall fence stretches, barbed wire at the top. It circles us, the buildings, and the individuals on the hill completely.

"Jack," Roth says behind me.

I look back at him.

His eyes widen as he examines me. "You don't look like you used to."

I peer down and check my arms and legs. I see nothing out of the ordinary. "What are you talking about?"

"There's a…glow around you. You're the only thing here that isn't gray. And the grass under your feet…it's greener than everywhere else. Around your head, the sky shows the faintest outline of blue. Near you, I hear birds in the trees."

I cock my head, recalling what Lutin has told me about his kind, *our* kind—we bring color back to the world, fill in all the gaps, all the cracks. Perhaps the Beretrum is one large crack, one that refuses to heal. Instead, it continues to split, widening forever.

"Shit," Roth says, his eyes leaving me.

I turn. All my muscles tense. The people on the hill are running toward us, far faster than seems possible. The lines in their faces become more apparent, their teeth visibly black and yellow, their thinness evident. They appear starved.

Several of them cry out.

"Save me!"

"Help us!"

Another movement catches my attention. Behind the running people, something white materializes. A creature appears from behind one of the buildings, like a spider stretching its legs.

My mouth drops, and my heart pounds. The image of a white thing on a vast ocean of black comes to mind—my vision in Roth's basement.

The Builder.

I retrieve the knife from my pocket that Roland has mixed with godsoul and tell the men to ready their weapons. "If you have a clean shot, fire at the Builder."

The strangers in prisoners' clothes are just fifty feet away. My army pushes forward to drive them back, but a man and woman break through and rush me. I shove them away. As I knock them to the ground, two more replace them, as if from thin air. They tear at my clothes, my face, my hair. The pain is overwhelming when my skin curls beneath their fingernails.

"Help us," one of them hisses. Spittle hits my ear. His eyes and teeth are yellow. Rotten breath washes over me and then disappears in the vast space that fills the Beretrum.

One of them bites me.

I shove them back and silently command Roth's men to pull them off me.

Hands yank them back, but more prisoners appear, swarming me. I drop my knife and am separated from it.

A prisoner grabs the knife and stabs one of Roth's men with a tribal tattoo on his arm. The tattooed arm lifts the gun and shoots the prisoner, who drops and disappears beneath a swarm of more prisoners.

"No!" I cry.

My arm is jerked to the left and twisted; it feels as though it is separating from the socket. More of them bite me.

"Get them off of me!" I scream.

Gunfire erupts, and people drop around me, disappearing as they hit the gray earth.

I fall to the ground, hoping to avoid the bullets. Crawling on top of several bodies, I make my way toward my silver and gold knife that is sticking straight out of the ground. I reach out and grasp it.

Someone lifts me—Roth. He drags me sideways, away from the scrambling people. We both run, escaping through the maze of his men and the Beretrum's residents. We stop beyond the perimeter of Roth's men, who are fighting the prisoners back.

The shining white thing, impossibly bright and empty, stands on the hill, as if watching the scene. The place where its face should be is blank. No eyes, no nose, no mouth. Though, I know that those features can form on the milky surface. I've seen it before.

My mouth dries, and I tremble at the sight. Something deep inside me seeks my childhood training, something that knows I must stop thinking and feeling to do what I need to do. I lunge forward, and Roth runs with me.

"Shoot it," I say.

We rush toward the white creature, my strength and courage having already abandoned me. Fear has invaded. I vibrate with it, wondering if I am actually here.

The Builder waits just a few hundred feet away. Then the creature turns its back to us. The surrounding reality shifts.

It is night. We are no longer on a hill but in the middle of a field. All around us, gunfire erupts like fireworks. Sulfur fills the air and coats my throat, sweet and dirty.

I search for Roth's men and see none. Behind us is a forest full of trees, not empty land. Strangers, men in dark garb, some of them on the ground, bloody and dead, stretch ahead. Others seem to be in the midst of battle.

"I've seen these uniforms before," Roth says. "In pictures."

"What pictures?"

He opens his mouth to answer and then freezes, dropping his jaw. Something white pierces the horizon. The Builder appears among the vast groups of warring men, its blank face peering in our direction, as if challenging us to follow.

I urge myself forward, away from Roth, and run. Men buzz around me, some of them pausing in their fight, their eyes widening as I rush past.

"Wait, Jack!" Roth calls behind me.

"Shoot it!" I yell.

"Wait!"

There's no time. The Builder is in front of us, and all we need do is pierce its heart with a bullet. Just one golden bullet, right in its heart.

The bright white thing seems solider, more substantial, unstained by the battle around us, as if with every wound, every bullet, every death, every drop of blood, it becomes cleaner, purer, whiter. Whiteness is darkness here.

My chest aches. My feet pound the ground, my thighs ache, and I launch myself even faster toward the Builder.

Roth calls out again, but I'm nearly at the thing, ready to pull my gun from my pocket and shoot.

The Builder's blank face changes. A mouth forms. Lips. Teeth. It smiles.

The world around me shifts. All goes quiet.

Night is gone.

Men are gone.

I stand on a white floor surrounded by a vast whiteness. I swallow, looking for Roth. "Roth!" I call. His name echoes, reverberating around me, then disappears as though sucked into a vacuum.

No response. I stand alone among all the white.

"Jack." The voice doesn't sound human; it's animal-like and robotic at the same time. I shiver in the echoes.

I turn.

Alex stands there.

His eyes are white, his clothes are white, his blond hair is whiter than ever, as though he has been scared out of his human colors. Eyelashes rim his white eyes like tiny white feathers.

Thousands of goosebumps crawl across my back, arms, and legs. I want to scream, but I force the urge down into my stomach, where it does a somersault and threatens to emerge as vomit.

"You're not Alex, anymore."

"Not the one you remember." He clasps his hands together. His tone and cadence don't resemble anything natural or human. "Just as you're not the Jack I remember."

I grit my teeth, forcing myself to stand still, not to run. There's no place to run to.

"It's too bad he brought you back," I say. "You've lost your humanity."

"And you exceeded yours. I wanted this, Jack. Did you not want what Lutin forced on you?"

I ponder his words. "Yes. Though I didn't realize it until later. It made me what I am."

He nods. "The same is true for me."

I suddenly wonder if we are merely chess pieces on a giant board.

Something in the white around me forms and rises. Bars about half a foot apart stretch up, farther than I can reach, and disappear into the whiteness above. A cage circles me.

I peer at Alex through the bars. Despite myself, my hands vibrate. I feel as though my head is filled with fog.

"What the hell have you released in this world?" I demand. My heart races.

He smiles. "The Builder was impressed with the army you created, made unstoppable by your power, by your blood. He decided to build his own army. Through me. So, like you, I dosed someone with my blood. Several people."

"And do you have your army?"

His white eyes, no pupils visible, turn to the vast white floor. "In my own way. In human beings, my blood did not have the same result as yours. But that's all right. We have done something else. We've constructed and hastened a plan of our own."

"What plan?"

He blinks, his eyelashes glistening. "To destroy the Earthly world."

A breath catches in my throat. I should've guessed that was his end goal, but I hadn't. Alex had always been about control—to control the world, to manipulate it, to gain from it—not destruction. "Why? Why would you want to destroy the only world you've ever known?"

"Because I belong *here* now. The old world is good food for the Builder, good food for me, and besides…there are other worlds to eat after this one is gone."

I swallow, wondering what Alex means by "other worlds." Does he mean the ferrics' home, or a reality beyond the one I know? Or both?

"The Builder is offering you a place beside us." Alex steps closer to the bars. "Help us destroy the world. If you accept, you will not die, and you will be able to travel with us."

I open my mouth to tell him he can go fuck himself, but an image comes to my mind, as if put there by another mind. It's an image of me, slightly colder, calmer, more resolute, untouchable. It is a version of myself that can never be harmed, only do harm, and there is something calming about the image. As though this is the me I should have been all along, before the route I chose softened and weakened me, made me too similar to the others. My path made me communal instead of individual, my own island. I should be the granite on which others break themselves.

I shake the image from my mind to say, "No," but my tongue won't form the word. Instead, another image arrives—an image of Cyrus,

Alex, and me, each powerful in our own right, each a third of a whole, coming together as one for the Builder. The piece of the ferric the Builder needs, the piece of the human the Builder needs, the piece of Himself the Builder needs, in each of us. It is almost as though it has been ordained by something much higher.

The pieces of the puzzle fit. Who am I to resist?

I grab my head, trying to stop the unwanted images and thoughts, and notice the milky white beyond the cage around me, like a vast ocean. I am deep in the Beretrum, where no ferric can ever willingly go, where no human has willingly gone. It is like I am submerged beneath the pressure of the largest sea, and there my mind is turning, just as Osric warned.

I want to join Alex. I want to join the Builder. I want to give in and let the me run out of me like bad blood and simply be beautifully blank and automatic, to let them tell me what to do.

I inhale deeply. I long for the empty me, but a nagging sensation, small, the size of a piece of fluff on the sleeve of an old jacket, whispers it isn't the right choice. The truth seems miniscule, but I feel it as though it is ten thousand times its size. The Builder—and Beretrum—is not the choice Lutin would prefer. It is not the choice I wanted when I dove inside. It feels right to tell Alex, "Yes, I'll join you," now, but it didn't used to feel that way.

I shake my head. "No." The word barely escapes on a light breath.

Alex blinks. He pulls back. "What?"

I double-down on my answer, perhaps the only link left to my reality. "No. I won't join you. Never."

Alex peers to his left, as if searching for an answer from something or someone I cannot see. "How was she able to resist?"

"Because I fight," I say. "I was raised to."

Alex turns back to me, his expression blank. "Fine." He turns and walks to my left, as though making way for someone. I take several steps back, and my heart rises to my throat. My eyes wildly search the place where Alex stood. I blink.

Patrick stands there, serene, quiet.

He is tall, slender, his piercing red hair perfectly arranged, his eyes greener than they have ever been, his skin creamy. A tailored black blazer and slacks with a white shirt ornament him. His black shoes shine. He clasps his hands. The image hypnotizes me. This isn't Patrick, and yet I can't help but believe it is.

"Jack," he says quietly, his eyes burning like green fire. The false-Patrick's gaze is far more pointed than any look Patrick would give. His eyes burrow through me.

My teeth clench, and a prickling sensation crawls across my back and arms. The whole time, the Beretrum has felt evil, but a fresher, purer version of it arrives. I feel bruised.

My chest burns right between my clavicles, and I slap my hand there. Something stings my palm, and I seize it and jerk it away.

It is Roland's cross. Shriveled and hot, it flashes red, as though it's been heated in a kiln. When I drop it, it tumbles to the white, away from me, like an ember right off a fire. It spins near the prison bars and stops. The white ground surrounding it hisses and steams.

Patrick watches it and then looks up and smiles.

"I'm going to kill you," I announce.

He rolls his eyes. "It's not quite that easy." He steps toward the bars. "And even if you did, for what? The Creator isn't going to return. Ever. You cannot save the world. Beings far more important than you, Jack, have prayed for Him to come to them, and He never has. I don't know where He is, even if He's still alive, and I know a lot more than the ferrics do."

I swallow. "I figure it's worth a shot."

He nods pityingly. "You remind me of someone. A boy by the name of Lucas. He was a hybrid, like you. The ferrics locked him away a century or so ago. They killed him when he was very young, within just a few years of imprisoning him. He was...powerful. Far more powerful than any other ferric. It's a shame they got to him before I could." His eyes search mine. "I can't help but wonder about the nature of the power you have. How long will you last in their grip?"

I don't respond, though curiosity pecks at me. Another hybrid? How many have there been?

"Who killed him?" I ask.

"The ferrics," he says, as though it is obvious. "They're not kind to outsiders. I should know. I've been around long enough to see it, to experience it. They'll never accept you. You are so beautiful, so perfect the way you are, and yet they'll torture and kill you, just like they did Lucas.

"I would like to help you, Jack. It's not without cost, but it will save you."

I blink and frown. "The ferrics would never torture me. They're not you. They're the good guys."

"Oh? There's a mirror in the ferric prison that tells me different. It's the one piece of their world linked to my home, and I can see everything through it, what they do and what they hide. Believe me. Good isn't *all* they are. When they wage war, they become unstoppable, and you won't win, not without my help. I've died in battle at least three hundred times. You yourself are facing at least that many battles, and you don't have the ability to self-resurrect like I do."

"I'm not you."

"True. But they don't see it that way. Do the smart thing, Jack. Do the right thing for yourself. I can protect you, and I will save you from them, if you do just one thing for me. Bring me some godsoul."

I nearly laugh and shake my head. I can't believe his brazenness. "Why the hell would I do that?"

He gazes at his fingernails. "I could mend Lutin for you."

My heart leaps at the mention of my savior. I picture his kind, dark face—the reason for my coming here—and a weight slips from my shoulders. I step toward the white bars. "He's not dead?"

"Of course not. That bargaining chip of mine is still very much alive, though perhaps nearing the edge between life and death. He's deep asleep, to protect his mind from the effects here. I can fix him though. I was there when the ferrics were originally made, and I know how to use the godsoul in ways the ferrics don't. With it, I can fashion the piece of his heart that Lutin is missing."

I cock my head, wary. "Why can't you just get it yourself?"

The Builder within Patrick smirks. "You haven't figured it out?"

"Figured what out?"

Patrick exchanges a look with Alex. He slides his hands against one another. "If you say yes and agree to get me the godsoul, then I'll save him. If you say no, then I'll wake him."

I lower my eyes. My mind pokes and prods at doors that will not open for me. I cannot logic my way out of this dilemma. My heart aches for Lutin and even for the other ferrics. An image comes to me of Lutin smiling down at me, smelling of chimney and cinnamon.

I know what I want, and I know what the Jack who entered the Beretrum wanted. My tenuous grasp on reality is slipping, but there is one word that maintains our connection. "No."

"You would prefer him to go insane?"

I look up.

"Trade with me," the Builder within Patrick says. "Godsoul for Lutin in mended condition and safe passage for you both alongside Alex and me. Ten pounds of godsoul should do the trick. And then…freedom."

There isn't enough time to think things through, not enough time to consider whether I've been cornered, whether I can move the chess pieces into a favorable position, but I'm betting that if the Builder wants this, it's wrong. Lutin, as much as I love him, would loathe me for trading godsoul to save him. I simply have to trust that I'm capable of finding a way out, even if I can't see it now.

"No," I whisper.

Patrick walks forward, hands in his pockets. "What are you doing, Jack?"

"The right thing."

"The long, arduous thing that won't get you anywhere," he says. He nods at Alex. "Your brother did me an incredible favor by spreading his blood to infect those people. As we speak, the virus is mining their souls, feeding me and killing them. You cannot stop the virus. None of you can. Not only that, but you can guess your fate. You won't end up in Domum, with the others. Because you're not like the others. Why would you maintain loyalty to a system that would sooner see you rot in my home than help you? What's the point?"

I swallow. "I don't care about pain. I don't care about uselessness. What I care about is right and wrong. To help you would be wrong. I would rather do the right thing and go to hell than the wrong thing and go to hell."

"But *why*?" he asks. "What's the point? If you just give in to yourself, your path becomes so much easier. I could help you."

"How could you possibly?" I say, shaking my head.

Before Patrick can speak again, I pull my knife from my pocket and strike the bars that surround me. They explode, fragments of white falling everywhere, liquifying before they soak into the ground.

Alex throws his hands up. I aim my gun and fire the bullets melded with godsoul at the Builder. They tear through his arms and chest. Where they pass, impossible round holes remain, but there's no blood. The Builder doesn't fall. He simply stands there.

Patrick drops his arms to his sides. Every hole in his flesh fills back in. His clothing repairs itself.

Shit.

It's time for plan B. I drop the gun and pull my backpack free. I open it quickly, retrieve the gramophone, and set the needle down on the record, which spins.

Patrick peers at the contraption, his eyebrows furrowed. "What are you doing?"

Big band swing fills the Beretrum, the trombones, saxophones, trumpets, and clarinets. The sound of it is sucked from the space as soon as it enters, so that the upbeat music arrives in a *whoosh*.

The white space around us reverberates, and the Builder looks around, startled. His form shivers and blanches before the image of Patrick disappears. A blank white face peers down at me. In a blink, he's gone.

Alex rushes to where the Builder stood. He peers to his left, then his right, unable to find what he's looking for. He turns to me, open-mouthed.

White goo flows down the center of the bell, and globs spill out over the white floor.

Alex shakes his head, tension releasing as his shoulders drop, as though comforted by the Builder's contraption. His quizzical expression seems to ask what I could possibly think I might accomplish by using it.

"Kill him," I say. The bell widens.

Alex's feet are swept out from under him. He lands on his back and jerks toward the gramophone, tugged by something invisible. I jump to my feet as the bell encompasses his shoes, his legs. Alex screams, his white mouth wide to bare white tongue, teeth, and palate.

The walls of the Beretrum reverberate again. An internal pressure pushes against me, compressing my lungs with such force I fear I will suffocate. Pain stabs my inner ears, and I press my hands to cover them, squeezing my eyes shut.

A roar drowns Alex's scream. It penetrates through my hands, so loud I can't think, can't breathe. I lose all sense of myself.

I pass out.

CHAPTER 16
CAPTUS

Patrick

My phone rang and vibrated on my car's dash. I woke up and I grabbed it to check the screen. Hank's name filled it. I answered, attempting not to mumble. "Hello?"

"I've been trying to contact you all day."

I rubbed my eyes and took note of the time. I'd slept for seven hours in the driver's seat. I moved the seat back into a sitting position, looked around, and groaned at the pain in my side and stiffness in my joints. So thirsty. "Something came up," I said, reaching for a mostly empty Ozarka water bottle on the car floor. I popped the cap off and swallowed the dregs.

Hank huffed. "I don't know if you've been watching the news or *what* you've been doing, but it's looking more and more like we've got a problem, a true international emergency, with this virus."

My mind reviewed the previous day—the cathedral, Donovan, the drugs, the gun going off like a cannon in my hand—and pounced on the image of the woman interviewed on television speaking of an individual becoming infected at a meditation retreat.

"Right," I said. I massaged my left ribs.

"The Board would like to move forward with formulating experimental drugs to try and combat the virus."

"I think the Board is right," I said. "I'm behind them one hundred percent."

"That's all I needed." He cleared his throat. "Just an FYI—the Dow dropped a thousand points today."

I frowned and poked my tongue against my cheek. "Why?"

"There have been inexplicable simultaneous outbreaks across the globe. Doesn't bode well for business. Restaurants are shutting down. Whatever it is, it moves fast. I'd stock up on supplies."

I chuckled. "My father's liquor room is still stocked."

"I'm serious, Patrick. Whatever this is, it's not going away. It's coming for all of us."

I examined the reflection of my eyes in the rearview mirror. "I know."

"I'll be in touch," he said. He hung up.

I dropped the phone on the passenger's seat and banged my head against the headrest. My gaze flicked through the windshield at my father's house. Beyond the gravel drive, blocks of cement led up to the house with lines of grass growing between them. The squares resembled a vast chessboard. In front of the giant casement windows, Siberian squill lined the bottom portion of the house, dabbing the exterior with porcelain blue. Two giant boxwood topiaries sat on either side of the porch.

Part of me wanted to go inside. Another part remembered my mother's rosary, disturbed on the nightstand beside the bed. Someone had been there. Was that "someone" human or a being of another sort? Like Jack or the creature I'd killed. Maybe something different than either.

I stared into the darkening sky and thought about how stupid it was of me to sleep right outside the house. Anyone—monster, human, angel, devil—could have attacked me while I slept.

I searched through my phone's call history for Jack's number. I tapped her name and listened to it ring, my heart steady, my jaw tense. The call went to voicemail. I didn't leave a message. I called again.

As the ring repeated, a movement near the house caught my eye. The front door slowly eased open, the entryway beyond invisible to me because of the angle. My skin prickled like a porcupine. I immediately pressed both the brake and the ignition button. As the engine came to life, I grabbed the steering wheel tight in my left hand, the gear shift in my right.

My tongue darted across my bottom lip.

Shit.

I couldn't remember if I'd shut the front door or not, or if I'd locked it. But it wasn't like me to leave the door open.

My right hand begged to throw the car in drive and get out of there. But where was I going to go? Who could I ask for help? Jack wasn't picking up, and anyone else would only be capable of hearing half-truths. Besides, I couldn't endanger people.

I gritted my teeth and swallowed, peering once again at my green eyes in the mirror. They appeared terrified.

A blur of color exploded on the front lawn. My heart thumped. My eyes flicked to the front of the house. Only the peaceful flowers, the house's yawning windows, and the open front door greeted me. But I could have sworn…I could have *sworn* I saw a flash of red.

My gaze returned to the rearview mirror, and I jumped. Someone stood behind the car. His face wasn't visible, nor were his legs, but a red double-breasted coat filled the rear window. The coat's red edges appeared on fire.

My hand shoved the car into drive. I floored the gas pedal, gravel grinding beneath the wheels until they finally found their footing and launched me around the front drive and out into the road. I swung the wheel to the right and sped along the open asphalt road that led to the highway. I slammed my foot against the gas pedal. The car gained momentum. The speedometer instantly registered sixty. Trees and tall grass whizzed by.

Some hundred feet ahead, something red moved into the road.

I slammed on the left pedal, and the brakes vibrated and screeched.

I came to a stop twenty feet from him—the same man who had stood behind the car in the driveway.

He was dressed from neck to feet in red—red pants, red shirt, red jacket. The jacket sleeves were rolled up; his hands and forearms were intensely black, as though they'd been dipped in coal or tar. So were his feet, which were bare. His face looked demonic. Black lines traced his eyes and the sides of his cheekbones. His hair was black. He resembled Jack when she was ill, though somehow different. A dark energy radiated from him, like he poisoned the air by breathing.

"Fuck," I whispered.

I put the car in reverse and pressed on the gas, looking backward over my shoulder.

A rumble permeated the car and road. Just fifty feet back down the way I'd come from, a black tupelo tree plummeted, then another, and another, uprooted one at a time, blocking me. I slammed on the brake, cursed, and put the car into drive.

The red man was closer.

I stomped on the gas and pulled the wheel to the right, determined to drive off into the field. The front wheels left the road, and then the car jerked to a stop. My forehead slammed into the steering wheel. An excruciating pain shot through my head and neck. I cried out.

The driver's door was yanked open. A pair of hands were on me, tugging me up and out of the car, as though I weighed nothing. The pungent scent of fire enveloped me, mixed with the smells of the uprooted trees and crushed grass.

Black irises with red tinges at the edges stared into mine. They traveled over me. "The smell of the Guardian is on you," he hissed.

I gaped at him, gripping his hands on my shirt, trying to loosen them. His fingers were like slender stones, unyielding and cold.

"I don't know what you're talking about. What the fuck are you?"

His thin lips curled into a wry smile. "I smell your life on your breath, and half of it is chemicals. Enough to choke anyone and poison the air. I'm not at all surprised that you are her friend." He kicked the car door shut with his leg and pressed me against it. Chains slithered from beneath the cuffs of his sleeves and crawled over my hands.

My chest tightened, my heart lodged in my throat. I couldn't breathe.

The cold, rough chains reminded me of a snake with dirty scales. The chain wound over my wrists and linked to itself. Light fluoresced, and then the red man released my shirt and grabbed the chain. I jerked back, momentarily freeing myself from his grip, but I couldn't shake free of the chains. They were bound to me, as though they'd been locked with a key.

Automatically, I clasped my hands together and slammed them into the man-creature's face.

My right hand popped, and I screamed. It was like punching brick.

Something collided with my cheekbone, and I fell to the asphalt.

"You dare strike me?" the man said. Though the words were threatening, his tone was amused.

I glared up at him from the ground.

"You're but a child," he said. He tilted his head to the right, blocking the sun, "and have no idea what damage you've done by following that hybrid." He bowed closer. "No worries though. Ven is here to help you."

CHAPTER 17
GEMELUS

Jack

I WOKE ON SNOW. IT spread out beneath me, freezing to the touch. Above, flakes drifted in a dark gray sky, collecting on my face and hands and quickly melting.

I sat up. Accumulated snow slid off my clothes.

Alex's body lay nearby, his empty white eyes staring up at me. The white gramophone goo remained attached to his legs, but it no longer moved, and the gramophone was nowhere to be seen. Alex's chest was still, as was his face.

A frisson ran through me. I rose to my feet.

I leaned to look over the edge of the Beretrum, but the black pit had closed in, leaving only white rock. I searched around the area for some clue to what had happened.

The Builder's scream reverberated in my mind, and a pressure deep inside me released.

Something had happened—something had changed.

I stared at the body beside me and nudged Alex's leg with my foot. He didn't move. The white goo that coated him slid off into the snow, becoming indistinguishable.

I swallowed and exhaled deeply, watching a vapor cloud bloom from my mouth like smoke.

I grabbed Alex's cold hand and pulled him away from the goo. Closing my eyes, I urged myself to return to our old home. The rock and snow and mountain colors swirled, until the hues disappeared, replaced by green and blue and brown. When the world righted, I was squatting outside Cyrus's mansion, Alex at my feet. My mind reeled. So many things had happened at once. So many disparate realities. But, most importantly, Alex was dead.

He was *dead*.

My shoulders released, and I nearly collapsed. The bastard was gone. He should have been gone months before.

"Roland," I whispered. I stood and dragged Alex toward the front of the house.

The front door swung back, and Roland appeared. As soon as he saw me, he cried, "I heard you call, from inside my head!" He paused at the top step. His eyes traveled down to Alex's body.

"Is that—?"

"Yes, but he's dead. And we need to make sure he stays that way."

Roland paused, his hand momentarily hovering just above his chest. He dropped it and came and clasped Alex's legs. We lifted my brother's body and walked him into the house.

"Where do you want him?" Roland asked.

I took a deep breath. "The furnace."

I GRABBED THE BLACK GRATE—THE same grate on which Shakespeare, our family dog, had been burned the year before, the same one on which the Guardian's body had burned—and pulled it out without any gloves. Roland watched, eyes wide, as my hand glided through the flames. The blistering metal didn't hurt me.

Roland and I lifted Alex's body onto the grate, Roland careful to avoid the bite of the hot metal before I pushed it back in.

I watched to ensure that my brother's body was not immune to the flames. We waited, breathless, as his white clothes caught. Slowly, his skin blistered and blackened, and I sighed in relief. I shut the furnace door and leaned against the opposite wall.

For too long I'd watched my brother transforming into a monstrous being, and for too long I'd had to endure his obsession with killing me. When Roth and I had worked together to lure Alex into a trap, I'd been certain that he'd died when I'd stabbed him. He had. But his body had collapsed on top of an *arca* that had brought him back to the Builder, where he was transformed. Now, finally, Alex was dead. I planned on keeping it that way.

"What happened?" Roland said, pulling me from my hard memories.

I took a deep breath. "I barely made it out. The men..." I shook my head. "They're still in there, somewhere. If they still exist...The Beretrum didn't spit them out like it did Alex and me."

"It spit you out?"

I nodded. "It shoved me and Alex out and closed itself. Temporarily, I think. It was trying to protect itself. Lutin's inside. Roth's inside. The entire army. They're all likely dead." My eyes wandered to the dirty floor. "When we first arrived, we fell into what seemed like the rings of hell. But Roth said he recognized the uniforms of some of the men in one of the battles we walked through. It was as though we were walking through Earth's past. Like the horrors on Earth were the rooms of hell, and the Builder lived there. I got to the center of the Beretrum, and my mind almost turned on itself. Alex invited me to join him and the Builder, and I nearly did. It... enticed me. But I said no. And then I...I used one of the Builder's *arcas* against Alex. The whole Beretrum shook around us, or maybe exploded. Alex died." I turned to Roland. "He had a piece of the Builder in him. I don't know if he will regenerate."

Roland searched my face.

"We need to keep the flames going," I said. "In case he self-resurrects, like the Builder. We can't have him coming back. At least, not while the Builder remains to be dealt with."

Roland nodded. "I'll make sure the flames remain strong." He paused. "What should I tell Cyrus about his son?"

I hadn't even considered that.

The house above us suddenly vibrated. It was as though something large had bounded upstairs. Dust dropped from the ceiling and fell in my eyes, irritating them. I shivered.

I pushed away from the wall. "Shit." I retrieved my gun and cocked it. Roland was right behind me. "You have to stay," I told him. "Make sure the body burns."

"You need help."

"While Alex crawls out of that furnace and finds us?" I asked, pushing him back. "I don't think so."

Roland's mouth twisted. He groaned and walked back to the incinerator. "I'll be here," he said. "Keep the basement door open and call if you need me."

I took a deep breath and bolted up the stairs into the house. I did a sweep of the empty room beside the garage and the hallway, listening for any new noise, my eyes wandering over the black-and-white tile with old scuff marks. I moved through the room quickly and paused at the threshold to the hall. Looking back and forth, I found it empty and crept to my right, toward the front of the house, where the sound had originated.

To the left of the front door, just beyond the staircase, my eyes caught the flash of red fabric. A crimson coat met crimson pants. The pants ended in tatters. The scent of smoke arrived with him, sweet though foreign, reminding me of a cigar. The ferric turned. He concealed someone behind him. Ven's wide black eyes bore straight into me, and I froze, my heart somersaulting. He pulled the person in front of him by the arm.

There stood Patrick, his head bleeding, his arms chained in front of him. Ven gripped his forearms. Blood dripped from the right side of Patrick's lower lip and landed on his blue t-shirt. The cut healed itself.

"Please, excuse my bold entrance into your beautiful home," Ven said. He grinned. He peered down like a snake at Patrick, who stood just a few inches shorter than him. "He bolted." He wiped some of the blood off Patrick's face. "But he didn't get far."

The last time I'd seen Ven, two of Roth's men were carrying his corpse into an elevator to be taken to the basement of the building. What the hell had happened?

Patrick's blood crystalized my vision. I went cold. I lifted the gun, my heart slamming into high gear, and I aimed at Ven, finger on the trigger. "How fucking *dare* you!" I hissed.

"Ah, ah, ah. That will barely slow me down."

"Oh? These bullets have godsoul in them."

Ven straightened his back. His grip on Patrick's biceps tightened, his fingers like black claws against the blue cotton. Ven's hands and bare feet looked like they'd been dipped in soot. "I should warn you, Jack. I didn't come alone this time."

The door opened. Two ferrics came into view on either side of the frame. One was the tallest being I'd ever seen. The other was a woman with a flat oval face and long black hair. I looked twice. I'd never seen a female ferric before.

"There are ten more in the front yard, ten more in the back. I don't think you'll be able to kill every one," Ven said. "And you certainly won't be able to save your friend, even if you do."

Patrick's haunted eyes shifted over his shoulder to Ven.

I could barely make out the figures on the front lawn. I warred with myself over what to do.

Ven lifted his hand, palm toward me, and closed it with a beckoning motion. My gun flew to him. He caught the weapon and opened the barrel. The bullets plopped into his palms, and he inspected them. "How did you get this godsoul?"

Patrick's eyes pleaded with me not to implicate him.

"I'm not telling you anything until you let him go."

"That's all right," Ven snarled. "We'll find out soon enough." His pointed chin lifted. He sniffed. "Have you been...to the Beretrum? I can smell it on you. It lingers, long after one leaves. It burns the nostrils."

"I did," I said. "And while I was down there, I killed my brother."

Ven squinted. The two ferrics on the front porch froze and looked at him.

"Killed him?" Ven laughed. "How did you manage that?"

I shook my head. "Nothing for you to worry about."

Ven smirked, his eyes bright and dancing with energy. "If you're telling the truth, bravo. But it won't save you. You're coming with us this time, Jack. We have your friend, and I'll hurt him terribly if you don't. And you must believe me that I know how to hurt people terribly."

I stiffened. I wished I could jerk Patrick free of Ven's arms and translocate us somewhere far, far away. But Ven was right. Too many ferrics surrounded the house, and I couldn't be quick enough.

"All right," I said, wiping sweat from my forehead. "You're right. I'll go with you."

Ven smiled like a victor. He beckoned with an open palm again, pulling me across the floor like a toy on a string. I landed at his side, barely avoiding tripping. He grabbed my arm, gripping it tight, and I readied myself for what I knew was about to happen. They were going to take both of us back to Ven's jail, and they'd play Patrick against me. For everything I didn't tell them, they would hurt him.

I looked at Patrick and mouthed the words "I'm sorry." He barely shook his head. Tears wet the edges of his eyes.

I heard Roland call my name. I faced the hallway, where I could barely make out his form before he bounded into the hallway.

The world swirled around us, the paneled hall, banister, stairs, and sunlight melding like wet paint and then disappearing. I shut my eyes, pressed my palms against them, and wished I could disappear into the darkness. When I eventually opened them, ten ferrics, Patrick, Ven, and I stood in a yellow room with cream tile and a singular bed. The smell of anesthetic stung my nostrils. To my right, a steady beep repeated from a machine delineating a pulse.

"What…where are we?" I said.

Ven pushed me toward a bed, where a young man lay, the same pale color as the sheets. His face, his eyelashes, his hair were blanched, like Alex's had been, far more progressed than Margaret. His hands and feet were bound to the bed. Was this a psych ward?

"I thought you were taking me to your prison," I said.

Ven smiled. "All in due time. First, we need you to do something." He pointed toward the man on the bed. "We need you to heal him."

I pulled my bottom lip between my teeth. "Why?"

"Because the council is desperate to discover something, or someone, that works against it."

"It?"

"Whatever godless disease your brother brought to this Earth when he injected his blood in these poor fools' bodies. Over two hundred thousand people are now infected."

"Two hundred thous… *Infected*?" I said, picturing Alex's body in the furnace, knowing that Roland had come into contact with it. "That's not possible. It's not a disease."

"Not an earthly one, which only makes it worse. It can pass from person to person. An immortal's blood, the Builder's blood, was never to be combined with any living thing. Just like the ferrics' power was not to be shared." He looked me up and down.

"Good Lord."

"Oh, it's much, much worse than that," he said, stepping close to me. His breath fell on my cheek like coal dust. "Because, you see, we ferrics can't eradicate it. We've tried *everything*." He drew this last word out. "Our presence, our blood, waves of our power. Everything we throw at these patients bounces off like powder against glass. They're not quite dead, but not alive. It seems as if no piece of soul remains in them to restore. They're only flesh now."

"You can't do anything?" I asked, recalling my failed attempts with Margaret. I'd hoped that the problem was that I was a hybrid.

Ven shook his head.

"Cyrus told me that a soul can always regrow," I said. "Lutin lasted ten years in Cyrus's basement."

Ven narrowed his eyes. "If there's a portion remaining, yes. But there doesn't seem to be any left. We are out of options…but we haven't tried you. You're a hybrid, and you might be capable of things we're not, in the same way that Alex is…*was*. The hybrids that were created before," he added, "always had something different about them. Sometimes, they had powers that we don't. And there have been rumors circulating about you. About what you might be capable of, about why Osric went to such lengths to end you. Why did he poison you, when he could have just as easily killed you?"

I swallowed dryly, afraid he might see through me, see what I was capable of. I shifted my feet. "I hate to break this to you, but I'm not capable of healing them. I tried…earlier, in Basille Hospital. I tried, and I couldn't."

"You'll have to forgive me, but I need to see that's the case, personally." He gestured toward the man in the bed again.

I sighed. There was no use trying to fight it. I walked to the side of the bed and surveyed the unconscious man. "Why is he restrained?"

"They become exceedingly violent in later stages of the disease," Ven replied, coming to stand on the opposite side. "If there's any soul left in these poor individuals, we can't reach it. Our presence does nothing to heal them."

I returned Ven's piercing gaze. "I'll help you, but I want you to get him out of here, now." I pointed to Patrick. "I don't want him catching this."

Ven's eyes remained locked on mine, and I realized that had been the point of bringing Patrick with us—Ven wanted him present, at risk. "Rightly concerned, Jack. But we will get both of you out of here as soon as you do what we ask. *Heal* him."

Rage boiled inside me. I wanted to attack Ven, finish all of them, but I was stuck, trapped as I'd always been by the people around me. I squeezed the bar of the hospital bed and felt the metal bend.

I stepped nearer to the young man and lifted his eyelid. No pupil was visible.

My thoughts whirred, not only at what Ven would do to me and Patrick when he found out I couldn't help but also in fear of what would happen to me if this time I could. Would the ferrics lock me in a basement and force me to heal anyone they couldn't? Part of me wanted to fake the test, but I understood that was impossible. They'd know whether or not I released my power. They could feel it, just like I'd felt the healing waves from Lutin and his brothers.

I rested my hand on the young man's forehead. I closed my eyes and willed the ball of power to coil within me. It spiked, like lightning caught in a globe. I shot the energy into his body. Immediately, it rebounded back into me, slamming me into the wall next to the bed. Black dots exploded in front of my eyes as my head bounced against it. I fell to the floor, breathless and disoriented from the pain.

"*Jack!*" Patrick yelled. He nearly bolted to me, but the tallest ferric grabbed him by his bound hands and jerked him back.

My mind cleared; the pain evaporated, as though it'd never been there. I slowly rose to my feet.

"I'm all right," I assured him. I ran my hands through my hair, pulling it back and tucking it behind my ears.

Ven's expression turned grim, focused inward, before his eyes zeroed in on mine. "Let's try your blood."

"It's useless," I said, turning my palms up toward him. "I've tried it. It doesn't work."

He nodded to the female ferric beside him, and she walked to me and grabbed my arm. Ven turned to the cupboards behind him and opened them, until he found what he wanted—a syringe. He opened the plastic package and inspected the needle.

"All right. All right. *I'll* do it," I grumbled, trying to push the woman away. Her hand was like a statue's upon mine. Ven nodded, and she released me.

I snatched the syringe from Ven, who then opened several doors and produced a tourniquet. I took it from him, tugged my sleeve up, and wrapped it around my arm. I tapped the vein and slipped the needle into the blue line. I pulled the plunger back, and blood flooded the cylinder. I released the tube, pulled the needle free, and handed the syringe to the female ferric. She inserted it into the line and pushed the plunger. My blood poured in and traveled down the tube to the young man's white arm.

Nothing happened. The power of my blood wilted in the man's body. I could sense it, like a flower closing its petals. I knew the others must be feeling it too.

Ven whispered a short, hot word in the ferric language. If I had to guess, it meant *shit*.

"You believe me, now?" I said. "I'm not your solution to this problem."

Ven compressed his lips. A dark shadow crossed his face. The fire in his body seemed to dim. "You think everything is about you. Do you not understand? If you can't heal them, and we can't heal them, there's only one thing left to do."

"What?"

"Get *rid* of them."

I frowned. I thought of Margaret in her hospital bed, blood draining down her forehead, the dozens of rooms on the fourteenth floor of Basille Hospital, the hundreds of thousands of infected. "What are you talking about?"

"In the early stages, before their hair and skin turn white, they can still be killed. After, they can't be, and the more that are infected, the stronger the Builder becomes, as the virus he created eats the tiniest bit of godsoul from each person. If we can't find a cure, getting rid of the infected will be what we resort to. We can't have the disease continuing to spread, for the Builder to continue to grow stronger. As for those in the later stages…" He shook his head. "We'll have to find a place for them. Perhaps the Beretrum."

"Wait wait wait," I said, not believing what I was hearing. "You said *two hundred thousand* people are infected."

"Yes. It moves incredibly fast. Soon, it will be a million."

I shook my head. "You can't send hundreds of thousands of people to hell."

"It's been done before. If we don't, even more people will become infected, and the Builder will be insurmountable, even with our stores of godsoul. If the council is unable to find a cure, they will come to me and require me to do what I am best at doing—eliminating. The human world and reality were not built for this kind of disease. It has to be eradicated."

I looked at the ferrics, their faces stone cold, as though seeing them for the first time. "No. No! You can't kill these people, can't doom them that way."

He raised his eyebrows. "Morality? From you?"

I took a deep breath, my gut clenching. "Look. I know we are not on good terms, but please, Ven, *just wait*. Wait for a little bit."

He shook his head. "For what?"

"Let me try and stop the Builder, stop all of this."

He grinned. "That's not possible." The other ferrics chuckled.

"You said this virus was impossible, and yet here we are. Sometimes, the impossible is possible. Look. If there's a way to save them, give me a chance. I think I'm almost there. I believe I can stop him."

"If you could stop the Builder, you would have done it already."

I shook my head. "I haven't had enough time."

The others laughed again, but Ven frowned. "That's what the rumors were about—that you, Osric, and the others had gone to try and destroy the Builder. Ludicrous. I didn't believe it. We have killed him hundreds of times, and it doesn't make a difference. Why would *you* make a difference? What is it about you?" he said, more to himself than to me. "What is it that Lutin saw in you? What is it that Osric saw that he wanted to destroy?"

I refused to look away, saying nothing.

"You won't tell me? Even now, at the world's potential end?"

"Me telling you about myself is *never* going to happen."

"You never know," he said. His gaze moved up the wall, and he straightened his shoulders. "Maybe I'll find a way to sway you." He nodded to those on either side of me.

A pair of handcuffs, as bright as the fire in my veins, slipped around my wrists and tightened, held there by the female ferric's hands.

"The Princeps Auctoritati, our council, has determined you will stay in the Vinclum until your trial for the deaths of Lutin, Osric, Flutri, Pepluv, Inarin, Semic, and me, for burning the body of the Guardian of the godsoul, and, we know, for having some role in his death."

He gestured toward Patrick and said something in the ferric language I could not identify.

The glowing red metal handcuffs contracted, sealed to my wrists as though skin to skin. My heart sank. There was no pain, but it felt as though my power had dampened, as if the cuffs were a vacuum that sucked my ability to heal, to translocate. I was left with only my humanness.

Ven lifted his palm and waved his fingers, pulled me toward him. When I was close enough, his hand grasped the bright rope between the two cuffs.

"You seem to be a weakness of hers, hm?" Ven said to Patrick. "Maybe she revealed things to you. You two are very close, after all. We'll find out what you both know."

Patrick's eyes met mine, wide with fear. "Oh fuck," he said. "Oh fuck fuck fuck. No no no. You can't do that. I haven't done anything…" Patrick continued to protest as Ven walked to the door of the hospital room and sliced his palm with a knife. He spread his blood around the frame and pressed his hand to its center. "*Patefecio carcerem in perpetuum,*" he said.

Light wavered beneath the door. Ven pulled the door inward. A dank, dark hallway smelling of mold and rot opened to us. The female ferric pushed me forward. Patrick called out, "Hey!" and I heard his stumbling footsteps. I looked back just in time to see him right himself before I was shoved again.

We walked down a hall lined with empty cells to both left and right. The cells did not abut but seemed to be individual cubes. Between those cubes were columns on which burning torches hung. At the end of the hall on the right was a mirror surrounded by an image of a woman leaning over the topmost portion, hair curling down her back. At one time, it must have had color, but dust had collected, and now it was mostly gray. We marched to the last cell, near the mirror, and I was jerked to the left.

On the other side of the wall, across from the mirror, was a metal door I hadn't noticed before. At least ten feet tall, a red glass square filled the upper portion. Ven tugged me toward it. I pulled back hard, trying and failing to free myself of his grasp. Ven yanked the door and pulled me inside. I stared, wide-eyed at the bright red tile surrounding us. It wasn't the glass in the door that was red.

Ven pushed me to the left, and I landed in a chair. He used a clip as bright red as the cuffs to latch me to one of the arm rests.

Patrick landed hard on the floor in front of me. I gasped and waited to see if he was all right. He lifted his head. Ven grabbed his bound hands and dragged him across the floor. He jerked Patrick up to his feet and pushed him into a chair opposite mine. Two ferrics came in, undid Patrick's ropes, and then tied him to the chair. A guttural yell burst out of me, and I screamed at Ven that I'd kill him. I tried to stand, but, if anything, my cuffs tightened. The ferrics left, but Ven and another with a tall stature, broad shoulders, and a Roman nose remained. The door swung shut.

Silence unlike any other expanded through the room. Ven's footsteps echoed, deep bass.

Ven approached a metal cart. He picked up a syringe and glanced back. "You know, Jack, no one has ever killed me before." He walked until he stood directly beside me and half-crouched. "Fortunately, though, my brothers found me." He looked at me with clear eyes and a complete, maniacal lack of fear. We were on his turf, and he seemed completely at ease. "It was intelligent of you—locking me in a lead-lined cell, blocking all the other ferrics from seeing me. But it wasn't quite good enough. We, too, are intelligent, and we've been waiting for you for a long while." He rose and held up the syringe. It was full of white liquid. "Do you know what this is?"

I swallowed.

His eyebrows raised. "It's blood from someone your brother infected."

He took several steps backward and handed the syringe to the other ferric, who held it like a cigarette between his fingers and carried it to Patrick. He clasped Patrick's shoulder, resting the plunger against Patrick's neck.

"*No,*" I yelled. I tried to drag the chair toward them, but it resisted, as though the chair was melded with the floor. The electric red rope tightened, feeling as though it would break my wrists.

"Can't escape those. Can't translocate," Ven observed, casually pacing around the room, as though he'd done this a million times. He lifted his hand and flicked his fingers toward me. An unseen force pushed me back into the metal seat. "Your only chance of stopping Hux from injecting your friend is to tell us." He faced me, crossed his arms. "What's so special about you? How are you different from the others?"

My heart pounded, and my hands vibrated. I looked from Ven to the plunger and Patrick's fear-stricken face and back.

"Let him go."

"I will. When you tell me."

I clenched my hands in fists; my fingernails bit into my palms. My breaths pulsed, short and restricted. I felt as if I might burst with rage and helplessness. I looked at Patrick—my friend, who had saved my life, doomed himself. He stared at me with wide emerald eyes, mouth open. Tears dripped down his cheeks. This wasn't supposed to happen. He was supposed to be invulnerable, protected. *I* was supposed to protect him.

But the Builder. My plan to kill and resurrect him couldn't be revealed. There was no way I could allow that.

I felt dizzy, and I shook my head. "I can't tell him, Patrick," I said. "I can't do it."

Patrick squeezed his eyes shut, his face flushed red. "Shit shit shit." His chin wobbled.

My heart pounded, a roar in my ears. "I'm so sorry. I'm so sorry." I repeated the words, unable to do more.

"Oh," Ven said, his eyes never veering from mine. "Just in case you haven't figured it out…" He pointed to the syringe between Hux's fingers. "This is where we *start*." Ven sneered. "After that, we've got a solid week before your friend here finally dies. And that means a week of this…" Ven lifted his arm and pointed to the wall behind Patrick.

Tools I hadn't noticed before, tools as red as the wall, hung on nails that stretched at least thirty feet high. They loomed above Patrick's head.

"What is it?" Patrick asked. His eyes were large and round like silver coins, his expression blank, like he knew what I was looking at without being able to see what was behind him.

I shuddered, a wave of nausea washing over me. Goose flesh prickled my arms. I couldn't stand the thought of those tools being used on Patrick. "Nothing," I said. "It's nothing."

When Patrick turned to look, the ferric named Hux grabbed his head and turned Patrick to face me and held him there.

If I had my gun, I could have ended everything.

Ven crouched down to Patrick's eye level. "Has she told you how she's different? What she's capable of? You can save yourself, you know."

Patrick's green eyes glared at Ven before he struggled to turn his face away. "I don't know shit about anything," Patrick said. "I haven't seen her in over a month."

"Now, see, I know that's not true," Ven replied. "I know Jack's been to New York, and I know she traveled to your father's house." He pressed a palm against Patrick's forehead. Patrick jerked back. Ven turned toward me, as though to ask, *Really? This one?*

"I thought you were supposed to be the good guys," I said. "No ferric I've ever met has been like you. Lutin would never do this. Osric wouldn't."

Ven smiled. "You're right about that. I'm not like the others, Jack. In some ways, I suppose, I am more similar to you than I am to them.

"The Princeps Auctoritati kept one, just one, ferric destined for the Beretrum with them." He pointed to his chest with both thumbs. "In a world without the Creator, we live in desperate times. I do all the things they need done but cannot do themselves."

Whatever unconscious credit I'd given Ven for being a ferric, for acting on behalf of ferric-kind, for inherently being better than me and knowing more, evaporated. My jaw dropped, and any reserve energy I had vanished. I drooped against the chair and stared at him with new understanding.

"I should've dropped you into the Beretrum," I whispered.

Ven rubbed his black palms together. "I guess you should've. It's too late for that now, though, so what's it going to be, Jack? Are you going to tell me, or is your friend here going to die?"

My eyes met Patrick's emerald ones. I shook my head. My chin trembled. My words crushed me. "I can't."

Patrick huffed. "It's okay, Jack." He nodded defiantly; his nostrils flared. "It's okay. Even when it's not okay." His chest rose and fell, faster and faster, as though he was at war with himself—part of him wanting to scream, the other part accepting that this was the way things were. "Fuck these guys."

Ven's black eyes flicked to him. He trapped Patrick's jaw with black fingers. "How dare you speak of us in such a way!" He squeezed Patrick's jaw so tightly his skin bled white. Then he released him. "Inject him."

My eyes shot wide open. "*Wait!*" I yelled.

Hux drove the syringe deep into Patrick's neck and pressed. The white disappeared beneath Patrick's skin. He screamed.

A blinding light exploded behind Patrick's head. The light expanded, threatening to blind me, as it flowed across Hux's arms, neck, face, skull, torso, legs. He transformed into a brilliant beacon of light. The encompassing radiance in an instant transformed into flames, glowing red and orange. Hux's body was engulfed. Slowly, the light died, collapsing in on itself, melting and blending in layers, until it puddled on the floor like lava.

I stared, silent, unbelieving.

Ven also gawked at the grim pool on the floor. Then he stumbled toward me and lifted my chin before his hand seized my throat. "*What did you do?*"

I shook my head, staring into his eyes, not knowing what to think or say. Black sparkles danced in my vision after the cruel light. I couldn't comprehend what'd happened. Hux had died, burned to nothing, and Ven thought it was me.

"*Is this what you can do?*" Ven said. He hit me. "*Is this what Osric tried to protect us from?*"

Elation sparked in my brain, louder than his voice. "Oh my God," I muttered, blinking.

Ven stopped, shoulders heaving, and clasped me by the throat. I gasped, my hands tethered to the chair, unable to reach up and stop him.

"I'm going to make sure you never leave here," he said. He squeezed my windpipe tighter.

My eyelids closed, and I heaved as hard as I could against the glowing red rope that bound me to the chair. Something popped, and my arms sprang free. I grasped Ven's wrist, bending it back, releasing my throat. I gasped a quick breath.

"It wasn't me," I managed, my voice barely a whisper. "It wasn't me."

The chair's arm dangled from the rope on my wrists, still connected by the bright red clasp.

"*Then how?*"

I nodded toward Patrick. Ven looked between Patrick, who sat shocked and speechless in the chair, and me.

The words left my mouth before I could fully comprehend them.

"He's the new Guardian."

CHAPTER 18
REMEDIUM

Jack

VEN GLARED AT ME, HIS eyes wild, angry.

"What are you talking about?" he barked.

"How is a new Guardian chosen" I asked, "when someone kills one?"

Ven shook his head. "Nobody knows."

I raised my eyebrows, relief flooding me. "We do now, Ven."

He looked back, and I gripped the dislocated chair arm in my hands. I kicked Ven backward and swung the arm down. It collided with his head, and he collapsed to the floor. He tried to get up, and I hit him again. Blood splattered my knees. I hit him again, and something to my right banged. The door. Ferrics raced into the room. One restrained me. Another lifted Ven and pressed a hand to his skull, where I'd slammed the arm of the chair. The wound sealed.

A ferric pinned me against the back wall.

My laughter echoed throughout the room. Every ferric stared at me as though I were insane.

"You guys really, really messed up," I crowed.

The ferric in front of me turned back to look at Ven. Patrick was still bound to the chair. His eyes were no longer distant, blank. Something behind them was quickening, propelling, gaining momentum. His clementine eyebrows furrowed, and he looked from the floor, where the black, lava-like substance that was once Hux's body pooled, to Ven.

"Release me," he ordered. Everyone froze. The ferrics sent desperate looks to each other, clearly unsure what to do.

"I *am* the new Guardian. She's right. The old Guardian came to me. In a dream. And blew gold dust on me. I didn't know what it meant until…" he paused, his eyes searching the floor as though he could see the face of the old Guardian in Ven's torture room. He slowly straightened himself, and a certainty turned his face stony. "Let me go. Or you'll *never* get another ounce of godsoul."

Ven's breathing slowed, and he stared down at the pool of Hux, scanning it. He opened his mouth, as though to say something, and then closed it. His Adam's apple bobbed up and down, his expression no longer resolute. He crept slowly to Patrick, so slowly that I feared he was planning to attack him.

Ven lifted his hand, towards the red wall with hanging torture tools behind Patrick, and a pair of red scissors levitated off the wall and traveled quickly and silently to Ven's hand. He brought the scissors towards Patrick, who leaned back. I went to step forward and was shoved harder against the wall. Ven paused. He clasped a piece of Patrick's red hair that had twisted up like liquorice, and he cut it close to the root. He dropped the scissors to the floor, where they clattered, metal on stone.

With his left hand, Ven held the sprout of Patrick's hair. He lifted his right hand up, just beneath the strands, and a small ball of fire emerged above his palm. The fire licked the strands of Patrick's hair, and I could only watch, ignorant of why Ven was doing this, my breath caught in my throat, every muscle in my body tensed.

After many seconds, perhaps a minute, of Ven holding the flame against the strands of red hair, the fire disappeared. The hair was just as it'd been before, not blackened, charred, and smoking like I expected.

Ven's shoulders dropped, his rigid body suddenly liquid. His black eyes searched the room. He tilted his head back, as though silently praying to the Creator. "His hair doesn't burn," he said.

"Shit," a ferric near the door whispered. The others' eyes were wide and unblinking, as they slipped to Patrick.

Slowly, Ven's head dropped back down. His fingers loosened, and the red hair floated like feathers to the floor. "It was you," he said. "Not her. You were the one who killed him." His stare was just as hard as Patrick's, but at last, he lifted his hand and reached in the pocket of his red coat. He rummaged and pulled out a knife, as though it were a key. He sliced one strap that bound Patrick to the chair, then the other.

Patrick rose, never veering from Ven's gaze. Ven stepped back, almost gracefully. Patrick pointed to me. "Let her go."

Ven pressed the tip of the blade to his thumb, where a drop of blood sprouted. "As you wish, Guardian." He lifted a hand toward me. The electric cuffs and rope loosened and dropped to the floor, the chair arm clanging as it landed.

At the sudden change in Ven, I momentarily gawked and then moved quickly. I went to Patrick and tugged on his arm. "Come on," I said. "Let's get out of here."

Ven's hands hung loosely at his sides, his face pensive, but he said nothing. The ferrics watched silently as we walked out of the room, our departing footsteps echoing against the walls. The bricks below us became illuminated, and the illumination flowed out and to the right, between sets of cells, down the hallway from which we'd come, providing us a path.

One ferric remained, just beyond the door. He moved to the side and gestured like a chauffeur would toward an open car door. "Our apologies, Guardian."

I released the breath I'd been holding and clung to Patrick's arm. We walked past the cells to the exit that I hoped against hope would open into the human world.

I grabbed the handle and turned it. Patrick and I stepped through the door without checking to see where we were going.

We landed on familiar tile floor in a brightly lit hospital room. The door shut behind us, and it was as though we'd never left. The beeping machines hooked to the man resting in the bed filled the room with a therapeutic rhythm. The scent of disinfectant wafted through the air. The young man remained unconscious, his skin as white as the sheets.

I sighed and hugged Patrick tight. He pressed his arms around me, and we held each other close. "I'm so sorry. I'm so sorry."

He shook his head against my hair. "Fuck. I can't believe what just happened."

We separated, and he leaned over, his hands on his knees, breathing huge gulps of air in and out. He appeared as though he might vomit.

I inhaled the hospital's medicinal air. "I'm so sorry."

Patrick came upright, running his hands through his bright red hair and then to his neck, where Hux had inserted the syringe. "Do you think I'm infected?"

"No," I said, shaking my head. "No. Nothing can kill the Guardian but a person who has never killed anyone before. Hux couldn't stop you, and neither can the virus."

I breathed deeply, grateful beyond words that Patrick had come into his own and been able to stand up to them, that we'd been able to escape.

"You did good, Patrick," I said. "You did good." I patted his arm. I leaned against the nearest wall and fell to a sitting position on the floor. I put a hand against my chest and willed my heart to slow. Patrick was safe. The ferrics wouldn't hurt him, couldn't use him against me. I squeezed my eyes shut and put my hand against my pounding head.

"You dreamt of the Guardian?" I asked.

"Yes," Patrick said. "But it wasn't just a dream." His eyes distanced. "God, I need a drink," he said. He crouched and placed his hands on the floor, half-falling to it, until he lay on his back. The beeping machine and our slowing breaths were the only sounds in the room.

"Yes, you do," I finally said. "And so do I. But, first, there's something you have to do."

"What are you talking about?" He stared at me as though I were insane. "We barely made it out of there alive."

That was true, but my mind was already whirring, thinking beyond the torture and death that Patrick had just barely managed to escape.

I wondered if he understood how different he was, now, how different his life was going to be. I certainly hadn't understood the significance when Lutin had given me a piece of his heart. I hadn't understood that it would change every facet of my existence. Looking at Patrick, I acknowledged the ludicrousness of life.

"*What?*" he demanded.

"You heard them. If they can't find a cure, they're going to drop two hundred thousand people, maybe more, straight into the Beretrum to try to resolve the disease, stop the Builder from growing and gaining power. There's only one thing they haven't tried on the sick." I nodded toward the unconscious young man on the hospital bed. "And it's the one thing you have access to."

Patrick's exhausted face became pensive, and he swiveled his head to gaze at the hospital bed. He nodded. "Oh."

"Yes. Oh. If we want to save them from death, save them from Ven and the torture of the Beretrum, we have to act now."

Wearily, I pushed myself up from the floor, using the wall to support me. I walked to the door through which we'd just escaped the Vinclum, my body still edgy and twitchy. With my knife I sliced my palm and again outlined the frame, finding my limbs to be clumsy and slow. I pressed my hand on the door's center and managed the necessary words. "*Patefacio tutor godsoul.*" Light glowed beneath the door, shining across the tile. I dropped my hand and stared at it, gathering as much consciousness as I could muster. I opened the door and stepped through, holding my bloody and healing hand out to Patrick. He stared at it and, after a brief hesitation, took it. I shut the door behind us.

Gold—Patrick the Guardian's gold—shined at the end of the royal purple hallway with the vaguest remnants of there being more in the walls beside us in the faintest gold cobweb climbing up the stone.

Patrick paused. His gaze wandered over the dripping luminescent plasma, the gilt reflecting in his emerald eyes. His nostrils flared, as though he were inhaling the scent of his own lair. As he walked to the wall, the air around him wavered, like a bubble about to pop. Then it stretched and let him through before it rebounded, solidified and again became invisible. It was as though the room had accepted him as its Guardian. Patrick didn't seem to notice. I wanted to test whether the invisible shield would prevent me from approaching and taking some of the wall, as I believed it would, but I didn't have the time. "How much do you need?" Patrick whispered. His voice barely reached me. He didn't turn away from the gold.

"To test my theory? Just a small speck."

He pressed his fingertips to one of the jutting edges and broke off a sliver. Patrick turned and tenderly placed it in the palm of my hand.

"Thank you," I said.

He nodded once. "I hope it works."

I turned and headed down the hallway. Before I opened the door, I decided that I would try something new. Instead of expecting that I would stumble upon the same hospital room as before, I instead thought of Margaret, closed my eyes, and willed myself to her. When I next opened the door, a darkened and different hospital room came into view. In a bed rested an older woman with white hair, white skin, and a bandage across her head. Beside her, the machines hooked up to her chest registered a flat line, just as they'd done the last time I left her. My experiment had worked. The door, just like my ability to translocate, could open upon any place I desired.

I stepped inside and shut the door behind me. Clasping the godsoul in my palm, I swallowed nervously and walked to Margaret's bedside. I mentally uttered a little prayer and used my left hand to open Margaret's mouth. I placed the godsoul on the center of her tongue and pressed her chin up.

She didn't wake. But her lips and tongue moved. The sounds she made in her throat were part-human, part-animal, and then she swallowed. Her breath became rhythmic.

I tensed, my hands in fists, as I waited, searching her body for any alteration.

Her skin color deepened as the pallor incrementally disappeared. Her white eyelashes turned dark again, and the white hair on her head returned to the previous deep maroon shade.

The heart rate monitor blipped—a hill bumped along the once-flat line. It blipped again. The rhythm steadied, and mountains and valleys appeared where they should. The blood pressure cuff hummed, filling with air.

Margaret's eyes opened. "Jack."

I smiled. "Margaret."

She gazed at me. "I feel…I feel…something. I feel better."

I undid the restraint that bound her hand to the bed, and she pressed her cool palm to my cheek.

"I told you I'd help you. No matter what."

"I never doubted it."

I wiped a tear from the corner of my eye. It seemed that all the fear in me, of Ven, of Patrick being tortured, and of Margaret's death, released all at once. I was instantly lighter. My knees buckled, and I caught myself on the bed's rail.

Margaret shifted upright in the bed and undid the other restraint, moving more and more freely, her sparkling eyes alight. "I feel so much better. So much more alive."

"Yes," I said, steadying myself. "You look it."

She peered around the room as though she'd never seen it before, her expression refreshed, serene. She stretched, moving her body smoothly. "I can't believe this. I can't believe that I'm better! I was so afraid it was permanent. It felt everlasting."

Her gaze settled on me. "My Jack. My Jack. Please tell me you finally got out of that house."

"Margaret, I *own* that house."

A knowing look came over her, as if she had something to say, but she didn't speak. She cleared her throat, looked at the door, and said, "What's the likelihood that the doctors let me walk out of here without a billion tests?"

"None."

"That's all right." She nodded. "It's a small price to pay." She swallowed and looked at her hands, as if taking them in for the first time. "What do I tell them, if anything, about how I was healed?"

The question surprised me. I'd never bothered explaining my actions to the broader, outside world. It was always elude, elude, elude and hope they didn't look too hard.

"Tell them…" I said, thinking of how we could camouflage the miracle. That was my gut reaction. As I searched my mind, however, I found no reason for it. I had no intention of hiding the fact there was a cure or leaving so many people sick. In fact, the faster the cure was distributed, the better.

"Tell them…" I said, letting my mind solve the problem for me. The solution hit, and my mouth dropped. I considered the possibilities. I looked at the hospital room door.

I turned back to Margaret. "Tell them this…"

CHAPTER 19
DEMETO

Jack

I RETURNED TO THE PURPLE and gold godsoul room and discovered Patrick rifling through various collections of capsules, vials, beakers, tools, and scales on the long gray marble counter that bisected the room. I couldn't help but think this same individual had been a drug addict for much of his life. He was used to beakers, tools, and scales.

Patrick noticed me and turned to face me. His exhaustion and terror had completely evaporated. It was as though we'd never met Ven, that Patrick hadn't faced being tortured. "Jack, there's something I want to show you." He beckoned me to the end of the island and a stack of books.

"You won't believe this," he said. He opened one of the books. I walked over, locking my news in my chest, and let him show me what he'd found.

"Look. The previous Guardian—Merrin was his name—kept a log accounting for every single piece of godsoul he ever gave out." I followed his finger to tiny sentences on the page denoting not just names of individuals but amounts. The figures were recorded beside the words *pondo unciam*, a measuring system I'd never encountered before.

"The last entries include you. See?"

He pointed to a set of names at the bottom of the page. They included all the ferrics, including Osric and Lutin, as well as "Jack Harper—hybrid."

My name was on the bottom of the page.

"Hybrid," I whispered. Merrin couldn't let the fact that he'd given godsoul to me go.

"Here's where it gets strange." He licked his lips and jigged a little on his feet. "My name's in here too. That means he listed me *before* I arrived."

Patrick turned the page. At the top was one name—Patrick Flannigan. The amount column beside his name contained three words in English. *To be determined.*

A chill ran down my back.

"He knew I was coming. And the look on his face makes so much sense now. When I got here, he expected me, Jack."

The importance of this discovery hadn't eluded me. Even more relevant, the importance of Patrick believing that he was destined to be there, whether or not true, hit me. The more he believed that, the less guilt he would suffer for causing the Guardian's death. I smiled, pushing aside any decision over whether I wanted to believe in this fate or not. It was psychologically important that I do so. "Fantastic!" I said.

"It *is*." Patrick surveyed the room. "I mean, I think I'm supposed to be here. I felt that when I was here. This is…this is *it*, Jack. Do you know what I'm talking about?"

I smiled. I understood more than he'd ever know. "I do. Yes. You have found your place."

He nodded, clasping his hands together. He seemed transformed— his skin had taken on a golden glow. I noticed new flecks of gold in his emerald eyes. He was one with his surroundings.

"How did it go with Margaret? Did it work?" His eyes were alight, his face full of refreshing innocence.

"It worked," I said, wondering if he was ready for the rest.

He slapped his hands together and hopped. "*Yes!*"

"And now we need to distribute godsoul to the sick. It occurred to me that you have the perfect means to do so."

He appeared to be deep in thought. Moments passed. "Lucient," he said.

"Lucient."

Goosebumps covered my arms. We needed the very thing Patrick had been given years and years before, which had belonged to his father. And I had cleared our path to unrestricted access several months ago, when Jonathon Roth killed Brian Flannigan. Perhaps, I thought, Patrick was right about fate, and not just in terms of the Guardian.

He bit at his thumb, the same thumb that he'd used to pluck free a piece of godsoul to give to me. His lips were now marked with gold. Already, patches of gold lit up sections of his arms. Golden dust coated his shirt.

"We could add godsoul to capsules, market it as an experimental drug made by…whatever company," I said. "Margaret is going to tell her doctors that someone from Lucient arrived and offered her the experimental drug. It's a hell of a lie, but I don't think anyone else has recovered from the disease. People are desperate and willing to accept strangeness in the face of life and death. At least, for a while. But, you know, eventually, at some point, researchers will poke and prod, and they'll see the fake drug for what it is—whether it's magic or a substance beyond previously understood reality."

Patrick nodded and rubbed his hands together. "They'll figure it out, yes. But that's okay, I think. My life is here now. I can sense it. And I want it. If they figure it out, it's fine. Whatever happens happens. Let Lucient burn. My place is here. Let's do it."

I smiled. "Maybe this is why you were meant to take over. Because you have the means of providing an immortal solution to an immortal disease. And you were willing to sacrifice your human life. Maybe that's why Merrin wanted you to come."

"Perhaps," Patrick said, pensively. "Or," he added nonchalantly, "maybe time isn't as linear as we think, and all the parts came to bear at the same time." He turned back to the wall, leaving me stunned. He hadn't sounded like Patrick then. "Two hundred thousand people, hm?"

"At least."

"And Margaret is already telling them that it was my company? They'll be knocking on Lucient's doors today."

"Yes."

"We have to get moving. Let me call Hank and get this underway."

"Of course."

He retrieved his cell phone and held it up, pacing around the room. "No reception," he said. "I guess that shouldn't surprise me. I'll call from home." He walked down the hall without a second thought or asking me to send him to his father's house. He opened the door at the end of the hall, which led directly to his father's office. The door had worked for him, just as it had worked for me, opening automatically to his destination. Patrick scrolled through his phone contacts.

I looked at the wall of gold. Relief flooded me. I set my elbows on the island and pressed my hands to my face, rubbing the skin, livening it. This was a disaster that was going to be averted. For a change.

Now having a moment to myself with the wall of gold, I stepped to it and went to grip a piece that jutted out at the bottom right. My hand stopped, inches from the wall, unable to go further. It was as though the air itself was compounded, thicker, compact and that I could not dip my fingers into it. I tilted my head and grabbed one of the chisels from the counter behind me. I jabbed at the wall, but the chisel could reach no further than my fingers had. I was right, when I suspected that only Patrick could access the wall. That was why the ferrics needed him, why I needed him, and why the Builder did, too.

I stepped back and placed the chisel on the counter. Looking at the various metals and implements that covered the counter's surface, I slid the book at the end in front of me, pressing my finger to Patrick's name, then my name, then Lutin's just above mine. The three of us, there together. I wondered if Patrick was right, if the Guardian had somehow known his end was near, if he'd willingly handed the responsibility over.

Or maybe he sensed the end of the world was coming, and he bowed out. The thought came to me unbidden, and I shook it off.

Patrick's footsteps resounded behind me in the hall. I turned.

"I told Hank that we only have a couple of vials of the experimental drug, which I'm calling *Numenus,* and to tell anyone who calls that mass production will be underway ASAP. The only questions now are how we're going to produce this medication. And what we are going to pretend it is. What strategy we'll undertake."

My mind called up an individual who was used to using my blood in both an asthma inhaler and insulin pump to heal himself. Jasper. He was still at Purdom, as far as I knew. "I know someone who might be able to help."

"Can he be trusted?"

I laughed. "You and I are working together—the Guardian and a hybrid. That forces everyone to be trustworthy."

I CALLED JASPER ON MY phone from Bryan Flannigan's office, as I ran my hands over the top of Flannigan's desk. Jasper picked up on the second ring.

"You're alive," he said, breathless.

I chuckled. "I'm thinking the same thing about you. You know that ferric I brought to Roth's building?"

"Yeah?"

"He's alive."

Jasper muttered a curse. "Didn't hear a thing. I'm so sorry, Jack. I should've stood guard."

"No. It's all right. Everything is all right tonight. You have no idea how close things came to working out the other way."

"Are you okay?"

"I'm...yes. I'm okay. But Roth and the men...I'm sorry to say they didn't make it. They're still in the Beretrum. I can't imagine they survived."

There was a long silence. "I guess that makes your job a little easier... down the road, I mean."

I did know what he meant. Had I really planned on keeping them alive for years, under my control? No.

"What about Alex and the Builder?" he asked.

I swallowed, recalling the image of a body in flames. "My brother's dead, at least for now. The Builder isn't."

"One down, at least. Finally."

"I hope. Look. I need a favor. I've finally found a cure for the illness that's spread across the country. It's the same substance that was in the bullets I handed out to the men before we went into the Beretrum—godsoul. But to get it out to at least two hundred thousand people, we need to make it look like a medication."

"Who's we?"

"Patrick and me."

"Ah." He inhaled and then whistled. "You're going to use Lucient. Of course."

"But no one can know how the pills are made. And we aren't sure, exactly, what our strategy should be to distribute them as invisibly as possible."

He grunted. "You can't hide it forever."

"No. Just long enough for it to work. Then…"

"Then you'll be gone."

"Yes."

Jasper cleared his throat. "Where should we meet? At Lucient?"

"That'll work. We'll be there by eight." I looked up to ask Patrick where we should meet, and he told me which building had survived the attack the month before. "The building that wasn't damaged in the explosion—4F—that's where we'll be."

"4F. Eight. See you then."

We both hung up.

I turned and saw Patrick shutting the door to the godsoul room. The dimness of the office dissipated, and light returned. "Are you ready?" he asked.

"I am." I held my hand out to him, beckoning him toward me. He came and slid his palm against mine.

I brought us to 4F at Lucient in barely any time at all. We stood next to a large gray building, lonely on a vast cement lot spotted with rubble yet to be removed. Black marks streaked the cement in numerous areas, the places where Roth had destroyed the buildings on the lot. Patrick retrieved his keycard and swiped it at the door. The lock's red light turned green, and the door clicked. Patrick slipped his hand around the door handle, turned it, and tugged it open. Warmth radiated from inside. We both entered the hallway.

The facility was larger than 1C, which I remembered from the last time I was on Lucient property. The hallway stretched ahead, several doors branching off on each side, for what seemed like eternity. Patrick led us down the hall. About halfway, he swiped his card at a glass door on the left, which led into an office. Opposite the door were windows that looked out on a large dim room. I walked to the window and peered down. Beyond a metal railing, identical machines stretched left to right.

Patrick retrieved his cell phone.

"What are you doing?" I asked.

He held up one finger, and I waited.

When he finished pressing buttons, he slipped his cell phone back into his pocket. "Turning off the surveillance cameras," he said with a smile. "No alarm this time."

"You can do that from your *phone*?"

He smirked. "You have no idea."

Patrick swiped his keycard, and the light turned green. He twisted the doorknob, turned to me, and winked.

He pulled the door open, and the bank of lights came on. He descended the metal stairs. I followed, shaking off the memories— the "box" that Bryan Flannigan had kept at Lucient, a large, coffin-like apparatus that bleached objects to white. Those objects, in the presence of a ferric, returned to red. The box had spit out the address where the ferrics were located. It was a brilliant mechanism, and Roth and I had been able to use it against Alex. We'd trapped him, I'd killed him, and everything had still gone to hell.

We arrived at the first machine, a tall metal hexagon. Its front section, at least on the upper portion, was encased in glass, with a side chute connected to a large bucket. At the top of the machine, a protruding tube connected to a metallic funnel.

"It's a multistation rotary press," Patrick said. "It makes hundreds of thousands to millions of tablets an hour."

"An hour?" It seemed too small for that.

He nodded. "Impressive, isn't it? All we need to do is place the ingredients up there." He pointed to the large tube leading down to the funnel. "Actually, we'll need to place them there, and there." He pointed to the machine next to it.

"Why?"

"American standard and European standard."

"Europe," I whispered, realizing that Alex had been all over the world. My stomach twisted. How long would it take to get the medication to all of them?

"Which means—"

"Which means," I finished for Patrick, "that you're going to need to extract giant pieces of godsoul to mix with other ingredients."

Patrick nodded. I pressed a hand to my cheek and walked between the two rotary presses. "Shit," I said. The idea of removing so much godsoul pained me more than I expected. I felt weak, weary, nauseous.

"You knew it was inevitable. If you want to heal all of them."

I nodded. "I didn't want to think about it." I pressed both hands to my forehead and rubbed. We couldn't save just a quarter of the people infected, or just half, right? How would we even go about choosing who should be given the cure and who shouldn't? And what did it mean for me, when I started weighing the possibility of dropping a hundred thousand people into the Beretrum and saving the other half? "What do you think?"

"About what?"

"Taking so much of the godsoul." I swallowed, my throat dry.

"There's no other cure. Right?"

I hated to say the word. "Right."

"Then what? We let them all die? Or…exist between life and death?"

"If that godsoul runs out, though, we're *all* dead."

Patrick shrugged. "Then we won't use it all."

Fear pierced me, fear like I'd never experienced before. I felt like a poker player, trying to figure out the other players' cards. But I'd gone blind.

"It worked on your friend Margaret," Patrick said. "It will work on the others. And you realize as much as I do that if we don't do it now, we can't do it at all. Because even more people will become infected. The choice is either kill two hundred thousand people or save them."

I winced and nodded.

"So we're agreed? We do this now?"

I swallowed and shivered, distressed by the fear of expending the godsoul and not having enough left to keep reality humming. But it was like Patrick said. What choice did we really have? No other cure existed, and the longer we waited, the more impossible it would become that our supply would be sufficient.

I took a deep breath and pressed a hand to my temple, feeling sweat. I licked my dry lips, trying to wet them and failing. "Yes," I said at last. "We do this now."

Boom.

The building shook. Particles of dust rained down from the ceiling and danced beneath the fluorescent lights.

"What was that?" Patrick asked.

I cursed. "I don't know."

The glass doors blew inward, shattering, showering us with shards. I bent low and pulled Patrick with me, covering him with my jacket.

When debris finally stopped falling, I stood, shaking off the heavy glass, and when I raised my eyes, I saw a ferric dressed all in red in front of me. His hand shot forward, and he grabbed my throat, pulling me close.

"*Jack!*" Patrick yelled.

Ven's eyes bore deep into mine. "They told me to let you alone. They warned me. But I can't. I can't allow you to destroy it all. You *will not do this.*"

I gasped, sucking in what little air I could. My face felt hot, full. My neck strained against the violation. I grabbed his hands and pulled myself up on tip toes, rewarded with a gulp of air. "There's no other way," I wheezed.

His hand squeezed tighter. "*Swear* you will stop, here and now, and I'll let you live. Otherwise..." He shook his head back and forth, his eyes growing as hot as the vines of fire in his veins. "You've gone too far."

A voice, very low and very near, spoke calmly, resolutely. "Put. Her. Down."

Ven's eyes flicked to his right. Patrick's face was close, and he edged even closer.

"Or what?" Ven said.

"Or I carve it all out. All the godsoul," Patrick warned, "and I'll throw it all away."

"I highly doubt that," Ven said. His fingers tightened on my windpipe, my neck muscles, blocking all the air. Black dots danced in my vision like fireflies. "A Guardian would never, ever do that. Something similar to maternal love has wound its way into your heart, connecting you to the godsoul."

"I'm not your Guardian. And fuck maternal instinct. I'll dump it all if you don't put her down right now."

Ven's gaze locked on Patrick. It seemed the two of them were playing a game of chicken, waiting to see who was the weaker. I felt like a rag doll hanging from Ven's hand. He was going to kill me. The fireflies quadrupled. Pounding pulse filled my ears, obscuring the buzz of the fluorescents.

"Ven," came a distant voice. "You must stop."

Ven's and Patrick's faces lifted to someone behind me, high above.

"You do not choose on behalf of us," another voice said. "You forego that long ago."

Ven's lips tightened, his eyebrows furrowing. The pressure abruptly released, and I slammed to the floor. I drew in a long, ragged breath and coughed before I could exhale. My throat itched and burned, but as I sat there, the pain withdrew, and I felt almost instantly better. I looked up at Patrick.

"You okay?" he asked, looking different. Certain, resilient, serious. He extended a hand to me.

"Yes." I grabbed his hand and pulled myself to my feet. He looked up at the balcony, and I followed his gaze to where three other ferrics stood. All three had short black hair and dark eyes. They wore long, black cloaks. They might have been some of the ferrics who worked with Ven in his jail, but I wasn't sure.

When they said nothing more, Patrick zeroed in on Ven. "*I* am the Guardian. *I* decide what happens to the godsoul. And *I* say that it goes to curing everyone the Builder has infected. Because you can't heal them, and I'm not going to watch you kill them."

"And what happens when there's none left, no godsoul?" Ven asked through clenched teeth, the visible muscles of his chest, arms, and neck taut. He seemed to be asking both Patrick and the three ferrics above. "We'll have nothing to fight the Builder."

"We won't use it all," Patrick said. "And what's left might regenerate, albeit slowly, if we leave it alone, according to what I read in the Guardian's catalog. But…" Patrick stepped toward Ven, face to face, emerald eyes scorching into black ones. "If you attack us again, I will dump it. I'm serious. If she dies, then everyone does."

"When it comes to godsoul, The Guardian's word is law," the middle ferric above us said. He didn't sound pleased to say it, but his posture, tone, and expression were resolute. He never blinked or even looked at me. It was as though just he and Ven were in the room. "We need him, you know. Or have you forgotten, Ven, as you have most everything else?" He paused, tilted his head, and breathed deeply. "You are not one to lecture others on obedience. You have been allowed a place with us, but its balance is precarious. It could tip at any moment. Do you want to be condemned to the Beretrum? After all these years of circumventing your fate?"

To hear ferrics defend me, defend Patrick, albeit on what appeared a technicality—that Patrick was the Guardian—filled me with awe and disbelief. Something fluttered deep in my belly, and I nearly barked with laughter. This was the first time that any of them, aside from Lutin, had spoken up for us.

Ven shrank back. His breath became shallow, and he curled his arms around his sides. "It won't regenerate," he said at last, looking helpless. "You two are children. And you have no idea…" He bit his lip. "You will be the end of everything." He ran a hand threw his hair and pointed a finger down at the floor. He looked between Patrick and the ferrics above. "Let it be known that I tried. I tried to stop it. So when the world does end, I can at least say I did what I could. And you were the cause of it."

"We are trying our best," I said.

Ven's eyes narrowed, and he sneered. "Try smarter." He pressed his fists to the side of his head and then wiped sweat from his brow. "Oh, and by the way," Ven said low, "that kill-for-hire who's been helping you…?" He shook his head. "His body's where you will never find it."

Enraged, I launched myself at him. But impact never happened. I stumbled and landed against one of the presses. I pushed myself off and released a frustrated grunt. Ven was nowhere to be seen. The three ferrics had also disappeared.

I closed my eyes and psychically searched for a hint of Jasper, willing myself to translocate to him. I felt nothing, no magnetic draw.

"What happened?" Patrick asked.

"I can't find Jasper." I shook my head. "Anywhere."

"Your guy? Did they kill him?"

I let out a shaky breath. "Yes. Or..." An image of the prison where Patrick and I had been held played in my mind's eye. Was it possible Jasper's body had been moved there? "The prison, maybe."

"What about the Beretrum?" Patrick asked.

The question was like a knife in my heart. "Maybe that, too."

I turned, looking up at the bent and broken glass doors. Sections of glass too large to fall through the grated balcony glittered atop the metal.

"What do you want to do?" Patrick asked.

"I want to find Ven and force him to tell me what he did with Jasper. But," I stopped, turned, and looked at Patrick. "That's probably what he wants—to distract me or lure me somewhere he can trap me."

Patrick nodded.

"It's just us," I said. "For now."

Our gazes returned to the machines.

"I guess I'll collect the godsoul, if we're going to get this thing going," Patrick said.

I grimaced. I loathed Ven, but his words had sapped my energy. I feared they were true. What if our plan didn't work, and the godsoul was depleted?

"How will you market it?" I asked, a little dizzy. "How will you describe the new drug?"

"An antiviral," Patrick replied. "It's the easiest."

I nodded, rubbing my chin. "And what will you mix the godsoul with?"

Patrick blinked. He peered at the various rotary presses, checking the clipboards attached to each of them. "Ibacitabine," he finally said, looking up at me. "An actual antiviral."

"And it will trick them? The doctors?"

Patrick shrugged and nodded. "Everyone is desperate. If Hank can lie well enough—and I know him, he can—then we can get this released tonight. Especially with Margaret's corroboration."

I nodded and bit my lip. There was no reason to delay any longer. "All right," I said.

Patrick came over and took my hand in his own. "We can do this, Jack. It will be all right. Even when it's not all right, it's all right."

I returned the smile, a sick sensation in the pit of my stomach. "Yes."

Patrick walked to the edge of the room to a closed door. He looked around and found a box cutter on a nearby table. He cut his palm and outlined the closet door with his blood. He pressed his hand to the center and muttered the words "*Patefacio tutor godsoul.*"

Light fluoresced around the frame. My hand shook. I gripped it into a fist.

Patrick opened the door, and the brilliant purple and gold room shimmered beyond. He beckoned me and entered. I followed, my feet soundless against the rock floor, the silence an apology for my presence and what I was about to do.

The island was just as Patrick had left it, cluttered with the tools for cutting and storing godsoul. Patrick lifted the large saw from the end of the island. He pressed beyond the invisible buffer that separated everyone but him from the remaining supply. He placed the blade against the golden rock and pushed it back and forth.

Golden plasma coated the blade and dripped to the floor in droplets, like blood. The rock seemed to jiggle, like ripe fruit or a fleshy organ. As Patrick worked, I stared at the gold that flooded the floor, splashed across the concrete, and reached my shoes. I stepped back. Part of me wanted to yell at Patrick to stop, but the logical part of me said *no*; this was important, necessary. When he finished, a substantial thirty-pound hunk of godsoul dropped to the floor. I half expected it to scurry away.

"Easier to cut than I thought," Patrick remarked. "There's something special about this saw." He walked to another section and pressed the saw against the wall. Again, golden blood dripped along his blade, coating the floor. Godsoul splashed down, flooding the floor and pushing the plasma closer toward me.

No longer able to watch, I turned and braced myself against the royal purple rock. Something inside me was screaming, and I couldn't get it to stop.

Beneath my hand, the purple rock crumbled. I pulled back, staring at my palm. It was coated in black, what looked like coal. All around me, the royal purple hallway hid tinges of black within it.

I turned to tell Patrick that he needed to stop. Something was happening.

Almost the entire wall was now trimmed back down to its roots. Exposed pieces of godsoul bled everywhere. Ten lumps, each perhaps thirty pounds, dotted the floor. How had Patrick worked so quickly? Again, I went to tell Patrick to stop, but then I thought of the number of people who needed to be saved, people like Margaret. Would I doom them? Would I have doomed her?

I swallowed bile and wished that I'd chased Ven, gone in search of Jasper. Anything was better than seeing this.

I felt like vomiting, but I wasn't going to show weakness. It was important we both believed in what we were doing.

"Excellent," I said. I forced a smile.

"Help me carry this into Lucient." He waved for me to come forward. I walked to where he stood and squatted. Barely able to look, I slipped my hands beneath the rock and gripped its flesh-like surface. It was like touching raw meat across bone. Patrick and I both lifted, our bodies and hands drenched in liquid gold. We slipped in the plasma and tracked it out of the hallway on our shoes into the darkened building. We lowered it to the dirty concrete floor. The godsoul glowed, sparkling.

"All right," Patrick said. "Just nine more. I'll cut off more after we finish the first batch."

I turned to him. "More?"

"Yeah," he confirmed. "This is maybe half of what we need."

A frisson swept through my body, though I tried my best not to show it. I reassessed what we were doing, who Patrick was. I remembered in that moment that he'd never had any self-control. Until recently he'd been a drug addict, through and through. And he'd thrown money every which way. Perhaps what we were doing was an extension of that.

"I know what you're thinking," Patrick said.

I swallowed dryly. "Oh?"

"That this is a lot. That we're in too deep. That we've done something wrong."

I winced and looked down at the chunk of godsoul.

"But there's no other choice, Jack," Patrick said. "It's like you said. This is the only thing that will cure them."

I pressed my gold-covered hands to my face. The severity of what we were doing overwhelmed me. The more I considered it, the more it woke me, and I was not used to being so awake. I began weighing the cost of two hundred thousand lives against the loss of the godsoul. At the beginning, the answer had seemed obvious. Now, all was blurred. It frightened me, more than I'd ever been.

"You're right," I said, imitating a resolve I didn't actually have. "You're right."

Patrick and I loaded the rest of the godsoul into the building and then fed it to a machine that ground it down and blended it with the ibacitabine.

CHAPTER 20
FRIGUS TORQUEM LOGISTICS

Jack

THE PILLS PATRICK'S LAB PRODUCED were cream colored, with a golden sheen, an unearthly luminescence. I cupped a pill in my hand and noted the sparkle. A lump formed in my throat, and my stomach turned. The wall of godsoul was nearly bare. Only one large piece remained, perhaps twenty pounds in total, if that.

It'd required nearly all of it to produce medication for twice the number of people we knew were infected to ensure we could eradicate Alex's disease.

Nearly twice.

As my stomach coiled, Patrick's cell rang. It was Hank, Lucient's VP. He told Patrick to turn on the news. Margaret's recovery and the treatment breakthrough were being broadcast. Patrick and I hurried to the second floor, through the broken glass doors into the office, where a television hung on a wall. We watched as Margaret smiled on camera, made up with black eyeliner and red lipstick, her hair once again maroon. She was beautiful and bouncy, telling everyone in the world about Lucient.

"A very special woman came from the lab—a woman I call my friend and savior—and…and she gave me the medication to fix the disease." Her eyes looked right into the camera, and it felt as though she saw me. "I owe everything to her."

Tears filled my eyes, and I wiped them away. My heart warmed, and I wished that I could reach through the television to hug Margaret. Seeing her healthy, knowing that I had made her healthy, eased the guilt that had fastened a noose around my heart. Patrick and I had saved her. And we could save more individuals just like her. We could save the world.

Harvesting the godsoul had come at an enormous a cost, but the infected individuals deserved to be saved, not fated for the Beretrum because they were infected. Patrick and I were achieving that beyond the existing rules and boundaries. Vindication and the knowledge that we had provided the world a cure it might not otherwise have, and saved so many people from Ven, eased the moral consequence.

Patrick sat at a desk and put Hank on speakerphone. I shifted my focus to his voice as he explained that hospitals and doctors all over the world, not just in Basille, Louisiana, were demanding Numenus. Patrick gave me a thumbs up.

"We'll get this loaded on the temp-controlled trucks for distribution," Patrick said.

"We're going to need GPS units in every vehicle. People are desperate for a cure, and you've got one. We don't want to lose any shipments," Hank said, his voice rushed. "You know as well as I do that three-quarters of all thefts occur on the road."

"Yes," Patrick replied.

"I'll make a few calls. We got fucking lucky, Patrick. Doctors talked about this being the next bubonic plague. We're going to make a fortune."

Patrick chuckled. He licked his upper lip nervously, but then his nervousness was replaced by cold resolve. "You have it wrong, Hank. We're not charging anything. The drugs are free."

The other end of the line went briefly silent. Then Hank laughed. "What?"

"They're free. People need them. We're not getting in the way of their cure."

"Wait, now. We need to discuss this." Hank spoke as though coaxing a suicidal man from the ledge. "I'm not talking about price gouging, but we've got to be reasonable here. We're a business, and businesses don't run on free."

"It's not a discussion," Patrick said.

"Then how are we going to recoup the production costs?"

Patrick cleared his throat. "Don't worry about it."

A nervous laugh trickled from the other phone, followed by a wheeze. Hank sounded as though he'd just been shot. "Patrick, I have to be frank with you. This is suicide, and you know, your father never would have—"

"Just get it done," Patrick announced. He ended the call and turned to me. "Don't worry," he said. "I'll make sure Hank has a respectable severance package when I sell Lucient."

I shook my head. "I don't care."

The equipment below us rumbled as it processed the godsoul. "The first round is nearly finished. It'll ship out soon," he said. He got up from the desk and left the TV on. The news program had moved on from Margaret's story. We returned downstairs.

Patrick lifted one of the white bottles of Numenus out of a box and tossed it to me. I caught it.

"In case you want to keep a bottle around for... What's his name? Roland?"

I pressed my thumb to the plain white label. Another use for the pills came to mind. "Yes. Thank you."

"Of course. Take several if you need to. Just in case."

I studied the insulated container that held about a hundred bottles of our deceptive drug. I claimed another and slipped both into my jacket pockets.

"Do you mind if I go now?"

"No." Patrick smiled and clasped his hands behind his back. I realized there was something else on his mind, sensed a desire to confide in me now that the fever throughout the country was finally about to break.

"What?" I asked, not sure I wanted to know.

He shrugged. "You might think this is strange, but I was looking at the hand soap in the bathroom while washing my hands after we finished moving the godsoul. It had a vanilla and bergamot smell."

"Bergamot?"

"It's a citrus with a heady—"

"I know what it is. I'm just surprised you do."

He nodded. "I know things, Jack."

"You do," I acknowledged.

"Anyway, the description on the back was 'gourmand.' An excessive scent for a glutton."

"They certainly know their consumer."

He barely chuckled. "It reminded me of our conversation…after I saved you. After we rested on the floor of my father's office. Do you remember?"

"Yes." Part of me didn't want to recall it, but I did—sitting at the kitchen table with Patrick, discussing my fear of failure. "We talked about our fathers and our inheritances. Their fear that we will spend it all."

Patrick studied the floor. "Do you think we've been gluttonous?" he asked softly. He shifted his feet. Beneath them, liquid gold coated the floor, drying in drops, splatters, like blood. It seemed as though the body of a giant, of a god, had been dragged through the lab. Gold splattered the machines that had ground down the godsoul.

I bit my lip and searched my heart. To my surprise, it didn't feel weighted. It felt free—released.

"Not since seeing Margaret on TV. Not after she thanked Lucient."

"I feel the same way. I feel like, for the first time, I've made a positive difference in this world." He pointed between us. "That we both have." He put his hands on my upper arms and gently patted and squeezed. Heat radiated from him, and I could smell a mixture of godsoul and cologne. Tiny droplets of gold decorated his black shirt.

"We did good," he said, leaning his forehead to mine. "I know you said I was a child…the last time we were at Lucient. But I'm hoping you'll rethink things. I'm different now."

I smiled and pulled free. This wasn't the time. "I'll be back," I said.

Patrick blinked. "I know." He didn't appear nearly as disappointed as I'd expected. He turned and walked down the Numenus production line, eyeing the working machines.

I exhaled deeply, wondering if he would have kissed me if I hadn't stepped back. More importantly, what did I want? I didn't know. I felt drawn to Patrick, but where, truly, was that going to go? When it came to romance, to love, to closeness I had zero experience, and I wasn't sure what the ultimate result was supposed to be. It reminded me of a complex puzzle with no guarantee of a solution. Even more troubling was the fact that being drawn to Patrick felt the opposite of my normal state of being, of the carefully pruned and drugged equilibrium that kept me going. I would kill for him, undoubtedly I would. How was that not the ultimate love? How could love be anything but this?

I turned away and readied myself to leave. It was best to shelve these thoughts and feelings because I could not yet give them the time they needed. As usual, I had things to do, and the fate of people's lives and safety rested on them. I closed my eyes and pictured Roland's kind face, urging myself to him. Lucient Pharmaceuticals blurred and sloughed away. Blackness took hold, and the familiar entryway of Cyrus's house appeared and established itself around me.

The place was eerily quiet. I paused, listening for any sound of life. Nothing.

My shoes thudded down the hall as I inspected each room. No sign of Roland or Cyrus.

"Roland!" I called.

No response.

I frowned and decided it would be best to go and check that the furnace had consumed Alex's body, to ensure that the fires were still going strong. Maybe Roland was down there. I slid open a drawer in the table near the entryway and slipped both the Numenus pill bottles inside. Tiny clicks, like marbles cascading, echoed in the hallway as I set them on their sides. I shut the drawer and headed downstairs.

In the furnace, I saw nothing left of my brother. The flames flickered, thick, hot, and fierce, as though determined that yes, damnit, yes, the body would be turned to ash. Alex wasn't allowed to come back.

"Jack," a voice said.

I jumped and turned, looking into Roland's face, half tempted to slap him. He must have come down the opposite hallway.

"You scared me."

"Sorry." He put a hand on my arm. "I'm so happy to see you." He pulled me into a hug. "I saw them take you and couldn't do anything. I sat and prayed. I prayed that something would happen and you'd be saved."

"I was," I said. I pulled back. "We figured it out."

"Figured what out?"

"A cure. To Alex's disease that's been ravaging this world. Godsoul."

Roland shook his head, and he beamed. He hugged me again, pulling me close, and I laughed, unable to help it.

"I brought you a couple bottles, in case you need them. They're upstairs in the entryway table drawer."

Roland nodded quietly, his smiling eyes creased with happiness.

"Where's Cyrus?"

"Upstairs sleeping," Roland said. "He knows…about Alex's death. He's been quieter than usual. I mean, he does whatever I tell him. But I can tell that deep inside him, the waters are not still. He's angry. He loathes us."

"As usual." I stared into the furnace fire. "I'm going to talk to him."

Roland patted my arm. "Be careful."

I nodded.

On the first floor, I paused at the foot of the stairs and then went the table where I'd stored the pills. I opened the drawer and took two pills from a bottle. I slipped them into my pocket and continued to Cyrus's bedroom.

The door was open, the bedside lamp on. Cyrus was in bed, wrapped in the cobalt blue covers, his mouth open, his silver hair mussed. Rarely had I seen him so vulnerable.

I cleared my throat and knocked on the door. His silver eyes opened, and he blinked several times, staring at the bedside lamp. He turned to me and froze, his eyes clearing.

"Are you all right?" I asked. It felt odd to ask this of him. He'd done so many horrible things to me. Maybe horrible things were all he now deserved. But I was trying to do something that transcended the horrible.

He sat up, propped against the tufted black headboard. "Yes."

"Your son wasn't your son anymore, you should know. The Builder changed him. His hair and skin were whiter than white. He had no pupils. His voice was robotic. It wasn't Alex. He was the Builder. And I know that might have made you joyful, but…" I shook my head, "the reality is your son was dead before I got to the Beretrum. He spread a sickness across this world, and it has—*had*—no known cure. But I and a friend discovered one. Over the next few weeks, it will be distributed to eradicate the illness."

Cyrus said nothing, and his silver eyes betrayed no emotion. They seemed as keen as ever, though sleepiness and loss had smoothed the edges.

I inhaled deeply. "I'm…sorry for your loss," I said. My mouth went dry, and the old aspect of myself that was wary and demure tempted me. I ignored it. "I know that you're likely in pain. I know you despise me, and you wish the Builder would rise up and destroy us all, but…I need to ask you a question that I hope you'll answer honestly."

Cyrus stared straight through me, expressionless.

I moved into the room and dragged the chair beside his bed closer. I sat. "It's something I've needed to know for a while now. And I'd like to ask you because…" I clenched my jaw and swallowed. "Well, just because." I let my eyes rise to meet his. "Am I your daughter? Biologically?" Within, I used what ferric power I had to urge him to the truth. I wouldn't be lied to.

"You are commanding an answer?"

"Yes."

Cyrus inhaled, his mouth open. He paused. He sighed and closed his eyes. And nodded.

My pulse thrummed, and I slumped forward. An unexpected relief flooded me. I'd never known my true origins but had been raised by Cyrus. I'd begun to suspect that he was actually my father when he suggested I take over Infinitum, but this proved my suspicions. Cyrus had just confessed the truth under the most powerful truth serum ever known—my immortal control.

"Then why did you pretend I was adopted?" I asked. "Why did we live as though Alex was your own and I wasn't?" My voice wavered, to my chagrin.

"Because," he said, "it nicely set up tension between you and Alex, ensuring that you would compete against one another, grow stronger from it. It also gave me more control over you. We were father and daughter only because I had decided we were, as far as you knew. And it shook the ground beneath your feet. That was useful."

"Was it?" I asked, half to myself. "Alex wasn't the one who stopped you. Maybe you brought the fever too high. It had to break." I leaned back. "I don't know how you had the energy for it all. I don't understand why we couldn't just…live. Just be."

"Because the Builder is going to win," Cyrus said. "And if we're not on his side, we're not on the winning side. He will destroy this world—if not with his *arcas* or Alex's disease, then with something else. And I was not going to allow us to end up on the losing side."

"Dying is not losing," I said. "It's life. Everybody dies."

"We wouldn't have. While I was in charge, we were above death. We could still be."

I shook my head. "You're not special to him. Alex wasn't special. I'm not special. Not really. He only makes people feel that way so he can get what he wants. I don't understand why I can see that but you can't." I bit the inside of my cheek. "The older I get, the less I understand you. The less alike we are. I suppose there's something to be said for that." I reached into my pocket and retrieved the pills. "I want you to take these."

Cyrus looked down, his gaze empty. "What are they?"

"Don't worry about it. They won't hurt you."

I wanted to see what godsoul might do to Cyrus. Was it possible that it would heal him in a way unlike any other?

"You are commanding me to take them?" Cyrus said.

"Yes."

He frowned and took the pills from my palm. He slipped them into his mouth one at a time and picked up the cup of water from his nightstand. He drank, eyeing me as he did.

I leaned forward and clasped my hands. His silver eyes flicked to me, and he set the cup on the nightstand table. He shifted under the sheets.

He pressed a hand to his stomach and tilted his head to the side, as if listening.

"What?" I asked.

"I feel strange." He lifted the covers and rose. He stretched and walked to a corner of the room, brushing a hand through his hair. His breath came quickly, as though he'd started jogging. He braced himself against a silver bureau.

"What did you give me?"

"What do you feel?"

He glanced around the room, then his eyes settled on me. He seemed woken, present, young. His lips parted, and he frowned. Tears welled. He winced and put a hand to his jaw.

I went over. "What?"

He backed away from me until he reached the wall. Sobbing, he mumbled behind his hands and rubbed his nose with a fist, trembling.

I moved closer.

"I hurt you," he said. His eyes pleaded with me. The irises were golden, no longer cold silver. "I hurt you. I hurt you…" He rocked back and forth, pressing his hands to his eyes.

I touch his hands, felt the tears on his skin. "Yes."

"I'm so sorry."

He slipped to the floor. He spoke between sobs in a voice that sounded like an entirely other person had entered him, possessed him. "I…I made you kill. I gave you drugs. I made you do and watch terrible things. And Roland. Oh God, Roland. And Alex. My son."

He gasped for air between sobs, his eyes wild. I bent down and put a hand on his arm. "Calm down," I said.

His breathing became slightly less ragged. His face was bright red, his eyes bloodshot, focused inward. He seemed to be rifling through his entire past with a new lens, able to recognize the morality he had soaked in gasoline and set fire to decades before.

"What do I do, Jack?" He grasped my arms like a needy child and clung to me.

I hugged him close, though I was unable to completely erase my wariness, my fear that all of this was a production. But I allowed the contact.

"Calm down and realize there's a new journey ahead for you. You'll learn right from wrong."

"But all the people I killed… All the things I did to you."

I reached within myself for unimagined strength. "We move beyond it." I brushed his silver hair away from his forehead. "We learn compassion, and we right the wrongs we can."

He shook his head, looking panicked. "I don't deserve a second chance." He started to push away from me, but I held him close.

"Relax," I said. "Rome wasn't built in a day, and neither will you be." He sank deeper into my arms, against his will.

Roland appeared in the doorway. His lowered eyebrows lifted up when he saw Cyrus's state. "What the hell is going on?"

"The godsoul works," I said.

Hearing Roland's voice, Cyrus looked up at him, tears streaming down his face.

Roland's frightened gaze shifted to me. "What are you talking about?"

"Cyrus is…different," I said.

Cyrus released me, shuffled to his feet, and stepped quickly toward Roland, arms outstretched. Roland slammed his hand into Cyrus's chest and swept Cyrus's legs out from under him with a foot. Cyrus dropped hard on his back. His eyes widened, and he moaned. He looked around his bedroom, starry eyed.

An urge to laugh rose from my belly and threatened to bubble up my throat. I swallowed it down and reached to help Cyrus up. He rubbed the back of his head and checked his blood-free hand. "I deserve worse," he said ruefully.

Roland stared open-mouthed at Cyrus. "I can't tell if this scares me more."

"I told you," I said. "The godsoul works."

My cell rang in my pocket. I argued with myself to let the call go, to be with my two fathers, to let the rest of the world figure itself out for a while. It rang a second time, and doubt nibbled at my resolve. I shoved my hand in my pocket. Too many important things were going on. I checked my phone. Patrick.

"I need to get this." I lifted my chin toward Cyrus. "Seriously, Roland. Take a look in his eyes. He's not the same man."

I stepped into the hallway and accepted the call. "Yeah."

"I just can't fuckin' believe it. We got the first three shipments out. One of the trucks is gone, Jack."

I froze. "What?"

"Stolen. And according to the driver…"

An image of the Builder shot to my mind.

"…two infected people stole it. They nearly killed the driver. He's at a hospital now. Doctors are giving him Numenus, just in case."

"Shit," I whispered.

"It can't be too bad, right? I mean…if they steal the pills and take them, that will cure them."

"Unless they're not stealing it for themselves."

Both of us were silent as realization settled in.

"I can give you their location on GPS. They're at…"

"Don't need it," I said, and I ended the call.

I returned to Roland, who spoke softly to Cyrus. He held Cyrus's hand between his, as might a Buddhist monk with a young student. Roland smiled with more joy than I'd ever seen. I hated to interrupt. "I'll be back," I whispered at the threshold.

Roland nodded vaguely, as though mildly annoyed at being interrupted. "Where are you going?"

"Just something I have to do," I said. "Shouldn't take long."

Slipping out of the room and back into the hall, I closed my eyes and let the boiling rage expand. I let it be the force that determined my destination.

The world around me swirled, dissolving like sand in deep black water. The hallway with its wooden floors, picture frame molding, and blue wallpaper swirled and faded into darkness. I floated in nothingness. Before me, out of thin air, appeared a short curtain, moth-eaten, smelling of reheated food. My knees bent, and I found myself sitting on a small reclining couch. A floorboard rattled beneath my boots. A vibration entered me, the sense of movement. Short walls surrounded me, the ceiling low. I realized I was in the back of a semi's cab.

Through the moth-eaten holes in the curtains, I made out white arms, the blank eyes of the driver, and then the holes closed in as the curtain repaired itself due to my presence.

I quietly pulled the curtain open a crack. In the driver's seat, a whitened man grasped the wheel. Only the dirt on his hands and his clothes had any color. The rest of him was as pale as a paper cup. In the passenger's seat sat a whitened woman who, in the dark, reminded me of a stone graveyard angel minus her wings.

I took a deep, silent breath and summoned all my energy and strength. I launched myself through the curtain and punched the driver's head. The semi swerved to the left, crossed the center line into the other lane. I yanked the wheel back and we jerked back in our lane. Car horns screamed as they passed. I kicked the driver's door until it broke free of its hinges, disappearing in the night. The sounds of the moaning wind and the whoosh of other vehicles exploded into the cab. Black pavement whipped past. White hands wrapped around my torso from behind as the woman screamed; she dug her nails into my ribs, and then my neck.

I pulled her arms free and shoved her backward with my elbows. As the driver turned toward me, I held tightly to the seat, lifted my legs, and slammed them into his chest. He flew out of the cab onto the pavement below like a white stone dropped on the road. He tumbled and disappeared from view.

The woman scratched the back of my neck and bit me. I grabbed her hair and pulled her off.

The truck swerved to the right. The cab shuddered, dropping me into the driver's seat, and the woman jumped on top of me. She clawed my face, and I screamed at the bright, fresh pain. I pulled my knees up and propelled her through the open door.

Her screams filled the night and then dissolved.

I sat up, grabbed the wheel, and slammed on the brakes. The semi zoomed to the right, off the hardtop, and toward a tree. I squeezed my eyes shut, pressed the pedal with all my strength, gripping the steering wheel tightly, and willed the truck to stop in time. I braced for impact.

The semi screeched to a stop. The tree loomed inches from the headlights, illuminated.

I released a big breath and let go of the wheel. I searched the inside panel for the gear shift, found it, and put the truck in park. Leaning forward, I explored my neck and hissed in pain. Wet, broken skin stung as I pressed. Blood coated my hand. I leaned my head back and breathed. The pain faded to a dull throb. I checked the skin again and realized with relief that the wound was healing. I sensed the raw edges seal. I sat upright and shook the other aches away before I hopped out of the cab. I landed on the pavement and peered down the road, where the infected pair had fallen.

I saw them coming toward me, the man in the distance, the woman quite close.

I hurried to the back of the truck and jerked the rolling trailer door up. Crates of boxes filled the space. I broke open one of the boxes, retrieving a bottle of pills. I turned and marched down the pavement. Cars passed on my right, headlights illuminating the glittery asphalt and yellow lines. The distance to the woman jogging toward me on the road shoulder shrank to a few feet.

She screamed at me, her arms wide. Blood coated her lips and teeth, dribbled down her chin, streaking her gray shirt.

My stride lengthened. "Where did you think you were going to take this, hm?" I yelled.

When we met, she dove at me. Turning quickly, I bent forward and used her force to throw her back when I straightened. She dropped to the ground, and I stomped my foot on her chest, pinning her. I ripped the cap from the Numenus bottle and shook several pills into my palm. I popped them into her screaming mouth and then forced her chin up with my hands. She struggled, clawing my arms, collecting my skin under her fingernails. As soon as the slices appeared, they closed again.

She swallowed.

Without waiting to see what would happen now, I stood and scoured the road for the driver. His outline was tiny in the distance. I appeared before him in the blink of an eye. The sudden translocation shocked me, and I froze for a moment.

He was whiter than white, bewildered, enraged. He threw a punch; I blocked it. I grabbed him by the throat and dumped several pills into his open mouth. I dropped the bottle and sealed his mouth with a hand. He clutched at my arms, but I had turned to stone, perhaps from the adrenaline, perhaps from immortal strength. He couldn't move me, couldn't stop me. He swallowed the drugs, and I released him. The welts he left between the fiery swaths on my arms vanished.

I bent over, hands on my knees, to catch my breath. Cottonwood seeds drifted in the strong wind like quiet snow. My pulse back to normal, I eyed the man whose skin regained color, whose eyes became blue and hair dark brown. I retrieved my cell phone and called Patrick.

He picked up on the second ring. "You okay?"

"Fine," I said. "The truck is safe. Get someone out here."

"Thank God," he said. "Police are already on their way. They have the GPS coordinates. You sure you aren't hurt?"

I tentatively tested the back of my neck. No blood, no pain. "I'm great," I said. "I'll stay here until the police arrive."

"And the infected?"

All the color had returned to the man on the ground. He cried, holding his head in his hands, looking at me as though he both feared me and feared himself, unsure which was scarier.

"Healed."

"Excellent," Patrick said, shuddering, his Irish accent surprisingly thick, perhaps exaggerated by his fear. "Tell them as long as they tell everyone that the Numenus healed them, we won't press charges."

"Will do. And Patrick…"

"Yeah?"

"You might consider putting guards on future trucks."

"Already on it."

I hung up, looked down at the man, and sighed. He seemed pitiful, as if he yearned to be comforted by me.

"Numenus healed you," I said. "Tell the police and anyone who interviews you that, and Lucient won't press charges."

He didn't nod, just stared at me open-mouthed, but I knew he heard. Slowly, I walked back to the truck, translocating to it. I suddenly yearned for a cigarette. It'd been a long time since I'd smoked.

I reached into my inside jacket pocket and felt for my pack of cigarettes. They were terribly smooshed, but I managed to tweeze one of the bent cigarettes free. I lit it with Cyrus's lighter. I stared at the lighter while I puffed, pressing my thumb to its golden surface, thinking of his tears and him hugging me. His emotions had been real. Right? They'd seemed so real.

The nicotine hit, sending me a momentary high. Simultaneously, the realization arrived that Cyrus—the Cyrus I had known—didn't exist anymore. All it had taken was a piece of godsoul.

Why hadn't the ferrics done that years ago, when I was still a child? Why hadn't they healed him? It would've saved us all so much trouble.

I settled on the back lip of the trailer, near the stacked boxes of Numenus, inhaling the scent of smoke and sweet, cool air. The grass beyond the road and the distant trees swayed in the wind. The moon waxed large and round, casting light on everything. Nearby, a bird twittered.

The tip of the cigarette brightened and died down. I dropped my hand to my side. In the distance, across the field, something bright appeared, drawing my attention. A thin line of white broke through the trees, seeming just as tall. The cigarette fell from my fingers.

More white appeared from behind the trees, and then a large creature clambered over the grass, tall and wide. It was impossible to tell how many legs it had, as though the white was shifting, creating and then disappearing however many it needed.

I froze. I stared deep into the white monstrosity, and it was as though I was in a black cave, darkness surrounded by pure white. I released a shaky breath and stood. My heart jackhammered. My hands trembled. Consciousness threatened to abandon me. The Builder was coming.

Sirens.

Red and blue swirling lights crested the hill to my right. They blinded me momentarily, and I lifted a hand.

I turned back. The white monstrosity had stopped. It remained where it was, as though recalculating. The whirling screech of the sirens expanded, the cars moving ever closer, and I readied myself—for what, I didn't know. I no longer had my gun with the bullets filled with godsoul.

The white creature shambled backward, slowly, and disappeared into the trees.

I sank to the ground and took several shallow breaths. What would I have done if the Builder hadn't stopped? And why did he leave? Did he not want to be seen? Even with the world ending? Why?

Perhaps he hasn't won, yet. Perhaps he knows that. Maybe the godsoul was correcting, rebalancing, the world. The medication that Patrick and I'd concocted might delay the end.

Just before the police vehicles stopped, I translocated back to Cyrus's mansion. I trembled in the hallway until Roland and Cyrus arrived and held me. Slowly, with the help of my two fathers, I returned to myself.

The Builder had retreated. Patrick and I were winning.

CHAPTER 21
ORATIO

Patrick

THE COSMETICIAN APPLIED CONCEALER TO my face. Bright lights and mirrors were set up around us. This wasn't the first time I'd worn makeup. The last time, a naked girl named Marissa had giggled and winked at me, expecting a wink back, a mascara wand in her hand. I'd pulled her to me, on top of me, close, and she'd swept the wand across my face, as though it would stop me. We'd kissed deeply. It had been snowing outside. She died of an overdose two weeks later.

To my left, a young boy named Hayden with brownish-red hair sat on a hospital bed. Crisp sheets were pulled tight across his chest. Another cosmetician, a woman named Rita wearing a bright green satin shirt and whose black, curly hair was done up in a twist, combed his hair with her fingers. Hayden's mother, Sandra—long cheeks, button nose, wrinkles at the corners of her lips—waited in the room's corner. Her exhaustion was evident in her eyes, but she smiled as she watched Hayden. Her smile resembled a break in the clouds on a stormy day.

Above us, fluorescent lighting hummed—an annoying monotone hospital sound that went on forever. A children's show played on a muted television across from the bed—Hayden's eyes occasionally wandered to it—and a metal IV stand with saline bags stood beside a table holding an unattached blood pressure cuff and LED heart monitor. An array of colorful get-well cards and several pink and white flower arrangements brightened a plain plastic dresser. The scent of the flowers and the cosmeticians' perfume mingled with the odor of cleaning supplies, hand sanitizer, and bland food.

In the hallway, a doctor was paged over the intercom. Two men in blue scrubs hurried past. The news crew bustled in, and a black and gray camera swung from a cameraman's back, nearly hitting Sandra's jaw.

"Careful," I said, grabbing the cameraman's shoulder. He turned his head to me, blue eyes wide, owl-like. I pointed to Hayden's mother. "It's a good thing we're in a hospital because you nearly knocked her right out."

Several individuals laughed. The cameraman apologized to Sandra. I walked to Hayden and smiled. The boy energetically beamed back at me. His fingers played with the edge of the bedding. The plastic hospital bed crinkled as he moved.

"Excited to be on television?" I asked him. The cosmetician followed me, dabbed cream under my eyes, and worked it in with a sponge. Could barely stand the sensation. How did women do it every day?

Hayden nodded and ran his tongue across his bottom lip. "What do I have to say again?"

"I don't think you have to say anything if you don't want to," I replied.

"Hmm. I'd hate to be on television and not say *anything*."

I chuckled. The statement reminded me of childlike desires. In a way, I'd never outgrown them. "That's a good point," I told him. "We should come up with something for you to say." I tilted my head. "What would you really like to do, once you get the all-clear from the doctors and get out of here?"

"Umm," Hayden said. His brown-green eyes wandered around the room. "I want to go swimming at John Jay. Mom said she'd take me."

"Swimming? That sounds *fun*."

Hayden grinned with his whole face.

"So how about, after I get done saying whatever these nice people tell me to say…" The cosmetician applying my makeup laughed. "You tell the whole world that you can't *wait* to go swimming."

Hayden nodded vigorously.

Someone cleared his voice. A set of papers appeared in front of me. I clasped them and looked sideways at Hank, Lucient's VP. The alpha dog look on his face, his hair semi-long with slicked-back sides, made me lean away when in the same space with him. He probably planned it that way. If someone were to gauge the destiny of the universe on his appearance alone, we'd be fucked.

"Remember to say that we've delivered Numenus to all fifty states and are working on international transport," he ordered.

I folded the pages and handed them back to him. "I know."

"And don't forget to say Lucient's name three times. Studies have shown that individuals remember a name they hear at least twice." He said it as though no one would remember the name of a company that saved the world if I failed at this task.

The cosmetician dabbed my face with powder, and my eyes burned.

"Where would Lucient be without you and your word repetition studies?" I asked, blinking away the powder.

Hank pressed his lips tightly. "The same place we'd be without your handsome mug. It's a good thing they're not filming me. The whole world would scream that the VP of Lucient had contracted an even worse virus."

I snickered.

Hank raised his chin. "You know, you don't look half bad these days, Patrick. You've got some color in your cheeks."

"You have gorgeous skin tone," the woman with the brush confirmed as she lightly dabbed my nose.

My eyes lingered on her for a moment before returning to Hank. "I'm…on a new diet."

"I'd heard. But to see it is another thing. Keep doing what you're doing." Hank folded his arms and began to walk away. He turned back. "And don't forget—"

"Don't forget to smile," I finished.

Hank winked, fired an air pistol while clicking his tongue, swiveled, and left, his heels clacking on the cream tile.

Hayden grinned again, rubbed his hands together with glee.

"Happy you're feeling better?" I said.

"Super happy." He scratched his nose. "Are you the one who did it?"

I winced as one of the camera lights was shifted to beam directly in my eyes.

"Sort of," I said, raising my hand to block the light.

Hayden jerked his sheets down, clambered over them, and hugged me. The line to the IV poked out of his tiny arm and swung back and forth. "Thank you," he said.

I placed my hand on his small back and pressed him close. To my surprise, my chest tightened. Tears came. When Hayden pulled back, one drop slid down my cheek. Hayden grabbed a tissue from a box on his bedside table and held it out to me.

I laughed and accepted it.

"Mom says you saved the world," Hayden reported. He slid back into bed and pulled the sheets over himself. "She said the doctors were surprised when the medicine you made worked. She was surprised too. Though I don't know why."

I cocked my head. "You don't know why?"

He nodded. "You're a good person. I can tell. Good people save the world."

"Takes a bit more than that, I think."

Hayden never blinked. "No it doesn't."

I fumbled with the folded papers. The truth of the story was buried in lines that didn't really say anything, didn't tell the world what Jack, Lucient, and I had really distributed.

"That woman likes you," Hayden whispered. He nodded toward the cosmetician. She'd moved to the other side of the room and sipped a Starbucks coffee. She glanced at us momentarily with a gleam in her eye, a knowing smile.

The part of my brain that typically itched when I met a woman remained oddly quiet. She was attractive, but she called to a part of me that no longer seemed to exist. I felt different.

"Maybe she does." I winked at Hayden.

"Do you like her?"

"No." I smiled. "I'm interested in someone else."

"What's her name?"

"Jack."

Hayden's nose wrinkled. "That's a *boy's* name."

I laughed. "I suppose it is."

"Why do you like her?" Hayden asked innocently.

I opened my mouth, assuming the answer would come to me immediately. It didn't. I recalled the first time I met Jack. The memory of my mother's repaired opal rosary, that she refused my kiss. Then how she'd materialized in my father's office, black lines along her skin. When I'd helped heal her, she seemed to be covered in gold. Fire fluoresced in those dark lines. "She helped me save the world. In fact," I confessed, leaning forward, "she did more of the work finding the cure than I did."

Hayden opened his eyes wide. "Oh." He looked deep in thought before he announced, "Never leave her."

"I don't intend to."

Someone called out that filming was ready to begin. I unfolded the papers, my mouth dry, and leaned in. "Ready?"

Hayden nodded. "Ready."

CHAPTER 22
GUTTA

Jack

PATRICK MADE SURE SURVEILLANCE CAMERAS were added to the trucks, as well as police escorts. In the following month, no others were stolen. Slowly, the treatment became available across the North and South America, Africa, Australia, and Eurasia. People Alex had infected were healed. Though the virus spread to tens of thousands more, Numenus was distributed to the infected in much earlier stages of the disease, ensuring that their symptoms never developed to the point that, like Margaret, they hovered between life and death.

The boiling point the world faced slowly tapered down, and news outlets lauded Lucient Laboratories for providing the medication for free. Patrick had spoken publicly. I watched him from Cyrus's living room as he related how happy he was that a select team of scientists had produced the antiviral medication in time and assured the public that Numenus would be supplied until the disease was wiped out.

I remained on alert in case any other trucks were stolen, but once the cameras and police escorts were in place, deliveries proceeded smoothly. I focused, meanwhile, on scouring the world, searching for Jasper, but I didn't sense him or find his remains. I'd gone as far as sending my power out into the world as I had when I resurrected Cyrus and Roland remotely, but nothing came of it. I felt like a failure and alone. To distract me from the loneliness, I shadowed Patrick, pretending my presence was necessary to ensure the safe delivery of Numenus.

It'd been worth the trouble, worth the pain of dwindling the supply of godsoul to one small section. When I actually slept, I had bad dreams that the supply evaporated because I was bingeing on it like golden cotton candy, ravaged by guilt when I consumed the last piece.

I shivered at the thought.

Often, I sat across from Cyrus in the living room, having discussions, as we often did lately, about how he'd developed as he had, where things had gone wrong. I found it endlessly fascinating and, in a strange way, insufficient. Nothing Cyrus told me seemed adequate to explain him, in the way reading recipe ingredients didn't convey its ultimate flavor. I had come to accept that he wasn't lying six months before, right before I helped free Lutin and his brothers to kill Cyrus. My mentor had told me then that although he'd been abused as a child by his father, that couldn't justify the path he'd chosen. The more I listened to him, the more I believed he was right.

"It's strange," Cyrus said. "Now that I'm changed, it's hard to recall how I was before. But, I think, I have come to understand it kind of like this…" He licked his lips and leaned forward in a lost, thoughtful way, so unlike his former cold, austere manner. "Without a higher power of some sort in my life, all manner of things—money, mostly, but also power, control— filled that empty slot on the roulette wheel. Where the ball landed was erratic and unpredictable, like my desires, but I threw myself at them full force. Eventually, the ball landed on the Builder. I think he could sense it in me—that I wasn't whole, that I hadn't settled on what would kindle me. I could imagine myself accommodating anything, doing anything. He decided to enter my life and offer himself as one of the options I could embrace, and I did. I wanted it so much. I would've done anything for what he offered.

"The fact that my choice punched holes in my soul only made me pursue him more. That, and the dark gifts he gave me."

I met his silver gaze and silently urged him to continue.

"I can clearly recognize that now. I sense something in the world that I didn't before. A connectedness. Bliss. Love. Joy. It's like I'm a child again. And I won't lose the connection this time. I'll give credit, and worship, where it's due."

"And where is that?"

He sipped his iced tea. He shrugged, as though it should have been obvious to him the whole time. "God."

I glanced at Roland, who stood across the room, leaning against the wall with his arms crossed. Our eyes met, and I could tell we were thinking the same thing. Though Cyrus said all the right things that made him seem changed, I reserved acceptance. He'd tricked me so many times that I couldn't let myself quite believe him anymore. I was burned out on belief, had moved entirely toward being. "It's very strange to hear you say that."

"It's strange to say it."

"I feel like the impossible has happened. This is…" I sought the words. "If this is a real change, it's miraculous. I wish godsoul was available to everyone. I wish I'd known about it before I had Jonathon Roth's men eliminate Infinitum. Those people could've been transformed, and that weighs on me now."

Cyrus settled his hand on top of mine. "Is there enough godsoul for everyone in the world, for every malady?"

I shook my head. "No."

"Then there's no reason for guilt. I feel fortunate that I am one of the lucky few who get to experience this transition." He tilted his head. "Perhaps the guilt is rightly mine. I don't deserve the transformation."

"It's not about what's deserved. It's about what's right."

Cyrus nodded. Tears came to the corners of his eyes, and he wiped them away. "You know…it's funny. I feel as though this sensation in me— this love, compassion, oneness with everyone and everything, as though I'm a part of a whole, rather than apart from it—is very similar to one I experienced long, long ago."

I tilted my head, wondering what he could possibly mean.

"It was long before I had you and Alex, long before I met Roland. I was probably still a teen, maybe in my early twenties. I happened to see a flier on a telephone pole." He laughed. "Now that I think about it, the idea of building a cult was probably part of me even then. Maybe I was sampling various groups, different followings and religious sects, to develop my own creation. The flier advertised a meditation group. I met several individuals and participated, just for one hour. On the way back to my apartment, I felt the most extraordinary peace. A calmness I had never experienced before. It was powerful, and it scared me. It was something I hadn't expected, and I didn't trust it. I ran. But the sensation of this godsoul—it reminds me of what I felt that day."

"I don't think I've ever tried anything like that." I looked at Roland. Was he still buying what Cyrus said or was he suspicious, as he usually was, as I always was? Was Cyrus fooling us? I didn't think so. It was as though my dark mentor, my dark father, had undergone a metamorphosis that could be achieved no other way than a miracle, by anything except the blood of a vanished or distant god. Yet, still, I felt unease.

"Do you think that meditation could have transformed you like the godsoul did?"

Cyrus seemed to consider the idea before he shook his head. "No. But only because I didn't want that. I would have fought against it tooth and nail. The godsoul overpowers you. You have no choice but to see the truth. It *forced* me to own my errors."

I nodded, pensive.

"Those pills you gave me erased hate. Greed. Memories of trauma." He tilted his head. "But now that I think about it, so did meditation."

Tears again washed across his eyes, as they had every day for the past month. Cyrus rubbed his hands together with a frown, shifting side to side.

"What?" I asked.

"How'd you get free?" He looked at me pointedly. "How is it that you, of all of my followers, escaped me?"

My eyes slipped back and forth between his as I considered my answer. "Because I was never actually yours."

He nodded and settled back in his seat. He pressed a hand to his mouth and sat there quietly for a moment, the room silent. Eventually, he spoke again. "May I ask, how are you doing in terms of making a plan to defeat the Builder?"

I ran my hand through my hair. I opened my mouth to speak, trying to decide what I should tell him, or if I should tell him anything. "I—"

My cell phone's ring tone pierced the air. I pulled it out of my pocket and saw a number I didn't recognize. I sucked my top lip between my teeth, trying to decide what I should do.

"Answer it," Roland said. "We have time for this later."

He was right. I took a deep breath and hit answer. "Hello?"

"Jack?" A woman's voice. It sounded familiar.

I shifted to the edge of my seat. "Yes?"

Her sigh of relief brushed against the mic like wind. "It's Margaret Wilhelm. I…I'm sorry to disturb you."

I smiled, relieved to hear her voice. I rose from my seat beside Cyrus. "Not at all. I'm glad to hear from you. I'm just…surprised."

"Well, I called Lucient and asked to speak to that charming devil who was on television. Patrick Flannigan. He gave me your number."

"Ah!" I said. "Of course, of course." I wandered out of the living room, shut the French doors behind me, and stood in the entryway, near the front door.

"I just…I was wondering if you could come by the house. I wanted to speak with you. We never did talk after you came by the hospital."

I beamed, content that Margaret was alive, healthy, and well enough to see me, that she'd returned home. "*Of course.* I'd love to," I said. "When would you like to meet?"

"How about today? If you can make it."

"I can." I paused, realizing that something about Margaret sounded… different. "Is everything okay?"

"Yes. I just…it would be better if you came by."

"Certainly."

She gave me her address, though that was unnecessary. My power could take me wherever I needed to go. I ended the call and replaced my phone in my pocket. On my way back to the living room, a wave of dizziness blindsided me. I pressed my hand against the wall and pressed my fingers to my nose, willing it to end. The vertigo continued, so I clung to the staircase and eased myself down on the bottom step. Slowly, I tamped the sensation down. The entryway righted itself. A tiny ball of nausea settled in the pit of my stomach, but nothing more.

What was that?

The question Cyrus had asked before the welcome interruption had shaken me. I was supposed to have an answer for the Builder, and I didn't. He hadn't appeared since I'd last seen him in the woods, near the stolen truck transporting Numenus. Since then, I'd spent most of my time on alert, in case another truck was stolen.

I felt unprepared, helpless. Maybe that had panicked me. That plus Margaret's surprise call, the strangeness of seeing Cyrus so at ease and complete.

I grabbed the banister and pulled myself to my feet. My vision was fine now. I cleared my throat, popped my neck, and returned to the living room. When I stepped through the door, I let Cyrus and Roland know I needed to leave.

One of Roland's eyes reflected the light coming in through the windows. The other remained dark. "Anything we can help you with?"

I shook my head. "Just visiting a friend."

MARGARET'S HOUSE, A TALL TWO-STORY, mint green and white Victorian, stretched between a cream-colored house and a robin's-egg blue home. It radiated history and personality, just like Margaret. The smell of the old wood was palpable where I stood.

I walked up the steps, the floorboards squeaking beneath me, to the wooden porch. To my left, a large bench swing hung, swaying slightly. An emerald blanket was bundled up on one side. A pair of sandals rested beneath the swing. Next to the swing stood an end table with a paperback book face-down. Its binding was well-worn; I couldn't make out the title. On the cover a shirtless man stood with a scantily clad woman, her hair windswept. I smirked and rang the doorbell beside the chestnut door. The glass oval panel featured carved roses.

The sound of heels on wood echoed, and a figure made her way toward me. The doorknob turned. I took a deep breath and smiled. Margaret opened the door. She wore a beautiful chambray dress, her bouncy burgundy hair pushed back from her face. She seemed like she was from a different time period.

She held out her arms, and I stepped inside them. We hugged one another tightly.

"Jack, I'm so glad to see you," she said. "And this time not in a grave! Either one of us!"

I laughed. "Yes!"

"Come inside." She shut the door behind me, and I looked around her home. The rooms were bright, some white, others mint green. Rose gold vases, pillows, and sculptures placed here and there brought warmth to the rooms. The scents of vanilla and buttercream rose from several candles on the living room mantle. Tufted white velvet couches sat across from one another, an antique coffee table between them.

"Would you like anything to drink?" Margaret asked as she moved down the hall. "Lemonade? Tea?"

"Warm tea sounds wonderful," I said, removing my jacket.

"Have a seat anywhere," she called back. "I'll return in a minute."

I settled on the closest couch, aware of how comfortable and inviting it was. On the mantle above the splendid fireplace a tiny golden birdcage rested among the candles. Across from me, on a buffet behind the opposite couch, was a ship constructed of coconuts. Shaved coconut shells formed the sails. I bent forward to analyze the details. It must have been very difficult, very time-consuming, to create.

"You're lucky," Margaret said at the threshold behind me. "I had just made a pot." She walked into the room, her blue skirt swinging free, and set a gold tray down holding sugar, cream, a variety of colorful tea packets, some napkins, and a steaming porcelain pot with a prairie scene depicted in blue.

I chose a packet of English breakfast tea, tore it open, and put the bag in my teacup. Margaret poured hot water over it.

"Thank you," I said.

She chose her own packet, dowsed it in steaming water, and set the pot down.

"So what is it that you want to talk to me about?"

"Straight to it, hm?" She winked.

I shrugged and waved my hands. "We can talk about *anything* you want to talk about. Believe me. I could listen to anything that doesn't have to do with…*well*…I mean, anything normal."

She laughed, and her white teeth beamed.

"You look so happy and healthy. It's so wonderful to see you feeling well."

She nodded and pressed her hands to the warm cup to take a sip.

"How *are* you feeling?" I asked.

"Well," she said, and she sighed. "That's something I wanted to talk to you about." She rested the cup on a knee. It trembled slightly, creating ripples in the liquid. She bit her bottom lip and looked at the corner of the room, lifting her hand and patting the air. "Everything was going fine," she said. "I felt so wonderful, so well. And I looked great. I mean, it was a miracle."

I tilted my head, troubled by her tone of voice, her use of past tense. "Right," I said, dragging the word out and giving it a lilt, asking her to continue.

"But…" She scratched her forehead. "Just a few days ago, I looked in the mirror, and…" She looked at her teacup and gripped it tightly.

"What?"

"My arm," she said. "The skin had gone white…again. Just as white as before."

I blinked. My heartbeat continued as though everything were fine, but my mind blanked. I checked her arms. The skin was the normal color. "You look fine."

She nodded. "I had visitors this morning. That's why I… Well, I'll show you."

She dipped one of the paper napkins into a cup of water and pressed it to her left arm. She rubbed. A creamy pink color transferred to the napkin, revealing white skin on her forearm.

My breath stopped. "No," I heard myself say.

She looked up at me apologetically.

"I…I didn't want to say anything to the doctors yet. I didn't want Lucient to get into trouble. It's just… The pills worked. They really did. But now I don't know. Maybe I haven't fully recovered."

Or maybe it came back. The thought slammed me, and I closed my eyes, suddenly dizzy again, and leaned back against the couch.

"I just…need another pill. I won't tell anyone. I'm so sorry to scare you, Jack."

An image of one tiny lump of godsoul remaining on the bleeding royal purple walls filled my mind. My muscles ached with unused adrenaline, my breath erratic. Vertigo made me gasp.

"Are you okay?" Margaret asked with concern.

I wiped burgeoning tears from my cheeks. I didn't want to betray what I was thinking, but at the same time, the need to hide any facts disintegrated. The need for *anything* disintegrated. I put my forehead in my hands.

"I'll be okay," Margaret reassured me. She smiled. "I will be. As soon as I get another pill."

I shivered, clenching my hands and thinking of Ven dressed all in red who had tried to halt me and Patrick.

Let it be known that I tried. I tried to stop it. So when the world does end, I can say at least I did what I could. And you were the cause of it, Ven had warned.

It was gone. All the godsoul was gone. And Margaret was not healed. Not permanently. That meant the others probably weren't either.

I forced myself to speak, to behave as normally as I could. "I'll have to get you some," I said, suppressing the trembling in my voice.

She nodded and smiled. "It's okay, Jack. I'm fine. Everything's fine." She laughed, rose from her seat, and came to hug me. "Lucient saved me once. It can save me again."

I hugged her back, suppressing a rising urge to scream. We released each other, and I nodded. "If you don't mind," I said, "I'd like to get right on this. Head to Lucient now."

"Of course," Margaret said. Her probing eyes searched mine. I tried to pretend everything was fine and that I felt better.

"Thank you for telling me."

She shrugged. "Who else would I tell?"

I walked past a few houses so Margaret wouldn't see me light a cigarette. I inhaled shakily and stood stock-still as I smoked. I finished the first cigarette and lit another. Then another. I couldn't do anything but stand and smoke.

My cell rang. I let it go, not moving to answer it. I felt as if I couldn't blink, couldn't focus my eyes, couldn't think. I kept repeating Margaret's revelation in my mind, observing her white skin.

My phone was silent for a few seconds and then rang again. It continued to ring as I stood on the sidewalk in the cool air, staring at the concrete in the space between two parked cars, beneath the shade of an oak tree. I looked up at the branches and listened to the birds tweeting, watched them hop from branch to branch.

My cell phone rang a third time. I blinked, in a daze, and reached into my pocket, retrieving my phone and pressing my thumb where I assumed the answer button was without looking. "Yeah."

A sigh on the other end of the line. "Jack, I got a call." Patrick. His voice sounded rough, cracked, like silk dragged through gravel. "I've got bad news."

I shrank, kneeling on the concrete. I swallowed without moisture.

"The cure isn't a cure," I said for him. All my energy evaporated.

"How the hell did you know that's what I was going to say?"

I took another drag. "Margaret Wilhelm invited me over, and we talked. She showed me her arm." I had to force the words out. "It's white. She's turning white again."

Patrick was quiet for several moments. I vaguely wondered at what he was doing. Was he staring at nothing like I was? "We don't have enough."

"No," I confirmed.

Patrick laughed. "I really thought... I thought we'd won. I don't understand how this happened."

When I swallowed, the saliva refused to go down. "So did I," I whispered. Then, remembering who I was speaking to, I rallied a little and chose my words carefully. "It's not your fault."

He laughed. "You expect me to believe that? I'm the fucking idiot who pushed for this. When you had your doubts, I pushed. Of all people, you know? I…I have to go."

I looked down at the phone. He'd ended the call.

"No," I said. I chucked the butt on the road. I stood and sent myself to Patrick. The concrete, the robin's-egg blue house, the picket fence, the cars on the street melded, a cyan color twisting among whites, grays, and greens. Black surrounded me, and I stood in the nothing. A familiar green carpet appeared, then golden drapes, a fireplace, a silver liquor cart, and a tall, thin man with licorice-twist red hair. The portrait on the left-hand side, above the silver liquor cart, was pushed aside, and Patrick was inputting a code into a safe. He caught sight of me.

"Jesus," he said. He bent over, slapped a hand to his chest, and straightened. "Don't fucking scare me like that."

"What did you think I was going to do?" I asked. I nodded toward the safe. "What's in there?"

He swallowed. "Doesn't matter." He tapped on the keypad. The safe beeped, a green light glowed, and he opened the black door. He grabbed a brown case, identical to the one that'd been in the glove compartment of his car the first time we met, pulled it free, and set it on his father's desk. "Something for the pain," he said. He withdrew a blue bottle and slid it toward me. It was, he said, the closest thing to laudanum his friend had produced.

"Patrick, don't."

"Why?"

"Your sobriety." It sounded stupid as soon as I said it. We were beyond the concerns of this world. We had descended to a new level of hell, and it was not in the Beretrum. It was here, in this hopeless situation, in the fact that a large majority of the population was going to die, the Builder's disease would continue to spread, empowering him, and there was no godsoul left.

His emerald eyes sent me daggers. "You're fucking nuts." He unscrewed the bottle, pressed it to his lips, and chugged until I jerked it from his hand. I threw the bottle at the window. The window exploded, and the bottle plummeted out of sight.

"What the *fuck*?" Patrick yelled. He charged toward me, stopping with his forehead nearly against mine.

"Why couldn't you have…why couldn't you have just…?" He waved at me with both hands, grimacing. "I never fucking *asked* for this, you know? I never wanted this, wanted to be this…this thing, this Guardian, or whatever the fuck it is. *You* brought this on *me*." He pointed at me. "*You* did this."

"I know," I acknowledged. "I did."

"And now I'm responsible for…for the fucking end of the world?" He pressed his hands to his eyes and shook his head. "No, I never asked for this."

"It's not your fault."

"But it is," he said, jerking his hands to his sides.

I didn't have time for this. I grabbed the bag from the desk and rushed toward the door. Patrick grabbed my free arm and spun me around. He jerked the bag from me. Syringes, a spoon, and bottles dropped to the carpet. "At least leave me a *little* solace." His face cracked into a sneer. "Maybe Ven was right. Maybe…maybe we *should* be locked up. If we had been, none of this would've happened."

I shook my head. I couldn't blame Patrick. I'd thought the same thing. "Maybe if a lot of things hadn't happened, this wouldn't have happened."

"That's how you're going to rationalize it?"

"*If I don't rationalize it, I don't work*," I yelled at him. My fury was like a loaded gun. The urge to hit him was powerful. "You know what?" I said, backing away. "You want to inject that shit, knock yourself out. I'm done being your babysitter. And this," I said, pointing to the mess on the floor, "isn't how I work. You get knocked down, you get back up. That's it. That's life."

"And how the hell are we supposed to get back up, Jack?"

I sighed, wordless, without an answer.

"That's right. You know as well as I do. We already took the final step." He ran his long fingers through his hair. "I suggest you join me. Because pain—pain is coming." He turned to the jumble on the floor and gathered every bit in his hands.

I shook my head. "You think you know pain?"

I turned away, opened the door, and stepped into the hall.

CHAPTER 23
INSANABILIS

Patrick

AFTER JACK LEFT, I INJECTED my body with every drug I had. I felt nothing. I lay on the plush living room carpet with the windows open. The cool air washed over me. I wished I felt something, anything, other than this stone-cold sobriety. I was locked into reality, and there was no getting out of it. Occasionally, I'd push myself off the floor and walk to the windows, stare into the lonely night.

"Fuck," I'd whisper randomly and then swig whiskey, which affected me as much as water. It was one thing to replace the Guardian when everything was going well; I could *help* others. It was another to be the Guardian and fail in every conceivable way, to lose the substance that could save the world, or at the very least keep it going. I'd dismantled the engine of reality.

I'd failed because, at heart, I was a user, a taker. Nothing in me could provide.

I dropped the whiskey bottle. The remaining dregs soaked the carpet. I grabbed my car keys and left for the garage. There, one of the Porsches awaited me. I drove along the road at a languid pace, no idea where I was going. I passed trees and street signs momentarily illuminated by the headlights. Insects hissed, audible through the open windows, and the air whipped through my hair, tickled my forehead.

The car was rarely used, and its still-new scent invited relishing. My heart, though, was like a stone and couldn't be moved. I passed the place where Ven had pulled the black tupelo trees down to block my escape. The red Maserati I'd once let Jack drive had been towed away. I left the skid marks behind and drove on into the night, feeling as though I were entering a void. Then I realized I was indeed going somewhere.

Twenty minutes later, I parked outside the New York Specialty Children's Hospital. More cars filled the parking lot than the previous time I'd visited. I locked the car. An ambulance with its lights swiveling reached the ER entrance. Individuals shouted above the sound of the engine. I walked over to the vehicle.

Paramedics opened the doors, and a gurney supporting a young child with short, white hair was tugged from the vehicle. Its wheels descended and locked in place on the driveway.

The gurney moved toward me. I made out the child's round face beneath an oxygen mask before the paramedics wheeled the gurney in. If anyone saw me, they said nothing about it. A woman climbed out of the ambulance and hurried behind the paramedics. I trailed them.

The hospital's interior was blinding and loud. Doctors circled the young child, pointing to a room across from the nearby nurses' station. They wheeled the child in and lifted him onto a hospital bed. Nurses and doctors snapped latex gloves on. A woman scribbled on the white board across from the boy in green Expo marker.

"Looks like the spiravirus," a bald, middle-aged doctor said. He used a word I'd never heard before for the illness. "I need two grams of Numenus."

"The supply hasn't been restocked yet," a nurse with short black hair replied, a fearful look in her eyes.

"Machine on the second floor still has some," a woman in green scrubs behind me said. "I'll go get it."

The woman who had climbed out of the ambulance brushed past me. She had dark red hair. She approached the hospital bed and gripped the railing.

"Ma'am, I'm going to have to ask you to step back. We don't yet understand how this thing spreads, and we don't need you to get infected," the bald doctor said.

"Sandra," I said. I spoke the name just as I recognized her. The woman turned. She looked at me, and her face brightened and cleared. She wiped her cheeks.

"Patrick! Oh, thank God." She grabbed my hand. Her palms were wet. Tears. "It's Hayden. He's infected again." Her eyes pleaded with me.

I stepped back without intending to, and my breath caught in my throat. My gaze passed from the boy, who'd once had red hair—reminding me of my own—that was now white, to the bald doctor standing beside him who seemed to suddenly recognize me, and then back to Sandra.

"I'm sorry," I said.

"It's okay. It's okay." She rubbed my arm. "Because they have Numenus here. I heard there are shortages—that Lucient can't keep up with the demand—but at least they have some here."

I nodded. I couldn't do anything else. My mind was blank, my mouth dry, my stomach hollow. In the background, a phone rang and alarms sounded at the nurses' station. The voice of a woman paging a doctor echoed in the hall, muffled and almost unintelligible. The paramedics relayed the boy's vital signs behind me. The filtered air and smell of antiseptic enveloped me.

"I'm afraid I'm going to have to ask you to leave," the doctor said again to Sandra. "You, too, Mr. Flannigan."

"I should be fine," I said quietly. "I've been taking Numenus regularly because I've been visiting hospitals for photos with the cured," I said. That wasn't true, but I wanted to see Hayden up close, to hold the hand of the boy who'd once been happy and healthy, to whisper words of kindness to him, whether or not he could hear them. "Could I have just a few minutes?" I asked. "I know him. He helped Lucient advertise Numenus just a little while ago."

The frowning doctor scrutinized each of us.

"It's okay," Sandra said. "I'll go. It's okay if Patrick stays with him for a few minutes."

The doctor pursed his lips. "Just a few."

As Sandra left, a new nurse entered and attached electrodes to the boy's chest. I stood near, my palms pressed together. Hayden looked tiny in the hospital bed. Without his red hair, he seemed like a different child entirely, which, considering how those with the virus behaved, he might as well be. I couldn't push my tears back. Several rolled down my face, and I wiped them with the back of my sleeve.

The doctor entered my peripheral vision, a peculiar look on his face.

"You must care a lot about him," he said.

"I do. About all of them."

The doctor crossed his arms and frowned. He spoke softly, probably to avoid being overheard. "Is any more Numenus coming?"

My pulse thrummed, and my hands went cold.

The doctor's eyes searched mine. "I ask," he said, "because no new orders by any hospitals anywhere that I'm aware of have been filled. And you look like hell right now. So just tell me, is any more Numenus on its way?"

The human part of me urged me to lie. What was the point, though? If everyone was going to die anyway, why bother? The doctor's eyes were serious, his expression earnest and genuine. I had nothing to hide from the world anymore.

"No," I admitted.

He winced. "I could see it on your face when you walked in." He pressed his hands to his temples and massaged them, his shoulders stiffening. "You've got to tell everyone. You've got to let the world know, so we can begin isolating new patients."

I ran my tongue across my front teeth and shook my head. "It's pointless."

"Why?"

"Because it turns out Numenus isn't a cure." Knowing it was one thing, saying it out loud another. My gut twisted.

The doctor opened his mouth to speak but sighed instead. His eyes searched the room before landing on Hayden. "Just make more."

"I don't know how to say it in a way you can understand, but that's impossible. What I, Lucient, used to make it…? There's no more."

The doctor blinked, waiting.

"Truly," I said. "I'm not lying."

He squeezed his eyes shut, shook his head. "Dear God," he whispered.

I swallowed. I wanted a cigarette, but I realized I wouldn't feel anything. I was barred from even that delicate high. I sighed, reached into my pocket, and retrieved the cigarettes from the pack I carried. I handed them to the doctor. "Here," I said. I rubbed my palm across my cheek.

He stared at the cigarettes, wrestling through the logical hurdles necessary to accept that information. "There's truly no more?"

I pictured the empty wall of gold, the spatter of gold plasma as Jack and I ground down the godsoul for the tablets. The floor and machines had looked like a golden crime scene. "No," I said. "It's all gone."

This new reality aged him. He opened his mouth to say something, stopped, turned away, and left the room. The nurse, oblivious to the exchange, followed, asking him where he was going. Hayden and I were alone.

I stood next to the boy's bed and pressed a palm to my forehead. His white hair was like strands of silk—beautiful, if not for the evil that created them. "I'm so sorry," I whispered. I repeated the phrase four or five times and wiped the tears that came. Part of me wanted to drop to my knees and pray for him, but I had no energy, and I'd already done too much to alter the boy's fate. It was better left to someone fit for the job.

Hayden's eyes opened. My stomach somersaulted. His irises and pupil were almost the same non-color as his skin.

He turned his head to me and smiled. "Guardian," he said. His childlike voice blended with something deeper, more resonant. "You will be one of the only ones left soon."

I stepped back, my heartbeat thunderous. I glanced behind me, hoping to see Sandra or the doctor or one of the nurses, but I was alone.

"Who are you?" I asked, turning back to the child.

"Has Jack not told you of me?" The boy grinned. His teeth and gums were as white as his skin.

"The Builder?"

Hayden nodded. "If you're willing to trade, I'll spare this boy for the last piece of untampered godsoul." His tone mocked, his smile wry.

My hands trembled, and I clenched them, willing them to stop. I wanted to run out of the room, but I couldn't bear the thought of turning my back on this creature. The way Jack had spoken of him, I wasn't sure how I was even alive in his presence.

"Is that a no?" Hayden asked.

I shook my head. "I suspect you don't know how to spare anyone."

Hayden blinked languidly. "It's only a matter of time, Patrick. Just a week, and the world will be mine. So will you."

Footsteps sounded behind me as a nurse entered.

"No!" I cried, trying to push her back. "It's not safe!"

"Sir!" she said as she sidestepped me, a cup in her hand. "Sir, what are you doing?"

I glanced back at Hayden and pointed. His eyes were closed.

I opened my mouth to tell the nurse he wasn't the boy, that something else was inside him, but the knowledge of how ridiculous it would sound tolled like a warning bell. I nodded. "Sorry. I'll leave. I'll leave. Just…give him the Numenus."

I turned from the nurse's wide eyes, her gaping mouth, and left.

I exited the hospital and drove back to my father's house, the image of Hayden possessed by the Builder on rerun in my head the entire trip. I shivered, coated in cold sweat that soaked my clothes. The chills from seeing the boy so perverted deepened the hollow sensation in my stomach. I felt as though a void had opened, was swallowing me whole.

When I got back to the house, swollen with the full understanding of the impossibility of my situation and the world's fate, I couldn't stand being alone there. I was responsible for Hayden, I was responsible for the downfall of the world. I had risked and lost the godsoul—the substance required to blockade the Builder—because I wouldn't allow the infected to be thrown into the Beretrum. Ven had been right, and I should have listened to him. Instead, I'd lost everything.

I went upstairs, chose one of my father's ties, and wrapped it around my hand. I pictured tying it around my neck, slipping the ends through the upper door jamb, slamming the door. I imagined tightening the makeshift noose, letting my legs relax, and allowing gravity to do its work.

I considered my Catholic lessons as I wound the green and gold tie over my hand—suicide would send me to hell. But hell had come to Earth. I'd brought it here.

I looked at the clock. How many minutes would it take to finish me? Ten? At least. I considered that I'd recently injected myself with every possible drug—amounts that would have killed another person—and felt nothing. I didn't need to try suicide to know it wouldn't work. I'd already attempted it in several ways and failed.

I leaned my forehead against the door and cried, sobs shaking my torso, consuming me. When I regained enough control to open my father's bedroom door, I stepped into the hallway. I wandered through the upstairs like it was a foreign land until I stood next to a door I hadn't opened in years. In the dark hallway, I gripped the knob, turned it, and pushed open the door.

A clean and empty room with pale pink carpet came into view. To my right stood a four-poster bed. At each of the posts, white curtains were attached. A white comforter and pillows ornamented the bed. Nightstands with detailed carvings of fairy tales sat on either side. Identical glass lamps, roses and carnations painted on them, rested in the center of the nightstands.

In front of me, two windows stretched tall, decorated with similar curtains as those on the bed. The moon was full and illuminated the room. Centered between the two windows stood a tall oak dresser. I could smell it, recalled how it infused clothing with its scent. To my left was a coffee table with a tufted cream cushion top and two plush lounge chairs across from it.

An image of my mother filled my mind. I longed for her. I longed for death to take me to her. It couldn't now, and never would. If I'd had an accidental overdose a year ago, I would have been able to join her. Now, that was no longer possible. Sobriety had not been the answer I thought it was.

I walked inside and pulled one of the chairs away from the table and placed it across from the door that led to the bathroom. Inside that bathroom, more than a decade before, I'd discovered my mother, her throat slit, in the bathtub.

Pressing the heels of my hands to my eyes, I tried to block the memory of so much red. Red on my mother, red in the tub, red on the floor, red on the walls and shower curtain. It reminded me of all the red when I'd killed the Guardian—red on the stone floor, on the gold wall, splattered across the island. Why had my father remained in the house all these years? Why had Jack come to me for help?

"Mama," I said, and the word returned me to myself, got me out of my head. "Mama, I'm so sorry. My entire life, I just wanted to be with you again. But now…now I wonder if it's for the best that you aren't here, that you can't see what I've done. It might kill you." Tears streamed down my face. I shook my head. "I wrecked my body with drugs the past four years. I've never learned how to take care of myself. I killed the Guardian of what's left of God. And I used up all His remaining pieces. I've doomed us. I've doomed…them. I'll be all that's left, since it seems nothing will kill me."

I looked up at the ceiling. "And I can't get rid of me. The Builder will find me eventually, and then I'll be in an even worse hell than I was before. A hell where it's just me and the Devil. Your Catholic son. Can you imagine? Why didn't your religion prepare me for this?"

I stared into the pitch-black bathroom. The darkness seemed to be open to me, receptive to what I had to say, as though it opened to a portal beyond, and in that portal was my mother.

"I guess," I said, my heartbeat slowing, "if I can't kill my body…and if I can't be with you…and I can't fix any of this…then I'll learn to let go." I swallowed, and my eyes stopped making tears. My shoulders and my hands relaxed. "Entirely."

CHAPTER 24
AEGER

Jack

HOPELESSNESS HIT ME, AND I paused, pressing my fingers to my eyes, wondering what I should do. Patrick was right. We'd fucked up, and I didn't know how to fix it. A memory of Lutin came to mind. His regal yet rebellious air, his smell. I wished I could speak to him. But I didn't have Lutin because I hadn't made a deal with the Builder. For all I knew, too much time had passed, and Lutin was dead.

I tried to squelch the tears that came to my eyes and urged myself to think, to choose something and move toward it as quickly as possible, lest I lose momentum.

Ven. Ven, who had gone to Lucient to try and stop us. Ven, who'd tried to lock us up. Ven, who'd killed Jasper. I knew where he probably was, or where he might be.

I wiped my eyes and translocated to Purdom, to Roth's office. The building was empty, doors locked, the office pitch black. I flicked on the lights. The once-buzzing space, where over a hundred men and I had once congregated to bring Infinitum down, was now stark. I turned to the elevator behind me. I slid my knife across my palm and framed the elevator door with my blood, then pressed my hand to its left side, over the elevator's heart. "*Patefecio carcerem in perpetuum.*" A wavering light shone from between the doors down low, at the floor. When I pressed the elevator button, the silver doors opened. A dusty walkway between multiple cells appeared. I entered, and the doors closed behind me, sealing me in.

I walked between the empty cells, eyeing the candles in sconces on the walls, the musty red brick, curious why this place—despite the presence of ferrics, who healed everything about them—was so unclean, so dank. Perhaps because it was built to be? Perhaps because Ven was destined for the Beretrum?

A wave of dizziness rushed me, and I clung to a jail cell bar. I suppressed the rolling nausea, urged it to leave me alone. I had to find Ven. I would rest later. My body, to my surprise, listened. The vertigo disappeared. I straightened my shoulders and took a deep breath.

I gazed around the jail cells, noting the familiar torches at each column, the door to the red room where Patrick and I had been captive. As I recalled the ferric named Hux injecting contaminated blood into Patrick, adrenaline and anger arrived, making my muscles ache.

At the end of the hall, Ven lay slumped on the floor, his head against the wall. I hadn't noticed him in the dark, hadn't heard anything. Had he noticed me? I rushed there and stopped at his side. He didn't move. I knelt and pressed a hand to his arm. "Ven," I said. I shook his shoulder. I looked behind me—was anyone here? But apparently we were alone.

"Ven, wake up. What happened?"

Ven's head rolled back. He grimaced and pressed a hand to the back of his skull, where it had been mashed against the wall. He zeroed in on me. "You," he said. He sighed, dragged his hips closer to the wall, and leaned against it, staring up at me deadpan. "What do you want?"

"What happened?" I asked. "I came…I came to ask for help. You were right. We shouldn't have used the godsoul. It doesn't help permanently. It has to be reapplied, and reapplied. We don't have enough, and…"

It didn't seem as though Ven was absorbing anything I said. His expression remained static. He was like a wall against which all my words died.

"What?"

"You don't know?" he whispered.

I shook my head. "Know what?"

Ven shifted again, bowing his head deeply. He pushed his black hair out of his eyes and shifted to try and remove his red jacket, grimacing. He freed one arm, then the other. The crimson trench coat fell to the ground, exposing the red shirt beneath it. He pulled his left sleeve up.

White strands snaked between the vibrant fire stripes in his flesh and the flesh itself, areas that seemed bleached. They curled around the back of his hand, his palm, and toward his elbow.

My knees threatened to buckle. All my energy, spitfire, momentum evaporated. I swiveled toward the closest cell door, hung onto the bars, and pressed my forehead there.

"Every ferric who came in contact with anyone your brother infected is also infected. And every ferric who came into contact with those ferrics is also infected."

"No," I whispered.

"We're all going to hell, Jack," he said. "The whole damned lot of us. You and I are not as alone anymore."

I couldn't look at him, couldn't look at the white of hell intertwined with his fire. "I'm…sorry."

"There's no more sorry," he said, sounding old, weathered.

I pulled myself upright and began to walk away. I had to get out of there, away from him, away from everything that'd happened. I gasped for air in the stale pit of the hall. "I'll be back," I said, unable to stand the idea of completely abandoning him as he lay there, clearly dying.

"There's no more coming back."

I burst out of the elevator into Roth's office. I pressed my hands to my face, the world spinning around me. The elevator door behind me shut, and the ethereal light shining beneath the elevator doors disappeared.

I sank to the floor, breathless. The ferrics had caught the disease. There was no way out now, no *back* or *sorry* or *redo*. All of humanity had been painted into a corner.

Tears dropped onto the backs of my hands. I noticed them, and then I tilted my head and sat back on my feet, holding my hands up to the light.

"Shit."

CHAPTER 25
MEDITOR

Jack

I urged myself somewhere out in the vast world, bright, close to the sun, where no people or ferrics could be found, to be alone. The room disappeared, replaced by blackness. When the world filled out around me, I found I'd translocated to the mountains.

Below, vast valleys and mountain ranges stretched. The only sound was the moving air, and it was cold and delicious. Above me, the sun shined down with heat, but clouds were moving in, and soon the sky would be overcast. In the distance, clouds swirled, dark and thick, rolling soundlessly closer, like a monster creeping in.

I examined my hands. In the bright sun, it was even clearer that they were splotched with white. The white interlaced with the fire strikes on my arms crept up beneath my sleeves.

The dizzy spells, the vertigo—they weren't from being overwhelmed or panicking about defeating the Builder. I was sick. The thing my brother had unleashed in the world had infected not just Margaret or Ven or the other ferrics, but me. Perhaps this was the end, the last of my moments. Even if I took godsoul, eventually, I'd be sick again.

Letting my hands drop to my side, I gazed out across the vast wilderness, empty of all feeling. Tears stung my eyes. "Creator," I said with barely any emotion. "Whoever you are. Please help me."

The silence was as vast as the scene before me.

"I know I belong to the Beretrum." I stared down at my white hands. "But I thought I could find a way out. I thought I'd be able to help people, be able to help Patrick. Instead, we used up what was left of the godsoul, and now we're all going to die." I winced and pressed my fingers to my eyes. I looked up into the darkening sky and felt tears on my face. "Do you care?"

Quiet.

Rain began to fall, though the sun still shone on me. It tapped on my clothes and on my splotchy white hands.

"Tell me what to do," I said, "and I will do it. I've always been good at that. I have…drive. I can get things done. I just…" I sighed and slumped forward, unable to continue.

I sat on the edge of the cliff and looked down at the drop below me. I closed my eyes and cracked my neck. "I was doomed from the beginning. And, stupid me, I thought I could still win. But it never lets up, does it? It just seems like it does for a while."

I thought about what Cyrus had said—that meditation felt like God to him. I didn't know how to meditate. It had something to do with clearing the mind. Maybe I could try?

The opposite of language was vision. I decided to rid my mind of language by focusing on images. I let an image come to mind. I didn't specify an image, but what arrived was a peacock. It stretched its feathers, which changed colors, and then the peacock turned into a pot of flowers. The flowers turned into a balloon, the balloon into a golden pyramid, and so on. I let the images shift at their will, and I demanded nothing. Each time I began to think, I brought myself back to the images and let them take precedence. The transitions of the images didn't make sense. I began to feel the literal, the linear, the reality that I normally encountered, disappear around me, replaced by the illogical.

The hum in my mind decreased. Fewer thoughts came to me, and when they did, it wasn't so difficult to free them. At least until they started asking, "What's the point of this? You've lost. Give up." Still, I returned to the images, ignoring everything but them. A lantern shifted into a thimble that shifted into a shoe.

My breathing became shallow, except for a few deep breaths here and there. I lost track of what my body felt like, could not remember how I'd positioned myself, what clothes I was wearing. Images shifted in my mind until I felt on the verge of sleep.

I wanted to force an answer to come to me, but this was no longer about will. This was about letting go and letting whatever was to come, come, to bring me whatever it wanted to bring. An umbrella turned into a cat, which turned into a candelabra. No rhyme or reason was attached to any of the shifts. My mind unlocked from the rational, and I sat in the in-between, detached from time, space, and reality.

The image shifted again, this time to a gramophone on a sea of white, then to the last of the godsoul of Patrick's lair, and finally to a bright red velvet box. A thought arrived, as though something within me had been working out the problem and discovered a solution. I opened my eyes, looking down on the scene below, more a part of myself than I'd been before.

You have a deal to make.

You can bring back anything, and it is yours.

"Oh," I whispered, as though the thought had come from a part of me—when I'd gotten out of my own way—that had known a solution all along. "That's true."

On the coattails of this realization, something else struck me—the Builder might have planned all this. If he knew Patrick was in charge of the godsoul, that he and I were at odds with the ferrics, he may have designed a disease none of us could kill, knowing that we would dwindle our resources down to nothing attempting to fight it. Well, not quite nothing. But nearly so.

There was still the possibility of a deal with the Builder, and there was still the possibility of killing him. I'd so been distracted from my original plan by the disease Alex spread that I hadn't considered that. But a part of me, deep beneath the conscious part of me, had been doing so.

I pressed my hands to the cold rock, pushed myself up, and scooted away from the edge of the cliff. I got to my feet and wiped my hands against my pant legs. Rain soaked me. It cleansed the air and livened everything around me. The smell of petrichor brought me fully awake.

If I hadn't chased after Alex's disease, trying to clean it up, had kept my sights on what was important, I might have been able to forge a different outcome.

I straightened my coat and willed myself back to Purdom, taking one last look at the vast beauty that surrounded me before it all melted to black. Once again within the confines of Roth's office, I redrew the lines around the elevator door and whispered the necessary words to take me back to the jail. The doors opened, and I entered the hallway. Ven was still passed out at the end of it, his hair bleaching to white.

Stepping into the last cell—the one where Patrick and I'd been kept—I looked into the mirror with its elaborate oval frame hanging on the wall beyond the bars.

My mind hearkened back to being in the Beretrum with the Builder, how he'd told me he knew what went on in the depths of Domum's prison, as he could witness it all through a mirror. As soon as I'd seen this mirror, when Patrick and I were dragged into the prison, I knew it had to be it.

"Are you there?" I asked my reflection. "I'm ready to make a deal."

I watched my image, waiting for it to speak. Lines were etched at the corners of my eyes. My lips were pale, my black hair sprinkled with white strands. I needed Numenus. And soon.

Behind me, Patrick came into view, his brilliant red hair and emerald eyes. I knew it wasn't him, but I turned and checked, just to make sure there was no one behind me. I returned to the reflection.

"You're not looking so well, Jack," Patrick said, dead pan, emerald eyes unblinking.

Something painful pierced my chest, and I remembered Roland's cross. I took it off and found that it now glowed hot orange. I held the necklace by its chain at my side.

"Do you want the godsoul or not?"

He smirked and gazed at his cuticles. "Why should I believe there's any left?"

"There is," I said. "I swear it. And I'll bring it to you. But I want to be healed, I want Lutin healed, and I want safe passage to another world for the both of us."

The Builder in Patrick's form tilted his head. "Do you *really*?"

"Yes," I said. A wave of vertigo hit me, but I forced it down. "Twenty pounds of godsoul is left. I'll bring it to you."

At the mention of godsoul, the Builder's eyes narrowed and hardened. Patrick's green eyes lightened to a barely perceptible mint green. His red hair blanched to faded pink. "Where?"

I swallowed. "Cyrus's house."

"We have a deal, then?"

I nodded.

Patrick walked forward to the edge of the mirror. He reached a hand through, and as it passed through the glass, the arm became pure white, plastic-like, as though belonging to a mannequin. The fingers were barely delineated.

"Let's shake on it, then," he said, his voice no longer sounding like Patrick's. The fire of hell was all but visible behind his eyes. His hair ruffled in a sudden wind, like flames.

I shivered, hiding my reaction the best I could.

I looked at the hand and then at the Builder in the mirror. "I'll meet you in twenty-four hours at Cyrus's mansion," I said. "You bring Lutin. I'll have the godsoul."

The Builder retracted his hand, and as it slipped past the glass, it returned to the color of Patrick's skin.

"Do not lie to me," he said.

"Never."

He nodded once.

I blinked, and the mirror returned to normal. I was alone in the reflection.

Down the hall, Ven's eyes were open, staring at me.

"What are you doing?" he said, barely audible. His eyes closed and opened, barely.

"Fixing it," I said.

"Oh? You think so? You think the Guardian will give the only remaining source of godsoul, after all this?" Ven chuckled softly. "Not if he's learned his lesson."

Ven had a point, but it wasn't a point I hadn't already considered. "I'm well aware. But I know him better than you do."

"What does that mean?" Ven asked.

"He just needs the right person to ask," I said.

I left the Vinclum.

CHAPTER 26
OBLATIO

Jack

I EXITED THE JAIL THROUGH the elevator doors and stared at Roth's office. My mind wandered, trolling through the world, picturing the place I wanted to go, the place I needed to go.

I imagined the swaying trees, the leaves blown across the grass, the large fence, and the gap Patrick had snipped, the way the dirt smelled, the tombstones, the large angel peering down upon a grave where Patrick and I had once sat.

Roth's office swirled around me, mixing like paint on the surface of waves. The light slowly diffused to blackness, and in that blackness, a tombstone entered. Beneath it, grass appeared. Above the grass and behind the angel were only the sky and a few stars. The smell of moist earth met me, sweet and thick. The vase beside the angel was filled with dead roses. I stood in Galloway Cemetery.

Rows upon rows of tombstones stretched out across the area. Not too far from here, I'd resurrected a man in one of the graves with the help of Jonathon Roth's league of murderous employees. Thinking of that moment, how I'd tried to dig the grave on my own and nearly collapsed of exhaustion, how Jasper had arrived at the edge of where I sat, helped me out, and proceeded with several others to finish my job for me, I felt nostalgic. I didn't know why. There was nothing wonderful about the memory. The smell of McFadden's corpse when they opened the tomb had been terrible. Shortly after that, one of Roth's men had killed me. When I was dead, I'd seen a vision of the Builder, overwhelmed by both terror and the hope of destroying him. Still, for some reason, I felt nostalgia. Simpler times.

I stared at the stone angel, the words *Deirdre Flannigan* on the tomb. Patrick's mother—she had been murdered when he was nine, and he'd been the one to find her. When he first brought me to the tomb, I had resurrected the roses in the vase.

This was something I should have done long ago.

But if I had, I would've lost a very important play.

My power filtered out of me, down into the earth, seeking the sensation of a corpse. Finally, it connected. My power floated over the body, feeling out the contours. I sensed its desire for reanimation.

That was new.

It wasn't only that I felt my own desire for life to return, or that I felt the ability to reignite life, the gap in the corpse awaiting my little spark, but rather a magnetism. The corpse was drawn to me.

We seemed entwined. I was supposed to bring it life, and it was supposed to accept.

I took a few steps back and lifted a hand, gesturing toward the dirt in front of me. A crevice broke in the soil ahead of my feet and traveled to the tombstone. As if the earth could not withstand the invisible strands of magnetism, the dirt surrounding the crevice tumbled up and away from me, dividing the soil even deeper, until, within seconds, the dividing line carved itself down six feet to the tomb. More dirt parted, revealing the burial vault, soil piled on either side.

My power lifted the lid, and the vault opened like a book, the cover resting against the dirt on the left. Within was a coffin with shriveled flowers on top. Color returned to them, and they brightened, plump. The coffin shivered, and then the top opened to rest against the burial vault's lid. Inside, a rotted corpse lay in a blue silk dress, the hands on its chest wrapped around a bouquet of flowers. The tips of the flowers shifted white, revealing roses. Their fragrant scent wafted up, along with the smell of the corpse.

The skin of the corpse paled, softened, returned to what should have been. The passion that surged through me willed it before I thought to. Soon, the corpse was no longer a corpse but a beautiful, red-haired woman with dark pink lips, cat eyes, and a pointed chin. Her hair ran down her shoulders in waves, and its color—neither quite orange or red—reminded me of Patrick's.

I carefully hopped down, landing beside the coffin to squat near the woman.

Roth's words came to me, the ones he'd said right before he killed Bryan Flannigan—he had called me *efficient*. Truly, I was. I was becoming even more so.

I scanned the curvature of the woman's nose, the lines at her eyes, her small frame, her ears. "Waken," I whispered, and I willed the power within me that felt like carbonation flowing down into her.

She gasped, her chest rising. Her emerald eyes opened and darted wildly. She clutched my arm, as though I'd electrocuted her. Her grip was hard, and her nails bit into the fabric of my shirt.

"You're okay," I assured her. "You're okay." I ran a palm through her hair, as though she were a child.

"Where am I?" she asked, sitting up, looking around.

"You're in your grave. In Galloway Cemetery. In New York City."

She turned to me, her eyes wilder.

"But you are not dead. Not dead, not hurt, not hurting, not dying. You are safe. I have you, and I will always protect you."

Her red eyebrows furrowed, and she crawled atop the coffin, as far from me as she could get.

"Who *are* you?"

I took a deep breath. "The simple answer? A friend of your son's."

"Patrick," she whispered, and she trembled.

I nodded. "The more complicated answer is that I'm what is known as a ferric. I can resurrect the dead."

"A fairy?" she said, looking me up and down.

I bit the inside of a cheek to stop from smiling. I shook my head. "No. Though I'm sure there must some correlation between your legends and what I am. But I'm a ferric."

"What have you done with my son?"

"Nothing," I said. "We're simply friends."

She sighed and looked at her hand with wonder as she flexed it. "Am I really alive?"

"You are."

She seemed small and vulnerable, and I dared not touch her.

"How long was I dead?"

I thought about that and answered, "Eleven years."

"Lord." She pressed a thumb to her bottom lip. "And why'd you bring me back?"

I thought about all that'd come to pass—the creation and failure of Numenus, the abundance of godsoul drained to nothing. "We are...at the end of the world, in a way. And your son needs you."

She tilted her head. "The end of the world?"

I nodded.

"Why bring me back if it's the end?"

What a question. I looked up at the stars, weighing my words carefully. "Things aren't as they were. Your son..." No. I restarted. "I wasn't always what I am now. I was human, like you. And Patrick isn't what he used to be. He is more now. In fact, he is precious, far more precious, I think, than any other creature on this earth. But he hasn't realized that. And I don't have enough time to wait for him to realize it."

"What is he?"

"He guards what remains of the Creator," I said. "We call it godsoul."

Her eyes searched mine, and she rubbed her upper arms, as though she were cold. "But he's only nine..." She paused, realizing that might not be true. "You said I've been here eleven years. So...he's twenty?"

I nodded.

"How did he...how did all of this happen? This can't be true. At all. This isn't the same world. I've woken up in a different one."

"Every moment is a different world. Every minute is a different universe, though we can't understand that until we're many universes down the line."

She stared at me incredulously, her mouth open.

I was also surprised by my words. "That's what I've learned, anyway."

She shook her head. "I still don't understand. Why did you bring me back?"

This was the moment when I'd learn if Deirdre would willingly help me or if I would have to force her. "I need what's left of God. I need the rest of the godsoul."

She shook her head back and forth. I worried she wasn't going to respond. She leaned against the burial vault propped up on its side.

"And Patrick won't give it to you?"

"I haven't yet asked. It was important to bring you back first. So you could…sway him. We had a falling out, and I don't have enough time to rebuild trust. I'm hoping you can serve in lieu of that. He loves you, Deirdre. He talks about you all the time. He is more connected to you than you could ever understand."

She stared at me with familiar emerald eyes. "What's your name?" she whispered.

"Jack."

"Jack. And you're going to do good things with this…this godsoul?"

I lifted my chin. "I'm going to try to save this world. One. Last. Time."

She swallowed. "Do you swear?"

"I swear."

"What will happen if you don't succeed? How will the world end?"

"The creature responsible for all evil will take over this world. His disease has already infected it. We will succumb. We will run out of godsoul, and we will all die."

"The devil?"

I took a deep breath. *Sure. Why not?* To a Catholic, that would make an impact. "Yes."

She rose and brushed herself, looking at the surrounding dirt walls. "He always was a stubborn child," she sighed.

Her words flooded me with relief. "He's just as stubborn now," I said.

I interlaced my hands and gestured toward Deirdre. She placed a foot in that cradle, and I lifted her up and down, building momentum. She pushed hard on the third rise, and I lifted her. She caught the top of the grave and stuck her toes in the dirt wall to slowly climb her way out. She stood there, staring out across the headstones, a thrilled look on her face. She looked down at me, smiled, and then kneeled at the edge, reaching down.

I didn't need her assistance. I leaped from one end of the grave to the other, jumped up the side wall, rebounded on the one across from it, and landed on my knees on the grass.

Deirdre gaped. She appeared both disheveled and proper in her blue silk dress and white shoes crusted with dirt. She pulled the high heels off and dropped them into the coffin, *clunk, clunk*. She removed her earrings and dropped them in as well.

"What about my husband?" she asked.

I nearly stumbled over my words. "He passed away a few months ago."

She blinked at me, considering that development. She did not seem to be suffering over the news. She put a hand on her hip. "Are you going to bring him back too?"

"There's no time, and we don't know where the body is." That could qualify as an excuse. She knew so little about me.

She pursed her lips. A soft wind brushed her, drifting her hair across her face. She pushed it back. "Did you do it?"

"What?"

"Is he dead because of you?"

"No."

An energy vibrated between us, two notes out of harmony. I felt it in the air and wondered if she felt it too.

"There are worse crimes, if you had," she said. She moved down the hill, pointing. "This way, I'm guessing."

I watched her for a moment before I jogged to catch up with her.

CHAPTER 27
QUID PRO QUO

Jack

When I caught up with her, I said, "No need for walking. I can take us straight to him."

Deirdre placed a hand on her chest. "Oh. Of course. You're...not human."

I nodded, attempting not to laugh. "I can translocate the both of us."

She tilted her head and raised her eyebrows questioningly.

"I can use my power to take us there."

She took a few steps back. "I'd much rather drive. No offense. I just...I don't know about that."

"It's not painful. I promise." I extended a hand. "Besides, I didn't bring a car."

Slowly, frowning, she slipped her hand in mine. I willed us to Bryan Flannigan's home, and the world around us disintegrated. We stood on black. Deirdre's grip tightened. Her eyes reflected the darkness. A mailbox appeared to our left, a circular drive, a large cream and white mansion, a fountain, trees. She gaped at the house.

Deirdre quickly ran her hands through her hair. Her short red curls bloomed and thickened.

"What's he like, now? Patrick."

I gave her a side glance, and then considered what I should say, what a mother would want to hear.

She laughed nervously. "That pause can't be good."

"I just don't know if you're ready to hear it."

"I can take it."

I sighed. "He's troubled."

"How?"

"Addicted to drugs and alcohol." I glanced at her. She revealed no sign of what she was thinking. "The memory of you, though, makes him feel guilty about that."

"Hmph," she said. "He's about to feel really guilty."

I smiled and recalled the first time Patrick and I met, when he'd been so erratic and crazy. We both had. Patrick always smelled like alcohol and cologne. His clothes were always new and fresh. And yet there was something toxic about him. I could sense it, beneath all the layers of wealth—the rot. I was drawn to it. Perhaps because I, too, was rotten. Or perhaps because half of me desired to renew rotten things. Potential came from carving out rot. The more rotten, the more potential.

Out of the corner of my eye, I caught Deirdre staring at me. "What?"

"You love him."

I shook my head and turned to the house. I chuckled. "Why would you say that?"

"The look on your face just then. You softened."

"Ah. That." I bit my cheek. "It's a consistent fault of mine."

We started toward the door, our footsteps clacking on the concrete path. "Your son," I added, "despite the drugs, is a good man. He can be. He will be." My hands clenched into fists. "He has to be."

We arrived at the front door. Deirdre was pale as she stared at the doorknob.

"What?"

Her large emerald eyes distanced. It wasn't a tiny fear, but a large one—one that could stop a person in her tracks. I wondered what could cause such dread. The answer hit me before she could explain.

She'd been murdered here. This was the location of the crime.

"You *died* here?" I said. I stared up at the house. "What? That doesn't make sense. Why the hell would Flannigan have stayed in that house? Kept Patrick in that house?"

Deirdre wrapped both arms around her small frame. She didn't reply. Her right hand moved toward the door, and she turned the knob. To my surprise, the door was open. She slipped inside and I followed her into the dark entryway.

"Patrick!" I called.

No response.

I took a deep breath and eyed both hallways—one leading to the living room, one to the kitchen. "Stay here," I said. I went to the kitchen first and called for Patrick. I walked to the dark living room and said his name. Nothing. I eyed the interior of the room, searching for a human form.

I returned to the entryway and climbed the stairs leading up to the balcony and, beyond that, Flannigan's office. No lights were on upstairs either. I proceeded down the carpeted hall to Flannigan's office door. I opened it and peered inside.

"Patrick?"

All was still and silent. A fire crackled in the fireplace, but Patrick was nowhere to be found.

I sighed and left the room. I scanned the hall and saw a cracked door. I found myself at the threshold and pushed the door open.

A four-poster bed appeared at the right, white curtains latched to each post. The bed was dressed in a white comforter and pillows. On either side of the headboard stood intricately carved tables with glass lamps. The glass shades that surrounded each bulb were painted with roses and carnations.

Across from the bed, two windows looked out onto the night. The moon cast beams onto the light carpet. A tall dresser stood between the two windows, its color indistinguishable in the dark. To the left of the dresser were a table and two chairs. It looked like a woman's room.

In one of the chairs, Patrick sat in profile. My heart jumped when I noticed him.

He faced left, toward a door that opened to a bathroom.

I shivered in the doorway. "Patrick, what are you doing?"

He didn't respond, but his right hand lifted a bottle of brown liquid to his lips, and he drank. As my eyes adjusted to the dim light, I saw that Patrick's empty eyes were framed by lines that dipped deep into his face. "Turns out, the drugs don't work. Nothing works. I can't even…cut myself. I can't bleed anymore."

I took a deep breath, released it slowly. "I'm sorry," I said.

Patrick turned to me. "There's no more sorry."

His words echoed Ven's. Everywhere I went, everyone I talked to, said it was the end of the world. All the doors to all the possible rooms were closing.

"I found her in there, you know?" he said, nodding toward the bathroom.

I looked where he gestured.

"That's where she was murdered." He grimaced and released a silent cry through his open mouth. Tears streamed down his cheeks.

"Patrick, I have something I need to tell you."

His gaze slipped to the floor. He swiped his cheek with the inside of his arm. "I'm tired, Jack. What do you want?"

"To make an amends."

He shrugged. "What for?"

I noticed Deirdre at the edge of the staircase out of the corner of my eye. I lifted my hand just slightly, warning her to stop. She did.

I took a deep breath. If I brought Deirdre to him right then, it might not go over as well as I was hoping. He would recognize her presence for what it was—an attempt at manipulation. Her return needed to seem heartfelt, more than motivation for him to retrieve the substance I needed.

I closed my eyes and stepped into the room. I opened myself to all the terrible things I normally suppressed and brought them into the moonlight. "I've caused you so much pain," I said. "For one, I'm the reason your father is dead."

Patrick stared at me.

I nodded, simply because my body seemed to require movement. "I allied myself with Jonathon Roth, and we set a trap for Alex. I didn't expect your father to arrive the same night that we were supposed to stop my brother, but he did. Roth killed him. I'm sorry. I lied to you before."

Patrick's stare was icy. His tears stopped.

"That's not all," I whispered. "Roth was also responsible for bombing Lucient. I told him where the *arca* was that turned the paint white, and he destroyed it. And…" I said, sighing, "I retrieved the money from the chimney…and your mother's rosary. I gave you the mended rosary to manipulate you so that I could see the *arca* waiting in Lucient. Also, the first time I met you…"

Tears came to my eyes. I willed them back down. A torrent of emotion roiled inside me, very much like the power to resurrect, and my stomach and heart felt like they would be crushed if I said what I was about to say.

"What?" Patrick said.

"I planned to kill you. Then take your money and resurrect you. Hell," I said, laughing through the tears because I couldn't believe that I was saying it, "maybe I should have. Because then I could have convinced you that I forced you to harvest the godsoul, that it wasn't your fault. It was mine. And maybe you wouldn't have suffered that pain and guilt." Emotions whirled inside me, more than ever before, as though they had always been there but I'd never freed them. I felt like another person entirely; I was foreign to myself.

Patrick sighed and slid a hand through his hair. "Fuck, Jack," he said. His voice sounded hopeless. He took several swigs of alcohol, alcohol he said didn't work. His eyes slid to the wall, and he stared. "What stopped you from killing me?"

I shook my head, searching for reasons and finding very little. "I just didn't."

"*Why?*" he demanded.

"Good God, I don't know," I said. "It was the apple, I think. The fucking white apple that your friend brought over."

Patrick scoffed and stared at me. "Saved by fruit?" He rose from his seat and set the bottle down on the seat. He tugged his fingers through his hair. "I need more than alcohol. I need…I need…release from *all* of this."

He headed toward the door. Quickly, I shut it behind me, barring him from leaving.

He pointed a finger at me. "*You* don't get to decide what I do," he yelled.

I shook my head. "I'm tired of you always trying to destroy yourself. I'm sick of it."

"You were going to *kill me!*" he snarled, throwing his hands wide. "What the fuck do you care what I do?"

"You have to understand what death is to me. It's temporary. It's always been. It was the way I was raised and the way I grew. If I'd killed you, I would have brought you back. But you…when you hurt yourself, it's permanent. That's worse."

Patrick rolled his eyes. "That's bullshit. All of this is. You only care about yourself."

"And you."

"Only insofar as I am a part of you. But me?" He hit his chest. "You don't give a shit about me, the *real* me." He reached for the door, and I shoved his hand away, pushed him back hard. He wobbled before he rushed at me and slammed his hand against the door. I pushed him back again, harder. He stumbled back into the chair, which tipped to the floor, spilling the contents of the bottle across the carpet.

He swung a fist at me. I automatically lifted my hands, swiping his fist with my left hand so his wrist landed in my right. Holding his hand tight, I put my left forearm on the back of that arm, forcing him to bend forward. I twisted his arm so that he could not stand up without pain.

"You're right to question whether I care," I said, "but I do."

"Let me go."

"Shut up and listen to me. From one terrible person to another, I give a shit about you. I do. I'm sorry I fucked up your life. If you want me to bring your father back, I will. If you want me to leave you alone, I will. But no more of these downward spirals. You are beyond this, and I won't watch you do it anymore."

"Yeah, because I can get you your godsoul, right?"

My jaw dropped and my hands nearly released him.

"Thought you were a step ahead, did you?"

I let go of him and pushed him back. He stumbled into the footboard of the bed, nearly falling back on it.

"You've got one more trick up your sleeve, don't you, to try to save us? And you need godsoul for it, which means you need me."

I bit my bottom lip, thinking quickly, feeling for an answer that was authentic and true. "*No*," I said. "Because you *are* godsoul."

He stared at me, apparently speechless.

"Don't you get it, you idiot?" I said. "I love you. I'd do anything for you. I'm not trying to save this world for myself. I'm screwed. I'm doomed to hell. I'm saving this world for you. For those I love."

Patrick snorted, his eyes wide. "Bullshit."

"It's bullshit, but it's true. You want me to sit here and let the world burn because you don't want to help me? Fine. That's your prerogative. I'll grab that bottle and we'll watch the world crumble together, if that's what you really want. Because I'm not going to kill you over this."

"You *can't* kill me, Jack."

"Oh, believe me. If I wanted to, I could find a way. I've been able to hack my way through every problem thrown at me, and if I really and truly saw you as a problem, just a problem, I'd eat through you, Patrick. I'd fucking eat right through you. But I don't because I love you, and I would never, ever do that." I bent over to catch my breath. "Dear God, you think *you're* tired? You don't know what tired is." I shook my head. "One day of my childhood… I wish you could have experienced just one day. If you want to give up, fine. We'll sit here and we'll waste away, and that'll be the end." I walked up to him, my face next to his face. "Fuck it."

I sighed, staring into Patrick's confused expression. "You say you didn't ask for this. You think I did? I could have blown my brains out years ago and saved myself so much trouble. So much responsibility."

I retreated and leaned against the wall on the other side of the room. We both panted, staring at each other.

Patrick sat on the edge of the bed. "You…you *really* love me?"

"Yes, motherfucker," I said, resting my head against the wall and closing my eyes. "I'd die for you. What happened with Ven," I shook my head, "wasn't about you. It was about something larger."

Patrick's breath steadied. "I'll get you the godsoul."

I slid down the wall to the floor.

"This is just so messed up," he whispered.

"Yes. It's the world," I said. His green eyes watched me. "It's the fabric of our reality, this chaos. It's partly our fault, of course. But it's just…in the air. I'm…I'm trying to change that. Trying to get the train back on the tracks."

Patrick shook his head. "I know." He sighed. "Sorry I took a shot at you."

I closed my eyes. "I'm sorry I thought about killing you and stealing your money when we first met."

Our breathing softened as we both relaxed. The entire house beyond us was silent. I wondered where Deirdre had gone, if she was standing right outside the door listening to us. I certainly sensed her nearby. I looked at Patrick. "I said when I got here that I came to make amends."

"You have," Patrick said.

I shook my head. "I did something…else."

He closed his eyes and pressed his lips together. "What?"

The doorknob turned, and Patrick popped upright. The door opened, revealing Deirdre Flannigan in her blue silk dress.

Patrick's expression reflected his shock.

"Mom?"

CHAPTER 28
PARITER

Patrick

I WRAPPED MY MOTHER'S RED hair around my hands and could not believe it was hers. I held her close to me. More than a decade had vanished since I'd lost her, but I knew her more truly than any other person.

"Good Lord, Lord, Lord," I whispered.

I pulled back. Tears streamed down her cheeks. She cupped my face, her green eyes searching mine. She said my name.

"Patrick. Look at you!" she said. "You're so *tall.*"

"And you…" I paused. Her blue dress flashed me back to her funeral. The memory arrived fresh. I could smell the flowers, hear the people crying around me, the words of the priest, feel the grip of my father's hand. My eyes met hers. "You're exactly the way I remember you."

"I can't believe I'm here."

"Neither can I." I opened my mouth to say more, but I didn't know what to add. "Jack. She must have…"

"Yes. She resurrected me." She pursed her lips and tucked a piece of hair behind her ear. "It was…miraculous." She hugged me close again. We embraced for a long while, rocking softly back and forth, side to side.

Eventually she pulled back, and her gaze wandered around the room. She focused on the bathroom door.

My mouth went dry. "We should get out of here," I said.

She nodded.

I took a step, and she put a hand on my chest. "Wait. Before we go, I need to tell you something."

I stepped back. "Of course," I said. "Anything."

My mother pressed her hands together, and her eyebrows rose into peaks. She hesitated. "You should know that Jack feels for you. A lot. She would do almost anything for you, I think."

My gaze dropped to the carpet. "I know. I mean…I realize that, now, what with you being here."

"And though she is capable of miraculous things, she isn't capable of everything. She told me that you, you *alone*, were made the Guardian of the remnants of God. That you're the only one with access to those remnants, that there is only one piece left. And that she needs it."

My stomach curled in on itself. I gripped the bedpost and lowered myself on the bed. The misery I'd quickly forgotten at the presence of my mother reared its head again.

"I trust her, Patrick. My intuition says she is trustworthy. Maybe not for everything, but for this. I know that you believe you've wasted the gifts given to you, and that may or may not be true, but I want you to search your heart. Is it that you do not trust her, or is it that you are tired of pain and you've shut down?"

I looked up at her, and she smiled consolingly.

"I'm tired of pain," I said. "I admit I do trust her."

My mother gripped my shoulders. "My dear, dear boy," she said. "I know you've been through so much. You were left with the wrong parent."

I searched myself, discovered this was the thing I'd always wanted to say and never had. How had she so quickly reached into my soul? "Yes, I was," I said. It felt like a question.

"And you are lucky to be *alive*, given you were left with him—your father. In fact, I think that's something you've always known, though you've never been able to face it. I think that's why you drank and drugged yourself, if what Jack said is true. It's because you've *known*, and you've tried not to know." She pursed her lips. The lines at the edges of her eyes crinkled. She smiled apologetically and grimaced at the same time. "I married the wrong man. You had the wrong father. And then you were left alone with him, and he didn't love you."

Of all the words I thought she might say, these were not them. But the words were right. It felt as though someone had reached into my chest and seized my heart, squeezing it and healing it at the same time.

"You are lucky he didn't kill you," my mother said.

I pressed my hand to my chest and bent low. It suddenly felt as though circulation had returned to my mind. The things I'd lived with that I thought I'd made up, results of misinterpretation and imagination, were validated.

"Oh, Patrick," she sighed. She sat on the bed beside me and pulled me close. I put my arms around her and cried into her neck.

"What was wrong with him?" I whispered. All my life, I'd wondered. The question had revolved in my brain along with others. What was wrong with my father? Why didn't he love me? What was wrong with me?

She rocked us back and forth. "He was a snake."

I licked my lips, wet and salty from my tears. "Jack killed him."

"I know."

I breathed deeply, and a shudder as big as ten years escaped. "I thought she was the problem. But she wasn't the problem." I sat upright.

My mom shook her head.

I pushed myself off the bed. I paced a few steps toward the bathroom and folded my arms. How had a woman so questionable and severe made so many right things happen? The answer came immediately. In her fearlessness, Jack became a catalyst. Fate could move through her in a way that it didn't move through the rest of us. Nothing stopped her from acting.

I turned to my mother, who seemed tiny on the vast bed, her hands resting in her lap.

"I'll give her the rest of the godsoul."

She smiled reassuringly and nodded.

I reached a hand toward her. "Let's go."

CHAPTER 29
COALESCO

Jack

DEIRDRE AND PATRICK STARED AT one another in silence. They met in the middle of the room and collapsed into each other's arms, breaking into tears. Patrick pulled back multiple times to look at his mother's face. She clutched the shoulders of his shirt, pressed her hands to his temples.

"Good Lord, Lord, Lord," Patrick whispered, his Irish accent suddenly thick.

Standing by the door, I noticed that the bottle of liquor on its side on the carpet still retained some liquid. I reached down, picked it up, and brought the bottle to my lips. I drank deeply, savoring the burn, hoping that even though it didn't work on Patrick, it would work on me.

I'd done what I needed to do. I'd played the necessary role to convince Patrick to do what I needed. But as I squatted on the backs of my heels, I realized that the line between pretend and real was difficult to distinguish. Every emotion I had released was mine. Every thought I told him about was true. Every regret existed. I couldn't tell whether I'd lied to him or I'd lied to myself. Perhaps I needed to feel as though I was lying to get the truth out. It was the only way it would come.

I drank deeply from the bottle again. A wave of exhaustion deluged me.

I rose from the floor and left the room, allowing Patrick and his mother privacy. I walked down the dark hallway and down the stairs toward the living room. I felt spacy, dizzy, my head in a fog. It wasn't the alcohol. It was the sickness. I'd expended too much energy on Patrick.

Collapsing on the couch, I felt my heart move, as though it jiggled, as though its various pieces were incongruent—part of my heart was not keeping time.

I took a deep breath, relaxed my neck, and closed my eyes. I drifted.

The world blurred, and when it cleared, a man wearing a black leather jacket and dark pants sat in front of me, his eyes cold, his hair trim, his face like a mutt. It was Jasper. He held something red and meaty in his blood-covered hands. The blood reached his elbows and dripped on the floor.

"Where are you?" I said. "I haven't been able to find you."

He shook his head, smirking. "Don't worry about where I am. You can think about that later. You don't have much time. You need to wake up."

"I am awake."

"No. Or I wouldn't have this." He lifted his hands; now they were coated in gold. He no longer held a piece of meat. It was a chunk of godsoul. "You're very ill, Jack. You're slipping. You need a piece to get you through." He offered what he held.

"It will be wasted on me."

"No. The rest is for you."

A hand touched my shoulder.

I jumped, strangled a scream, and spun around. I expected to see Jasper, but it was Patrick. I was lying on a couch in Patrick's dark living room. I hadn't heard him come down. How long had I been unconscious?

"We should go," Patrick said. "Mom told me it's urgent."

I was aware of the dried salt at the edges of my eyes, my weariness. "It is."

He nodded. "I understand. You brought my mother back to me. This is the least I can do."

"Thank you."

I rose, circled the couch, and approached what I assumed was a closet door in the living room. I retrieved my knife, intending to cut my palm. Patrick stopped me. He peered closely at my hand. "What's wrong with you? Are…" His breath caught in his throat, and his eyes widened. "You're sick. Like the others."

I nodded.

"Oh, no. Jack, no. Jesus Christ. You should've told me."

"It's fine," I said. "I'll be fine."

Patrick looked stunned, like he didn't know what to say. I put the knife to my palm again, but he stopped me. He plucked the knife from my fingers. "I'll do it." Deirdre appeared behind him, quiet and calm. Her green eyes studied me.

Patrick cut his palm, gasped, and hissed as the blood streamed. He outlined the door, imitating what I'd done many times before. He pressed his bleeding hand against the door's heart. "*Patefacio tutor godsoul,*" he whispered.

The room dimmed, and a miraculous light fluoresced, wavering like the fire in my own body. Logically, I knew Patrick was the Guardian. Seeing it this time, though, was different. Patrick had crossed some sort of line, was beyond the human. I hadn't completely realized it before then. Perhaps the severity of the moment made me drink it in fully. He wasn't just my friend, anymore, and I felt a strange new guilt for attempting to manipulate an immortal creature, especially if my plan didn't work, and this was the last time we saw each other. We were both beyond what we were.

He gripped the handle and opened the door.

Royal purple rock stretched across the entire back wall—evidence of our greed and failure.

Patrick and I went inside. Deirdre tentatively followed.

I waited as he walked forward, past the threshold that divided others from the godsoul. He looked back, as though waiting for me, and his eyes traced the white lines in my hands, the white strands in my hair. "Go ahead," I said.

A knowing look crossed his face, a look that seemed to say he knew he was supposed to be there, doing what he was doing. A look that said he belonged to the ship, even if the ship went down. Just like me.

He turned blankly, almost mesmerized, toward the rock, and gripped the final piece of godsoul, the size of a small pillow. He reached for the saw and sliced it free. Then he carried it to me, gold coating his hands. The blood of the Creator dripped down his wrists to his elbows.

"This is it." he said. It sounded final.

"Thank you, Patrick."

He blinked, and his green eyes seemed flecked with gold.

"Eat it," he said. "Make yourself better."

"I will. Just not right now." I breathed deeply. "I want you to stay here. Stay safe. I'll be back, if all goes well."

Patrick nodded calmly. Something was different about him. Something had entered him that was not him, that was more than him.

"I love you too, Jack," he said.

I smiled and nodded. Another wave of tiredness washed over me. I said goodbye to Deirdre.

I left.

WHEN I SHUT THE DOOR, the room returned to its normal light level. I took a deep breath and imagined Cyrus's front porch. I shut my eyes and willed myself there, the godsoul gripped tightly in my hands.

The world swirled around me, dissolving into black and then resolidifying. Cyrus's mansion stood before me, the crickets of Basille, Louisiana, humming all around.

If Roland saw me as I was now—diseased—it would shock him. I broke a tiny piece of the rock I carried off with my teeth. I chewed the honey char taste, the solid and liquid melding together, and swallowed. A thrill went through me, easing my weariness, relaxing my muscles, reigniting my mind, awakening and reviving me. The white marks on the backs of my hands disappeared. The white hair that I could see out of the corners of my eyes shivered to black.

I took a deep breath, moved to the front door, and opened it.

"Roland!" I called.

He appeared to my right in the hall, a brown book in his hand, which he fumbled with when he saw me. Behind him, in the living room, Cyrus rose. It was the first time I'd thought of him since I'd left. The image of Margaret's whitening arm came to mind—the realization that the godsoul only worked for a short period of time. Was that also true for Cyrus?

"What is it?" Roland asked a little breathlessly. His gaze shifted to the large piece of godsoul in my hand.

I licked the remaining godsoul from my lips.

"I need your help." I lifted my chin toward the hall. "The basement," I said. I looked at Cyrus. "You stay here."

Cyrus looked ready to speak, but he paused. "All right."

I walked the familiar path down the hall, to the left and down another hall, through the small room to the wooden door, down the steps to the basement, and then into the wine room. Roland followed closely. I set the chunk of godsoul on the island surrounded by wine, took his warm hand in mine, and squeezed, coating his hand in gold.

I walked to the metallic vault door and gripped the handle. It unlocked itself for me, just as it had before. Roland's mouth opened. "How did you do that?"

Still not ready to say what I was capable of, I nodded toward the hallway beyond the door. "I'll tell you in there."

I pulled the door open, collected the godsoul from the island, and entered the hallway. When Roland, too, entered, I shut the metallic door. I stepped to the right, to the first door, gripped the giant crystal knob, and turned it. Beyond the door, the empty, dusty room appeared exactly as I remembered. The hearth gaped, no fire heating it; the familiar worn chair in the middle of the room faced it.

In that room, some eight months before, Lutin had saved my life. I scanned his prison, remembering my own in the basement of Roth's building.

"What are we doing here?" Roland asked.

I took a deep breath. "Making things right, yet again." I handed him the godsoul. He took it with a quizzical look on his face. Gold dripped down his palm and arm. It seemed as though he held a heart, not a rock.

"Do you remember how I killed Ven, and then Alex, with the gramophone?"

"Of course."

"The *arca*…it wasn't just any machine. I destroyed it and brought it back from death. When it killed Alex, it was doing so because it *obeyed* me."

"What are you saying…? You…you can control more than just people?"

I nodded. "Yes. I'm sorry I kept it from you, but I was afraid to say so." I took a deep breath. "The thing is, after I killed Alex, the Beretrum closed, spitting both Alex and me back out." I looked into Roland's eyes. "That *arca* hurt the Builder. It just wasn't…strong enough to do the trick."

I took my coat off and laid it on the chair.

"Okay," Roland said, absorbing the new information. "So what's the plan?"

I squatted, held my hands over the brick floor, and closed my eyes. I sought the sensation of carbonation building and bubbling and spilling over within me, simultaneously picturing the item that had terrified me throughout my childhood—Cyrus's red box.

I willed its particles—any tiny specks—to find me in the room. I couldn't sense any, but I nevertheless bore down, willing the *arca* into existence. I breathed steadily in and out and released my power. It erupted from me, and where it landed, Cyrus's red box appeared.

Roland cursed.

"Shut the door," I said.

He looked panicked, but he did as I asked. "Are you insane? There's no reason for you to be bringing that thing back."

I nodded. "There is. We now have a device we can use against the Builder. But I have to make it stronger."

Roland's wide eyes searched mine. He was catching up. I could see comprehension in his gaze.

"And that's why you brought the godsoul here? To feed to the box?"

"Maybe," I said. I winced. "I don't think it will be able to consume the godsoul itself though. The box was built to mine it from human beings. We can try to see if the box will accept it, but I don't think it will."

He tilted his head. "And if it doesn't?"

I sighed. "Cyrus was able to expand the box's power by feeding it pieces of Lutin's soul. Our only choice then would be to grow it the same way."

Roland looked from me to the box and the godsoul. "Then I'll be the one to do it." He stepped forward toward the box. I put a restraining hand on his shoulder, and he turned to look me in the eye.

"You're not a ferric," I said softly. "I am. Well, I'm a hybrid. I might be even more powerful, capable of much more. I'm going to feed the box."

Roland shook his head back and forth.

I reclaimed the godsoul from his hand.

"You're going to make sure the box stays open, continues to feed on me, while I renew myself with this. We're going to make this *arca* more powerful than it's ever been, and when the Builder comes, we're going to use it on him."

Roland's eyes filled with tears. "I can't let you do this."

"It's our only shot. We…I…Patrick and I messed up. The godsoul didn't work as a permanent cure for the disease that Alex spread, and now our supply is gone except for this last piece. My army is gone. The ferrics have also caught the disease. We're out of options. It's either try this or die."

We looked down at the dripping rock. "I had no idea," Roland said, "that everything had gone to hell. Your face showed dread when you came into the house, so I did wonder. If…if you think this is the way it has to be, then I accept it. But I still think it should be me."

I nodded. "I know you do." I was grateful to him for the offer. "When I open the box, don't let it close." I licked my lips, took an edge of the rock between my teeth, and bit down to break it off. I ground the stone and swallowed. Fluid coated my tongue and throat. The fire in my limbs fluoresced, bright enough to illuminate the entire room.

I gripped the box. Roland circled around me to stand behind me.

The worn velvet was smooth against my fingers, preternaturally so. I flipped the latches open and braced myself.

I'd never seen what was inside.

CHAPTER 30
DEGULO

Jack

I OPENED THE ARCA. A white cloud launched toward me from inside, whipping past the godsoul and slamming me to the floor. Expanding above, it obscured my view of the room. Its edges sharpened into points, as though made of white needles, and the whole mass grew and shrank, expanded and retracted, as though breathing or beating. One large needle dropped down and pierced my chest, pinning me to the floor.

The needle began sucking. Bits of my flesh floated up into the cloud. Pain stabbed my chest and filtered out through the rest of my body. I could feel myself being emptied, shredded, until only a few pieces of me remained. I looked down at myself and saw the lines in my body grow faint orange. The tendrils of Alex's disease spread and brightened.

Roland lifted the godsoul from my hand and brought it to my lips.

"Get out of its way," I warned.

"*Eat.*"

Feeling myself nearly completely empty of energy, life, or soul, I bit off a chunk and chewed and swallowed, forcing the metallic grit down.

My being filled in again, as though my soul were once again whole, like a wilted flower returned to full bloom.

The needle expanded in my chest. A hollowing pain beyond anything that had ever existed swept through my core, unraveling me. I tried to breathe and couldn't.

Roland pressed the gold to my lips. I bit and chewed. As I swallowed and renewed myself, a sound echoed in the room.

"What are you doing here?" Roland asked.

Pain entered deep into me, as though it'd become my marrow. I forced myself to turn toward Roland, to ask him what he was talking about.

A familiar form stood in the doorway—tall, slender, captivating. Silver hair gleamed beneath the low lighting.

Cyrus. He held the key card in his hand.

His eyes wandered over me and the white cloud. He stood fearless. In his right hand was a knife.

A shiver attempted to pass through me, but the hollowing pain cut it short. I took a quick bite of the gold from Roland's hand.

Renewed. Fresh. Invigorated.

I chewed, and metallic blood oozed down the sides of my lips. "Drop the knife," I whispered, barely able to get the words out.

Cyrus held the knife out to his right. The blade dangled between his trembling fingers, reflecting the overhead light.

My strength vanished, and pain returned. The cloud above me grew, and the white blade that penetrated my chest expanded. I gasped.

Cyrus's hand steadied, his palm wrapped solidly around the hilt.

I prepared to bite off another piece of godsoul.

Cyrus lunged.

Roland dropped the gold and stood to parry Cyrus's knife hand. Cyrus stumbled against the back wall and flipped around. Roland squatted, bringing his arms to chest level, a wild gleam in his eye. He panted, his right hand coated in gold, and veered to the left as Cyrus circled.

The godsoul sat to my left, leaking metallic blood across the dirty cement floor. I called up all my remaining strength and reached for it, trying to get my body to move.

Someone's foot knocked the godsoul a few feet away.

Shit.

"Roland," I whispered.

Fighting sounds, grunts and hollers, ricocheted off the walls. Shadows melded and struck one another.

I forced my eyes open, forced myself to reach for the golden chunk an inch from my outstretched hand. My breath was ragged. Moving even an inch pressed the preternatural blade against my rib cage. It burned.

"Unngggh!"

I dug my nails along a jagged edge of the godsoul and dragged it toward me. I brought it to my lips and bit off a chunk, hardly aware of my teeth grinding it down, hardly tasting the gold blood. I was completely numb, aware of my vulnerability. I was only temporary. Powerless. Nothing.

When the godsoul refreshed me, awareness flooded my mind. I could hear, feel, sense again.

Two bodies collapsed beside me. As Cyrus swung the dagger down, Roland crossed his arms, braced for the blow. The blade sliced through his left arm. Roland screamed.

"Stop!" I ordered Cyrus as my strength began to fade.

He wavered enough so that Roland could heave Cyrus off; Cyrus fell backward on the floor but quickly regained his feet.

The cloud above me expanded, covering most of the ceiling in stalactite crystals. The room shifted to white—concrete floor, dust, fireplace, brick walls. The basement room became a white cave.

I took another bite of the godsoul, chewing and swallowing. Momentarily, the slightest hue returned to the room, but it quickly faded, just as quickly as I'd lost my grip on Cyrus.

Fear invaded my mind. I stared at the red box and willed it to stop what it was doing.

It didn't even shiver.

I had no control over Cyrus, I had no control over the *arca*. I was too weak.

"Roland," I gasped. "Close the box."

Cyrus swung the blade at Roland, and Roland barely dodged it. Blood coursed down his arm, soaking his white shirt and dribbling to the floor, where it whitened. Cyrus's clothes bleached. Everything was too bright, like we'd all been launched out of the mansion into some alternate reality—a side room in the Beretrum.

I fumbled, barely managing another mouthful of the godsoul. Awareness returned to me, consciousness returned, but momentarily, lasting not nearly as long as it once had.

Roland failed to knock the knife from Cyrus's hand, and Cyrus swung around and stabbed Roland in his leg. He screamed.

The spindly white cloud expanded to the ceiling, obscuring everything. Like ice crystals on glass, it spread across the walls, fireplace, and door, closing it firmly.

I nibbled another small piece of godsoul. The hollowing sensation returned within seconds.

At my feet, the red box was open, a smoky twisting spiral connecting its interior to the cloud.

I tried to edge closer to it, and the blade in the center of my chest sliced upward. I screamed. Another two spikes appeared above my legs, entering my thighs. My legs were now immobile.

"Roland. Please," I whispered, energy abandoning me again.

My mentors continued to battle. Cyrus knocked Roland against the wall, and his head smacked loudly. He dropped to the ground, motionless but alive, his chest expanding, retracting. Heaving, Cyrus stood over him.

White spikes framed them. Their skin lightened. Cyrus's hair, which had always been silver, started to lose its sheen. The blood on his hand turned white.

Roland glared up at Cyrus, waiting for the last blow.

I blinked. I could no longer think, no longer breathe.

Cyrus dropped to his knees. The knife, the blade and handle now white, clattered to the cement. He clutched his chest. Roland did the same. We were all dying.

I tried to command Cyrus one last time but had no breath to form words. All that came out was a low moan. A whooshing noise filled my ears. My vision blurred.

Cyrus toppled to the floor. He reached one hand forward, then another, crawling across the white cement, past me. He reached the box and slipped his hand behind the lid. He heaved.

Black dots speckled my vision.

He pulled the lid forward. Slowly, like the lid of a jewelry box, it dropped. Wood connected with wood, and my pain vanished. The white cloud vanished, as did the spikes.

I gasped, turned on my side, and pulled my legs to my chest. I moaned.

Two other moans followed.

A puddle of gold pooled on the floor amid all the white. A ring of gray cement circled it. I crawled forward and licked it, took a gulp, tasting the metallic flavor. I swallowed, and a little bit of consciousness returned. I lifted the hand that had held the godsoul to my mouth and licked my fingers, swallowing as much as I could. My vision cleared. My heartbeat steadied and strengthened. I stopped shaking.

I rested my head against the floor. The aching fever subsided. I opened my eyes.

Cyrus's face was a foot from mine. He lifted his arm, the knife in his fist. As he drove the knife down, my arm shot up and stopped his, mid-strike, as though I were catching a feather.

"Stop," I commanded.

His body went slack.

"Drop the knife."

He released it. It dropped inches from my head and clattered against the white cement.

I took a shaky breath and relaxed.

Roland lay against the wall, quivering and bleeding. Red pooled beneath him.

"What the hell is that?" he asked between heaving breaths, pointing to the red box.

I pushed myself upright.

A red aura swirled around the bright red box on the floor—the only thing in the white room with color. A low whistling sound, like wind in the skies, circled it.

I rose unsteadily to my feet and carefully went to the supernatural machine. Ignoring the fear that exploded in me, I bent over and quickly pressed a hand against one of the locks. I lifted the latch, hooking it, and pressed down until it clicked. I did the same for the right latch.

The red box glowed bright, then softened, then brightened again, a neon-red halo circling around it.

Satisfied, I moved toward Roland's bloody, trembling form. I pressed my hand to his arm to stop the bleeding. Wherever tiny bits of the godsoul touched, the wound closed.

He moaned.

"We'll need to do that a few more times," I said. "Use my soul to feed the box."

His eyes widened. "Good Lord," he said.

I leaned against the reddening brick wall, nodding. "But we'll give it five minutes." I looked at Cyrus. "You're so goddamn wily," I told him.

Cyrus stared at us, not speaking, not moving. He'd nearly destroyed us, nearly allowed the Builder to win. He may not have realized it. I was lucky he knew so little about my abilities. I was lucky he wanted to survive.

"Has the box ever looked like that before?" I asked Cyrus, nodding over to the glowing, noisy *arca*.

"No," he said without a blink.

I relaxed against the wall. "Good."

CHAPTER 31
ITERO

Jack

We locked Cyrus in the basement room next door. I healed Roland's wounds, and we completed another round of building the box's power, until I couldn't stand it anymore and needed a break. I smoked a cigarette in the open garage and stared out into the night, thinking of the last time I'd dealt with the box—when I'd freed Lutin, and his brothers had burned it.

Part of me would have done anything to have Lutin there, helping me. Another part of me, however, felt that the wish was selfish—he should never have to see the basement room where he'd been held for ten years again, and he shouldn't have to deal with the red box, anymore. He'd done his time. It was time for me to do mine.

Roland and I worked two more rounds of building the box's power. By the end, my body was numb, filled with a frisson I couldn't explain. I took one more bite of godsoul to repair myself. Even after that, I needed to rest. I climbed the stairs out of the basement, and Roland followed, carrying the arca. In the living room, I collapsed on the couch.

Roland set the red box with the glowing aura on the coffee table.

"Now what?" he asked.

I looked up at him. "Now we wait for him," I said, all my nerves frayed. My voice cracked. "And we hope."

CHAPTER 32
MUNITOR

Jack

Around nine in the evening, we heard a knock on the front door. I stood in the hallway, Roland at my side, and inhaled. As I hesitated, hand on the doorknob, my heart jackhammered. I opened the door.

A white creature, as if from a horror film, stood there silently, the purest white that had ever existed. The Builder's body looked like a plastic statue. His clothes were also white and reflected the light, as though made of the same material as he. The face was completely blank, and my gaze swept over it, seeking human features. His presence obliterated reality. Around him, all color disappeared from the door's wooden frame, the gray porch, the yellow light.

Lutin, his dark eyes closed, lips parted, head drooped, hung limp over the Builder's shoulder. The lines in his body were black, the fire extinguished. I wanted to rush to him and hold him, wake him from death. His love had enveloped me, returned me to myself, made me who I was.

The scar on the back of my right hand—the one that had healed in the presence of Lutin and his brothers—returned. The wood floor beneath my feet aged, scorched by burn marks.

A mouth took shape on the Builder's face, and a voice far lower and more layered than any human's said, "Hello, Roland."

Roland stiffened beside me.

The cross on my neck began to burn, and I jerked it free and set it on a nearby table. The red heat scorched the wood, which sizzled. Smoke rose in the air.

I reached toward Lutin. The Builder lifted a nub that formed into a hand. The hand twisted and opened the palm toward me. "The godsoul," he said.

Lutin's face slid down the Builder's shoulder. Where his skin touched the Builder's white jacket, cracks formed in his skin.

I invited him in with a wave of my hand. "This way."

In the hallway, I waited for the Builder to follow. He leaned to fit through the door. As he entered, his blank face turned like a beacon to his right, toward the living room. For a long time, he simply stood.

The mouth formed on the blank white surface of his lower face. "Cyrus is…here," he said. For the first time, I registered a hint of emotion, as though he'd said the name of his favorite pet.

Nervously, I wondered how he'd sensed Cyrus.

I looked sideways at Roland. His eyes widened momentarily, a gasp catching in his throat.

"He's downstairs," I said. "Locked in one of the basement rooms."

The Builder tilted his head. "Why would you bring him back? If you were responsible for his downfall and death?"

I took a deep breath, searching for the right words, words that would make sense. "After I met a man named Jonathon Roth—"

"The kill-for-hire," the Builder confirmed.

I swallowed dryly. "Yes…After I met him, I became nostalgic for home. For Cyrus."

The Builder's featureless face aimed straight at me, eyeless, noseless, mouthless.

"What was your intention?" he asked.

"To try to make him good."

"A useless endeavor."

My eyes flicked to where the cuts had been on Roland's arms and legs after his battle with Cyrus. "Yes."

"I want to renegotiate. Lutin, you, and Cyrus come with me when we leave this world."

I shook my head. "We can't renegotiate. We've already made the deal."

"I can *always* renegotiate." He audibly sucked the atmosphere toward him. The walls around us creaked, threatening to implode.

"Why Cyrus?" I asked.

"As a replacement for your brother, whom you stole from me."

I shook my head. "No."

"Then we no longer have a deal."

I pulled a hand through my hair. "Roland too, then."

A long silence stretched. The Builder turned toward Roland, seemed to study him. "Fine." His blank face swiveled back to me.

I continued the long walk down the hallway, with Roland following. The Builder shifted Lutin, letting him drop from his shoulder and positioning him in the crook of his arm like a doll. Lutin's feet dragged against the floorboards with each step the Builder took.

We passed through the basement and the wine room into the hallway that led to Lutin's old cell. Roland followed.

As we neared the cell, the Builder inhaled. "A big piece," he whispered.

A shiver crawled down my back. "Like I said. Twenty pounds."

When I opened the door, the Builder entered and dropped Lutin to the floor. Lutin's head bounced when it connected with the cement. I winced and suppressed the desire to run to him. Roland stood just to my right, and the look on his face said that he'd had to stop himself, too.

Hands and fingers expanded from the Builder's nubs. He hurried toward the last of godsoul in the center of the room, picked up the chunk, and began to take bites.

The box sat on an orange velvet chair to my left, the latches open. I reached for it, ready to bare its contents.

The Builder stopped chewing when he noticed me reaching toward the box. He lifted a white hand. The red box flew away from me, the Builder its target. He smiled a triumphant smile, gold in his teeth, dripping down his face, as the airborne box came to rest in his hand.

"I figured," he said. "Just like with the gramophone in my Beretrum." He filled his lungs and then released a stream of air toward me. I felt it and smelled it. The white striations on the backs of my hands reappeared, reversing the godsoul that had healed me. I felt faint.

"You did something to my *arca*, didn't you?" he hissed.

I shook my head but couldn't answer. All sense of myself and my surroundings disappeared. Looking into his white face was like looking into a void that stripped me of everything I'd known. The world beyond his face began to spin.

He flipped the red box in his hands. "It doesn't feel the same. No. It's powerful, greatly powerful, but it is not mine."

"Jack," Roland said. He grabbed my hand and jerked me out of my trance.

I refocused on the Builder, who carried the godsoul in one hand and the box in two others, one of which had just sprouted.

"How did you learn to tinker with my creations?" he asked. He strode toward me, the basement floor vibrating with each step. Merely two feet away, he towered above me and then bowed his torso toward me. "How did you do it?" White spittle hit my cheek. I wiped it off with the back of my hand.

Somehow, he'd unraveled my plan. But I realized he still didn't know the whole truth—the truth about *how* I'd altered the box or what made me different from the other ferrics.

I took a deep breath. "Can you really fix Lutin?"

"I was there when the ferrics were first made. But that doesn't mean I will."

I looked down at Lutin on the floor and longed for him to wake.

A fourth arm propelled from the Builder's core and slammed into my sternum. I hit the wall, filled with pain. "*Now tell me*," he commanded, "*how you altered this box.*"

I took a deep breath and composed my face. Focusing on the box, I said three words. "Open. Kill him."

The box dropped from the Builder's hand and fell to the floor. The two latches released, and it opened, releasing a white cloud. It expanded toward the Builder, forming icicles midair. When recognition crossed his face, the merest suggestion of eyes took shape, as if to confirm the spiky cloud.

The cloud pierced the Builder's chest, white within white, and inhaled pieces of him, incorporating them into the vapor. He reached out toward me. Another spiky cloud sprouted and pinned his arm. His white body faded and thinned. The Builder lifted the godsoul to his mouth. The box pinned that arm to the Builder's chest. Roland reached forward to claim the godsoul.

The Builder scrambled on his remaining limbs, trying to take the gold from Roland, but the *arca* held him in place. Fresh spikes pinned his arms and legs. The Builder freed one arm, which stretched impossibly long to follow Roland, fingers extended toward the godsoul. Roland dodged free and tossed the godsoul to me.

I caught it, broke a piece off, welcomed it in my mouth, and chewed and swallowed with relief.

The extended arm stopped three feet away from me. And then the Builder began to collapse.

"You idiots," he growled. "*When I return, I'll kill you.*"

My arms and legs trembled uncontrollably, as I watched and waited for it to be over.

He still didn't get it. We already knew. Roland came to stand beside me.

I kneeled next to Lutin and broke off a piece of the remaining godsoul. I spread his lips and placed it under his tongue, hoping that somehow, someway, it might help him.

The Builder's body completely deflated, sucked completely empty of whatever soul he'd had. His unearthly moan boomed against the walls, sending vibrations through the brick and air. Roland clapped both hands over his ears.

I gasped. A mighty expansion, maybe the power that the red box had gained, now surged through me, as though its power was *my* power.

A high unlike any I'd experienced took over. Throughout my childhood, I'd been given all sorts of drugs to allay my guilt, my fears, my trauma, but this was beyond that. Elation washed through me, in spite of all the horror, or maybe because of it. There seemed to be no further boundaries. Everything had liquified. Everything that had once caused me pain now gratified me, and I slipped under the euphoric waves.

"Jack," a voice called.

"Hm?"

I deflated a little and returned to the room. Roland stared at me. "He's dead now, Jack. He's been dead for several minutes. Are you going to bring him back?"

I noticed that Lutin was on the floor near my feet. Farther away, the empty sack of what used to be the Builder was collapsed on the concrete. Strangely, I didn't feel the need to resurrect him, to kill the devil to save the world. I felt no connection to Roland, no connection to Lutin. I knew that I should, but I didn't.

"We've got to *hurry*," Roland pleaded, his eyes begging.

Was something wrong?

I blinked several times, trying to remember the point of it all. "Why?"

Roland seemed at a loss. His hand passed through the air, as though trying to make his point for him, before it dropped. "Something's wrong with you," he moaned. He backed away.

I tried to figure out what he meant. Life had never been better. Once the box was full, so was I.

"I'm sorry," I said. "I just…don't remember what all this was supposed to be about. I don't remember the point. Maybe I just don't feel it."

I looked at the walls, which were foreign to me. The house was alien, as were Roland and Lutin. I knew who they were, but I didn't feel connected to them. I remembered their faces but nothing more.

Roland came to me and held my hands between his. "I do," he said. "Will you trust me? *I* remember."

I stared into his eyes, feeling blank. I became aware of myself, as if I saw me through another's eyes. Something was wrong with me. I didn't know what, but it felt huge and all-encompassing. We had something important to do, whether or not I realized its importance.

Something had invaded me, and it couldn't be trusted.

Roland seemed thousands of miles away, as if on a different plane of existence, but I called to him. "Yes. I trust you. What do you want me to do?"

He winced. "You've got to resurrect the Builder."

That seemed unimportant to me, and distant. I felt reborn in some way, as if my blood had been replaced with a new, purer element.

I grasped his arm—my one tether back to reality—and nodded. "All right."

I dropped the godsoul and reached my arms out toward the Builder. I let the building sensation of carbonation filter through my body, rolling in on itself, twisting, compressing, folding, until it held the explosive capacity of a bomb. I shot that energy toward the white paranormal pool of a creature on the floor. The numbness that had infused me vanished. The body filled out, shifted, shuddered. The Builder lay on the floor, breathing, but didn't move.

Roland shut the red box.

I bent over and gasped. The sensation of otherness was gone. As soon as the lid slammed down, I was once again me.

"Thank God you were here," I whispered, looking at Roland with gratitude.

"You weren't yourself."

I shook my head. "But I am now. I swear it. We're destroying that thing as soon as possible," I said, pointing to the box. I strode to the Builder's shapeless mass and stared down at him. One of his appendages twitched. I nudged it with the toe of my shoe, and his body jumped. Impossibly quickly, he launched to his feet, rattling the room.

His blank face shifted focus from Roland to the box to me. A mouth formed on his face, and he laughed. The deep laughter echoed off of the brick walls. He peered down at me and grinned.

"I told you I can't be killed."

I blinked. "I never said you couldn't."

The Builder grabbed me by my neck and lifted me off of the ground before I could think. He was faster, stronger, than before. I feared that I'd made a mistake, that I, so small in comparison, could have no sway whatsoever over him, no matter my power. He was older, stronger, made by the Creator. He was privy to the inner workings of the ferrics, of the godsoul, of the world beyond.

Who was I in the face of that?

"Stop," I commanded.

The Builder froze. The mouth on his white face disappeared like a mist.

"Let me go."

Slowly, his arm lowered. My shoes met the floor. He released me.

He looked at his hand as if it were not his own. "What is this?"

"It's me," I said, relief flooding my heart. I stumbled back, and Roland was there, steadying me with his hand.

The Builder cocked his head. "What do you mean it's *you?*"

"I control the things I resurrect, and I resurrected you."

I sensed he was about to swipe at me, and I ordered, "Don't. Don't move."

He leaned back, as though surprised I knew he'd strike. I walked around him, studying him, waiting to see if he would or could rebel against me. He stood in the center of the room, as still as a statue.

Roland's worried expression relaxed. Dark circles beneath his eyes emphasized them, but the fear had left. "My God," he said.

I inhaled deeply and released the breath.

I circled back to face the Builder.

"Now," I said, indicating Lutin. "Fix him."

CHAPTER 33
UNA

Jack

THE BUILDER FELL TO HIS knees and collected the godsoul from the floor. He broke off several pieces. His hand became a hammer, and he shattered the pieces into golden mud.

The Builder's hands quickly shifted into a variety of white instruments. Scissors, knives, hooks, sewing needles, and other implements sprouted from his fingers, working the muddy godsoul into a round shape. When the Builder finished, he flicked the mound, and the ventricles of a heart pulsed and assumed a regular beat. The Builder held it up to me, silently, as if to show me he was done.

I crawled to Lutin and carefully rolled him onto his back. Lifting his shirt, I winced. Black dust from the extinguished lines in his skin marked the fabric of his cream-colored boatneck shirt. His bare chest now exposed, I beckoned to the Builder.

"Fix him," I said.

The Builder approached, the passage of his white body bleaching the floor beneath him. He held the heart in his right claw; his left hand formed into a knife, and he used it to cut open the center of Lutin's chest. The cut was deep and oozed blood.

The Builder slipped the golden beating heart into the cut, widening it so that the skin stretched and creased. He pushed his hand up under Lutin's ribs.

Lutin's eyes flew open. He gasped, and his whole body jerked.

He was awake.

When his eyes took in the Builder, he screamed before he grabbed the Builder's arm, jerking the white hand out of his chest. Lutin rolled over and crawled away, spilling his blood across the floor.

"Stay still!" I yelled at the Builder. He froze. Along his arm, Lutin's blood bleached to white.

I scrambled over to Lutin and attempted to hold him still. As he struggled, fire fluoresced throughout his body, as though the engine of his being were firing. The stomach wound sealed as I watched. Lutin gasped and clutched his chest. He pressed his forehead against the concrete, his eyes squeezed shut.

"It's over," I assured him.

His ribcage heaved as air flowed in and out. He looked from me to Roland to his stomach and the Builder.

"It's okay. It's done. Thank God you're all right." I stroked Lutin's arm.

Gold from the godsoul I'd put in his mouth coated his lips. He licked it and pressed his hands to the floor to lift himself to his knees, and then he rose to his feet. He focused on the Builder, as though Roland and I weren't there.

He said something in the ferrics' feathery, light language, a language I didn't understand.

The Builder responded in the same tongue.

Lutin's eyes shifted from the Builder to the floor, then to me.

"I had him fashion a heart for you out of godsoul, so you wouldn't die," I said.

The hardness in Lutin's eyes vanished. His gaze embraced me. "That's what he just said. I didn't know it was possible."

"He has a few tricks up his sleeve. I'm sure there's much we don't know."

Lutin released a breath. He came and pulled me to his chest, holding me tight. I pressed my face into his neck and inhaled deeply the scent of cinnamon and chimney.

"You resurrected him."

"Yes."

"And you're still alive."

I nodded. "Yes."

He tightened his hug before he released me. Tears wetted his eyes. He beckoned to Roland. Roland took a few steps forward, but only a few steps.

"I'm not going to hurt you," Lutin said.

"That might be true, but it's hard to believe. I deserve it. Keeping you down here for Cyrus's sake for so many years."

Lutin's sober gaze took in the Builder and then me. "Things appear to have worked out," he said. "You had a part in that." He beckoned again, and Roland stepped forward into Lutin's embrace.

When they released one another, Lutin turned to me. "Are you all right?"

"I…" I looked down at my hand, worried that the white striations might be there. But they weren't. My skin and the fire in my limbs appeared healthy, normal.

I smiled. "Yes."

He nodded. Concern was etched in the contours of his face. "Even if you aren't, I'm here for you. Always."

"I know." I smiled. "And I for you."

CHAPTER 34
REDITUS

Patrick

Seeing my mother within the purple room striated with gold struck me as surreal, impossible, and inevitable. I blinked several times, trying to wake myself, but she remained, as did the room. It felt alien, but also realer than anything I'd experienced. Something permeated the air—a mist, rising from the depleted wall, crystallizing and perfecting every atom. I inhaled it, feeling rejuvenated, healthy, for the first time ever. My mother did the same and beamed.

Her blue dress swayed. She walked to the wall and inspected the areas where I'd chiseled away the gold. She pressed her hand against it and closed her eyes. Her chest expanded slowly and then retracted. The edges of her lips curled upwards. "Oooh, Patrick," she whispered and turned to me. "This is unbelievable."

I nodded and looked up at the top of the wall, which disappeared into black oblivion overhead. At some indistinguishable point, it faded away.

"There was so much of it," I said. "But we used it all."

My mother pursed her lips. She came to me, and we embraced. Her warmth melted my fear and resentment. "Perhaps it was all for a reason," she said. She pulled back.

My gaze wandered over her cheeks, chin, forehead, eyes. "Hm," I said. "Perhaps." My mind landed on a new, more positive perspective. As difficult as it was to know that everything might end, I did have my mother back. I was more than human. I stood in the midst of a protective inner world where everything felt right. I'd been delivered from suicide and a drug overdose, and I had—even if only for a short while—saved the lives of hundreds of thousands of people.

"Say that Jack's plan works and she saves the world, that you and I are okay. What would you want to do?" I asked her.

My mother smiled, breathed in, and hummed. Her eyes focused inward. "I'd want to go to the Maldives. Stay there for a while, put my toes in the sand and listen to the waves crash. Drink mojitos. Watch the sun rise and set. Feel the warm wind against my skin. Watch lantern fire dance in the night."

I smiled, felt the warm air on my skin.

"And then," she said with a sigh, "I would like to travel in the mountains somewhere. Somewhere I can feel the ice, until it's painful and my hands go numb. I want to sit by the fire and drink hot cocoa. I want to ski and make snow angels.

"And I want to skydive," she added. "I want to scuba dive. I want to go see every show on Broadway. I want to…to pursue the medical degree that I gave up so long ago, when I married your father. And I want to…to open a women's shelter, where abused women can stay for free and be safe while they get back on their feet. I want to donate money to animal shelters and open my own animal sanctuary, and I want to grant scholarships to youth in need who are struggling to make it through college. I want…oh, Patrick, I think I want to do everything." My mother's earnest eyes turned to me, alive and beseeching. "I hadn't thought about it until you asked me, but I do. I want everything. I want it all." She inhaled deeply, absorbing the reviving air in the room.

I smiled. "I think you will have it all." I meant it. Looking up, I watched twinkling pieces of gold float through the air. "I think we both will." I slipped my hands into my pockets, and my fingers encountered something familiar. I wrapped my hand around it, aware of what it was, and carefully retrieved the object.

My mother walked to the other side of the room and slid her hand against the wall. She looked at the gold transferred to her palm. She tasted the substance, marking her maroon lips with gold.

I considered the opal rosary in my hand, the lightning strikes of greens and reds and blues in the stones. It'd traveled from my mother's hand, to my hand, to the carved-out pocket in a chimney, to Jack who had stolen it and mended it, and back to me. Now it was time for it to return to its owner.

I approached my mother. "Here. This is yours," I said softly.

She turned, her attention on the rosary in my palm. Her lips parted when she gasped. "You kept it," she whispered. She plucked it from my hand, rubbing it between her fingers.

"Of course. It made me feel close to you."

When she smiled, tears rimmed her eyes. She pressed a palm to her forehead. Her eyes rolled back and she collapsed forward. I caught her, and we both dropped to our knees.

"Are you all right?" I asked, my heart pounding.

"Yes. Yes. I'm just…overwhelmed." She wiped her tears with the back of a wrist. "It means so much to me that you kept this. It was my mother's, and her mother's before that. It's passed through a long line of women. I'd hoped to eventually give it to you, so you could pass it on to your children." She clasped the rosary to her chest. With her other hand, she reached toward me.

"Will you pray with me?" she asked. "For us? For Jack?"

"Of course."

We settled on the floor, and I crossed my legs. My mother sat on the backs of her heels and bowed her head. I bowed mine. Together, we said the Apostles' Creed. The words felt strange in my mouth. It'd been so long since I'd uttered them.

As we recited the prayers of the rosary together, my mind wandered, as it often had during this Catholic meditation. I took a step back, out of my life, and was able to see it from an aerial view, at a distance. Its peaks and valleys were not linear. They formed a circle without end and, from an even higher view, a singular spot, like a thumbprint. Each line of the print was too complex to be understood at once; it had to be unraveled, experienced a section at a time. From this vantage, joy, glory, love, and luminosity balanced tragedy and trauma. Nothing was wrong. Everything was interlocking and interlocked.

We moved to the Our Father, then the Hail Mary, the Glory Be, and the Hail Holy Queen.

We both inhaled in unison to begin again, but the ground beneath us rumbled.

The walls around us shifted.

CHAPTER 35
CONVENIO

Jack

"How did you get the godsoul?" Lutin asked as we shut the door on the Builder's cell, locking him inside. Roland headed upstairs for some much-needed liquor, leaving Lutin and me alone.

"It will make you cringe."

"Not now. No."

I looked up into his dark eyes, black circles around them, and relaxed. "I had Patrick kill the guard, and he took the godsoul, brought it to me, saved my life. And then…" I paused. "Why don't I show you?"

I retrieved my knife and cut open my palm. I drew an outline around the door and placed my hand on its heart. "*Patefacio tutor godsoul,*" I said. The hallway dimmed, and light sparkled from beneath the door. I gripped the handle as my hand was healing and opened the door. Lutin and I stared down a familiar royal purple hallway. At the end, a golden wall appeared.

To my left and right, the hallway of purple rock had changed. I saw new cracks that had not existed before, and in those cracks glowed the tiniest hints of gold. The spots of black were gone.

"What the hell happened here?" Lutin asked.

I glimpsed red hair by the wall beyond the hall.

"Come," I said. I took Lutin's hand and led him down the hallway toward my friend. Patrick noticed us and turned away from the rock. His hands, arms, and neck were coated in gold dust. His eyelashes flashed gold. To his left, Deirdre stood by the wall, turning from it as though she'd been studying it.

"Jack!" he exclaimed. He dashed over and embraced me. I hugged him back. "It's over?"

I nodded.

He pulled back. "I knew it. Look." He walked to where godsoul had once been plentiful. "It's growing."

I stepped forward. Golden peach fuzz had sprouted all along the rock. As I watched, I could swear I saw it thickening.

"It just started," Patrick said. "And when it did, I could feel it. Some dark thing's presence lessened. Everywhere. It was like a weight I didn't know existed until it was gone."

"I felt it, too," Deirdre said. She came to me, and we embraced. As we parted, I gave her hands a comforting squeeze.

Lutin wore a horrified expression as he stared at the wall where the godsoul had been cut away. "Believe me," I said. "This is an improvement." I cleared my throat. "Lutin, this is Patrick and Deirdre Flannigan. Patrick and Deirdre, Lutin."

Patrick's gaze studied Lutin, and he reached out a golden hand. Lutin took Patrick's hand in his own and shook. The fire in his veins fluoresced.

"Patrick is the new Guardian."

Lutin looked at me, confused. He opened his mouth momentarily and then shut it. "The *new* Guardian," he said. It began as a question but became a statement. He turned to the wall and broached the barrier. "That would make sense."

Patrick's hand struck out and caught the edge of the island.

"What is it?" I asked.

"I could swear that…I could swear…" He turned to us, his emerald eyes flicking between us.

"What?" I asked.

"I could swear that I sensed the rock growing."

"Growing?"

He nodded. "I could feel it expand. I thought I was going crazy. But then…" He pointed toward the royal purple hall. "But then I saw it start to spread out of the walls like vines."

He eyed Lutin, "I feel it *needs me* here."

Lutin placed a hand on Patrick's shoulder. "You are needed. Though," he said, gazing around, "I suspect you will not have to live your entire life like the other Guardian. There will be less to guard it from, now." His gaze briefly held mine.

"There's something I'm supposed to do," Patrick said, a wild look in his eye. "Something I'm meant to do."

The normal, joking Patrick had disappeared beneath an all-knowing, a deeper Patrick.

"What?" I asked.

"I don't know yet," he said, "but as soon as I do, I'll tell you."

He returned to the wall and ran his fingers over it. He whispered something unintelligible.

Deirdre Flannigan stood at the end of the island, gaping at her son, clearly puzzled. I caught her attention. *Thank you*, I mouthed silently.

She smiled. Her eyebrows rose. *Thank you*, she replied.

Lutin tugged at me, beckoning for me to follow. We bid farewell to Deirdre and Patrick and walked back down the hall and entered the door into Cyrus's basement. I shut the door behind us.

"You should know there's no release for the Guardian," he said, "except death."

"I figured."

"And Patrick now has total control over the most ameliorative and lethal substance, the most important remnant of our Creator. What kind of man is he?"

My mind replayed my various experiences with my friend. "He's harmless," I finally settled on. "He's funny, and ridiculous, and harmless."

Lutin's shoulders relaxed. He nodded and leaned against the brick wall. He took in his surroundings. "What happened to my brothers?" he asked, his voice both firm and apologetic.

"I don't know. They were in the Beretrum last time I saw them. With you. I think the Builder killed them."

"If they died in the Beretrum, they're gone."

I took his hand. "I'm sorry."

He nodded. "I'm sorry for what they did to you. But they were mine, and I loved them. And it's not as though their absence would slow you down."

I smiled. "Lutin, you've missed a lot."

"I bet."

"I used the resurrected gramophone on Alex inside the Beretrum. It killed him. I was shot out of the hell."

"You resurrected the…gramophone?"

I nodded. "And could control it. When I discovered that new part of my power, I resurrected Cyrus's red box, fed it pieces of my soul to grow it larger as I ate godsoul. The same way that Cyrus grew his box using you. Then I used it on the Builder. That's what killed him. And I brought him back to life."

Lutin's dark eyes took me in. He whispered something in his language.

"What does that mean?"

"Thank you for your bravery."

I shook my head. "It wasn't bravery. It was the only choice."

He pulled back. "Just take the compliment."

CHAPTER 36
TOTUS

Jack

A MONTH AFTER I'D ENSLAVED the Builder, I received a parcel in the mail from Patrick. I had to check twice to believe it.

Inside was a note on a piece of cream stationary trimmed in gold.

The miracle pulses now, it read.

Something rattled, and I reached inside and retrieved an orange prescription bottle. The label read *Meridiem*. Inside the bottle were thirty or so pills. A tiny speck of gold glinted in the light and disappeared as though it'd never been there.

I blinked, wondering what Patrick had done. A vision of Lucient Pharmaceuticals popped into my mind. Had he concocted another medication with the godsoul? He would've had enough to do so. It'd flourished since the Builder's imprisonment.

Lutin approached me, and I placed the bottle in his hand. He looked down at it, then back at me.

"There's certainly enough godsoul now for any purpose he might choose. It's doubling almost every day," he remarked.

Lutin was pondering the same thing as me: was dispersing the godsoul as medication to the world a wise decision? But he'd have to admit what I was already thinking—it was no longer the same world.

As soon as the Builder was locked in his cell, I had him connect with his followers across the globe to return his *arcas* to him. One by one, he'd destroyed them, melting each of them down into nothing.

The Builder's removal from the world had resolved many problems. The first result was eliminating the disease Alex had spread. It simply evaporated, including from my own body. It was as though his tendrils connecting him to all disease had been chopped, uprooted. Violence had decreased. People had become conscious in a way they were not before, suddenly aware of their actions, not tempted by the usual crimes. Violent crime, assault, battery, kidnapping, homicide, rape, war, torture—all had diminished significantly.

Cyrus had also changed. It was as though whatever acid was keeping his soul at bay vanished. He'd become apologetic to me and Roland without my willing it, without constantly ingesting the godsoul. It was strange to see this, and sorrow, and what seemed like love—the whole emotional spectrum, in fact—in him. Even Lutin admitted he was not the same man who'd existed before. I'd considered releasing him from his cell. The only thing that stopped me was it did not feel as though enough time had passed. My instincts told me to wait.

Considering all of this, the way in which the world was changing without the Builder's influence, why not disperse godsoul?

Lutin set the pills on the table beside the door.

"What do you think?" he said. We walked into the living room of Cyrus's mansion to the velvet purple couch in front of a wall painted gold. He lowered himself to the cushion and motioned for me to sit beside him. Sunlight streamed through the window. Two weeks before, we'd replaced all of the living area furniture with pieces we chose.

"I don't see a problem with it."

"Neither do I. The world has been healing itself." Lutin smiled. "Now that the primary source of evil is locked away."

"And will remain so. Forever."

Nodding, Lutin retrieved a small piece of paper, rolled up and tied with twine, from his jacket pocket. "I have something for you."

I tilted my head and held my hand out. "What is it?"

"Read it first."

The paper was surprisingly soft between my fingers, like silk. I tugged the string, and it slipped off like water. I unrolled the sheet. Two words with a slash between them filled the page.

"Domum / Beretrum."

I looked up at Lutin. "I don't understand."

"That is your fate, Jack. From the Princeps Auctoritati themselves."

I frowned as I tried to make sense of it.

"You are destined for both. One foot in heaven. One in hell. You always were."

I looked into his dark eyes. My heart thrummed like a bird's wings.

I blinked. "So, did my fate shift?"

"No," Lutin said. "Osric lied to you. Well, he told you a half-truth." He winced. "I warned you to trust no one but yourself, to see it through. This is one of the reasons why. People have their own version of the truth. Osric had his. And he told you only the part of the council's decree that validated his beliefs. In reality, you are connected to both the Beretrum and Domum simultaneously and also not at all. You move through these worlds as no one else can. That is what your fate means."

I stared at the sheet of paper, overwhelmed by it. A surge of emotion exploded in my chest, and tears came to my eyes. I hugged Lutin, and he returned the hug, holding me tight. I wasn't bound for the Beretrum, after all. And the council's decree was description, not prescription. It was relief to me not because I feared the Beretrum—after all, I controlled the Builder and, thus, controlled what might happen to me in the Beretrum. It was relief in that I'd not been outcast, relegated as belonging to the Builder and the Builder alone, of deserving him. "Thank you," I said.

"Now, you know the truth. And, you live in a new world, one you have helped build. It takes some getting used to. But we can do so together."

For a long time, he held me, and I pressed my face against his shoulder, breathing him in and feeling his fierce warmth. At last, when I'd regained composure, I let him go. "Both? Truly?"

He nodded. "You are not alone, Jack. As for Ven, the council apologizes for his actions and hopes that, in time, you will forgive their use of him against you. They admit they didn't understand the extent of who you are or what would constitute your link to the Beretrum."

"And what do they think of me now?"

He sighed. "They are ever closer to viewing you like I myself view you—as the system correcting itself."

I weighed his words, cocked an eyebrow. Lutin had never explicitly said this was how he viewed me. He always gave me the sense he believed I was integral but had never put words to it. It made sense to me, now, why he had fought so hard for me, if he truly believed what he said. "Forgiveness might take some time."

Lutin smiled. "I have no doubt. Take all the time you need."

I looked out the window at the emerald green grass that surrounded Cyrus's mansion, my mansion, Lutin's mansion. "Imagine," I said. "The Builder's influence is over. Not just in my life, but in everyone's." I looked at the piece of paper, rolled it up, tied it, and placed it in my pocket. "No more people torturing dogs in the night."

"No more people torturing dogs," Lutin agreed. He tilted his head. "You will have to forgive me, but...I must ask this. In the face of all that you have accomplished and done the past month, do you feel all right? You would tell me if it's otherwise?"

I momentarily recalled the high I'd felt as the resurrected *arca* had been used on the Builder, to my numbness at the concept of right and wrong, to the glee that blossomed during destruction, as though no piece of Lutin's heart had ever taken hold. I hadn't told Lutin about it, and I never would. That moment, like the Builder, was locked in a cell beneath the house. If it escaped, it wouldn't be my doing.

"I do. I would," I answered.

"We mustn't forget that evil still exists in this world, even as good blossoms. The Builder is still here, even as Patrick spreads the Creator's soul and blood."

"Yes, but *I* exist in this world too."

"As do I." He smiled. "But we mustn't forget."

"I won't. Never."

"Never is a very long time. And I have a proposition.

"Why don't you release all of this for a little while, trust me that I will remember for you, that I will remind you, that the Builder still exists. And, for a moment, just for a little while, act as though he doesn't. Be in the moment, this moment, with me, and relax. Trust that I will waken you, if the time comes to wake."

"Why?"

The corner of his lips quirked upward. "Because it's something you've never had, and it's the one thing I long to give you—release, freedom, to lift the weight."

I looked at him, and love filled me. "You don't have to do that, Lutin. But thank you. I'm doing just fine."

His expression never shifted. "Yes, you are. But just think about it." He lifted a cup of tea from the table and sipped, looking content.

I imagined for a moment doing what he said and releasing myself from the knowledge that the Builder still existed, locked away. I let the idea of an improved and constantly improving world permeate me. A substantial tension I didn't realize I carried in my shoulders eased, if briefly.

Perhaps one day I could set the load down for longer, but today was not that day.

While the world had brightened, one dark corner remained cordoned off, and what kept it secure was me. I wasn't one to let things get out of hand.

I glanced at Lutin. He smiled as he sipped his tea. The light in his fiery veins flickered, dimming slightly, then returned. Wrinkles appeared at his eyes, aging him, before they disappeared. It was as though the wiring in him had momentarily failed.

I watched, waiting for another flicker. The fire coursed through him as though it had never shorted.

My throat clicked as I swallowed dryly. I smiled back.

Acknowledgments

Here we are, at the end of the third book of the trilogy. Jack's journey as catalyst is complete. As she has gone through her journey, I have gone through mine, though perhaps my own journey has been less bloody, less lurid.

When I first spoke with Wayne and Ryan—two wonderful individuals who helped me with these books, and whom I thank immensely—I didn't know a damn thing about writing a book. I had thrown myself into the fray of fiction and, truly, became disoriented in the first draft of my first novel. It read that way. I knew I could write—I've been a writer all my life, and I had written tons of papers, short stories, even a published academic journal article—but I didn't yet know how to write this. Wayne and Ryan knew it—not in any judgmental sense, but just in its reality. Anyone would, as it was obvious. Nevertheless, they gave me a shot, something they didn't have to do, which gave me permission to swim beyond my depth and find a way, through many hours in the ocean of this, to stay afloat and to learn to trust myself.

Originally, when I first started revising that well-written mess of a first draft, I'd felt a bit guilty about the whole thing. I didn't want to waste anybody's time, and if I didn't unquestionably know how to do something, perhaps I should fess up and leave, no? It was not something I thought about consciously, but it was subconscious, as I put forth my solid efforts day-after-day. Instead of giving in to that unconscious doubt and fear, I persisted in learning "on-the-job." Of course, now I know I am not alone in this strategy. This is the way a lot of people learn to accomplish a lot of things. They find something completely out of their depth, they refuse to give in, and they end up creating something that could never have been foreseen.

There are quite wonderful things that can happen in the writing process that I didn't even know existed until they happened to me while finding my footing. There is a moment, for instance, in all books when, if someone were to sit down and just start reading the manuscript, he or she goes, "Whoa. What is this?" There is a turn, a swivel, a shift, a pivot in a book, where it is no longer like you're sitting down reading a book, but that you have suddenly entered a world, or the book itself has created a world, done something to you. It is almost as though the 2-D world becomes 3-D. This moment does, I believe, have something to do with the interconnection of plot or character—a moment where the book is interlaced with itself. It's a moment that wakes you up. And it doesn't matter if that book is still a manuscript, or in a hardcover, or on a thumb drive, or on some crumpled-up sheets of paper one finds on a park bench. When you're reading it, it doesn't matter if you're in your living room, a hotel, camping, or waiting in a doctor's office. When the "Whoa. What is this?" happens, you're suddenly plucked from your surroundings… and you're also maybe not quite entirely in the book. You are relishing what is possible. Or, maybe, you are relishing what has become possible.

From the writer's perspective, when the book really starts finding momentum, you can have those moments fairly often—when it's working, it's clicking, and it's almost writing itself, as you're kind of in a swoon or flow, and you feel like a passenger as another part of you develops it off-the-cuff expertly. You watch yourself write and become the audience while you're writing. Whoa, you think, what is this?

These are the moments where, published or not, awarded or not, read or not, the book is nevertheless born. It is something. And it can be really neat, sometimes, to experience that alone. Or... perhaps not alone, but first. Sometimes, when you try to tell others about the book, you're not trying to tell them about it; you're trying to tell them about the moment of it being born—the aha moment in the quiet room, when a door opens to a different world, on a dark night.

Perhaps as a result of this, I have understood the importance of giving the writing its own autonomy and admitting that it isn't all me. There's something else there.

Writing the third book for me was different than writing the first two. *Pivot* and *Perish* were born simultaneously, as they were originally the same book, two different time periods of Jack's life. I built up each book and then split them and then did another long revision on each of them. Then, while simultaneously working on these, I was developing a dark fantasy book in my MFA program for my thesis. Technically, that dark fantasy book was my third book, and it taught me quite a bit about worldbuilding. After I finished my MFA, and Bob at California Coldblood Books offered me a three-book deal, it was then time to create *Peak*, the last of the trilogy.

Peak went more smoothly than the first two novels. I only had to pause three times or so in the development of the original manuscript to go back through and re-strategize (compare this to having to write over 1,000 single-spaced pages of trial-and-error revisions to produce *Pivot*). According to one of my beta readers, *Peak* read differently (smoother) than the first two novels, as well.

In that initial manuscript for *Peak* that I submitted to my publisher, the point of view never veered from Jack. When Bob took a look at it, though, he offered up an idea that I ultimately ran with—why not have chapters from Patrick's perspective? As I thought about it, why not, indeed? It made sense. Patrick evolved with Jack, became his own (immortal?) being at the same time Jack did. So many important elements of the book happened with him. Thus, the chapters involving Patrick were born, and I am grateful to Bob for this suggestion. The end result was worth it, and many scenes that we as readers would not have been able to enter if we stayed with Jack became accessible.

One other thing that I must thank Bob for is the moment when, after reading *Peak*, he told me, "You obviously know what you're doing." It was an eye-opening moment because I had worked very hard for six years on figuring out just that—what I was doing—something that is quite difficult when, as I said before, writing has its own autonomy. Additionally, considering a book never has to be written a certain way, finding something that nevertheless works for the first, then second, then third book felt miraculous. Bob, though, might have pointed out something that I hadn't truly realized—I was further along than I had been six years prior. I, perhaps, had more tools in my toolbox, more experience as a detective/surgeon of plot and character. This is not the only thing I have to thank Bob for, of course; he opened a door for me and saw something in my work that was worth investing in. "Thank you" will never cover it.

This is also true for Wayne and Ryan. They gave me a chance and saw the potential and value of what I might be/am capable of, as well as provided me amazing pointers and notes for revisions. I also want to thank my agent Jonathan for his pointers, advice, and being willing to give me a chance. It is because of these individuals that Jack and I have had our amazing journeys.

Many thanks to Nancy Holder, Liz Hand, and Elizabeth Searle at Stonecoast for helping me develop my craft. In particular, many thanks to Nancy for her craft book advice, seminars, and kindness.

I am very grateful, as well, to Sue Ducharme who helped me tremendously with copyediting these three novels. I couldn't have asked for a better first-experience with a copyeditor. Sue has well-honed magic at her fingertips!

I would also like to express my utmost gratitude to the preeminent Emma Galvin for doing such justice to Jack and her story through the audiobooks.

Others who I want to thank are my friends for their tremendous support. I didn't know it was possible to feel so supported by a group of people. Adam, Eric, Jennifer, Stephanie, Ryan, Stewart, Lisset, Justin, Michele, Jeannie, Jen, Christi, Braxton, Kā, Elizabeth, Stephanie M., Joe, and Tim, thank you for celebrating with me. I love you guys.

Adam, in particular, I want to thank. I can only imagine what he was thinking when I submitted the first twenty pages of Pivot to him to look at seven years ago. If the word "writer" didn't exist, I'm sure all writers would be deemed insane. I thank him for not losing sight of "writer" as a descriptor for me. I thank him for getting excited by those first twenty pages, for reading all the versions of all the books, for talking with me about ideas, and for listening to me complain about the many tough moments, over pie and coffee.

In addition, I want to acknowledge my family, who has been so supportive of me as I have worked so diligently. Joyce, Janine, Kristin, Kevin, Stacy, Phaedra, Steve, the Kline and Schiurring families, Rachel, Catherine, Joycelyn, and Saundra, thank you.

I thank my Mom for her spectacular support, excitement, and encouragement. I am so grateful for my Dad who, though he has entered the great beyond, was like sunshine and showed me what it means to truly love and value people and exhibit gentle strength, even while suffering from multiple illnesses for many years.

My gratitude goes to Weston Ochse for encouraging me to listen to my heart when I wanted to pursue writing fiction, for encouraging me to pursue an MFA program, and for reading Jack's story and lauding it.

My thanks also go to Josh Malerman for giving my books his time. In this regard, I would also like to thank Yvonne Navarro, Rena Mason, Eric J. Guignard, Frederic S. Durbin, and Rodman Philbrick.

And, finally, reader, I thank you, as well. Thank you for seeing Jack's story through. Thank you for giving her journey your time. There are so many other "Whoa. What is this?" moments out there, in other worlds, in other books. Thank you for experiencing this one.

About the Author

L.C. Barlow is a writer and professor. Her work has been published in a variety of magazines and journals and garnered praise, winning multiple awards. Barlow lives in Dallas, Texas, with her cats Smaug and Dusty.